Assassin's Code

Also by Jonathan Maberry

Jonathan Maberry

Assassin's Code

St. Martin's Griffin
New York

ASSASSIN'S CODE. Copyright © 2012 by Jonathan Maberry. All rights reserved. Printed in the United States of America. For information, address St. Martin's Press, 175 Fifth Avenue, New York, N.Y. 10010.

www.stmartins.com

ISBN 978-0-312-55220-6 (trade paperback)
ISBN 978-1-250-00667-7 (hardcover)
ISBN 978-1-4299-4234-8 (e-book)

First Edition: April 2012

10 9 8 7 6 5 4 3 2 1

This one is for the mothers of all nations and for the three

Americans who were illegally arrested and jailed in Iran:

Shane Bauer, Josh Fattal, and Sara Shourd.

Glad you're home safe and sound.

Our children are not weapons of war or politics.

To the memory of John B. Maberry, who earned the

Congressional Medal of Honor at the Battle of Gettysburg.

And, as always, for Sara Jo.

Acknowledgments

Thanks to Steve Yetiv; Philadelphia police officer Bob Clark; the men of the 1-111 Infantry Battalion, Recon Platoon, with 36th Brigade, Iraqi Army Recon; Michael Sicilia of California Homeland Security; Michael E. Witzgall; Ken Coluzzi, Chief of Lower Makefield Police Department in Pennsylvania; Ted Krimmel, SERT; folklorist Nancy Keim-Comley; Archaeological Museum of Aruba; social media consultant Don Lafferty; Javier Grillo-Marxuach; Emilia Filocamo; Victorya Chase; Danny Evarts of Shroud Publishing; and Father Joseph Bordonaro of the St. Joseph Roman Catholic Church in Warrington, Pennsylvania.

And, of course, my agents, Sara Crowe and Harvey Klinger; all the good folks at St. Martin's Griffin, Michael Homler, Joe Goldschein, Matthew Shear, Rob Grom; M. J. Rose of AuthorBuzz; and Matt Snyder of Creative Artists Agency.

Part One
Acts of War

*Those who say religion has nothing to do with politics
do not know what religion is.*

—MOHANDAS GANDHI

Chapter One

Starbox Coffee
Tehran, Iran
June 15, 7:23 a.m.

She said, "Look down at your chest."

I held the cell phone to my ear as I bent my head. Two red dots, quivering slightly, danced right over my heart.

"You are one second away from death," said the caller.

Chapter Two

Starbox Coffee
Tehran, Iran
June 15, 7:25 a.m.

I didn't know the voice. She was a stranger. I didn't know her name. Didn't know anything except that she had my cell number. Ten seconds ago I was about to go into Starbox—yes, they really call it that in Iran—for a cup of bold and a couple of pastries. The street outside was empty.

I looked up. The shooters had to be in the building across the street, maybe the fifth floor. Didn't really matter, the range was a hundred yards and even a sloppy marksman could punch my ticket at that distance. I doubted these guys were sloppy. And there were two of them. I was also pretty sure I knew why they were after me.

"Okay," I said.

"I need you to confirm your name," she said in Persian. She had a very sexy voice for a psycho killer. Low and smoky.

"Why?"

"Because I have to be certain."

"Geez, sister," I said, "if this is how you ID your targets then I don't think you're going to get that contract killer merit badge."

The joke didn't translate well but she made a sound. It might have been a laugh. Glad she was amused. Sweat was pouring down my spine. The two little laser sights gave me no chance at all to run.

"If this was simply a matter of killing you," she said, "then we'd have done it and taken your wallet for identification." She had a European accent but she was hiding it by trying to speak Persian like a native. Kind of weird. Not the weirdest thing going on at the moment.

"Um . . . thanks?" I said.

"Tell me your name," she said again.

There had to be three of them. Two shooters and her. Was she the spotter? If not, there could have been one or two others, spotting for the gunmen. Or it might have been the three of them.

"Ebenezer Scrooge," I said.

"No games," she warned. "Your name."

"Joe."

"Full name."

"Joseph."

One of the laser sights drifted down from my chest and settled on my crotch.

"Once more?" she coaxed.

"Joseph Edwin Ledger." No screwing around this time.

"Rank?"

"Why?"

"Rank?"

"Captain. Want my shoe size?"

There was a pause. "I was warned about you. You think you're funny."

"Everyone thinks I'm funny."

"I doubt that's true. How often do you make Mr. Church laugh out loud?"

"Never heard of him," I lied.

Now I was confused. Up till now I thought she was part of a team looking to take me down for the little bit of nastiness I got into last night. Echo Team and I went into a high-security facility and liberated three twentysomethings who had been arrested a year ago while hiking in the mountains. The *Iraqi* mountains. An Iranian patrol crossed the border, nabbed the hikers, and started making noise in the media that the three hikers had illegally trespassed and therefore they were spies. They weren't. One was a former Peace Corps team leader who was there with his animal behaviorist girlfriend who wanted to take photos of a kind of rare tiger to help her with her master's thesis. *Acinonyx jubatus venaticus*. Asiatic cheetah. Also known as the Iranian cheetah. No, I'm not making this up.

The hikers had been used as pawns in Iran's ongoing policy of stalling and disinformation regarding their nuclear program. Normally we'd let the State Department and world opinion exert pressure on the Iranian government . . . but the third member of the hiking party was the only son of one of America's most important senators. The real twist is that the senator was a key player on several committees crucial to the U.S. war effort. Everyone with a spoonful of brains knew that the Iranians staged the whole thing to be able to turn dials on Senator McHale.

And it was starting to work. So the president asked Church to make the problem go away. We were Church's response.

"So, who gets to slap the cuffs on me?" I asked.

This time she did laugh.

"No, Captain Ledger," she said, "here's how it's going to work. As soon as I am done speaking you will turn off your cell phone and remove the battery and the SIM card. Put the SIM card and phone into different pockets. Walk to the curb and drop the battery into the culvert. Then I want you to go into the café. Order a coffee, sit in the corner. Do not reassemble your phone. Do not use the store's phone. Write no notes to the staff or other customers. Sit and enjoy your coffee. Read the newspaper. Ahmadinejad is insisting that the dramatics at the prison last night were the result of a boiler explosion. You should find that amusing. Do not make any calls. Maybe have a second cup of coffee."

"Do you work for Starbox? If so, I can't say I dig your new marketing strategy."

She ignored me. Her resistance to my wit was almost as disconcerting as the laser sights on my junk. Almost.

She said, "In a few minutes a person will enter the café. A man. He will recognize you and will join you. The two of you will have a conversation and then he will leave. Once he has left, you will wait another ten minutes before you reassemble your phone. You are on your own to find a new battery. You are supposed to be resourceful, so I imagine you will solve that problem without my advice."

"Then what do I do?"

"Then," she said, "you will do whatever you judge best."

"That's it?"

"That's it."

"When do I meet you?"

"You don't."

"I'd like to."

"No," she said with another little laugh, "you would not."

"Tell me something, miss, why go to these lengths? This could have been arranged with a lot less drama."

"No it could not. If you are smarter than you appear, then you'll understand why in a few minutes."

"These laser sights going to be on me the whole time? It's a lousy fashion statement and people *will* talk."

There was a moment's silence on the other end and then both sights vanished. I had to control myself from collapsing against the wall. I was pretty sure it would be two or three weeks before my nuts felt safe enough to climb down out of my chest cavity. My heart was beating like a jazz drum solo—loud, fast, and with no discernable rhythm.

"The clock is now ticking, Captain Ledger. Once I disconnect, please follow the instructions you have been given."

"Wait—" I said, but the line went dead.

I held the phone in my hand and looked across the street to the office building. Even without the sights I knew they could take me anytime they wanted.

There were no real options left. Just because the laser sights weren't on me didn't mean that I was safe. I think they'd used them for effect. It was broad daylight; they certainly had scopes. So I did as I was told. I dismantled my phone and put the SIM card in my left coat pocket and the empty phone casing in my jeans. With great reluctance I walked to the edge of the pavement and stared for a moment down into the black hole of the culvert.

"Crap," I said, and dropped the battery, which vanished without a trace. All I heard was a dull *plop* as it landed in the subterranean muck.

Before I turned to go into the store I scratched the tip of my nose with my forefinger. I was sure they'd see that, too.

Chapter Three

Starbox Coffee

Tehran, Iran

June 15, 7:39 a.m.

I went into the Starbox and ordered my coffee.

The waitress, a slim gal with a blue headscarf, glanced at my hands, which were visibly shaking. "Decaf?" she asked.

I screwed a smile into place and tried to make a joke. It fell flat. I repeated my drink order in a low mumble, paid for it and a French edition of the *Tehran Daily News*, and took them with me to a table where I could watch the street. It was pretty early, so the place was empty. There were two leather chairs in a corner and I took one, aware that there was no place in the café where a shooter with a good scope couldn't find me.

Last year I'd been in a coffee shop when a strike team tried to take me out. You'd think I'd have learned by now. My best friend and shrink, Dr. Rudy Sanchez, constantly tells me that I drink too much coffee. He says, "Caffeine will kill you," all the time. He'll be delighted to hear me admit that he was very nearly right.

I crossed my legs as if that would offer my groin any real protection from a high-velocity sniper bullet and tried to read the paper.

Apparently America is still the Great Satan. What a surprise.

The main headline was about last week's assassination attempt on the nation's Rahbare Mo'azzame Enghelab—the Supreme Leader. A man dressed as a Shia cleric had attended a prayer session at Mashhad, which is the second largest city in Iran and one of the holiest cities in the Shia Muslim world, over five hundred miles east of Tehran, near the borders of Afghanistan and Turkmenistan. It's the resting place of the Imam Reza, seventh descendant of the prophet Muhammad and the eighth of the Twelve Imams. I've been there. It's a gorgeous city, and home to the most extensive collection of Iranian cultural and artistic treasures. Millions of

Muslims make the pilgrimage to Mashhad every year, as do scholars and tourists like me; and that's been going on since medieval times. The saying is "The rich go to Mecca but the poor journey to Mashhad."

So, after a few introductory speeches, the Supreme Leader stepped up to lead the people in prayer and discuss matters of faith. Problem was, the fake cleric whipped off his coat to reveal a vest packed with Semtex. A group of young men grabbed the bomber and tried to drag him outside before the bombs went off. They only partly succeeded, and though the mosque was not destroyed, it was damaged. The Supreme Leader received minor injuries, but sixty-four people died, and the effect was like cutting a scar into the flesh of Islam.

I'm not a Muslim, and I'm not deeply religious even with my Methodist upbringing—not like my father and brother whose butts have worn grooves in the pews in our church back in Baltimore—but there is something that disgusts me on a deep level when someone makes a deliberate attack on the faith of another person, or in this case on an entire people. I don't like it when it happens to Americans; and I certainly don't like it when Americans do it to each other. Can't say I'm much in favor of it anywhere in the world.

Who was to blame for this particular hate crime?

Hard to tell.

Lately there's been a weirdly sharp rise in hate crimes throughout the Middle East. Five times as many suicide bombers, a 300 percent increase in political assassinations, plus car bombs, pipe bombs, and even a rash of people found murdered with their throats completely torn out.

At the best of times the Mideast was never known for its easygoing tolerance; lately it's like everyone has gone just a little bit crazier. My boss, Mr. Church, has been monitoring the escalation of violence, and although he hasn't come out and said so, I'm certain that he's suspicious of the rising body count. My friend Bug, who runs the computer resources for the Department of Military Sciences, told me on the sly that Church wanted him to run a thorough background search on the victims, even the ones who appeared to be innocent bystanders.

"Why?" I asked.

"'Cause the boss thinks there's a hidden agenda," answered Bug.

"He always thinks there's a hidden agenda," I remarked.

"He's usually right, though, isn't he?"

And I had no argument for that. Like the bumper stickers say, "You're not paranoid if they really are out to get you."

I'd been following this in the local and national news, and I scanned the paper to see if they had anything on the mosque bomber, but this rag was pretty heavily slanted toward the ultraconservative view, which pretty much concludes that if a bird shits on a statue in Iran it's a U.S. plot. The reporter, probably quoting a government directive, claimed that this was the latest act in a series of escalating terrorist attacks by America. Completely ignoring the fact that half of the recent victims in the Middle East were Americans or allies. Go figure.

The rest of the paper was local stuff. No cartoons. No *Doonesbury* or *Zits* or *Tank McNamara*. No crossword puzzle.

Time crawled by. A few people came in for coffee.

I debated rolling sideways out of the chair and shimmying behind the counter, but if I did that and the snipers opened up I'd be the cause of civilian casualties.

Besides . . . after all this I kind of wanted to see who was going to walk in the door.

While I waited, I went over everything that had happened last night. This thing with the woman and the snipers didn't seem to fit, but . . . how could it *not*? We did a lot of harm last night . . . Somebody must want some payback.

I sipped my coffee. It wasn't Starbucks, but it was hot and black.

I could almost hear the echo of gunfire in my ears . . .

Chapter Four

Afa Police Station
Tehran, Iran
One Day Ago
June 14, 7:20 p.m.

The trial was set to start in two days, so to avoid the crowds near the capital building that had been a constant since the mosque bombing, the military moved the three hikers to a secure location on the outskirts of Tehran. The move was also likely done to reduce the risk of having the press ask any questions of the hikers, and there was an army of reporters from all over the world in Iran right now.

This whole thing worked for us. It gave us a window we otherwise would never have had.

The new location was a small jail near a residential district; no one would think to look there. Except we were already looking there. Our computer, MindReader, was plugged into the Iranian military police network, courtesy of Abdul Jamar, an Iranian on the CIA payroll. Abdul's older brother had been murdered by the secret police for writing essays in protest of the nuclear program. This was his form of payback.

When Mr. Church formed the Department of Military Sciences he built it around the MindReader computer system, which was his sole property. Bug, our head of computer operations, hinted that Church may have written some of its more advanced software packages, but Church refused to confirm it. Actually, Church simply ignored the question, which was his style. MindReader has a lot of functions, but two stand out and make it the most valuable tool in the intelligence arsenal. It is designed to look for patterns, and though computers can't generalize, MindReader comes damn close. It gathers information from other sources, including many that refuse to share their intel with the DMS. That doesn't matter to MindReader, and that's the other reason it's so valuable. It is designed to intrude into virtually any other computer system without tripping alarms, and when it backs out, it rewrites the target computer's software so that there is no record that it had ever been hacked. The system is proprietary and no one outside of a select few DMS senior staff has access to it; and no one has full access except Church.

My team and I were staying in a seedy hotel near the center of town—one that allowed dogs—and my dog was currently waiting there for us. When we got word about the transfer, we began tracking the move through a series of high-security-coded e-mails. I had half of Echo Team with me for this: my number two, First Sergeant Bradley "Top" Sims; the big California kid, Harvey "Bunny" Rabbit; the professorial Khalid Shaheed; the laconic former LAPD sniper John Smith; and the newbie, Lydia Ruiz, who was in the navy's first covert group of women SEALs.

Khalid was, among other things, a makeup artist who could have gotten work on Broadway. When we arrived at the hotel room, among the equipment delivered for us was a professional stage makeup kit. Khalid used it to transform us all into Iranians. Luckily a lot of people in Iran look like their European forebears. Khalid had to tone down his own darker Egyptian complexion. Bunny and I both got our fair hair dyed black. Lydia was Latina but had the olive skin of her Madrid ancestors; with the right eye makeup and a modest chador with a headscarf, she would blend right in. John Smith was already dark-haired, so Khalid gave his pale face a little more color.

Top was never going to look like either an Iranian or an Arab, but that was okay. There were plenty of African Muslims in Iran, and Top could speak Somali and Persian with an African lilt. Except for Top, we all dressed in military police uniforms.

We let the transfer happen and gave it about three hours for all the hubbub to settle down. Top, dressed like a factory worker, came into the police station to report that someone had stolen the tires off of his car while he was out to dinner with his wife. Lydia was the wife. Top was not hysterical but still managed to be loud enough to draw attention, and no matter what he said, Lydia contradicted and corrected him. The officers found it all very amusing, though they dutifully took the report.

The rest of us watched all this on tiny monitors built into the faces of our wristwatches. Very Dick Tracy. One of the last toys Mr. Church got from his longtime friend Steve Jobs. Stuff was three years away from hitting the commercial market. They'll be going out as iSee, and Apple will make another gazillion off it. Pretty handy for the military, especially when married to the high-definition digital camera built into the middle button of Top's shirt.

We were parked in two cars, one in front, one in back. The streets were empty. It was nearing the time for *Isha'a*, the evening prayer, last of the five prayer times of the day.

Eight men in the police station's front room. Top made sure to show us as he turned to appeal to one officer after another in his distress about his tires. MindReader provided us with a floor plan. One door in front, one in back. Ten cells. Thermal scans from a satellite confirmed the eight men up front and four more in the back, plus three thermal signatures in the holding area. The hikers each separated into different cells.

Twelve to five, and if we blew the snatch or let them raise the alarm, we were going to fill those empty cells. Even though none of us carried any ID, and although our fingerprints and DNA were in no databases anywhere, thanks to MindReader, it wouldn't be a stretch for anyone to guess where we came from. We were potentially bigger political currency than the three college kids, even if one of them was a senator's only son.

"Okay, Top," I murmured as we got out of our cars. "Party time."

The easiest way to do this would have been to kick the doors, toss in a couple of flash-bangs and kill everyone in a uniform. That would also be barbaric. We weren't at war with Iran, and we certainly weren't at war with a small regional police station. The officers in there were nowhere near the policy level. They were probably working schlubs like me and my guys; like my brother back in Baltimore PD.

So we went with Plan B.

The flash-bangs? Yeah, okay, we did that. But, hey, everyone likes party favors.

When I gave the word, Top and Lydia jammed their palms against their ears, squeezed their eyes shut and dropped to the floor. Khalid came through the station's front door and lobbed a flash-bang in a softball underarm pitch that arced it over the intake counter and landed it right on the duty officer's desk. I was right behind Khalid and I had a second's glimpse of the officer staring in unbelieving horror at the grenade.

Then . . . *BANG!*

The flash-bang is designed to temporarily blind and deafen anyone in the blast radius. It feels exactly like getting hit in the head with a sledgehammer made of pure light. You don't shrug it off. You scream, you go temporarily but intensely deaf and blind, and roll around on the floor. If you're up close and personal it can burst your eardrums.

Everyone in the room was staggered.

I raised a Benelli M4 shotgun and opened up. I wasn't firing buckshot—my gun was loaded with beanbag rounds. That sounds fun. It isn't. The rounds are small fabric pillows loaded with #9 lead shot. They won't penetrate the skin, but it feels like you've been punched by the Incredible Hulk. You do go down and you do it right now.

There was one officer who hadn't gotten his eggs scrambled by the flash-bang and he had a pistol halfway out of the holster. I put a round center mass and knocked him into a row of filing cabinets. He rebounded from the cabinets and fell flat on his face making tiny croaking sounds. Khalid and Top flanked me, drawing and firing X26-A Tasers, which have a three-shot magazine with detachable battery packs. The twin sets of fléchettes struck their targets and the battery packs sent fifty thousand volts into each man. The men dropped and the shooters released the battery packs to allow their guns to chamber the second rounds. The packs would continue to send maintenance charges through the fléchettes until the batteries ran dry, say about twenty seconds. Four down, four to go.

Lydia pulled another shotgun from under her billowing black chador and hammered an officer into the wall with the beanbags. I pivoted and fired two shots at a screaming cop trying to crawl toward a desk with a phone on it, hitting him once and missing once because he went down that fast. Khalid and Top used the Tasers on the other two.

In the space between the flash-bang and my first shot, I heard an explosion in the cell area. Bunny blowing the back door off its hinges with a blaster-plaster. Then the sound of shotguns and Tasers.

And that fast it was over. Eight men up front, four in the back. All of them down, no fight left in anyone.

I turned. "Warbride, secure the door. Sergeant Rock, Dancing Duck— bag 'em and tag 'em."

We were using combat call signs. Lydia was Warbride, Top was Sergeant Rock, Khalid was Dancing Duck. I was Cowboy.

Immediately Top and Khalid produced plastic flex-cuffs, which had been designed to hold pipes together but have become a staple of law enforcement worldwide.

One of the officers began to stir. Maybe the Taser fléchettes hadn't lodged deeply enough for him to take the full shock, or maybe he was one of those rare types who can bull their way through it, but he lunged at Lydia and tried to tackle her. Lydia is five eight and one forty. Solid for a woman but far smaller than the cop. However, she stepped into his rush and hit him three times—nose, solar plexus, and groin—in less than a second. The cop went down like he'd been poleaxed. Lydia spun him onto his stomach and cuffed him, then bent and whispered, "Next time, *pendejo*, don't let your balls get your ass in trouble."

Once he was down, my team cuffed the officers by the wrists and ankles and then connected those cuffs, leaving everyone hog-tied. Sponge balls with elastic cords were used to muffle voices. The cops would be able to spit them out once they got their wits about them, but I intended for Echo Team to be a memory by then. Lydia locked the door and pulled down the slatted metal security shutters. Then she started ripping out phone lines, smashing laptops, and crushing cell phones under her heel.

I ran past her, through the security office and into the holding area. Bunny was finishing the last of the hog-tying while John Smith searched the officers for keys. He found them and tossed the set to me as I ran past.

"Green Giant," I yelled to Bunny. "Talk to me."

"Last one."

"Chatterbox, watch the door."

John Smith nodded and crouched down by the shattered rear doorway. There were people on the street, poking their heads out of doors and second floor windows to see what the fuss was about.

"Drawing a crowd," he said.

"Out front, too," called Lydia. "*Truchas!* Neighbors are coming!"

The three hikers were in the cells. They looked terrible. Haunted faces, emaciated bodies, fresh bruises, and healed-over scars. However, I noticed that the jailers had provided each of the young prisoners with a big plate of fresh food and plenty of clean water. It was a small courtesy, but it said a lot about the men we'd just roughed up. Human beings. They couldn't do anything about what had been done to the hikers, and they had no say in what was planned for them—a bullshit trial and either execution or life in a much more terrible state prison—but here, on the street level, these were frightened, starving young people and the cops did what they could to take care of them. They'd even rigged blankets on the bars to give the girl, Rachel, a measure of privacy and dignity. Top saw me looking at that and when I noticed him looking, he flicked an eye to the front room and nodded. I nodded back. There was nothing else to say or do.

The college kids, however, were jabbering and screaming and yelling. The panic was such a huge thing for them that they'd lost all control. Bunny kept trying to calm them down, but his voice was lost beneath the barrage of theirs.

From the doorway, Top yelled, "*Shut the fuck up!*" with all the volume that his leather-throated drill instructor's voice could manage.

The hikers shut up at once and stared at him, goggle-eyed.

I said, "We are United States Special Forces. We're here to take you home."

They started yammering again, rushing the cell doors before we could even open them.

"Stop!" I snapped, and they did. Scared as they were, they paid attention, which I knew was going to help make this work. Hysteria would get everyone killed. I was also reassured by seeing them all on their feet. I've heard horror stories about prisoner rescues where the people the Spec-Ops forces liberated were broken and catatonic wrecks who had to be carried out.

One of them, the only woman among them, stepped forward. She wore a scowl that was half anger and half hope. "They tricked us once with something like this. How do we know—?"

"Smart question. When you were ten your mom gave you a guinea pig for your birthday. You named it Olivia."

Her eyes stayed hard, but they grew wet as well. She nodded.

"God, thank you—" she began, but I cut her off.

"Listen to me. We will get you out of here but you need to do exactly as you're told. No questions, no talk."

Khalid produced a PDA and called up photographs, matching them against the faces of the prisoners. "Three for three," he confirmed and handed the device to me.

I unlocked one cell and handed Top the keys.

"Each of you will go with one of my team. You'll get into separate cars and you'll be taken out of the country. You're going home. This is for your own safety," I said. "If any one car gets stopped, the others will get away. Now, no more talk . . . let's move."

When I said the word "separate," they looked terrified and suspicious, but they did not panic. I found myself liking them. I'd had reservations at first—like a lot of people, I guess—because they had put themselves in harm's way by going on a science field trip in a war zone. But now I understood. These were very tough young people. Resourceful and capable. If they had a fault, maybe it was that they had too much faith in people. I'm not about to slam anyone for thinking that other people will aspire to their higher values. It's just too bad they got caught in a moment when the Iranian soldiers were not listening to their better angels.

Khalid stepped into the cell with the senator's son. "Jason McHale?"

The young man saw Khalid's Arab face and hesitated, but I stepped close.

"He's an American soldier. Go with him or stay here. Decide fast, kid, 'cause your dad's waiting for you in Kuwait City. He wants to see 'Ranger.'"

That did it. "Ranger" was Jason's nickname as a little boy. Tears welled in his eyes and he tried to hug me. I pushed him gruffly back. I felt for him, but this wasn't the time.

"Sorry," he said.

"No need to be sorry, brother," I said. "When we get out of this I'll buy the first round."

He smiled. It was a good smile, conflicted in the moment but that was a veneer over a clear and evident openness. "The next one's on me." He allowed Khalid to guide him out of the cell.

Top entered Rachel's cell and held out a hand toward her, palm up. An invitation rather than a command. "Come on, darlin'" he said in the fatherly way he has. He's the only Echo Team member with kids. "You can tell me everything I need to know about rare tigers on the way to Kuwait."

Rachel stared blankly at him for a moment. He had warmth, and you knew on an instinctive level that it was genuine. Then she smiled— maybe her first real and unguarded smile in months.

"Asiatic cheetah," she corrected as she took his hand. He grinned back at her.

The kid in the last cell, Bryan, was the youngest of the three. His twentieth birthday had happened behind bars. He was also the most clearly damaged, and he stared through the open cell with sunken eyes. It was pretty obvious that the experience had fractured something inside him. Maybe—with luck and the right doctors—he'd find his way out of the dark. Top put a hand on his shoulder.

Top started to say something, but Rachel stepped past him.

"It's okay, Bryan," she said. "Nobody's going to hurt you anymore. We made it. We survived. We're *free*."

He took a small step forward but that was all. Then Jason stood next to Rachel and said, "You beat them, Bry. Remember what we said after they took us? We're innocent and no matter what they did to us we were going to stick to the truth. You said that, and Rachel and I went along with you.

Well, check it out, brah, you saved our asses with that. You held the line for all of us. Now they're here to take us home."

Bryan's empty eyes gradually filled with something. Hard to put a name on it, because there was a lot of wreckage in the way. Maybe he had gone inside his head to hide from what they were doing to him, but here, in this moment, I think he looked through the shadows and saw the faint light from the door he'd left open.

"Tick-tock, *Jefe*," said Lydia quietly, and I nodded.

Bryan took a ragged breath and then took a step forward, reaching through his personal darkness. Taking Rachel's hand, taking Jason's. Top helped guide him out of the cell, and I could see the broken boy becoming the man who had walked through hell and survived.

As he passed one of the cops who lay trussed on the floor, Bryan suddenly knelt beside him. At first I thought he was going to lash out at him, but he didn't. Instead he rolled the man onto his side so that the restraints didn't cut as deeply into his wrists and ankles. Either kindness to local cops who had been relatively kind to the prisoners, or a statement that compassion should be a factor whenever one person has power over another. It was a small thing, a minor kindness in the middle of a dreadful experience; but it might be the defining moment in the entire experience for the young man.

I was proud of him and I saw the looks in the eyes of Top, Khalid, and Bunny. This was why we do what we do. Not to punish the bad guys, but to make sure the good ones have a real chance.

The silence in the cells was cracked apart by the sound of sirens approaching.

The prisoners looked toward the rear door, new fear blossoming in their eyes.

"Okay, everybody out of the pool," said Bunny, dialing up the wattage on his Southern California smile. Bunny has a great blend of impressive size, movie-star looks, and surfer-boy charm; but at the same time you know you're safe with him. It takes a lot of guys to outnumber someone like him.

The sirens were coming fast.

"Warbride?" I called.

"We're drawing a crowd," she reported tersely. "We need to get into the wind most riki-tik."

I ran to the door and peered out. People were pouring out of their houses and converging on the police station. Half of them were yelling into cell phones.

"Dark and stormy night," I said to Smith, and he nodded. He fished out a smoke grenade and threw it. And another and another. Dense black smoke boiled up from each one. Lydia lobbed flash-bangs into the smoke. Between the thick smoke and the sudden explosions, the crowd screamed and began to scatter, running in every wrong direction, colliding, creating very useful panic.

"Go! Go! Go!" I barked.

Top, Khalid, and Bunny, each guiding a freed hostage, flipped down their infrared visors and ran like hell for the cars we had parked on different side streets.

People were still in the streets but when they saw men with automatic weapons, they stumbled backward toward their houses.

Lydia ran behind them, and immediately cut left and vanished into an alley. The plan was for her to circle the block and reenter the scene as a pedestrian. She looked like every other woman in this conservative part of town. She'd blend in with the crowd and help confuse things with a little whisper-down-the-lane distortion of the facts. Were there six men or twelve? Didn't they drive away in a white van? The men were bearded. Was that Afrikaans they were speaking? Any good crowd of confused and angry people could be worked like a conductor with a baton.

John Smith covered everyone with his rifle and infrared scope. He was good with every kind of firearm, but as a sniper he was the hammer of God. If anyone made a move on our teams they would get the real thing, no beanbags, no Tasers. Now was not the time to play.

My earbud buzzed and I heard Top's voice. "One away."

"Two away," said Khalid.

"Down the road and gone," said Bunny.

But by then John Smith and I were already in motion. Our visors showed the heat signatures of the fleeing civilians. And it also showed the heat from the engines of at least a dozen police cars coming at us from different directions. They were closer than we anticipated, and that was not good news. Our window of escape had slammed shut. In twenty paces we were going to be out of the smoke and as visible as gnats on a bedsheet.

"Chatterbox," I growled, "escape three. Go!"

We had four different escape strategies. The first two were now for shit, and number four involved shooting our way out. Three was less lethal but not much more comforting. We split up, went for the first cover we could find to get off the grid as quickly as possible. It meant dumping all of our gear. Everything.

We each popped a final smoke grenade and ran into the cloud. As they burst, we hit quick release buttons on our belts and shed holsters, cross belts, bandoliers, and harnesses packed with expensive and very useful equipment. Even the iSee devices and earbuds. It all clattered to the ground. When I dropped my helmet I lost sight of John Smith. I crouched while running and tugged at the seams of my trousers. With a screech of Velcro, the pants split apart and flapped behind me. I repeated the action with the shirt. The last thing I did was to grab the medallion hanging around my neck and press the sculpted design in the center. It sent a signal to the gear—weapons, equipment, and even clothing—that released hundreds of tiny thermite micro charges. I heard the *whoosh* as all of it exploded into flame. Then I yanked off the medallion and tossed it away.

When I staggered backward out of the smoke, faking a cough, I was an Iranian in ordinary street clothes. I yelled in Persian and bellowed for the police, pointing toward the smoke and flames.

Just like every other ordinary citizen was doing.

Chapter Five

Starbox Coffee
Tehran, Iran
June 15, 7:41 a.m.

That was how it ended. At least for me. Top, Bunny, and Khalid still had to get the college kids out of the country, but circumstances cut me from that team. I knew it was going to be a nail-biter for the guys, but Top was the best team leader in the business. If there was a way, he'd see it done.

I made it back to my hotel room without further incident. John Smith and Lydia weren't there, but I hadn't expected them. Each of us had a different bolt-hole and pickup point for a ride out of town.

I didn't have much in the way of weapons or equipment left at the hotel.

Our local contact, Abdul, whom I hadn't yet met—had come by and cleared everything out. All that was left was my suitcase filled with locally made and purchased street clothes and my shaving kit.

Abdul wasn't scheduled to pick me up until noon. *Plenty of time*, I'd thought. *I'll just go get some coffee and a roll and read the paper.*

Jeez.

While I waited I thought about the conversation with the mystery lady. She was clearly working for someone—possibly the person I was now waiting for—but there was something extra hinky about the way she "confirmed" my identity. It felt more like she didn't know who I was and was fishing for that information. And yet she'd known enough about Church to make a crack about how tough it is to make him laugh. Did that mean she knew Church? Or was that a slice of information she'd been given to use to convince me that she knew more than she does. Apparent omniscience is frightening; it intimidates people into saying things they shouldn't. Cops use it all the time, mostly faking it, to get suspects and witnesses to open up.

So, what did she know about me? That I was a smart-ass. That's not exactly the best-kept secret in the world. That I worked for someone named Church who didn't always appreciate my humor? That was a single fact that *suggested* intimate knowledge. At the time, out there in the awkward moment of having laser sights on me, it encouraged me to perhaps read more into it than was necessary.

The fact that she knew about Church at *all* was spooky. I was certain that Church's name was fake. Since I've known him I've heard people call him Colonel Eldritch, the Deacon, Dr. Bishop, Mr. Priest, and a few other names that were equally phony. I knew of only one person who definitely knew his real name; and one other—his daughter—who probably did, but even I wasn't certain about that.

Another question was how she found me?

Either I was spotted on the street, ID'd, and followed—which I don't think is likely, not given how elaborate this all was. Or my hotel was being watched and they'd acquired me there. Safer to brace me on a city street than in my lair. They couldn't know that the only thing I had in my "lair" was a hungry dog, an extra pair of clean boxers, and a shaving kit. No James Bond gadgets. No lurking ninja army waiting to spring to my defense.

The real bitch was the fact that she had my phone number. That's really hard to get. It's not like I'm listed in the phone book under "DMS team leaders with a wacky sense of humor."

So that was all disturbing on a lot of levels.

Minutes limped by and no visitor. People came into the Starbox for coffee, but most of them left again, joining the burgeoning flow of office drones heading to work. They shambled in like zombies, ordered tea or coffee, and shambled out again with barely a word spoken. It was the same here as it was everywhere else in the world. People are people and most of them have enough on their minds with family, jobs, bosses on their ass, bills to pay, kids to raise, and futures to get to that they don't give much of a shit about the things that go on in my life. Back in the States we tend to think of Iran as an evil place because we don't like the extremist ruling government. But . . . we don't like *most* ruling governments, and even the ones running the countries that we *do* like don't give much of a shit about us. The one percent at the top of the money heap care about each other, or hate each other, but they all play with each other. The rest of us go about our jobs, and raise our kids, and do our best to stay out of it all.

I watched them come and go. Just folks. I never saw one person that looked alien or evil to me. Not one.

Until *he* arrived.

This was the guy I was here to meet, no doubt about it.

"Uh-oh," I murmured.

No need to worry about them reading my lips—they'd probably expect me to say exactly that.

Chapter Six

Starbox Coffee
Tehran, Iran
June 15, 7:56 a.m.

He was late forties, average height, with dark hair and fair skin. Iranian without a doubt, and the European heritage was there in the aquiline nose, green eyes, and non-Semitic features. Iranians aren't Arabs. Most people don't know that, especially the mouthbreathers who lump all

Middle Eastern peoples into one group so they can be more easily de-spised. The name "Iranian" comes from "Aryan," but the culture draws on ethnic lines from Europe, Asia, and elsewhere. Lots of nice diversity in a generally good-looking people.

This guy could be a soap opera star. Women would swoon. If they didn't know who and what he was. If they did . . . well, I think even the president of the antigun lobby would pop a cap in him and laugh while he did it. The stakes on this bizarre morning encounter jumped about ten-fold.

I *did* know who he was.

He was accompanied by a second man who might as well have had "thug" tattooed on his forehead; he shooed away the only other custom-ers, a pair of middle-aged men, and positioned himself at the door to pre-vent anyone else from coming in.

The man I was here to meet bought a cup of coffee, told the girl behind the counter to go into the back room and stay there, and then he walked over and stood in front of me. He wore a blue sport coat over a white dress shirt with only the top button undone, khakis, and a pair of hand-sewn Italian shoes. He looked down at me and I sat there; I smiled affably, hold-ing my coffee between my palms, resisting the urge to kick his kneecaps off and stomp him to death.

"Captain Ledger," he said. Not a question.

When I didn't reply, he nodded toward the other chair.

"May I?"

"Sure," I said. "It's a free country."

His mouth twitched a little at that. He sat, perching on the edge of the chair like a nervous Chihuahua ready to bolt. He looked around and then stared out through the window for a moment, then nodded. Not sure if it was to the mysterious woman or the shooters or to himself. This was his home turf, so I was curious why he should be skittish.

He looked at me looking at him. "You know who I am?"

"Yes."

"If we were in your country I imagine you would like to arrest me."

" 'Arrest'?" I said, tasting the word. "No . . . not really."

"Then—"

" 'Kill'? Sure, that would work."

He had eyes like a hunting hawk. Piercing, fierce, and almost unblinking. "Why do you believe that it is up to you to judge whether I live or die? I have never killed anyone. I have not spilled a single drop of human blood. Not ever."

I crossed my legs and leaned back in my chair. "Jalil Rasouli," I said. "I always thought that was kind of funny. Same name as the artist. I *like* the artist. He brings something to the world. He uplifts."

"As do—"

"If you say that what you do also uplifts I will rip your throat out," I said in a conversational tone, my smile unwavering. Rasouli shut up. I let a couple of seconds pass. I said, "If you know who I am then you should be able to guess that I've read your file. Not the public profile, but the real stuff. You say that you don't have any blood on your hands?"

He said nothing.

"Vezarat-e Ettela'at Jomhouri-ye Eslami-ye Iran," I said quietly. His eyes bored into mine. I translated it just to put it out there. "The Ministry of Intelligence and National Security of the Islamic Republic of Iran. MISIRI. Pretty unfortunate acronym."

Nothing.

"You were the deputy operations chief during the 1999 chain of murders. CIA, Interpol, even some spies in your own government name you as the man behind the whole shebang. No blood on your hands? But how many murders did you green-light? Car accidents, stabbings, shootings in staged robberies. Oh, and all those faked heart attacks—what was it you used for those? Potassium injections? And who were the targets? Soldiers, enemy combatants? No. You went after writers, translators, poets, political activists, ordinary citizens. Iranian citizens. The intellectual class, the ones capable of phrasing a compelling argument against the extremist government. You get that idea from reading Stalin's biography?"

Jalil Rasouli brushed some lint from his jacket sleeve. "Your Persian is very good; you speak it like an Iranian. Excellent."

"You should hear my pig Latin."

He didn't seem to know what that was and shrugged it off. On a different and mildly perverse level, I was pleased by the compliment. I have a talent for languages and Persian was one of the first I learned. Before I joined the DMS I sat on wiretaps as part of Baltimore PD's role in Homeland. Listening to endless hours of people talking about ordinary things helps a linguist smooth out the edges of their own command of the language. On the other hand, I'd rather have my fingernails yanked out with pliers before I let Rasouli know that I appreciated his approval.

"Most of the world press thinks you're going to make a bid for the presidency," I said. "Oddsmakers say you even have a shot. Not sure it would be an improvement over the current psycho in office."

He yawned. "You want to provoke me? What do you think I would do? Attack you?" He jerked his head toward the thug. "Or order Feyd to do it?"

"Don't count too much on that moron."

"He is very good."

"His coat is buttoned and he's leaning against the wall on his gun-arm side. He tries anything, you'll be dead before he can draw his gun, and then I'll feed it to him."

Rasouli considered his bodyguard and gave a noncommittal shrug. "If I am the man you believe me to be, then I could have sent a squad of soldiers here."

"Maybe you should have."

He smiled. Son of a bitch had a great dentist. I wanted to knock his caps down his throat. I had to covertly take a calming breath. This guy was not bringing out my best qualities.

Rasouli cleared his throat. For a moment he looked almost embarrassed by his own threat, which I found confusing. With a clear change in his tone of voice he leaned forward and placed his elbows on his knees. "I am risking much in meeting you here."

I resisted the urge to prove him right. Instead I gave an encouraging nod.

"I could not go through the regular diplomatic channels," he continued in a quiet and confidential tone, "for reasons that should be apparent to you."

"Because your regular diplomatic channels are staffed by vultures, thieves, cutthroats, and scumbags," I said. "And your own people would sell you out for the price of a bowl of lentil soup."

"No," he said, "my own people would sell me out, that is not a question, but it would be for very much money."

"Ah. So you *know* that your ambassadors and diplomats are as crooked as a barrel of fish hooks."

He smiled. "There is a saying: 'Trust a thief before a diplomat.' "

"That says it."

"There is a matter of great importance and equally great complexity that needs to be dealt with, but it is so . . ." Rasouli waved his hand as he searched for the word.

"Fragile?" I suggested. "Volatile?"

"Either will do. Both, I suppose."

"And you thought it would be easier to discuss it by ambushing me with snipers?"

"Would you have agreed to this meeting without them?"

"Probably not."

"Of course not," he said. "Besides . . . the snipers were already here, preparing for another task. I . . . borrowed them." He paused, then added, "That other task is now canceled and will likely be abandoned."

"What was the other job?"

Rasouli considered, then shook his head. "No, it would confuse things to discuss that. What we are here to discuss is much more important."

"Before we get to that—why me?"

He spread his hands. "You came highly recommended."

"By whom?"

"A mutual friend."

"Give me a name."

A strange, fierce light flared in his eyes and he studied every inch of my face before he answered. "Hugo Vox."

Rasouli couldn't have hit me harder if he'd swung a baseball bat at my face.

"You're shitting me."

"Not at all."

I swallowed a lump the size of a football. Hugo Vox. Now if there was ever an "enemy of god," then Vox had my vote. Pretty much my vote for "actual supervillain" too. Vox used to be one of the most trusted men in the

United States anti- and counterterrorism community, trusted by the kind of people who don't trust anyone. Vox was a screener for above-top-secret personnel and the director of Terror Town, the most effective counterterrorism training facility in the world. To be "vetted by Vox" was the highest honor and a seal of absolute trust. Unfortunately he turned out to be a murdering psychopath and a founding member of the Seven Kings, a secret society that we believed to be behind everything from 9/11 to the London hospital bombing. A very conservative estimate of the deaths that could directly or indirectly be laid at his door was somewhere north of twelve thousand. I wanted his head on a pole, as did most of the law enforcement agencies in the world. My boss, Mr. Church, most of all.

"How do I know that you really spoke to Vox?" I said in a quiet growl.

Rasouli offered a thin smile. "He said that you might ask that, so he gave me something to say. I suppose it is a code phrase that will mean something to you. It means nothing to me."

"What is it?"

"Vox told me to say, 'I vetted Grace and she was clean. She wasn't one of mine.'"

I had to work really hard to keep what I was feeling off my face. It cost a lot.

Grace.

Damn.

When I'd first joined the DMS a year ago, Church's senior field officer and my direct superior was Major Grace Courtland. She was as beautiful as she was smart and tough. She had been the first woman to enter Britain's elite SAS team as a field operative, and she helped build Barrier—Britain's elite and highly secret counterterrorism rapid response force—and was later seconded to Church when Congress gave him approval to build the DMS. Grace and I went into combat together, we worked together, and we fell in love together. We never should have done that, it was against common sense and every rule in the book. Then, last summer, a professional killer's bullet took Grace away from me. She died saving the world. The whole damn world. I still hear her voice; still catch glimpses of her out of the corner of my eye. Still feel the absolute yawning, cavernous absence of her in my heart.

She had also been vetted by Vox before coming to work for Church.

Some people on both sides of the pond tried to use that to smear Grace's good name. Church had words with a few of them. I had words with a few others. Word got around and people shut the hell up.

Hearing her name on the lips of this monster filled me with a rage so intense that black poppies seemed to bloom before my eyes. Rasouli watched my face and I could see the delight he took in what he saw. He was like a vampire, feeding off of my pain.

The voices in my head all screamed at me to drag Rasouli to the floor and . . .

. . . I closed my eyes for a moment.

Grace.

Thinking of her tricked me into a memory of her speaking my name.

Joe.

The black flowers of hate withered and blew away, leaving a strange, cold control. I smiled at Rasouli and after a moment his smile faded.

"Vox," I said quietly.

"He spoke quite highly of you. I think he likes you . . . and he certainly admires you. He called you 'tenacious.'"

I leaned toward him. "Hear me on this. If you are working with Vox to bring any harm to the United States or its people, I will make it my life's work to tear your world apart. I'm not talking about government sanctions, and I'm not even talking about a black ops hit. You'll go to sleep one night and when you wake up it'll be you and me someplace where you can scream all you want, because believe me you will want to scream." He started to smile at the brash phrasing, but I leaned an inch closer. "If you're here then you know who I am, and what I've done. You know that most of the wiring inside my head is already fucked. It wouldn't take much to push me all the way over the line. Look at me. Look into my eyes, tell me if I'm lying."

His mouth tightened into a hard line as he cut a glance at his bodyguard, who was cleaning his fingernails with a toothpick, and back to me.

He said, "You are correct, Captain Ledger. I do know who—and *what*—you are. And it is for that reason that I risked so much to meet you."

"And Vox?"

Rasouli's lip curled as if he suddenly smelled dog shit on his shoe. "He is an insect to be stepped on. If you are asking if he and I are conspiring together, then no. I would sooner let a desert camel have its way with me."

"And yet you can call him up for favors any time you want?"

He thought about that, shrugged, took a pen and notebook from his pocket, wrote a string of numbers, tore off the page, and handed it to me. "All I have ever had for him is a phone number. It's a cell number that we have never been able to trace."

I looked at the number. "What are the chances that Vox will answer this call?"

"I do not know and do not care," he said. "Vox is your concern. If you can use that number to find him, then do so with my blessings."

"Is this the party line?"

Rasouli shook his head. "No. Vox has friends among the ayatollahs, but you probably know that."

"Is he in Iran?"

"I have no idea."

We sat for a moment with that floating in the air between us. Then I slipped the page into my shirt pocket. "God help you if you're lying to me."

Rasouli frowned, but it wasn't a fear reaction. It looked as if he was considering another aspect of what I'd said. Perhaps it was the reference to "God." Whatever it was, he nodded.

"There are times, Captain, that people who share as many ideological and political differences as do we can share a compatible view of something else. In prisons, for example, even the most hardened murderers cannot abide a molester of children."

I said nothing.

"Before we continue, Captain Ledger, let's be clear on something," he said. "I know that it was you who freed the spies last night."

"Don't even try," I warned. "Those three kids were hikers. They're as close to being spies as I am to being a prima ballerina, and believe me I don't look good in a tutu."

He arched an eyebrow. "Are you really so naïve that you believe their cover story? I would think someone of your caliber would be in the loop."

"I am. They're not spies."

"This isn't the first time we've encountered this kind of thing," he said. "You always send 'kids' to spy on us. You think the veneer of innocence is more convincing than it is. The Peace Corps was created with CIA money. Doctors Without Borders, the World Health Organization . . . they're all fronts and everyone knows it. It's not even an 'open secret' anymore."

"Horseshit." I said it loud enough to finally provoke the doofus body-guard, Feyd, to take notice. I wanted to see how he reacted. He straight-ened and looked around like an old dog that had just woken from a deep sleep. Rasouli watched me watching and waved Feyd back with an irrita-ble flick of his hand.

"Of course, you would deny it," Rasouli snapped. "You deny it be-cause you think I'm wearing a wire?"

"I don't care if you brought a film crew." I took a sip and set aside my cup. "What's the play here? Did you really set this whole thing up, the snipers and all, just so you could debate politics with a tourist?"

"Ah," he snorted with a sour smile. "'Tourist.'"

"Ah," I said with a nod in his direction. "'Human being.'"

"The spies—"

"Hikers."

"'Hikers,' whatever, are not the issue, Captain. We will get them back."

"Not a chance."

"Are you sure?"

"Pretty sure. If I had to guess, I'd bet you a shiny ten-rial piece that they're eating lunch at the U.S. embassy someplace safe. Kuwait, maybe."

"Then why are *you* still here?"

"I'm doing touristy things. I even went to a few museums. Want to see my ticket stubs? Right now, I'm doing nothing more sinister than having a cup of coffee and reading the paper."

"While waiting for a pickup car, perhaps?" His smile faded. "Captain, let's not—what's the American expression? 'Jerk each other off'?"

I grinned.

"Frankly I don't much care about the *hikers*, even though I know you were involved."

"Yeah? How about the mosque bombing? You don't want to try and hang that on me, just for shits and giggles."

"I have no interest in arresting you for anything."

"Better for everyone," I said. "You wouldn't survive the attempt."

"You are very sure of yourself," he said.

"Yes," I said. "I am. I'm not saying that your guys couldn't take me—we're in your country, not mine—but not with you still sucking air. Might even be worth it, though."

If Rasouli was frightened by my threat he managed not to show it. "We are wasting time neither of us has."

"Okay. So why are we here? What do you want to talk about?"

His eyes glittered like cold green glass. "Let us talk about saving the world."

Chapter Seven

The Agriculture Building, 7th floor
Tehran, Iran
June 15, 7:59 a.m.

"We have to go," said the tallest of the four women. She was a blocky Serbian with a knife scar across her mouth.

"You go," said the Italian woman by the window. Although she was younger by twelve years than the Serbian and had less field time than either of the other two—a Castilian brunette and a French blonde—the Italian was the team leader. "I want to watch this."

The others nodded and began packing their gear—disassembling their sniper rifles and scopes—but the Serbian lingered. It was her laser sight that had danced over the heart of the American agent; it was hers that had wandered down to burn with ugly promise over his crotch. She would have taken that shot, too. Without hesitation or remorse. Now her black eyes bored into the younger woman's.

"Another team is already on Rasouli," said the Serbian. "They'll pick him up when he leaves the café. Why are we wasting time?"

The Italian woman turned slowly away from the window and fixed her gaze on the tall Serbian. She held that stare for five full seconds, not blinking, not allowing a trace of emotion to change her expression. It was an old trick, one of Lilith's—something her mother had used on her countless times—and it worked now, too. The Serbian's eyes held for four seconds and then slid away.

"I want to watch the American," said the Italian, letting her gaze linger a moment longer before she turned without hurry back to the window.

She made sure not to turn or acknowledge as the three other women finished packing.

After the other two filed out, the Serbian lingered in the doorway. "The American isn't our—"

"I'll decide who is and isn't our concern," snapped the Italian. When she was angry her tone was identical to her mother's, and it shut the Serbian up as surely as a slap across the face. It did that with everyone. The Italian gave it a few seconds to set the mood, then she said, "Set up a surveillance post. Two cars. If Ledger leaves the café I want to know where he goes and where he's staying. Upload surveillance photos and data to my personal file on Oracle."

The Serbian nodded so curtly that it looked painful. "And then?"

"And then go back to the staging area until I call you." The Italian made sure that her voice carried every bit of Lilith's icy command. It was an illusion, borrowed power, but it was a useful skill that she'd begun cultivating before she was ten years old.

The other women mumbled something and went out.

When she could no longer hear their footsteps on the stairs she waited another thirty seconds, and then sighed, her shoulders slumping.

Was it ever like this for Lilith? Probably, she thought, and wondered how long her mother had to fake being tough before she actually became the stone-faced, stone-hearted monster she was now.

Knowing her mother as she did, that transformation had probably happened at a much younger age, maybe before she had been abducted by the Upierczi. If it hadn't been there already, Lilith would never have escaped the pits, never have escaped the breeding pens.

For her own part, the Italian woman did not yet feel that hardness developing within her own soul. Perhaps it all came down to how many people she had to kill, perhaps there was a line that, once crossed, burned away all softness. At twenty-five, the Italian woman could still count the numbers. Every head shot, every cut throat, every garroting and poisoning. Lilith? If even half of the stories were true, then her kills could fill a medium-sized office building. Or an entire graveyard.

The woman believed that *all* of the stories told about her mother were true.

Every last one.

And everyone in the sisterhood expected her to be her mother's daughter in every sense.

She murmured a brief prayer in Latin as she bent to peer through the sniper scope at the two figures seated in the coffee shop.

Joe Ledger and Jalil Rasouli.

Why had she lingered to watch?

The question flitted around in her head, fluttering like a bat after moths.

Why?

The obvious reason was to maintain surveillance on Rasouli, who—she hoped—did not know that the team he had hired had been actively surveilling him for three months. The Italian woman's team was one of several who kept tabs on Rasouli and other key players in the Muslim world. Just as other teams kept a close watch on significant persons in the Christian world. Adding to the general store of information about Rasouli's whereabouts was the obvious answer to the question.

Obvious, but a lie.

The truth was something that she could never put into a field report. She would not know how to phrase it anyway. A gut instinct. A feeling. In her personal lexicon she called it a "flash."

They did not happen often and sometimes she never understood what they meant. However, there were too many times in her life when a flash—a moment in which her entire mind and heart were locked onto a single person—proved to be a turning point. Sometimes those flashes saved her life.

Sometimes they forged an instant and inexplicable connection between her and the person who she was destined to kill.

She stayed there, seated on a folding chair, her sniper rifle resting on a bipod which in turn rested on a stack of small, sturdy crates. Not watching Rasouli.

She watched the American. The man who had identified himself as Captain Joseph Edwin Ledger.

She liked the name.

And she liked the man, which surprised her.

Not for the obvious reasons, and even she was aware of that much. To be sure, Ledger was tall and fit, handsome in the rugged way athletes often are. Some rough edges, a few visible scars, a lean waist, and muscular shoulders. That wasn't it, though.

It was his eyes.

Her sniper scope was of the finest quality. Very precise and powerful. Through it she had looked into the man's eyes while he joked with her on the phone. She knew that he'd been afraid. Who wouldn't be with laser sights on him? But he wasn't afraid in the right way. His was a practical fear, of the kind that only warriors have.

Warrior. She tasted the word. It was grandiose and yet it seemed to fit him quite well. More than that, though, was the hurt she saw in his eyes. Not hurt from anything related to this incident. Deeper hurt, older. That was something this woman understood more intimately than anything else. Her world was built on pillars of pain and suffering.

Was it possible that this man's soul dwelt in a similar tower? Was that why she felt the flash at the moment when she and her team had first trained their laser sights on him?

If so, then it would genuinely hurt her to have to kill him.

Chapter Eight

Starbox Coffee
Tehran, Iran
June 15, 8:03 a.m.

I stared at Rasouli. "Saving the world from—what?"

He pursed his lips thoughtfully. "Consider this. If scientists discovered than an asteroid was hurtling toward the earth and was likely to strike in one year, would it not be possible that the best and the brightest from all countries would drop their hostilities and work together to prevent a shared disaster?"

The comment was so weird that it jerked my head into an entirely different place. At the same time my heart started doing another jazz riff. "Christ! Is *that* what this is about?"

"What? Oh, no . . . no," he said, looking genuinely surprised. "I speak hypothetically about the nature of our response to a shared threat too large for any one country to handle alone."

"Next time say so. You almost gave me a frigging heart attack."

He smiled at that. Jackass.

"Okay," I said, "Given the right kind of potential catastrophe, then that kind of cooperation is possible. Even so, red tape would be a bitch."

"And yet the red tape could be cut if the threat was more imminent, yes? Say that this hypothetical asteroid was due to strike in a month? The need for immediate and uninhibited action would necessitate a quicker exchange of information so that the situation could be handled. After all, global extermination trumps individual ideologies."

"In a rational world, yes," I agreed. "Where are you going with this?"

"There is a matter that will require very great and very careful cooperation."

He removed a cell phone from his jacket pocket and played with the touch screen to bring up a photo, then handed the phone to me. "Do you know what that is?"

I stared at the picture and my mouth went as dry as dust.

"*Good God . . .*"

"Indeed," agreed Rasouli.

I knew all about them, of course. I had to. I knew the history, studied them for my job, read the field reports. I had seen them in museums and textbooks and on the Discovery Channel. Knowledge may be power but at that moment I felt as weak as a child. Even as a picture on a phone— small and frozen in a snapshot moment of time—it was terrifying to behold.

A nuclear bomb.

"It is a Teller-Ulam design hydrogen bomb," said Rasouli quietly. "It has a yield of fifty megatons, which is equivalent to fourteen hundred times the combined power of the bombs dropped on Hiroshima and Nagasaki. Or, if you look at it another way, it has ten times the combined power of all the explosives used in WWII."

"Where is it?" I snarled, causing Rasouli to recoil from me.

"Please," he said soothingly, "this device is not on U.S. soil."

"Then why the hell are you showing me this?"

"Because I need you to know that this is something larger than the political struggles between our countries."

"Your country has been trying to build this for years, asshole—" I began, but he cut me off, and again had to wave back his guard.

"You don't understand," said Rasouli in an urgent whisper, "this is not *ours*."

I stared at him. "Then *whose is it*?"

"I . . . do not know," he said. "That is one of the reasons I wanted your help. It's likely the device is one of many that have gone 'missing' since the end of the Cold War and the collapse of the Russian economy."

"Just so we're clear," I said, "you—Iran—you're afraid of terrorists with a bomb?"

"Yes." His mouth was a tight line, "and I'll thank you not to smirk. This is a very real threat that could cause untold damage."

"You have any suspects?"

Rasouli shrugged. "We are not a popular country, Captain Ledger. It is the price of being powerful, as you Americans well know,"

"Yeah. Seems like every five minutes there's a fundamentalist nut job coming at us with a vest of C-4 and the name of God on his lips. Ain't that a bitch?"

All that earned me was a contemptuous sneer. "This is hardly on the level of car bombings, Captain. Whoever is behind this is organized, extraordinarily well-financed, and subtle. I have reliable sources within Hezbollah, al Qaeda, and the Taliban and I am convinced they are not involved."

"They aren't the only players."

"No, but they are the ones most likely to consider such a radical plan; and the smaller cells and splinter groups could never make one of these."

"They could buy one," I said.

"Of course, but it would be very expensive. Prohibitively so. Most organizations do not have that much money."

"Hugo Vox could buy one of those with his beer money."

"Why would he? His day is over."

"Why? Because the Seven Kings are off the board?"

"No," said Rasouli. "My sources tell me that Vox is ill."

"What do you mean?"

Rasouli's green eyes glittered. "He has cancer, didn't you know?"

"Shit."

It was good and bad news at the same time. Good news because it was nice to think about Vox rotting away. Bad because that was a much easier exit strategy than he deserved.

"Could be his last blast," I said, meaning it the way it sounded.

I thought about what I said but then dismissed it. Vox is many things, but he has never struck me as vindictive. Murderous, to be sure, and merciless, but not petty. To detonate a bomb in frustration for dying of cancer . . . ? No, that would be cheap, no matter what the death toll.

I tried to build a case for it in my mind, but gave it up. It didn't fit Vox's pattern at all. For him, killing was only ever a pathway to profit. Even so, I'd want to run this past Mr. Church, Rudy Sanchez, and Circe O'Tree. They built the profile on him that was being used by every law enforcement agency in the world.

"If it's not Vox," I said, "then we're looking at someone who has as big a bank account."

"Would you like me to recite a list of nations who would love to see Iran reduced to scorched earth?"

"Not really, because you'd start your list with the U.S., Israel, and Great Britain, and they don't need to buy black-market bombs."

He shrugged. "That is not entirely true. A case can be made for why such countries would want to have bombs that could in no way be traced back to them. Bombs from former Soviet countries, perhaps."

"Fair enough. But is that your pitch? Are you saying that it's America or one of its allies?"

"No," he said tiredly. "If I thought that, then this discussion would be held in the world press, backed by all of the considerable outrage which it is possible for our propaganda department to muster. The Ayatollahs would probably enjoy that."

"Bottom line," I said, "can you tell me where this thing can be found?"

"Much worse," he said. "I know where *four* of these things can be found."

The whole world froze around me.

"Jesus Christ," I said.

"Worse still," Rasouli said in a voice that sucked the last shreds of peace from the morning, "there are at least three more that we have not been able to locate. And one of the others might even be on U.S. soil."

Chapter Nine

He was the King of Thorns.

The King of Blood and Shadows.

He lived in a world of darkness, and that darkness was so beautiful. So subtle. It hid so many things from those who lacked the power to see. It was his mother, his ally, his weapon. It was the ocean in which he swam, the sky through which he flew, the dream in which he walked.

Darkness did not blind him. Even down here in the endless shadows. Buried beneath a billion tons of rock and sand.

Darkness held no surprises for him; he knew its secrets. They had been handed down to him, generation upon generation, and he had shared those secrets with the other pale bodies that moved and writhed and burrowed beneath the earth.

A single candle burned, its flame hidden behind a pillar of rock so that only the faintest of yellow light painted the edges of walls and glimmered on the golden thread of ancient tapestries. A single candle was all the light he needed. More than he needed.

He rose from a bed of fur and silk and broken bones. Ribs cracked beneath his feet. Cobwebs licked at his face as he moved from chamber to chamber. Water dripped in the distance, and the sound of wretched weeping echoed to him from down one of the many corridors his people had carved from the living rock. He paused to listen to the sobs. A female voice, of course. A babble of nonsense words and bits of prayers which combined to make sense only to the mad. There was so much pain there, so much hurt and loss.

It made him smile. It made his loins throb with a deep and ancient ache.

He closed his eyes and leaned against the closest wall. The limestone was cool and damp as he pressed his cheek against it, savoring the rough texture. A tongue tip the color of a worm wriggled out from between his teeth and curled along the thin contours of his lips.

It was as if he could taste the pain, and he craved it, wanting more of it, wanting the freshest and choicest bits.

He was there for a long time, lost in memory and expectation.

"Grigor," murmured a voice, and with regret he opened his eyes and pushed himself away from the wall. He turned to see Thaddeus, his eighth son, standing a few yards away. The boy had made no sound at all. Excellent. He was learning, he would be ready soon.

"What is it?" asked Grigor.

"*He* is here."

Grigor smiled again. "Good."

And it was good. In the distance the weeping continued unabated, and that was good too. Soon, Grigor knew, there would be more weeping. So much more.

How delicious that would be.

And how soon.

It was almost time to make the whole world scream.

Chapter Ten

Starbox Coffee
Tehran, Iran
June 15, 8:05 a.m.

I almost came out of my chair and went for Rasouli.

"Where?" I snarled. Feyd was halfway across the room before Rasouli held up his hand to freeze the moment.

"I don't know," he fired back, cold and hard. "Listen to me, Captain, I am here as a friend—"

"Bullshit."

"As an ally then. In this matter, we are both in danger. Now please, listen for a moment."

I stayed in my chair. Feyd gave me a hard look and slouched back to his post. Rasouli let out a weary breath.

"You said that there was a device in the States," I said very quietly. "*Where?*"

"I don't know where. I'm not even positive there *is* one in America. Please, let me tell you what I do know." He gestured to the phone that I still held. "We believe that this device is somewhere inside the Aghajari oil refinery."

"That's yours," I said. "That's in Iran."

He nodded. "We don't know exactly where they've placed it. However, I have managed to get some degree of verification through an operative with a radiation detector. I have not risked a full-blown investigation yet for fear that if we started looking it would alert whoever planted the devices that we know about them. That might be a fatal misstep."

"You think there's a mole inside your government?"

"There are many moles inside my government, and not all of them are yours, Captain. It is in the nature of what we do that there are spies, and I have very good reason to believe that some of those spies work for whoever has these bombs." Before I could interrupt him he held up a finger. "What little information I have came to me in a way that has effectively shut the door to investigation. My agent was found dead, the victim of a savage beating. Many of his bones were broken and his internal organs ruptured. My pathologist says that the injuries were apparently delivered with hands and feet. Whoever did it made it last and that suggests either someone with a taste for it or someone who wanted information that my agent was unwilling or unable to provide. However, during the autopsy the surgeon found this." Rasouli reached into his pocket and produced a flash drive. "He had apparently swallowed it."

"And didn't give it up during the beating?" I remarked. "Tough man."

"Very. One of my best agents. You . . . would have admired him, I'm sure, but disliked him." He paused. "The beating is not what killed him, however."

"What did? A bullet in the back of the head?"

"His throat was torn out," Rasouli said.

I paused. "When you say 'torn out'—"

"My people did a thorough post mortem, including all of the appropriate tests for trace particles. Blades leave microscopic metallic residue, and even with plastic knives there are signature markings. There was nothing like that. The pathologist did a reconstruction of the man's throat and determined that the flesh was torn out by teeth."

"What kind? Dog?"

Rasouli studied me for a moment. "I don't know. There were traces of saliva in the wounds that my physician could not immediately identify. I would like to have had DNA testing done on it, but that would raise too many flags." He fished in his pocket and produced a small metal container the size of a Zippo lighter. "This contains a skin sample packed in CO_2. Your employer has access to more sophisticated equipment than I do. The body has since been cremated, so that is the only remaining sample. I'm trusting you, Captain, and I ask only that you share your findings with me."

"How?"

He produced his notebook again and wrote a second number; however, he did not give me that sheet of paper. Instead he held it up for me to look at. "That is my private cell. Memorize the number. If you have to call, let it ring once and then hang up. I'll return your call when I can do so safely."

I nodded and he produced a pack of matches and burned the page in an ashtray. I glanced at Feyd, but either he didn't notice or didn't care.

I pocketed the metal sample case.

"When my agent's body was found, the police investigators concluded that he had been murdered elsewhere and then dumped where the remains could be found. They reached that conclusion because there was very little blood found at the scene, and such a terrible wound would have bled profusely."

"So?"

"I believe the police drew the wrong conclusion. I believe that he *was* killed where he was found."

"And the blood?"

"This is not the first time there has been a murder of this kind, Captain Ledger. There have been others. Many others, if the reports I collected are correct. Here in Iran, and elsewhere. Syria and Lebanon, Palestine and Jordan. I had to dig deeply and quietly to learn that much, but my sources are reliable. In each case the throat was mutilated and the bodies exsanguinated by unknown means. All of the deaths have some political or religious connection, even if tangentially so." He gave me a strange look. "What do you think of that?"

I sipped my coffee, which was getting cold. "If it's not a serial killer, then you have a freak. A contract hitter or rogue special operator who has a screw loose. Someone who has created a very specific style for his kills."

"Why would someone do that?" he asked. "What would be the gain from so grotesque a form of execution? There is no political or religious significance to it, and therefore no message which can be conveyed to an opposition party through it. Do you understand what I mean?"

"All too well."

We sat there, a pair of gunslingers, fully aware of the graveyards of enemies we'd each buried. Like me, he knew all sorts of killers, from those who pulled the trigger for God and country to those who killed for the sheer joy of it. More than a few of those were drawn to military service or covert wetworks because of the opportunities provided to kill while being afforded the umbrella of official sanction. Not most, of course, but enough so that military psychs and screeners were always on the prowl for them. Either to weed them out or to recruit them. I'd like to say that "we don't do that sort of thing," but that would be a lie.

I had my own inner demon who liked to roll around in the enemy's blood. Mine was on a leash most of the time, but once in a while he got out. If the public at large ever saw that side of me, I'd be labeled a monster and locked up. Looking into Rasouli's eyes, it was clear that he was thinking the same things about himself.

We were sitting there, a couple of monsters contemplating something worse than either of us.

I cleared my throat. "Bombs," I said.

He set the flash drive on the table between us. "Because the man swallowed the drive, there has been some moisture damage. I was able to salvage about ten percent of the information. Enough to scare me to death. Enough to make me want to risk this encounter we are having."

"You said there were seven of them? One in America?"

"I *believe* there is one in America. One of the documents on the drive gave a list of potential targets in your country. The file was corrupted and there is nothing to indicate that a bomb has definitely reached your shores. That is, as you well know, a difficult thing to accomplish."

"Don't look so sad about it."

He sighed again. "Captain, we may be on different sides of many issues, not the least of which is nuclear power and arms, but I doubt either of us is a fool or an absolute bloody-minded madman. We are entering into a new Cold War, a new arms race, but just as neither America nor Russia launched bombs at each other, no matter how badly they wanted to or how many they had to spare, neither do we. What we *want* is to be safe, and if having weapons of mass destruction insures that we will never be invaded by a conquering army, then that is only fair. And . . . more to the point, there is nothing to be gained by mutual extermination. Nothing. Even the most extreme ayatollahs know that, no matter what comprises their public rhetoric. Besides . . . surely you, a soldier of some reputation, understand the difference between being only able to shout loud and shake a fist and to speak quietly and shake a spear."

"Walk softly and carry a big stick," I said.

"Yes. Theodore Roosevelt. The smarter of your two Roosevelts. He understood that one must have power before one can effectively enter into war *or* peace."

I studied the picture. The picture showed a bomb the size of a central air conditioning unit for a medium-sized suburban house. The walls around it looked like bare rock; the floor was poured concrete. There were no other details visible. Not on a phone image a couple of inches square. "This is a big unit. It's not built into a warhead, or at least this one's not. How are they planning on transporting these devices?"

"I doubt they are," said Rasouli. "The fragments of information on the drive suggest that as many as four devices are already in place. The ones here in the Middle East. The last time I spoke to my agent, shortly before he was killed, he said that he did not think that any bombs were currently inside the borders of the United States. That was, alas, all that he said on that topic. I ordered him to bring me all of his findings, but he was apparently abducted on the way to my home. Another fragment of a file obliquely mentions America, but there are no other details. Merely the hint that America may be a target. "

"Where are the others?"

"I don't know. Possibly in Iraq, or India. It's conjecture though, based solely on similarly cryptic references. One message fragment makes reference to 'the seven devices.' That's all we could recover."

"Shit," I said, and if I wasn't scared enough before I was really starting to sweat now. Given a choice of knowing for sure that there was a bomb in the U.S. and not knowing, I'd prefer certain knowledge. At least then we could start some kind of proper search. "What's the endgame for all this?" I asked. "What does this accomplish?"

"I don't know. From a practical stance, I believe they are planning to destroy a significant amount of the oil reserves in the Middle East. Not just what is in the refineries, but in the actual oil fields. Underground devices could ignite much of it—wherever there is sufficient venting for oxygen, and what isn't burned would be contaminated. Not to mention the destruction of everything that lives and moves on the sands above."

I shook my head. "Four nukes couldn't do that. Not sure if seven of them could."

"Four would be sufficient to disrupt the majority of production. All other refineries would be shut down or scaled down as safety measures. It might takes months or years before each facility could be properly and thoroughly checked, and longer to build newer security systems that would guarantee the safety of the remaining fields and refineries. Think about the impact on the global market. The cost per barrel from noncontaminated fields would be astronomical. The blow would be as much financial as material."

"You know," I said, forcing a smile, "that's just the kind of thing your pal Hugo Vox would cook up. Financial gain was the reason the Seven Kings arranged to have Bin Laden and the Saudis fly planes into the towers, and it's why they blew up the London Hospital. Have you asked him about this?"

"In a roundabout way, yes. He appeared to know nothing."

"He's good at that, the lying sack of shit."

Rasouli spread his hands. "Now you are where I am, armed with dangerous knowledge and no clear set of answers. In the wake of Vox's betrayal, I doubt you will be able to completely trust everyone in your government. But you have Mr. Church and the considerable resources at his disposal."

I grunted. "What made you call Vox in the first place? To arrange this meet, I mean."

Rasouli showed me his expensive white teeth. "I had been troubling over how to proceed with this matter when the reports came in about the 'hikers' being liberated. There are several countries that have teams capable of such an action, but most of them would not risk it, even for as staunch an ally as the United States, therefore it must be an American black operation. Who knows more about that sort of thing than Hugo

Vox? I knew that he would know who was responsible and I made a call. He already knew about the action. He did not tell me how, though we are both adult enough to accept that he must still have operatives active in the United States covert community. He gave me you, and now we are here."

"What would you have done with the flash drive if there had been no drama last night?"

"Have it sent by private courier to your embassy, I suppose. Addressed to Mr. Church."

I took the drive and closed my fist around it, but I nodded toward his phone. "The photo you showed me? If your agents haven't put eyes on this thing, then where'd that come from?"

"It was on the drive, too, but I never got the chance to ask how my agent obtained it. There are several badly damaged image files. This is the cleanest one."

We sat for a moment, looking at each other while so many unsaid things swirled around us. I mean, think about it. Here was a guy I would have gladly killed ten minutes ago. Without hesitation or remorse. I could have cut his throat and then gone to work with a light heart.

And now?

I opened my hand and studied the flash drive. An ordinary device, probably bought at whatever passes for Staples in this part of the world. Now it's little memory chip was filled with horrors beyond imagining.

Nukes. Under the Middle East oil fields.

"So that's it?" I asked. "You—pardon the expression—drop this bomb on me and walk off?"

"That is a disingenuous remark, Captain. I risked much coming here. My president and the Rahbare Mo'azzame Enghelab do not know that I am here."

"And you don't entirely trust Ahmadinejad and the Supreme Leader? Wouldn't they have the same fears as you? I doubt they want to reach paradise atop a mushroom cloud."

Actually, I deliberately mispronounced his name as Armanihandjob, but Rasouli did not so much as crack a smile.

"I am not in their inner circle," he said with a philosophic shrug. "They know I have ambitions and the president in particular would not cry if

I was found dead with my throat torn out. Besides, in government nothing is as hard to protect as a state secret. They have people that *they* trust, but I do not know if I can trust the same people."

"Yeah," I agreed, "but you have to admit that it's pretty weird that you're bringing this to us."

He cocked his head at me. "You may neither believe nor care, but I respect Mr. Church. And you, if what I've heard about you is true."

I said nothing.

Rasouli smiled. "I am not fishing for a reciprocal compliment."

"Good thing. Fishing hole's pretty dry."

He shrugged, then asked, "Tell me, do you know the name Salāh-ed-Dīn Ayyūbi?"

"Sure. Saladin. General during the Crusades."

"He was a sultan," corrected Rasouli. "A great man, a hero of Islam."

"Wasn't he a Sunni born in Iraq?" I asked with a smile.

Rasouli shrugged. Iran was no friend of Iraq and 95 percent of Iranians belong to the Shia branch of Islam.

"My point is," he persisted, "Saladin viewed the world from an eagle's perspective. What you would call a 'big picture' view. It was never his desire to exterminate his enemies, only to defeat them and drive them from the Holy Land."

"Ah. So, we're supposed to shake hands like two worldly wise warriors, setting political differences aside for the betterment of mankind. Is that about it?"

"Something like that," he said without a trace of embarrassment.

I nodded and shoved the flash drive into my shirt pocket.

Rasouli looked down at his shoes for a moment, breathing audibly through his nostrils. Without looking at me he said, "There is one last thing. It's also on the drive."

"More bombs?"

He shook his head. "I am not entirely sure that it is related to this matter, but then again I'm not entirely sure it isn't." He tilted his head and cut an upward look at me. "What do you know of the *Book of Shadows*?"

"Isn't that a CD by Enya?"

His mouth twitched. "What about the *Saladin Codex*?"

"Nope. What are they?"

He turned toward me now and his eyes looked different. Older. Sadder. "They are two sides of the same very old coin."

"Meaning?"

"As you do not know what they are, then it is all I'm prepared to say at this point. Mr. Church will see the references on the drive. Perhaps he will know if they are pertinent."

Rasouli stood up and offered me his hand. I stood and looked from it to him.

"I know you despise me, Captain Ledger, and I do not care much for you. For now, however, we must rise above our individual beliefs and politics and do what we can for the common good."

"You're not Saladin," I said. "And I'm sure as hell not Richard the Lionhearted."

The hand did not move.

So, I shook it. Fuck it. It didn't cost anything except a little pride and disgust, and I had a bottle of Purell in my pocket.

"Remember," he said, "that you have been instructed to wait for ten minutes after my departure before leaving this coffee shop."

With that he turned and left. Feyd opened the door for him and gave me a single withering stare, which I managed to endure without dying of fright. I stood by the glass and watched them walk around the corner of the building out of sight, presumably to a waiting car.

The next ten minutes took about ten thousand years.

Chapter Eleven

Driving in the City
Tehran, Iran
June 15, 8:17 a.m.

The passenger in the limousine rolled up his window as the tall American agent stepped out of the Starbox. The limousine idled one hundred feet down the side street, mostly hidden by a sidewalk stand selling dried lentils and wheat flour. The American agent looked up and down the street and then turned away and headed in the direction of the hotel district.

The passenger slid open the glass door between the front and rear seats. "Sefu, follow him. We need the name of his hotel but for God's sake don't let him see us."

"Sir," grunted the driver. Sefu was an Egyptian Christian who had worked for many years in this man's service. He was not in the habit of letting anyone spot him when he tailed them, though he was circumspect enough not to say so. He put the car in drive and eased into traffic three cars back from the one closest to the American.

In the rear seat, Charles LaRoque, a French businessman and one of the world's leading brokers of fine Persian rugs, pushed the button to close the soundproof glass partition. He cut a look at the rearview mirror to assure himself that the driver was not watching him, then he fished a small compact mirror out of his pocket. He opened it to reveal that both top and bottom held small mirrors. LaRoque studied his face in one mirror and then the other, back and forth for several moments, tilting the compact and changing his expression over and over again. A strange little laugh burbled from his chest.

"Delicious, delicious, delicious," he said to the alternating images. There was so much to see there, so many faces. His father and his grandfather. The trickster and the priest. The Red Knights with their red mouths. The King of Thorns. It was all so very delicious.

"Oh yes it is," LaRoque said, and laughed again.

A soft musical tone filled the car. Not the ringtone of his regular cell but the much more elaborate encrypted device given to him by a friend of his father's.

"I'll talk to you later," LaRoque said to his mirror and shoved it back into his pocket, then closed his eyes and composed himself before he reached for the cell phone. When he opened his eyes he felt composed and ready to play his role.

"Yes?" he said into the phone, his tone serious and sober. Even so, LaRoque almost giggled and caught himself. He took a breath and forced himself to *live* his role. On this call, and in this matter, he was no longer Charles LaRoque. He was the Scriptor of the *Ordo Ruber*, the Sacred Red Order. The Scriptor did not giggle. The Scriptor was stern, decisive. That was how the old priest wanted him to play it.

"Was it Ledger?" asked Hugo Vox. "Was he there?"

"Yes," confirmed LaRoque. "Just as you said."

Vox laughed. He had a bass voice and a rumbling grizzly laugh. "What happened? What'd they talk about?"

"How would I know?" said LaRoque in a waspish voice. "I was outside in the bloody car, wasn't I?"

"Charlie," replied Vox with false patience, "don't fuck with me. You heard every goddamn thing they said and we both know it."

LaRoque cut a guilty look at the headphones lying next to him on the car seat. He debated lying to Vox. There was no strategic benefit to it, but lying was fun. But, he sighed instead and grunted. "I listened."

"And?"

"It wasn't what we thought," said LaRoque. "It had nothing to do with the Red Order or the Holy Agreement. Well, at least not much. Rasouli mentioned the *Book* and the *Codex* at the end, but he didn't tell Ledger what they were."

"Hunh. That's interesting as shit," said Vox sourly. "What *did* they talk about?"

"Some nonsense about bombs."

"What kind of bombs?"

"Nuclear bombs."

There was a heavy silence at the other end of the line. "Really." Vox said it more like a statement than a question. "Tell me exactly what they said."

As well as he could, LaRoque repeated the conversation between Jalil Rasouli and Captain Joe Ledger. Vox did not interrupt, and when LaRoque was done there was another ponderous silence.

"It's not our concern," LaRoque said into the silence.

"Yeah," said Vox, "I think it fucking well is."

"I don't care about that sort of thing. All I care about is whether Rasouli signs the Holy Agreement so we can get back to business."

"Seriously?" asked Vox. "I mean, holy shit, Charlie, I knew that you were no rocket scientist, kid, but I didn't think you were actually challenged. Rasouli is bending you over a barrel and dropping his shorts."

"Nonsense."

"You said that he gave a flash drive to Ledger. How do you know that it doesn't have the whole damn story of the Agreement on it? It could have the name of every Scriptor and Murshid, every action taken by the Red Order and the Tariqa for the last eight hundred years. You *gave* Rasouli that information."

"Not all of it," LaRoque said defensively, and despite what he'd said to Vox he was beginning to think the uncouth American traitor might be correct.

"Enough of it, damn it. Enough to have you stood against a wall and shot. Christ, Charlie, if this gets out old ladies and nuns will want to cut your balls off, let alone the Americans and NATO. You should never have—"

"Stop lecturing me, Hugo. I don't appreciate it and—"

"What would you prefer I do? Leave you to the wolves? Your father and grandfather were friends of mine. I made promises to them that I'd always be there for you, no matter what."

"You mean, 'no matter what silly insane Charles did'?"

"If the shoe fits, kid."

LaRoque looked out the window, trying to catch his reflection in the smoked glass. He needed to see one of his other faces. One of the stronger ones. Or, maybe the face of the old priest. As the car rounded a corner to follow Ledger, LaRoque thought he caught a glimpse of the wizened features of the priest. Just a flash and then it was gone.

It was enough, though. It steadied him.

He drew a breath and let it out audibly. "Very well, Hugo. What do you advise?"

"Good," Vox said, and LaRoque wondered if the American had also seen the priest. Could Vox do that, he wondered. Did the priest appear to everyone? Or to a chosen few? Or just to him?

"Let's go on the assumption that Rasouli gave Ledger information that could hurt the Order," said Vox. "Start there 'cause that gives us a game plan for safety."

"What plan is that?"

"A very simple one because we need to do two things and they can both be done at the same time," said Vox. "We have to get the flash drive back and we have to kill Joe Ledger."

"Only that?"

Vox paused. "To start, yeah. Then we have to decide what to do about—"

Suddenly Vox's words disintegrated into a terrible fit of wet coughs. Vicious coughs that broke from deep in his chest. The coughing fit lasted nearly a full minute before winding down to gasps. When he could finally speak, Vox cursed.

"Good lord, Hugo, are you all right?"

"Yeah, yeah, yeah, shit," Vox wheezed. "These chemo treatments are kicking my ass."

The Scriptor took a moment to make sure that his voice was filled with concern, even if his mouth was trembling with a smile. "Are you in much pain?"

"A bit."

"I'm sorry." He almost said, "Oh, goody."

"Yeah, well. Life's a bitch and then you're dead for a long time." Vox cleared his throat. "Look, the bottom line is that you have to get that flash drive back and you have to do it right fucking now."

"Why the hurry? I looked him up in our database and he appears to have been competent, yes, but not—"

"Don't be an idiot. You only have his army and police records. I'll send you his DMS file. It makes interesting reading."

"You're saying he's a threat?"

"I'm saying that he's Mr. Church's pet psychopath. Don't underestimate him. Ledger's a weird cat, but he's sharp and he is fucking relentless. He's also got some freaky mojo."

" 'Mojo'?"

"Luck. Son of a bitch is either lucky or unlucky, depending on how you look at it, but he always seems to be in the thick of things. Should have been dead a dozen times, but even though bodies stack up around him the cocksucker keeps finding a way through to the other side."

"An angel in his pocket?" mused LaRoque. He looked down in surprise to find that his hand held the little compact mirror even though he had no memory of removing it from his pocket. He watched as his manicured thumbnail popped it open.

"You need to send a knight after him," said Vox, and LaRoque almost dropped the compact.

"What? No. You have whole teams of Sabbatarians in Tehran—"

"Forget those fruitcakes. Ledger would have them for lunch."

"Don't be absurd."

"I'm not. Ledger and his team dismantled my Kingsmen last year, and no one's ever done that before. And I have it on good authority that Ledger beat Rafael Santoro one-on-one."

That made the Scriptor pause. Santoro was the chief assassin of the Seven Kings, a man whose utter ruthlessness was only equaled by his nearly matchless skills as a combatant. Santoro was one of the very few ordinary men who might stand a chance against a knight. Not a full-blooded knight, of course, but one of the trainees.

"Ledger killed Santoro?"

"I . . . don't know," admitted Vox. "All I know is that they fought and then Santoro was gone, off the radar. And it's not the first time Ledger's beaten the odds. Don't risk a Sabbatarian team. You have the Red Knights. Use one of them."

The Scriptor looked at the two aspects of his face in the mirror, angling the compact one way and then the other, back and forth as the silence grew. The bottom mirror showed his own weak mouth, the top showed his indecisive eyes.

"Charlie—?" prompted Vox.

LaRoque flipped the mirrors forward and back, over and over again until the top image *changed*. From one heartbeat to the next the image changed from his own reflection to the face of the priest. Wrinkled skin, a slash of a cruel mouth, and eyes that were a strange swirl of colors—leprous brown and ophidian green.

Do it, whispered the voice in his mind. The voice of the priest.

LaRoque took a steadying breath. "Very well, Hugo, I'll do it. I hope you appreciate the great faith I'm showing by trusting you."

A snort of laughter came down the line. "You're showing great intelligence by trusting me."

"Others might disagree, considering what happened to your organization."

"Nothing happened that I didn't want to happen," Vox said with a little edge to his voice. "I *used* Ledger and Church to turn a losing situation into a winning one."

"Winning?"

"Am I in jail? Am I dead? Fuck no. Did I stroll away with a hundred billion dollars in numbered accounts? You bet your left nut I did. Am I *still* raking in about a couple of mil a week from that shit? You can bet your right nut on that one. So, yeah, I put the DMS to work for me and they don't even know it."

"Not even Church?"

"Maybe Church," Vox conceded after some thought, "but he can't do jack shit about it. He can't want to kill me more than he already does. So, call me when Ledger's dead."

Vox disconnected.

For several moments LaRoque held the phone to his ear with his right hand and stared at the face of the priest in the compact mirror he held in his left.

Then it was gone. LaRoque blinked. The mirror now held only his own reflection.

"You made the right choice," said the priest.

The Scriptor slowly raised his eyes and stared at the wizened figure who now sat across from him in the back of the limousine. The priest had eyes the color of toad flesh, and his skin was as sallow and thin as old parchment. When he smiled, his teeth were white and wet.

Charles LaRoque smiled back.

"Thank you, Father Nicodemus," he said.

Chapter Twelve

Golden Oasis Hotel
Tehran, Iran
June 15, 8:28 a.m.

I walked back to the hotel, and with each step I tried not to scream. I wanted to run back, but I didn't dare draw attention to myself. It was bad enough I was sweating and probably looked nervous and guilty. There were so many ways this could play out, most of them bad, and I didn't know how we were going to play it.

Inside my head the word "nuke" kept echoing.

About every third car on the street was either a police sedan or a military jeep. Even though the rescue of the hikers wasn't in the morning papers, it was clear from the activity on the street that the government was mobilized. Although the hikers had been illegally arrested and unfairly held, Iran had never budged from its stance that the kids were spies and that they'd crossed the border. At the time Echo Team went wheels-up to come here, the State Department had not yet decided how to announce the event. A lot of it, I knew, depended on whether we were successful, on the physical and mental condition of the rescued hikers, on the degree of resistance during the raid, and whether we got caught. The mission had gone by the numbers except for the end; and though I had no doubt Top had managed to get the kids out of the country, at least one American still had boots on the ground here.

If John Smith or Lydia had missed their rides, then the math got more complicated. The local government needed only one of us to create a media shit storm. The fact that there wasn't *yet* that storm suggested that none of my people were in the bag. I did not want to be the one to let the team down; and I had no illusions about Church dispatching a team to haul my ass out of jail. There was no political profit in that. He'd disown me and wipe my records.

That's exactly as comforting as it sounds.

I knew that Church was advising the president and the secretary of state about how to spin this thing. Spin control for global disasters was one of his most endearing talents.

And, of course, there was the whole nuke thing. Talk about skewing the math. Rasouli oversaw much of the nation's misinformation and propaganda and he was the one who wanted me to find the nukes. Did that mean he was influencing the manhunt process? No one had a physical description of me, at least no one attached to the rescue; but Rasouli and his sniper psycho babe were able to spot me and put a laser sight on me at a coffee shop. How'd that happen? Even with Hugo Vox advising them, how'd they know where to acquire me?

"Joe," a voice said.

I spun around, sure that someone stood right behind me, whispering in my ear. But I was alone on the street. The voice . . . I knew that voice.

Her voice.

"Grace?"

My heart was pounding and the ground under me felt like it was tilting. But there was no one close enough to have spoken my name.

Chances are that no voice spoke and that I was crazy as a loon. Chances, not guarantees.

Grace.

I searched for the echo of her voice, of that one word, inside the fractured darkness of my mind, but it, like she, was gone. Tears wanted to burn their way out of my eyes. I wanted so badly to find a place of shadows, a doorway or the back of an abandoned car, somewhere I could hide. Ever since Rasouli dropped the first two bombs on me—Hugo Vox and Grace Courtland—I felt like things were starting to unravel inside my head. It made me feel as if everyone was looking at me, as if everyone knew who and what I was.

I used every ounce of strength and will I possessed to compose my face and show absolutely nothing. It cost me, though.

The Israelis operated a news and cigarette shop a block from my hotel and I stopped by there and browsed the papers until the shop was empty. Then I drifted over to the counter. The man who ran the place looked and sounded Iranian but I knew for a fact that he was Mossad.

"Carton of cigarettes," I said. "Do you still carry Bistoon?"

He smiled. "We get no call for it, I'm sorry."

It was the proper call sign and response that identified me as an American agent. We both glanced around the shop to verify that we were alone.

"What do you need?"

"Cell phone battery." I showed the phone I had, which was a DMS design built on a local model. Even though my unit had some extra goodies built in, it was designed to work on a standard cell battery that could be found anywhere in Iran.

"I can have it for you in half an hour. Will you wait or do you want it delivered?"

"Delivered." I told him my hotel and room.

He studied my face and frowned. "I will not ask what is troubling you, my friend, but it appears that you are having a bad day."

"You have no idea."

Before I left I bought a pack of goat jerky. I had a hungry dog waiting for me in my hotel and if I didn't come back with food he'd sulk all day.

I paid for the goat.

"May your day improve," said the shopkeeper.

"Yeah," I said from the doorway. "Here's hoping."

As cops and soldiers cruised by and peered at every civilian with suspicious eyes, I forced myself to walk normally. I willed myself not to be noticeable. I needed to punch and pound the fear and grief and paranoia down into its little box. Walking a few blocks seemed to take absolutely forever. By the time I reached my hotel my hands were shaking so badly I had to jam them into my pockets.

I climbed three flights of stairs, dropped my keys twice, and finally opened the lock. As soon as I was inside I closed and relocked the door and fell back against it with an exhale that came all the way up from my shoes.

My dog, Ghost, was waiting for me, wagging his tail and looking at my hands to see if I'd brought him anything. He's a big white shepherd, 105 pounds of muscle and appetite. Ghost was cross-trained in a variety of useful skills from combat to rescue; and though he was useful in ordinary bomb detection, he couldn't disarm a nuke.

I knelt down and hugged him. I kissed his furry head.

"This one's going to be a bitch, fuzzball," I told him.

He looked at me with those liquid dog eyes that always seem deep and wise. He whined a little, catching my mood or perhaps smelling my fear. Then his whole body went rigid as he stared past me. Not to the closed door, but to an empty space on the wall. I followed the line of his gaze, willing myself to see what he saw, but a dog is a dog and they see things we can't. No matter how much we want to.

I listened to the silence, wondering if I'd just heard a soft voice whisper my name again.

But, no . . . there was nothing.

When I looked at Ghost, he was no longer staring at the wall.

"What is it, boy?"

Ghost, being a dog, just looked at me.

I mean, really . . . what had I expected him to say? My palms were sweaty and I wiped them on my thighs. Then I fished some dried goat strips out of my jacket pocket and dropped them on the floor. Ghost is peculiar in that he eats his food delicately, one piece at a time, making it last.

Minutes crawled by as I waited for the Mossad shopkeeper to send over the battery. The thought of those moments being chipped off the block of time remaining until those nukes went active was making my heart hurt. I was sweating and it wasn't the heat in that stuffy little room.

I fished for more goat and my fingers scrabbled over the flash drive. That drove everything else out of my head.

Rasouli said that there were four nukes scattered throughout the Mid-east oil fields, and three more unknowns. Maybe one in the States.

"Holy God . . ." I breathed. Ghost cut a sharp look at me and gave a soft *woof.*

Chapter Thirteen

Southwestern Iran
Twenty Kilometers from the Kuwait Border
Ten Hours Before . . .

First Sergeant Bradley Sims saw the army truck stop at a crossroads at the far end of the valley. Roadside lights cast the area in a golden glow. He turned off his headlights, slowed his car, and pulled behind an abandoned grain warehouse where he could observe the street through a chain-link fence. The soldiers began off-loading sawhorse barricades.

"No! Oh, god, no!" cried the young woman beside him. Rachel had a cinnamon colored shawl wrapped around her head and face, but the eyes that peered out from under the shawl were bright with new tears. "God, please don't let them take us back."

Top pasted on a smile that was filled with far more confidence than he felt. "Not a chance, darlin'."

He removed a small pair of high-powered night-vision binoculars and steadied his forearms on the wheel as he peered at the men: checking their uniforms, their weapons, their body language, and apparent combat readiness. You can tell a lot about soldiers by how well they go about ordinary tasks. Mediocre ones slouch through it, as if laziness were the best part of down time. The best ones did everything with a degree of polish and professionalism so that even something as simple as erecting a roadblock was done right and done right the first time.

The men at the crossroads did not appear to be a gang of slackers.

Not good.

He tapped his earbud. "Sergeant Rock to Road Trip. On me. No lights.

Stop and listen." Behind him, scattered hundreds of yards apart, the other two cars crept slowly through the shadows, running without headlights.

"Okay, ladies and gents," Top said into his mike, "this is about to get fun. Here's what I need and I need it now. First, I need a volunteer—snake oil salesman, feel me?"

"I'm in," said Khalid.

"Roger that, Dancing Duck. Green Giant, that means you're Jack-in-the-box."

"Rock 'n' roll," agreed Bunny, and he sounded happy about it.

"Converge on me. I'm Santa Claus."

He tapped out of the channel.

Rachel grabbed his sleeve. "What was all that? What's happening?"

Top held up a finger. "My orders are to get you three over the border and into Kuwait. To do that I have to get past that roadblock. I'd go a different way but every other route keeps us in country for at least an hour, and we don't have that hour. I'll be straight with you. Best guess is that Iranian military helicopters will be here in fifteen, twenty minutes—we need ten to make it to our LZ and that's going all out, balls-to-the-walls crazy."

" 'LZ'?"

"Landing zone. We got our own helo coming, but it can't come this close to a town or we'd start a war that nobody wants. That means that we have to get through that security checkpoint down there."

"They'll know who I am!" she yelped. "They'll just take me back to that awful place. You don't know the sort of things they did to us in there."

"I pretty much think I do, darlin'. That's why we're not going to let you get taken. I need you to do what I say, and help me help your friends. Can you do that?"

Her eyes were huge and filled with fear, but the young woman was tough and she took a breath that steadied her trembling hands. She nodded. "Okay."

"Good. Here's the plan." He told her what he had planned, and her eyes went wide with fear and doubt.

The other cars pulled in behind Top's. Doors opened and immediately Khalid and Bunny quick-walked the two young men toward the lead vehicle.

"Everyone in the back," said Top. "Stay together and stay down. Things might get loud but you will be safe. No questions now. Let's go."

Before he closed the door he made brief eye contact with Rachel, and she nodded and even managed a brave smile. She guided the two young men through the shadows into the back and then squeezed in. There was just enough downspill from the warehouse's pale security lights to see as she made sure everyone was buckled in tightly. Rachel kept talking to the others, soothing them, calming them. Top reached out and gave her shoulder a single squeeze, then closed the door. He stepped a few yards away and consulted briefly with Khalid and Bunny, and then climbed back behind the wheel of his car.

"What's happening?" asked Senator McHale's son.

"Rachel will tell you," said Top. "Then I need you all to be real quiet. Don't ask questions and absolutely do not talk to me or interfere with me until I say it's all clear."

"Okay," assured Rachel, and the two young men nodded.

Top turned away as Khalid switched on his headlights and pulled his car onto the road.

"Where's the other man?" asked the girl. "The surfer guy?"

Top chuckled at that. "Oh, you never can tell where Farmboy's going to pop up."

He gave Khalid's car a long lead, then switched on his lights and followed.

The sergeant at the crossroads held up his hand and then patted the air, indicating that Khalid should slow down and stop. Two soldiers converged on the front of the car from either side, using the flashlights clipped to their rifles to sweep the vehicle. The other three soldiers walked around back, their lights and barrels pointed at the trunk.

Top's jaw was tight with tension. Timing was going to be critical. If Khalid made an error, he'd be dead in the next few seconds, and then everything would go to shit. He cut a look into the rearview mirror, at the faces of the three freed hostages. They had been held for a year. A whole year carved out of their lives because Ahmadinejad liked using kids as chess pieces in his political games.

Top knew that firing live rounds would likely result in a major political incident, possibly even a renewed threat of war. But there was no way on earth he was going to let Iran take these college students back.

He gripped the steering wheel hard enough to make it creak.

"Papers," ordered the sergeant, shining a small flashlight directly into Khalid's face. "Name and destination."

Khalid squinted into the light as he handed over his papers, which were in a cheap vinyl folder of the kind most people in Tehran carried. His car was a late-model sedan, suggesting that he was at very least someone of note. Moneyed, or perhaps attached to the massive political machine that squatted over the whole country.

One of the guards looked in through the passenger window, peering into the footwell and the backseat, but there was nothing to see. Khalid gave them the false name that matched the ID, and spun a quick story about going to have an early breakfast with a business associate in a small border town. If the soldiers had a computer uplink and ran a check, everything would be there to verify the story.

"Open the trunk," the sergeant said as he handed back the papers.

"Certainly," said Khalid and he reached down to pop the latch. Instead he pulled the pin on a flash-bang and simply dropped it out the window at the sergeant's feet. The sergeant stared down it, totally shocked despite his training. He started to yell a warning, but instantly the flash-bang burst with tremendous force, battering the sergeant away from the car.

As soon as Khalid dropped the device he threw himself sideways and pressed his hands against his ears. The flash filled the night with a brilliant white light. The accompanying bang caught one of the soldiers in its blast radius, and the man screamed and spun away in an awkward pirouette. The other three soldiers whipped around toward the blast and never saw the trunk flip open and two more flash-bangs whip up into the air. The grenades burst five feet above the car hood, catching all three soldiers with its terrible burst of blinding light and crushing noise.

Then Khalid kicked open the door and Bunny rolled out of the trunk. The soldiers were on their knees or leaning against the car, holding their heads. One of them tried to fight through the pain and bring his rifle up, but Bunny drove an uppercut into the man's stomach that lifted him ten inches off the ground. Bunny pivoted and grabbed the other two closest guards, knotting his huge fists around the backstraps of their Kevlar vests. He pulled them off the ground, swung them apart, and then slammed them together with a huge bellow of effort. The helmets collided with a sound like a church gong and the men instantly went slack.

On the far side of the car, Khalid kicked the dazed sergeant in the groin and then hammered the top of his helmet with the bottom of a hard fist. The sergeant dropped on his face and Khalid stepped on his back as he dove at the remaining soldier, who was staggering backward, shaking his head, and trying to pull his shoulder microphone. Khalid slapped the mike out of his hand, grabbed his helmet, and yanked the man's head down onto a rising knee.

And then it was over. Five men down, and down hard. Alive, but they wouldn't feel lucky about it when they woke up.

Top watched all this with narrowed eyes and no trace of compassion. Like the rest of Echo Team, he'd had some compassion for the cops in the police station. For the soldiers? None at all. The military had been in charge of the hikers for a year and had abused and starved them. If Mr. Church hadn't given a no-live-fire order, Top knew that his guys would be cutting throats.

Now was the not the time to play "what if," though. He gunned the engine and rocketed toward the crossroads, reaching it only seconds after Bunny kicked the barrier out of the way. There was a roar behind them and Top saw Khalid's headlights flick on.

The two cars raced through the night; the third vehicle abandoned back at the warehouse. As they drove, Khalid pulled ahead and took point. The closer they got to the rendezvous point, the better the chance that they might meet the kind of resistance that wouldn't be stopped by a couple of flash-bangs and some fisticuffs.

"Are we safe?" whispered the young woman in the back seat. "God . . . are we safe?"

Top said nothing. There were miles to go before he would know the answer to that question.

Chapter Fourteen

The last thing the businessman in the bad suit did that day was open the door to his hotel room. He was undressing to take a shower when he heard the soft knock and padded barefoot to the door, a frown creasing his jowly face. He was neither expecting nor wanting a visitor of any kind. His frown deepened when he saw that it was a woman who stood outside, her face hidden by a modest chador but burdened with a heavy black canvas equipment bag whose strap was slung across her torso.

"Who——?" began the businessman, and the woman shot him in the chest with a pistol that had been hidden beneath her flowing sleeve.

The businessman gave a single croaking bleat, and then his eyes rolled up and he fell backward onto the floor. The woman kicked his legs out of the way, checked that the hall was still empty, stepped inside, and closed the door.

The Italian woman knelt and pressed her fingers against the businessman's throat. The pulse was there, steady and rapid, though she knew it would slow down within seconds. The gun she used was a Snellig gas-dart pistol, its tiny glass projectiles were loaded with horse tranquilizer.

She unslung the heavy bag, laid it on the bed, unzipped one of its many compartments, and removed a scope. Then she crossed to the window and put the scope to her eye. The Serbian subcommander of her team had followed Ledger after the meeting with Rasouli had ended, tailing him to a store and then to the Golden Oasis Hotel. After determining the floor and room number, the Serbian gruffly asked for further orders.

"Go back to the staging area," answered the Italian. "File your report and wait for me."

She hung up before the Serbian could ask another question.

It was an easy matter to decide on a vantage point from one of the surrounding hotels. She used her Oracle computer to hack the booking records for each hotel until she found a perfect spot. Now she controlled a safe vantage point and peered through the scope to count floors and windows until she found the right one.

At first all she saw was a balcony, sliding glass doors, thin sheer curtains beyond which a bleak room was occupied only by Joe Ledger and a large dog. Ledger sat on the floor, petting the dog. She adjusted the scope to study the animal. It was a beautiful white shepherd, and that made the Italian frown. Was the dog's color a coincidence or was there another element to this man? Was he tied to the Sabbatarians? Was that a fetch dog?

That question would need to be answered, because it might mean that Ledger would have to die right now.

Still frowning, she removed her sniper rifle from the canvas bag. The rifle was not in parts. She had spent too much time carefully sighting it in to have it all spoiled by disassembling the weapon. Only the stock was detached and she clicked it into place and then mounted the weapon on a tripod. Like most professionals in her craft she preferred shooting from a prone position, or kneeling with a bipod, but she had no idea how long she would have to wait here in this hotel room, so a tripod was more practical. It reduced the risk of muscle fatigue.

She mounted the scope onto an American McMillan Tac-50 bolt-action sniper rifle and loaded it with .50 caliber Browning machine gun rimless cartridges, lean and long and completely lethal, even if she was forced to take a body shot instead of the preferred head shot. Not that she would have. The Italian sniper had not missed a kill shot in many years. She had learned the craft from the greatest shooter who ever lived, Simo Häyhä, the legendary Finnish shooter known in international sniper circles as the White Death, and rightly so. During the Winter War between Finland and Russia in 1939 and '40, Häyhä had racked up 705 confirmed kills. Five hundred and five with an iron-sighted bolt action rifle, the rest with a submachine gun. Häyhä endured murderous subzero temperatures as low as minus forty Celsius and in less than one hundred days had been an angel of slaughter to the Russians, sometimes stuffing his mouth with snow so his breath did not condense and reveal his position. Even after taking a bullet to the face he survived and escaped capture.

Häyhä had been one of many tutors Lilith had hired to prepare her for the life she led. And though he was ancient and near death, his mind was sharp and his lessons profound. Häyhä had been a master killer, and yet his eyes were always calm, always peaceful. The Italian never understood that. When she looked in the mirror she saw the eyes of some vile thing. Something tainted and impure. Something evil.

She sat in a folding chair in the shadows of the hijacked hotel room. No lights except the indirect light from the open window. Above her, a rickety ceiling fan turned continuously and there was a breeze from outside, but the curtains did not move. They were weighted down with rocks she had brought upstairs with her for that purpose. Blowing curtains could spoil a shot and they draw the eye. She did not want to attract any attention.

Ledger still sat on the floor.

The sniper leaned back from the rifle and removed a small leather case from her bag, unzipped it, and propped it on the night table. The device was the size of an e-book reader but it was a very powerful portable computer with a satellite uplink. The sniper booted the device, entered her password, and activated the voice interface.

"Authorize Arklight field protocol five."

The monitor flashed several times and then settled on a screen saver with the smiling face of the Mona Lisa.

The Mona Lisa spoke.

"Oracle welcomes you."

The Oracle computer had been designed by a man named St. Germaine but re-programmed by her mother; the voice was hers as well, though with a slight alien quality when composing unique phrasing. The sniper had added the animation of the Mona Lisa to give it a less threatening feeling. She loved her mother but, like everyone else who ever met her, was deeply intimidated by her. Even the other two Mothers of the Fallen deferred to her.

"Access all data for mission coded Arklight eight-one-one-seven."

"Accessing. Do you want to update your field report?"

"Yes." She gave the computer a detailed report beginning with the phone call from Rasouli that morning and the resulting change in the mission for which her Arklight team had been contracted. At the conclusion of the report she said, "Collate data. I will want a set of probabilities."

"Collating," said Oracle. *"Is there anything else I can do for you?"*

"Yes. I want everything you can find on Joseph Edwin Ledger. White male, early thirties, American."

"There are ninety-seven unique instances of living people named Joseph Edwin Ledger; one-hundred and sixteen for deceased—"

"Stop. Subject is likely military or ex-military. Possibly law enforcement."

"There is one instance of a Joseph Edwin Ledger with the Baltimore Police Department in the state of Maryland. There is also one instance of a Joseph Edwin Ledger with the United States Army Rangers. Personal identification numbers and Social Security numbers match."

"Open a file on him. I want everything. Ledger's background. Service record, awards, citations, reprimands, psych profiles, his politics. Anything you have."

"There is already an active Arklight file on this subject."

"When was the file opened and who opened it?"

The computer gave an open date from July of the previous year. *"The file has an L1 code."*

L1. Lilith.

"My mother opened that file?"

"Yes."

"Summarize the content of that file."

Oracle began reading out information regarding several matters of grave international importance. The Seif al Din plague, which coincided with the opening of Ledger's file. There were others, all high profile. The shutdown of the ultrasecret vault in the Pocono Mountains of Pennsylvania; the famous Jakoby-Mengele file; and others, leading up to the Seven Kings event last December. The records were spotty and included more speculation and unofficial information than hard evidence. As the Italian woman well knew it was virtually impossible to prove anything about the DMS. Very often files of this kind suddenly vanished from even encrypted hard drives. There were rumors of a DMS supercomputer called Mind-Reader that had an aggressive search and destroy subroutine for ferreting out this kind of information.

"Oracle," she said, "have you been attacked in any way since this file was opened?"

"No."

"Isn't that unusual?"

"There is a note in the file stating that any questions of this kind be directed

to Lilith herself. Your mother does not permit additional speculative notes to be added to the file. Would you like me to pass along a request to your mother?"

"God no," said the sniper before she could stop herself. "No," she corrected.

"Shall I continue reading the subject's service record?"

"Yes."

Ledger reached out and pulled his dog toward him, wrapping his arms around the animal and laying his head on the dog's shoulder. What an odd thing for a man like him to do, she thought. A strangely *human* act, totally at odds with the things Oracle was saying: that he was emotionally fractured, that he was utterly ruthless in a fight, that he had killed people with guns, knives, explosives, his hands. However, the way he held his dog and stroked the animal's fur and spoke to it—even though she could not hear his words—made her smile.

"Oracle, stop report," she said. "How did my mother obtain the information for her file on Ledger?"

"That information is in a subfolder marked eyes-only. Would you like to request temporary clearance to read that report?"

The sniper took a breath, then let it out slowly. "Yes."

"That request has been forwarded to the Mothers."

"Continue report."

Oracle moved from the bland details of an unremarkable military record, through a moderately interesting though short police career. The sniper found nothing of real note there, however, except that Ledger had been scheduled for enrollment in the FBI academy. There were no records of his having actually entered the academy. What really caught her interest, however, were Ledger's psychotherapy reports and transcripts of sessions with Dr. Rudolfo Ernesto Sanchez y Martinez. Ledger was a deeply damaged individual who had a minimum of three and possibly as many as nine separate personality subtypes living in his head. Dr. Sanchez's records indicated that Ledger had found a way to balance these personalities and even put them to work, like a committee, within his fractured mind. It was not a unique occurrence, but it was very rare; and rarer still for such a man to be accepted into the police department and, apparently, the Department of Military Sciences.

"Stop. Who recruited Ledger into the DMS?"

"Unknown, though there is a high probability that he was recruited directly by St. Germaine."

The sniper's pulse quickened as it did every time she heard that name. St. Germaine.

That was one of the many names for a man currently using the name Church. St. Germaine was the name her mother used for the man. The sniper had never met him, but other Arklight agents told wild stories. She doubted most of them were true, but all of them were fascinating.

"Oracle," she said, "why might St. Germaine risk using a field operative with Ledger's psychological profile?"

"Unknown."

"Speculate. Access all known data on St. Germaine and cross-reference."

"There are one hundred and three separate field reports that include the man code-named St. Germaine under twenty-eight aliases. Twenty-six of those reports indicate a tendency to use agents with unpredictable or unstable personality types. Four of the six analysis reports uploaded by senior Arklight operators postulate that Mr. Church uses said unpredictable personalities to introduce random elements to missions."

"An X factor?"

"That is the theory most commonly postulated."

"What is the probability that Mr. Church sent Ledger to Iran knowing that he would become involved in my current mission?"

"There is insufficient data to calculate a complete probability model."

"Fuck."

"I am unable to perform that function, as you well know," said Oracle in her mother's dry voice. It was one of the messages Mama had added to the database. An attempt at humor.

"What is the likelihood that Rasouli knew my team was associated with Arklight?"

"Unknown, however the mission for which your team was originally contracted has multiple connection points to the Mothers of the Fallen and—"

"What is Rasouli's connection with Joseph Ledger?"

"Unknown."

She processed that as she made some minor adjustments to her rifle.

Why had Rasouli wanted to meet this man? Was he an intermediary? Or, more likely, was Rasouli trying to recruit him as a double agent?

Despite the poverty most of the people in this country endured, the government was very rich, with pockets deep enough to tempt saints and angels. The sniper had seen that firsthand in the absurd amount of money Rasouli had paid to have her team provide security for half an hour in a coffee shop.

"Oracle, give me a probability estimate on Ledger's loyalty."

"That question lacks specificity."

"Based on Joseph Ledger's psych profiles, can he be bought? Could Rasouli buy him away from the DMS?

"Unknown."

"But we can't discount it?"

"That would be unwise."

She peered through the scope. Ledger was still sitting on the floor with his dog. Was he crying? The blowing curtains on Ledger's window made it impossible to tell, but the American looked like he had something on his cheeks. Tears or dog slobber?

"How dangerous is this man?"

"To others or to himself?"

The question did not surprise the sniper. She was more than half-convinced the marks on Ledger's cheeks were *not* there because of his dog.

"As a fighter and field agent," she said.

"According to psych profiles and all other available data, Captain Joseph Edwin Ledger should be considered a Class-A threat."

The sniper found that very interesting.

There was movement. Ledger abruptly straightened and looked at the closed door against which he sat. Then he and the dog climbed quickly to their feet. Ledger reached inside his jacket but after a moment brought his hand away without a gun. It was clear that someone had just knocked on the door, and it seemed apparent from Ledger's body language that the visitor was expected.

But who was it?

Rasouli?

Another of St. Germaine's agents? The Sabbatarians?

Or one of those unholy bastards in the Red Order?

"Oracle. Stand by."

"Standing by."

As Ledger reached for the door handle, the sniper leaned her shoulder against the stock of the rifle. Her slender finger stroked the cold metal rim of the trigger guard.

Chapter Fifteen

Golden Oasis Hotel
Tehran, Iran
June 15, 8:47 a.m.

When the delivery man knocked on the door I nearly jumped out of my skin. I leapt to my feet and spun toward the door. Ghost gave a low growl and took up a defensive stance next to me. He was too tactful to mention that I spent five seconds scrabbling inside my jacket for a pistol I wasn't carrying.

I peered through the peephole and saw a teenage boy in a kufi.

Before he could knock again, I opened the door and he handed me a package, accepted a tip, and departed without saying a word. He threw some cautious looks at Ghost, though, as if aware that this was a ferocious mankiller for whom a packet of goat strips would not assuage a savage hunger. Ghost apparently had the same thought and glared at his retreating back until I closed the door and told him to knock it off.

Inside the package was a carton of Bistoon cigarettes, which I threw out. The other items in the paper sack were the battery and a cell-phone charger wrapped together with a blue rubber band.

I sat down on the edge of the bed and slid the battery into the phone and was delighted to see that it was already charged. I should have given the kid a bigger tip.

Our DMS phones have a USB port, and I fished out the flash drive and plugged it in. It did not look particularly damaged from the outside, but then again the outside was plastic. I was more than a little surprised—or maybe "suspicious" is the appropriate word—that Rasouli gave me the original rather than a copy. I was glad he did, though, because once I uploaded what I could I was going to find a way to get the flash drive into a diplomatic pouch for an expedited trip across the ocean. Once Bug got his sweaty little hands on it I was sure the drive would yield up everything there was to find.

Could Rasouli have had that in mind? Did he know about Mind-Reader? Sure he did, he knew Vox.

My gut turned over. Every time I thought I had a grasp on how much damage—past, current, and potential—that could be laid at Vox's feet, something came along to broaden my perspective. MindReader was an ultrasecret system and part of its strength lay in the fact that the bad guys didn't know about it, or if they did they didn't know what it could do. Vox did. That meant that anyone he told, every government or terrorist organization, would be scrambling now to upgrade their computer-security protocols. Common knowledge of MindReader's intrusion properties could easily create a new spike in security technology for computers. Grace Courtland once told me that the whole Chinese GhostNet program was their response to *rumors* that something like MindReader existed. And Vox himself had clearly financed some big-ticket research because he had provided the Seven Kings with the only cellular phone system that MindReader couldn't trace or crack. Bug, the DMS computer hotshot, said that designing such a system could not have been done by accident, it had to have been created specifically to thwart our computer.

I plugged the flash drive into the USB port on my phone and immediately got a bunch of read-error messages. The thing had been in someone's stomach, so that was no surprise. However, I went through the steps to do a forced upload of bulk data and soon images were whipping across the screen too fast for me to see. Damaged or not, there was a lot of stuff on the drive. The upload failed twice and I had to repeat the steps, but eventually I got the UPLOAD COMPLETE message.

I scrolled back through the contents at a slower speed until I found a series of JPEGs, one of which was the picture Rasouli had showed me. It looked so innocent, so nondescript in its metal case. And though I know that machines have no personality, I could not help but ascribe the word "evil" to it, as if the malign intent of its creators had been somehow transferred to the device during its construction.

I took a breath, engaged the code scrambler, and punched a speed dial. The phone rang three times.

"Go," was all Church said, which is more than he usually gives when he answers a phone.

"Boss, I have a Firehall One situation."

"Is there a finger on a trigger?" His voice sounded as calm as if I asked him who pitched for the Orioles last night.

"Unknown. But . . . from the vibe I got from my source I'd say this is something coming at us rather than already here."

"Tell me."

"I just uploaded the contents of a flash drive to the server. It's damaged goods. It's filed under my name and coded for you, eyes only."

I could hear him tapping keys on his laptop as I spoke.

"Okay, I have the data. Where did this originate? Who's your source?"

"You're going to love this," I said, and told him everything. He did not interrupt once, and I hoped that he was alone because this was going to really test his Vulcan calm.

After a short pause, Church asked, "Were you able to verify his connection to Vox? Could Rasouli have simply thrown the name at you to win your trust?"

"I don't think so. Vox told him to tell me that he vetted Grace and she was clean. He said 'She wasn't one of mine.'"

There was a longer pause. "Interesting."

"Isn't it, though?"

"Rasouli made no move to arrest you?"

"Just the opposite," I said. "Rasouli teased me by saying that one of the devices might be in the U.S. He couldn't have been more vague if he'd spoken in code, though."

"You don't believe him?"

"I'm not sure I'd believe him if he said the desert was made out of sand. But . . ."

"Where are you?"

"My hotel room."

"Bug might be able to salvage more of the damaged files. I'll reroute a local asset to pick up the flash drive. Wait for his call."

"I don't think I should leave the country while—"

"You're not. You'll be taken to a safe house you can use as a staging area. We'll evaluate the situation so be prepared to go after that device in Iran. I'll have Echo Team rendezvous with you there."

"Speaking of my team . . . did everyone make it out okay?"

"Everyone but you. Safe and sound and over the border."

"Outstanding. What about the packages?"

"The three young people are with their families. They'll go to London for a thorough physical, and we'll have them home in forty-eight hours."

"Not seeing anything in the news."

"Iran hasn't acknowledged the incident. There's some question here about how they'll play it. Fifty-fifty split between them producing dead soldiers and claiming that we launched an illegal attack that resulted in casualties; or they reach out to us on the sly and agree to a public statement that they worked with us to insure the safe release of suspected spies who have since been cleared. My money is on the latter. State is prepping a variety of responses," he said.

"Be nice to have the good guys win. Those three kids were pretty tough. They didn't break, and we both know the Iranians didn't go light on them."

"Admirable," Church agreed, and that was about as sentimental and weepy as he ever gets. "What do you need, Captain?"

"I'm equipment-light. I need weapons and gear. Can your asset drop that stuff off?"

"I can arrange weapons, but he won't have a field kit. Echo Team will bring the party favors. And I'll have Bug send you the latest disarming protocols."

"Once last thing, Boss," I said. "Do you think this is the return of the Seven Kings?"

"Impossible to say at this juncture," he said. The line went dead.

In my best impersonation of Church I said, "Why, thank you, Captain Ledger, damn fine work." Ghost gave me a look and went back to his dried goat.

I studied the picture of the bomb. Jesus. Someone wanted to nuke the entire Mideast oil fields.

Understand, I gave just about half a warm shit about the whole oil wars thing. I cared even less about the politics of it. But there were hundreds of millions of people in the region. I thought of all the people coming and going in the café. Their families, their kids. All of them. Working, eating, sleeping, loving, and living on top of four, maybe six, nuclear bombs. Maybe more.

I stood up, swayed for a moment, then ran like hell into the bathroom, dropped to my knees in front of the toilet and vomited. It was so immediate and desperate that I could hear myself screaming as I threw up.

My stomach spasmed on empty and I dropped the lid with a bang. Ghost was in the doorway, barking at me, scared and nervous. I pulled some toilet paper off the roll and wiped my mouth.

"It's okay," I gasped, reaching out with a trembling hand toward Ghost. He gave my knuckles a nervous lick. "It's okay."

I flushed the paper and used the sink to pull myself upright. I ran the water on cold and stuck my face down into the spray. I rinsed out my mouth and tried to spit out the taste of terror.

The shakes hit me then and I had to ball my hands into fists as I walked into the bedroom. You can only play it like Mr. Cool for so long before the realities of emotion and brain chemistry show up to kick your ass and prove to you that you're just as human as everyone else. Maybe Mr. Church has a lock on invulnerability, but I haven't cracked the code yet. I sat down on the edge of the bed and tried not to cry.

In the movies, Bruce Willis doesn't cry. He's a stoic. He's also working off a script that he *knows* has a happy ending. I wasn't. What if it came down to me to stop these things? Me and what I can do pitted against the potential loss of life that numbered several hundred million. I'm one guy. A year ago I was just a cop.

"Jesus Christ," I said, and I could hear the raw horror in my own voice.

Chapter Sixteen

The Hangar—DMS Central HQ
Floyd Bennett Field, Brooklyn
June 15, 12:49 a.m. EST

Mr. Church typed his personal code into his laptop and brought up the Rasouli files. He scanned the index and then began viewing the files one by one. His face was relaxed, composed, without expression, as data, charts, diagrams, lists, and photographs came and went, came and went on his laptop screen.

The room was still except for music playing softly. "Smokin' At The Half Note" by Wynton Kelly Trio with Wes Montgomery. The current track was Tadd Dameron's "If You Could See Me Now." Mr. Church appreciated the simple intensity of Wes Montgomery's guitar work on the track, and he let it play through before he did anything.

Mr. Church selected a vanilla wafer from a plate, tapped crumbs off of it, and took a small bite. He munched quietly for several seconds. He was a large man, broad-shouldered, strong and blocky. It was generally believed by those who knew him that he was north of sixty, but people agreed that age did not seem to touch him. The gray in his hair was the only real mark; and the scars on his face and hands suggested that his years, no matter how many they were, had not been idle.

His eyes were half-closed behind the tinted lenses of his glasses as he looked inward, assessing what Ledger had told him, working through the implications of the information on Rasouli's flash drive. If anyone had been in the room they would have thought he was a man lost in the subtleties of a piece of classic jazz. There was no outward sign of agitation.

A slender cell phone sat on the desk blotter next to his laptop. The image on the laptop's screen was the one Joe Ledger had sent via e-mail. When the song ended, Mr. Church picked up his cell and opened it, punched a number, entered a code that engaged a 128-bit scrambler, and waited for the other party to answer. After three rings, a man's voice said, "Hello?"

Mr. Church said, "Mr. President, we have a situation."

Chapter Seventeen

The Kingdom of Shadows
Beneath the Sands
One Year Ago

The fat American sat uneasily on the edge of a metal chair that was draped with red velvet. He was not accustomed to being uneasy. For most of his life it was other people who were uneasy around him. The other man—if "man" could accurately describe the pale figure who sat opposite him— was not like other people. The American doubted this creature feared anything.

Their chairs were identical, ponderous wrought-iron monstrosities looted centuries ago from a desecrated mosque. A single small candle in a shaded sconce cast the only light, and its pale glow was far too fragile to hold back the enormous walls of darkness that closed in on them from every side. The American could only guess at the size of the chamber in which they sat. During the long and convoluted walk down here from a hidden entrance in the city above, the American could see that it had been carved out of the living rock, and was forever filled with shadows that dripped and whispered. The black mouths of tunnels trailed off into darkness all around them. The American knew that there were guards in those tunnels—creatures equally as pale and strange as this man—but he could not see them.

He could, however, *feel* them. And he caught glimpses of luminous red eyes staring at him with suspicion and pernicious hunger.

The American and the pale man sat in silence for long minutes. Studying each other with the frankness of butchers.

The pale man was tall and gaunt, dressed simply in black trousers and a collarless shirt the color of old rust. No shoes on his pale feet, no jewelry on his hands, and only a crystal locket on a silver chain around his neck. Long white hair was brushed back from a narrow, ascetic face. When the American had first met him, the man looked like a starving albino, but on closer inspection there was a ferocious vitality in the thin face and long-fingered hands. A lupine, predatory quality. The American adjusted his opinion: this man was not wasted by hunger, but defined by it. Made powerful by it.

When the American had been ushered into the room he had brought with him a heavy metal briefcase which he set on the bare rock floor between them, equidistant between the chair provided for him and the three-step dais on which his host sat. The pale man regarded the case but did not ask that it be opened or inspected.

"So," said the American, "LaRoque wasn't bullshitting me when he described you."

The pale man said nothing.

"I believe his exact words were," continued the fat man, " 'the King of Thorns.' I thought it was some kind of lurid nonsense at the time. Some bit of poetry that he was using to try and spook me. But . . ."

"The Scriptor," said the pale man.

"Beg pardon?"

"You will call him 'the Scriptor.' We do not use his daylight name."

"You may not, chum, but I do," laughed the American, but his smile was fragile and fleeting. "Okay, yeah. The Scriptor. Silly damn name, though."

"So says the 'king of fear,'" murmured the other. "Or am I mistaken about who you are, Mr. Vox?"

Hugo Vox straightened in his chair and eyed the pale man shrewdly for a few seconds. "Yeah, okay, cards on the table. Call me Hugo. What do I call you, though? 'King of Thorns' is a bit clumsy for a casual chat."

"You may call me Grigor."

"Good. I prefer first names when I do business." Vox pursed his lips. "If you know about me, then I guess that means you know about the Seven Kings."

"Yes."

"Who told you? The 'Scriptor'?"

Grigor shook his head. "The Scriptor does not choose to come down here. He calls when he needs his Red Knights."

The pale man's voice was strange, heavily accented, and controlled, which made it a challenge for Vox to read inflection and subtext. Even so, he could detect an edge of contempt in Grigor's phrasing in that last sentence. Certainly disapproval, and maybe more than that.

"So, what, he phoned in about me? Just up and broke his word to me? He told you the secret he swore on his life that he wouldn't share with anyone?"

The pale man smiled and made a small dismissive gesture with one hand.

"No, uh-uh," persisted Vox, "we don't just drop that. How do you know about me?"

"It is the business of the Red Knights to know everything—"

"Yeah, cut the sales pitch. I'm not a rube and you're not at one with the universe. This is supposed to be a very hush-hush meeting and you are not supposed to know who I am. That information was mine to share or not. The fact that you do know makes me pretty goddamn twitchy about the whole deal. My business associates—"

"Your associates are terrorists, corrupt officials, and mass murderers, Mr. Vox. Let's not pretend they are anything else."

"And you're what? Kermit and the Muppet Babies? You really want to measure dicks to see who gets the bigger boner from screwing the public?"

Grigor looked amused. "What the Red Knights have done, and what we continue to do, has the blessing of the church."

"Bullshit. It has the blessing of one twisted fuck of a priest who is even scarier than you and me put together, and I know for a fact that the Vatican has no clue what he's giving his personal blessing to. If they did, they'd go Old Testament all over the Red Order, the Red Knights, and Father-frigging-Nicodemus, and you can put that in the bank."

Grigor said nothing. He steepled his long fingers and simply stared at Vox. Around them the shadows echoed with the scuttle of rat feet and the distant weeping of women.

"Fuck it," said Vox and stood up.

"The priest."

Vox stared at him. "What?"

"The Scriptor did not betray your trust. It was Father Nicodemus who told me your name. It was he who told me about the Seven Kings and what you and your mother are planning. Weaponized versions of the Ten Plagues of Egypt. Father Nicodemus thinks that it is a beautiful plan."

Vox narrowed his eyes. "How does he know about that?"

"He did not say."

"No," muttered Vox. "He wouldn't. Spooky bastard."

Vox remained standing for a moment. He looked around and saw milk-white faces watching him from the tunnel mouths. The watchers seemed to be cast in black and white except for their eyes. Like the man on the dais, everyone down in the shadow kingdom had dark red eyes. Vox was only half sure that it was stage dressing designed to create exactly the reaction he was having. Naked fear.

To the pale man, Vox said, "Which means that LaRoque—excuse me, the *Scriptor*—probably knows, too."

"The Scriptor and the priest do not have secrets from one another. That is one of the pillars on which the *Ordo Ruber* was built."

The Red Order. Vox did not speak the translation aloud, but he knew what it was. LaRoque's grandfather had told him the whole story decades ago. That sharing had been a betrayal of the strict rules of the Red Order, and knowledge of it was supposed to be a death sentence for anyone not initiated into their ancient brotherhood.

"Okay," he said, "then let's both lay cards on the table. You know who and what I am? Fine. Turns out, I know who, and much more importantly, *what* you are."

The pale man looked skeptical. "Then who and what am I?"

Vox smiled thinly as he spoke a single word. "Upier."

He heard gasps and angry mutters from the surrounding shadows. Grigor's eyes widened briefly and then narrowed to dangerous slits.

Vox held up a hand. "If you're planning on giving me one of those 'men have died for less' speeches, save it for the tourists. We got off on a bad foot here. I'm appropriately skeeved out by you and your troops down here, so you can put that in your win category. Still—to make this completely fair, I think you should be a little more afraid of me."

Grigor smiled at that. "The Scriptor said that you were brash, but he neglected to tell me that you were a fool."

"The Scriptor is a paranoid schizophrenic and a fucking moron who couldn't find his own dick with both hands and a set of printed instructions," said Vox. "And just so you don't think I'm blowing smoke up your ass, take a look at what I brought."

He nodded to the briefcase. Grigor stared down at it with sudden suspicion, his pale lips parting slightly, but he made no move toward the case. Vox nodded approvingly.

"We both know what's supposed to be in the case," said Vox. "Contact info for every arms dealer on three continents, and some of my untraceable cell phones. But, since I'm not hideously stupid, the contact information is on a password-protected laptop and the cell phones can't be activated without a special access code."

Grigor's eyes narrowed to lethal slits. "You did not bring them?"

"No," said Vox, "I did not bring them down here to your deep, dark ultrascary secret lair. Like I said, I'm not stupid. What I brought instead, is a bomb."

He removed his right hand from his pocket and raised it to show the small black plastic device he held.

"Yup. Detonator. The case also has two pounds of C-4 in it. Probably won't kill everyone down here, but it'll turn both of us into clouds of pink mist and bring down a hundred tons of rubble on the rest.

Grigor's pale face went whiter still and he took an involuntary step backward, forking the sign of the Evil Eye at Vox and barking out a few sharp words in a language Vox could not recognize.

"Okay," said Vox in a hushed tone that did not carry beyond the small circle of lamplight in which they stood. "Now we know whose dick is bigger. Let's cut right to the chase. You think I came down here as a gofer for the Scriptor. Pretty apparent now that it isn't the case. Though the Scriptor thinks it is. He thinks I'm kindly old friend of the family. I can't begin to tell you how fucked up LaRoque is. He has no insight into people at all. He's known me his whole life, knows about the Seven Kings, and still thinks I'm just some guy he can send on errands."

He took a step forward. Grigor tensed, clearly debating whether to attack or run, but Vox showed him the trigger. A red light glowed beneath the arm of the detonator. "Dead man's switch. I die, you die. Stop thinking bad thoughts and let's see if we can talk serious business."

To his credit, and to Vox's appreciation, Grigor's body gradually relaxed and he held his ground. Still on the dais, a king of death looming above the king of fear.

"Why have you come here, then?" asked Grigor. "What do you want?"

"I'm here because you need me."

Grigor smiled, revealing his unnatural teeth. "What I need from you I could take."

Vox shivered despite himself. "Christ, don't do that, you big freak. I'm trying to talk business here."

The candlelight glimmered on the wicked points of Grigor's fangs. Vox licked his lips. It felt like the cavern floor was tilting under him. The moment was as terrifying as it was surreal, but he stood his ground even as sweat poured down his face and stung his eyes.

Finally, Grigor allowed his smile to fade and the fangs slowly vanished. He sat back in his chair. "Then talk business."

Vox let out a tremendous sigh. "Jesus H. Christ," he growled. "You really groove on your own mystique, don't you? Shit." He used his free hand to mop his forehead with a handkerchief, and despite the fact that every nerve he possessed screamed at him to run, he took a step closer to the foot of the dais. Grigor arched an eyebrow in surprise, or perhaps in appreciation for the nerve that such an action displayed. Vox said, "Since you know about the Kings, then it's only fair that I tell you that I know *everything* about the Red Order, and I do mean everything."

He watched Grigor's eyes, saw them jump in surprise, and saw how Grigor looked quickly away to hide his reaction.

"That is between you and the Scriptor," said the pale man.

"No it isn't," replied Vox, and Grigor's eyes settled once more on him. "When I say that I know everything about the Order, that means *everything*. That means I know about the Upierczi."

Grigor leaned forward. "And what is it that you think you know?"

"I know why you really want the names of all the arms dealers . . . and it's not to buy guns, no matter what LaRoque says."

"No."

"What's a gun to someone like you? Maybe twenty years ago, maybe before you guys got your 'upgrade.' Yeah, don't look so surprised, Grigor. I told you I know all about you. I know how strong you've become. I don't think Charles LaRoque has a fucking clue."

Grigor did not correct him this time.

Vox took another step. "I know that despite being called a 'knight,' the Red Order thinks of you as a slave. They treat you like slaves. You *are* slaves."

In a pale and dangerous whisper Grigor said, "What else do you know?"

"I know that your slavery is about to come to an end. You want to break the chains. You want to stage a slave revolt that will make Spartacus and the gladiator rebellion look like a frat party." Vox smiled. "Don't you?"

Grigor's eyes burned with red flame. "Yes."

"And," said Hugo Vox, "I want to make sure that happens. That . . . and so much more."

Chapter Eighteen

Tactical Operations Center (TOC)

The Hangar

Floyd Bennett Field, Brooklyn

June 15, 12:49 a.m. EST

Jerome Williams—"Bug" to everyone—sat amid a web of computer terminals, screens, coaxial cables, encoding buffers, and other equipment, and all of it inside a big glass box. Two inches of reinforced glass and a sophisticated multiform entry scanner separated him from the fifty other people in the sprawling Tactical Operations Center. The TOC was a monument to computer-driven sophistication, and rising like an obelisk was the primary processing tower of MindReader. That, too, was safe behind the bulletproof glass and guarded by two unsmiling soldiers with M4s.

Bug glanced up from his keyboard at the flow of people in the TOC. Some were hunched over workstations connected through monitored sockets to MindReader's servers; others spoke on phones or milled like frenzied insects, going about the thousand crucial tasks related to the current crisis.

Despite the constant flow of cool air into his fishbowl, Bug was sweating heavily. Six rogue nukes. Just the thought of those weapons hidden out there terrified him. Violence was such an alien concept to him, despite where and for whom he worked. Most of the time it was an abstraction, a crazy concept no more real than the aliens, monsters, orcs, and zombies he battled in video games. He *knew* that the problems the DMS faced were real, but they weren't real to him. He had never heard a shot fired in anger, never saw the enemy anywhere but on a computer screen. It was easy to stay detached if you lived like that.

Bug was a small man. Thin, spare, slightly hunched from a life spent at the keyboard. His work for the DMS was usually pure support. Crack a code, break through an anti-intrusion firewall, steal some guarded information. Fun stuff. Even when providing real-time intel for the field teams there wasn't much actual pressure on him. After all, MindReader was the fastest computer on the planet. The basement of the hangar had a cold room lined wall to wall with a supercomputer cluster. The primary computer block was made up of three thousand premarket upgrades of the Tianhe-1A system which flew at a speed of 2.507 petaflops. That was more than thirty percent faster than the Cray XT5 Jaguar. Sometimes Bug would sit with his palms flat on the MindReader obelisk and *feel* the power surging through him. That was real to him.

But today . . . the real world seemed to have found a way past all of his personal anti-intrusion systems. Fear was like an unbearably shrill sound in his ears.

"Find those other devices." That's what Mr. Church had said to him before the Big Man went in for his conference with the president. Not "try" to find them. *Find them.*

It was on him.

Him.

He closed his eyes and breathed in long and deep through his nose. The air in the fishbowl was ripe with the hot-wire smell of ozone. A beautiful smell.

"Come on, baby," he said aloud as his fingers hovered above the keyboard. "Come on, my baby. Don't make me do this alone. Talk to me . . ."

Almost as if in answer to his plea, a bell softly pinged.

Chapter Nineteen

Park Avenue and McMechen Street

Bolton Hill

Baltimore, Maryland

June 15, 12:53 a.m. EST

The bedside phone began ringing at precisely the wrong moment. Circe O'Tree was naked, covered in sweat, painted by candlelight, and on the verge of screaming as she moved in a frenzied pace up and down. Her black curls danced above her bouncing breasts as the rhythm drove her up and up and up toward the crest of climax. Beneath her, drenched and straining and grimacing with the beginnings of his own orgasm, Rudy Sanchez growled out her name over and over again.

The phone kept ringing.

They ignored it. They were only aware of it on some distant level, their immediate need transforming the intrusive sound into a mere component in the symphony of sounds and sensations. The music from the speakers, the sounds from the street outside of Circe's window, the creak of the bedsprings, the urgent slap of flesh against flesh, and their marathon panting breathing were all parts of something much greater.

"Oh, *God*!" cried Circe as the orgasm reared above her like a dark wave of velvet beauty, and she screamed incoherently as he came too. Together they spun to the edge of the precipice and plunged over, crying out each other's names, saying meaningless words, making sounds provoked by sensations that were beyond even the most precise articulation.

The phone rang through to voice mail.

Circe collapsed onto Rudy, showering his face with many small, quick kisses as beads of crystalline sweat dripped from every point of her onto his skin. He gathered her in his arms and kissed the hot hollow of her throat and her cheeks and her eyes and finally her lips.

The phone began ringing again.

They ignored it.

It rang five times and stopped.

Circe could feel Rudy's heart beating as insistently as hers. She clung to him, her body wrapped around his.

"I love you," she whispered.

"Te quiero," he murmured.

Then his cell phone began ringing.

They both glanced at it.

"Let it go," she said.

"Yes," he agreed. They did not move as it rang through to voice mail.

There was silence. Circle let herself fall off of him in delicious slow motion, his arms around her to catch her fall and keep her close. Rudy looked at her. Lean and yet ripe, tanned skin a shade lighter than olive, and eyes that held more mysteries than he could count. She was the most beautiful woman he had ever touched; the most beautiful woman he had ever seen. Movie-star beauty coupled with a fierce intellect and a personality as complexly faceted as a diamond. He took a strand of her hair and held it to his nose. It smelled of incense and wood smoke and sex. He wanted to tell her all of this, but in more poetic terms, and he fished for words that would convey what he felt without sounding like lines cribbed from old movies.

"I—" Rudy began, and then her house phone started ringing.

And her cell.

And his cell.

All at the same time.

"Damn," Circe said.

Rudy cursed quietly in Spanish as he stretched an arm over and picked up both cell phones. Circe took hers and answered first.

"Dr. O'Tree."

"Where are you?" asked Mr. Church.

She closed her eyes and mouthed the word "Dad."

Rudy looked at the screen display on his. It said TIA. Aunt. Aunt Sallie. He nodded to her.

"I'm home," she said.

"How quickly can you get to the Warehouse?"

"Why? I'm off this week. I have to do revisions on the chapter on—"

"That can wait."

"But it's important."

"Not as important as this," said Mr. Church.

Circe sighed and considered smashing the phone against the wall.

Then Mr. Church said, "Bring Dr. Sanchez with you."

Before she could ask a single question, he disconnected.

All of the phones went silent.

"What?" asked Rudy, and Circe told him. Then she buried her head against his chest.

"I hate this," she growled. "I hate that he can just pick up a phone and ruin a perfect moment for me."

"I expect," said Rudy, "that he hates it too."

She looked at him for a moment, reading his eyes. She sighed again and nodded. "Damn it."

Five minutes later they were in Rudy's Lexus breaking speed laws all the way to the Warehouse.

Chapter Twenty

Warbah Island

The Persian Gulf, Near the Mouth of the Euphrates River

Kuwait

June 15, 8:57 a.m.

Top Sims sat on the edge of the open door of a stealth helicopter. The helo was a model Top had never seen or heard of before last night—a Nightbird 319, a prototype variation on the OH-6 Loach used by the CIA during Vietnam but updated with twenty-first-century noise reduction technology, better construction materials, and radar-shedding panels that made the craft look like it was coated in dragon scales. The Nightbird had skimmed a few yards above the sand as it crossed the Iranian border, flying well below radar and inside the bank of total darkness provided by the rocky landscape. Almost totally silent beyond two hundred feet, it used special rotor blades that thrummed out a much softer vibration signature than that used by regular helicopters. If the pilot had not sent Top a locator signal, the two cars would had driven right past them in the night.

Echo Team abandoned the cars and crammed themselves and the rescued college students into the chopper, but then they had to endure a terrible two minutes of waiting and praying as a phalanx of Iranian Shahed 285 attack helicopters came sweeping across the star field above. Top was very familiar with those birds. Each Shahed was rigged with autocanons, machine guns, guided missiles, antiarmor missiles, air-to-air and air-to-sea missiles. Seriously badass, and Iranian helo pilots were no fools.

However, the helicopters swept past and then split into two groups, heading north and south along the border, their surveillance systems looking right through the bird on the ground.

"Jesus, Mary, and Joseph," breathed Bunny. The three former hostages were panting like dogs. Khalid was murmuring prayers in Egyptian.

Top felt every one of his very long, very hard years settle over him as he exhaled a deep breath and closed his eyes.

"We're clear," said the pilot over the intercom. The rotors spun up to a higher whine—though still eerily quiet—and the Nightbird lifted off. "Next stop Kuwait. First round's on me."

That was ten hours ago.

Now the three freed American college students were with their families. Laughing and weeping, hugging each other, kissing their families and each other. A happy ending and for once no one had died. Despite his weariness, it made Top feel like there was some clean air to breathe in the world.

Bunny sat nearby on an overturned milk crate, sipping Coke from a can. Khalid was throwing grapes into the air and catching them in his mouth. Lydia, who had found her own way out of Iran, had her boots off and her feet in a bucket of cool water.

The three of them looked like they were at a picnic, but Top wasn't fooled. He knew every trick in the book about the "fake it till you make it" approach to regaining personal calm. All of them were feeling it. Anyone who ran this kind of game or played in this league felt it; but all of the nerves, the fears, the existential doubts were wrapped tight in affectation and shoved out of sight of the rest of the world.

To let it show would be to admit openly that they were human, and they couldn't do that. Not on the job. Not in front of people. Not when there was another mission ahead, and another after that.

Top ached for the cigarettes he'd given up fifteen years ago. Or maybe a nice cigar. That would give his hands something to do, and concentrating on the smoke rolling down into the lungs and then swirling out again was something orderly and controllable. Even if the cigarettes were killing you, the process of lighting, inhaling, holding, exhaling, watching the smoke, shaping it with lips and tongue as it flowed out, and tapping the ash—all of that was deliberate process. Process was part and parcel with calm. But he didn't have a smoke and promised his ex-wife that he would never start again. So, instead he chewed a piece of gum very slowly and precisely, and he grinned at the hikers and their families.

It was Bunny who finally spoke, starting the process of talking about it. "Smith should be here pretty soon."

Top nodded. Smith had called from a border post right before climbing into a jeep with a Kuwaiti sergeant. "Any time now."

A few seconds blew by on the hot wind.

"You think the Cap's okay?" Bunny asked.

Khalid caught two grapes in his mouth, bobbing and weaving like a boxer to get under each of them. "Cowboy's always okay."

"Uh-huh," agreed Top. It was a lie, though. Their captain spent as much time being stitched and splinted as the rest of the team put together. And they all knew that he was half crazy. Maybe more than half crazy. No one had the details, but rumors had leaked out in DMS circles that Captain Ledger had a party going on in his head. Not that it mattered to them. As far as Top was concerned, the captain could have the entire Mormon Tabernacle Choir singing "Ave Maria" in his head and it didn't change a thing. Ledger was their captain and their friend, and they'd follow him into hell. Top thought about that and smiled ruefully. They *had* followed him into hell.

His earbud buzzed and he tapped it. "Go for Sergeant Rock."

"Sit rep," said Mr. Church crisply.

"Sir, all quiet on the western front. Waiting on Chatterbox and Cowboy."

"Give me a status report on combat readiness," interrupted Church.

Top winced and almost cursed aloud. He was bone weary, and he ached for a hot bath, a cold beer, and twenty hours of sleep. Preferably with someone curvy, brown, and warm snuggled up against him.

"Always ready to rock and roll, sir," he said with energy in his voice that was a total fabrication. "What's the op?"

Khalid and Bunny shot him looks that went from inquisitive to surprised to murderous in the space of a second. Top spread his hands in a "what can I tell you" gesture.

Bunny bowed his head and sighed. "Oh, man . . ."

"We are at Firehall One," said Church. That rocked Top and slapped all the fatigue from his nerves. Firehall was DMS combat code for a nuclear threat.

"Jesus . . ."

"Acknowledge," snapped Mr. Church.

Top stiffened and the others caught the sudden jerk of his body. They clustered around him.

"Acknowledge Firehall One, sir," said Top, and the others exchanged stunned looks. "Echo Team is ready to respond."

"Then listen closely," said Church. "Time is critical . . ."

Chapter Twenty-One

The Kingdom of Shadows
Beneath the Sands
One Year Ago

The King of Thorns rose from his chair and loomed above Hugo Vox. In the dense shadows pale figures crept closer, surrounding Vox with burning red eyes and hungry mouths.

Vox turned in a slow circle, looking at the twisted figures. Some were vastly old, with crooked bodies and crippled limbs; some had the blank moon faces of deeply inbred retardation; but seeded throughout the crowd were creatures like Grigor. Taller, whole, and powerful, their skin the color of milk, their eyes blazing with intelligence and an unnatural vitality that seemed to burn into Vox, threatening to steal away his life and breath.

Vox held up the detonator. "Careful now," he murmured in a ghost of a voice. "Let's all be very, very careful."

"I am not afraid of your bomb," sneered Grigor. "The Upierczi do not fear death."

That annoyed Vox and he snapped, "Don't lie to me, Grigor. Not to me. Everyone fears death. Even monsters like you. And . . . monsters like me. I'm not here to bring death and you damn well know it. I brought the bomb because I need to speak openly with you. No coy bullshit. We don't know each other enough for trust, so shared fear is a good platform. Tell me I'm wrong."

Grigor ran his tongue over the serrated ridge of his teeth.

"Talk," he said.

Vox took another step, which brought him to within reach of Grigor, but the pale man remained motionless, his eyes glittering.

"The Scriptor and the Red Order don't give a shit about you unless they need you to do their dirty work," said Vox. "To do the work they are too weak and too afraid to do themselves. Isn't it time to stop being their dog?"

Grigor's eyes seemed to blaze with real heat. "Yes." He hissed the word, filling it with endless hatred and cold fire.

"Yes," agreed Vox.

"I know what happened to you. I know that eight hundred years ago Sir Guy LaRoque, the first Scriptor, sought out the Upierczi because the Order had a need for killers. Not any killers, but the best. Better than the *Hashashin* the Tariqa were using for their part of the so-called Holy Agreement. Nicodemus told LaRoque where to look, and he found an Upier in England, in Newburgh. He found another in France, and more in Italy, Poland, Russia . . . all through Europe. Not a community of you. Individuals. Hunted, wretched, hungry. Persecuted by the church. Condemned as monsters, as demons, as the unholy. LaRoque brought the Upier back to Nicodemus, and the priest created the Order of the Red Knights. Must have sounded pretty great at the time. To those poor, miserable fucks who had been hiding out in crypts and forests and ruins—to them it must have felt like they were *people*. Like they mattered. And, I guess they did matter; but only in the way a bullet matters if you want to shoot a gun. That's what the Upierczi were, no matter what fancy-ass labels the Red Order hand out. Tools, weapons, slaves. For you guys, all three words mean the same thing."

Grigor gave a single, slow nod.

"But the Order hit a snag with you. Something Sir Guy and Nicodemus didn't foresee. You guys can't breed worth shit. There are no female Upierczi, which screws things up from the jump. You guys are genetic freaks, a sideline of human evolution that didn't pan out. The genes that make you what you are rarely present in females, and when they are the females look human and they sure as hell don't want to breed with you. Not by choice. That meant that the Red Order had to start a forced breeding program. How many women did they take over all those years? Ten thousand? A hundred thousand? More? And every one of them had to be forced. Eight hundred years of rape isn't a legacy to be proud of."

Grigor sneered. "They are women. Who cares?"

Vox smiled. "Yeah, I'm the last person to throw stones. Anyway, the breeding program hit some of its own snags. Turns out only one in fifty or a hundred women was able to give birth to a healthy Upier. Most of the babies were—how should I put it? Less than successful? Stillbirths, freaks. Once in a while one of the breeding slaves popped out a half-breed. Always female, though, right? Whaddya call 'em? Dhampyr?"

"Abominations!" The word rippled through the darkness, spoken by a hundred mouths.

"Glass houses, stones. Any of that ring a bell?" asked Vox, amused. To Grigor he said, "The real bitch of it all was that the Red Order focused their breeding program on those few women who *could* produce Upierczi. They bred them and their children, over and over again, which left a pretty shallow fucking gene pool." He gestured to one of the Upierczi who had mongoloid features and a vacuous expression in his eyes. "Inbreeding didn't work for the Hapsburgs, and it sure as hell didn't work for you."

"That is the past," growled Grigor.

"I know," said Vox, smiling broadly. "I know that really goddamn well, which is why I'm here. Charlie LaRoque's dad, who was probably one of the better Scriptors, as far as that goes, decided to try something different. Genetics. Gene therapy, gene splicing. Not rebreeding but a careful and deliberate remodeling of the Upier DNA. Very smart, very expensive, and very illegal. Which is how *I* found out about it, because if it involves science and it's against the law, I'm always involved, I'm always making a buck on it, and I *always* find out about it."

"What is it to you? What is any of this to you? You have the Seven

Kings. You are their King of Fear. You are more powerful than most of the governments in the world above."

Vox reached up, threaded his fingers through his hair, and revealed a bald pate that was blotched and unhealthy.

"I'm a walking dead man," he said. "Cancer. I'm done. Best-case scenario gives me eighteen months."

Grigor's eyes glittered like rubies.

"Nobody knows. Not the Kings, not my mother. Not the Scriptor. Nobody."

"Why come to me? Do you want a quicker death?"

"No . . . I want to live. You see, the *other* thing that I know about is what the scientists discovered while they were engineering the new generation of Upierczi. They cracked your DNA. They found out why you never get sick, why you lucky pricks live for so damn long. They know what makes you as close to immortal as living flesh and bone is ever going to get."

Vox took a last step closer to Grigor, well within reach.

"I know about the treatment. I know about Upier 531," he said fiercely. "And I fucking want it."

"It isn't for your kind. It would kill you."

"It *might* kill me," corrected Vox. "Or it might make me live forever."

Grigor laughed. Low and soft. If a wolf could laugh, Vox thought, it would sound like that.

"Why should I give it to you? What could you possibly give me in return?"

"I can give you the whole fucking world, Grigor. I can make *sure* that no one and nothing can put you in chains again. I can guarantee it."

"Prove it," demanded Grigor.

He and Vox stared at each other for a long minute, their faces less than a yard apart.

Vox raised the detonator between them. He turned it over and slid back a small panel on the bottom, revealing a nine-digit touch pad. Vox showed this to Grigor and then slowly and deliberately punched in a complex code. The LED light glowing under his thumb faded to black. Hugo Vox raised his hand, palm out, offering the inert detonator to Grigor.

"All hail the King of Thorns," he said.

Chapter Twenty-Two

Knowing that Church was working on finding the nukes was a tremendous relief. Even I don't have a sense of all the forces he can bring to bear at need. His connections and his political clout are considerable, and he doesn't allow red tape to slow him down. With Vox in the mix? Well, let's just say that I pity anyone who got in his way today.

Having handed off the ball, I switched my focus to the second part of Rasouli's message. The *Book of Shadows* and the *Saladin Codex*. I had no idea what they were and I did not believe for a moment that they were entirely tangential to the nuclear issue. Rasouli had been a little too casual about mentioning them.

I called Bug. He wasn't good with computers—he was a freak. When 9/11 happened Bug was still in high school, amusing himself by hacking into the school board computer to give everyone he liked a 4.0 average and to put the school disciplinarian on a sex offenders watch list. A couple of years after the planes hit, Bug tried to hack Homeland, believing that if he had access to their data he could find Bin Laden. The next day Grace Courtland and Sergeant Gus Dietrich—Church's personal bodyguard—showed up at his front door to offer him a choice: jail or a job with the DMS. Bug made the smart choice.

Since then he'd become the high priest in the church of MindReader. And back in 2011 he got his wish by helping track Bin Laden to his Pakistani compound.

He answered the call with: "Hey, whaddya know, Joe? Heard about the hikers gig. Echo Team kicks a-a-a-a-ass."

"Thanks, Bug, but listen up. Something else is about to hit the fan. The Big Man will be calling you any minute about—"

"I know, the nukes. I'm looking at it right now. Frigging scary as shit, huh?" Bug said with the kind of excitement you hear from video gamers who have found a challenging new level. I sometimes wonder if Bug knew that he *didn't* exist in a purely virtual world.

"So you're already tied up?"

"Nah, this stuff is crap. Got to run it through a bunch of filters and a clean-up program before we can do much with it. That's going to take a couple of—"

"Good. Then, before you get swamped with that I need you to start a database search for me. It's part of the nuke thing; but it's a different arm of the investigation and to tell you the truth I don't have a clue how it relates. All I have are the names of two books. No authors, no other data."

"Fire away."

"The *Book of Shadows* and the *Saladin Codex*."

"Saladin, as in the sultan who—?"

"Presumably. Rasouli dropped his name during our little chitchat, so I figure that was some kind of hint."

"Okay. Wait—there's something about them on the drive. No . . . forget it. Stuff's corrupted as all shit. Reads like some kind of gibberish. I'll have to see if I can translate it. What do you need?"

"Anything you got. General and specific. I had to dump my tactical computer and PDA, so send it to me via e-mail so I can read it on my phone. You ring any serious bells, call me directly. If I don't answer, hit scramble and leave it on my voice mail."

"You got it, Joe."

I disconnected, and again I could feel another layer of stress crack and fall away.

Ghost came over and leaned against me. He does that. I know it's more of a greyhound trait and the fuzzmonster is pure White Shepherd, but Ghost isn't one to pass up a trick that might get him petted. I ran my fingers through his fur.

"I don't suppose you know how to sniff out a nuclear bomb, do you?" I asked him. "No? Guess I'd better do it."

He wagged his tail to show that he believed me to be Captain Invincible who could find those pesky nukes and crush them in my hands of steel. That or he thought I had more goat strips in my pocket.

I debated taking a shower and maybe drowning myself. Might be a tension breaker.

Instead I called Rudy Sanchez.

"Cowboy!" he said instead of hello. "Are you home?"

"I wish. Where are you?" I could hear wind rushing past the phone.

"On the way to the Warehouse. Mr. Church called ten minutes ago and told us to come in right away. Can you tell me what's happening?"

We were both on scrambled phones, so I gave him the highlights.

"*Dios mio!*"

"No kidding."

"How are you doing with all of this?"

His question, I knew, had very little to do with the mission and a lot to do with my overall mental health. Rudy and I have a lot of history. When I was a teenager my girlfriend Helen and I were jumped by a gang of older teens. The guys completely trashed me, breaking bones, rupturing some stuff inside. While I lay there coughing up blood they took turns with Helen. That image is seared onto the front of my mind. I see it every single day.

Helen and I healed from the physical trauma. I got involved in martial arts and made myself as tough and as ruthless as I could. Helen wandered down a few dark corridors inside her head and never found her way out.

We met Rudy during his psychiatric residency at Sinai in Baltimore. Helen was having one of her frequent breakdowns and Rudy did some amazing work with her, pulling her back from the brink time after time. He also helped me work on my internal wiring. Unfortunately the darkness was too much for Helen, and one day she let it take her.

I kicked in her door and found her.

Her death nearly killed me. Nearly killed Rudy, too. He'd never lost a patient to suicide before. We were already best friends, and that friendship probably saved us both. Since then we've become closer than brothers— certainly closer than I am to my own brother. Rudy is the only person in whom I place total trust.

He's also the person who helped me make sense of the wreckage in my head. As I healed, I began to realize that I was not completely alone inside my mind. Over time three distinct personalities emerged. One was the Civilized Man, and Rudy says that he is my idealized self, the version of me that I wish could survive in this world. Optimistic, compassionate, nonviolent; and he's been taking a real beating over the last couple of years as I hunt bad guys for Mr. Church. Then there is his complete opposite, the

Warrior. Or, as I sometimes think of him, the Killer. He's the part of me that was born on that day when the children that Helen and I had been were destroyed. He is ruthless, highly dangerous, and unrelenting. His bloodlust is intense and constant, and although he can be glutted, his hunger will eventually come back. I have to keep a real eye on him, especially while working for the DMS, because the more evil I see in the world the harder it is to rationalize putting him in a cage.

The third personality is the one that I believe truly defines me. The Cop. He's not a cynic or a wide-eyed idealist. He's rational, cool, calculating, and balanced. He emerged even before I joined the police; in a lot of ways he has a Samurai vibe. Skilled, but self-controlled.

They're always with me, and Rudy taught me how to manage them. How to make them more fully a part of a whole rather than disparate entities. I'm not entirely convinced I've managed that.

I trust Rudy's judgment, though. In that and in most things. When I got my gold shield with Baltimore PD, my father—then the commissioner—arranged a consultant's position for Rudy, which later expanded into a full-time gig. Rudy specialized in trauma cases, which is something he really dug into after Helen's death. He was in New York after the towers fell, working with survivors and families and with the legion of heroes who risked their lives to search through the rubble. He was in New Orleans and Mississippi following Katrina, in Thailand after the tsunami, in Haiti, and in Japan. He knows that he can't save everyone, and every lost soul gouges a deep mark into his own soul, but he saves more of them than anyone else.

When Mr. Church hijacked me into the DMS, Rudy became part of the deal. I often think that he does a lot more good with quiet conversations and a patient ear than I do with a pistol. Which is very much as it should be.

"I'm okay," I said. Rudy grunted, knowing that I was lying. He'd let me get away with that as long as I was in the field, but once I got back home I'd have to fess up. I'd need to by then.

"Joe—Mr. Church called me late last night and told me about the hikers."

"Yeah."

"That was well done," he said. "That one will really matter."

"All part of the job."

"No," he said, but left it there. Knowing Church, he would probably have Rudy sit down with the hikers.

"Why'd Church call you in on this?" I asked.

"I think he wanted Circe more than me. This is her field more than mine."

"Not if the nukes go off," I said.

"Mother of God."

"Speaking of Circe—how's she doing?"

Dr. Circe O'Tree was a PhD in a handful of overlapping subjects including Middle Eastern history and religions, cults, anthropology, psychology, and a few others I'm probably forgetting. She has more letters after her name than anyone I've ever met. She was also Mr. Church's daughter, a fact that was shared by only a few people and that I'd only found out by accident. Although Circe now worked for the DMS, she and her father had been estranged for years. I was under very specific orders from Church not to mention the family connection. To anyone. Ever. He didn't actually come out and threaten to disappear me, but I didn't want to push the issue.

"She's wonderful," said Rudy.

I smiled. I've never seen Rudy happier. Even though I hadn't yet heard him throw around the L-word, whenever he looked at Circe there were little red hearts floating all around him.

"Tell the missus I said 'hi.'"

"Cowboy," he warned, but I laughed at him. Laughing felt good. It felt like I was still in the real world.

My phone pinged softly. Someone else was trying to reach me.

"Hey, Rude . . . I have another call coming in. I'll talk to you soon."

I disconnected and looked at the screen. No caller ID. Church said he would have Abdul, our local asset, call me, so I punched the button.

"Hello," I said in Persian.

"I see you got a new battery for your phone," she said in English. "Sorry I made you throw out the last one."

Chapter Twenty-Three

It was *her*. Same voice, same hint of an Italian accent. A bit more pronounced now. I fought the urge to check my body for laser sights. There were none, but I moved out of the line of sight of the hotel window.

"What is it now?" I asked. "You want to set me up for a playdate with Satan?"

She laughed. At least *someone* thought I was funny. "No," she said, "you said you wanted to meet me."

"I do." I tried not to sound too eager. I used my thumbnail to slide back a panel on the side of my phone. I pressed a button that activates a trace. "Name a place. I'll buy the coffee."

"Sorry . . . it will have to be over the phone. I want to ask a question."

I almost laughed. "Why on earth would I want to answer one? Last time we chatted, you put a laser sight on my balls."

"I could have shot your balls off. I did not. You can check if you like. I'll wait."

"Okay," I said, "admittedly you get some Brownie points for not blowing my balls off. Thanks bunches, but it's hardly a basis for enduring trust."

" 'Brownie points'? You are a strange man, Captain Ledger."

"You have no idea."

"Maybe I do."

Before I could respond to that she came at me out of left field. "What did Rasouli give you?"

"What makes you think he gave me anything?"

"He *said* he wanted to give you something."

"Okay, there's that. He's your boss, why don't you ask him?"

She made a gagging noise. "God! I would rather shoot myself than work for such a cockroach."

"Didn't look that way an hour ago."

"Eh," she said dismissively. "It was contract work. Believe me, Captain Ledger, it is all I would ever be willing to do for him." With her accent she pronounced my last name as "La-jeer." I liked it. Made me feel exotic and mysterious.

"Even so," I said, "why not ask him?"

"He doesn't know me. I'm a voice on a phone to him. Why would he trust me?"

"Why would I?"

"I am asking very nicely," she said.

Despite everything, I laughed. She did too. "I'll think about it."

"I promise not to shoot you."

"Yeah, that earns you those brownie points, but so far you're only a sexy voice on a phone line. You don't have enough points to buy much more than civility."

There was a short silence as she considered this. I looked at the display on the side of my phone. The trace was about halfway completed.

"Maybe I can earn some extra 'brownie' points," she said.

"How?"

Instead of answering she asked, "Can I call you 'Joe'?"

I smiled and shook my head in exasperation. Ghost looked at me in disgust. He would have hung up a long time ago, I suppose. "Only if I have something to call you."

"You have to know that's impossible."

"Then give me anything. A nickname."

"I have a thousand names."

"Yes, that's very 'international woman of mystery' of you, but I only need one."

After a few seconds she said, "Violin."

"Violin," I said, testing the name. "That's pretty."

"Thanks."

"I'll bet you are, too."

"No," she said, "I'm a monster." And in those four simple words her tone changed from playful humor to something else. She packed that word with such intense sadness that I was momentarily left speechless. Before I could fumble out a reply the line went dead.

I stared at the phone. The LED tracer went from green to red. Trace incomplete.

"Okay," I said aloud. "That was surreal."

Ghost stared at me with huge doggie eyes. Sadly he offered no wise insights into what the hell was going on.

Chapter Twenty-Four

The Kingdom of Shadows
Beneath the Sands
One Year Ago

They walked through the shadows, two incongruous figures that did not look like they belonged in the same century let alone the same reality. Vox found it very amusing even while it was frightening. He admitted to himself that Grigor scared him. In Vox's estimation, Grigor—with his pale skin, black clothes, and otherworldly demeanor—would scare anyone. He wondered how much of it was window dressing to sell the idea of immortal monsters, and how much of it was the real deal. Not knowing the difference is what made the fear sweat run icy lines down Vox's back.

After all, Grigor *was* in many ways the real deal. He was one of Upierczi, the reigning king of his kind. Ancient by any ordinary standard and, if the stories the Scriptor's father had told him were true, faster and more powerful than any of his followers—and they were faster and stronger than . . .

Than what? He asked himself. *Than humans?*

As they walked, Vox pondered that question and his fear grew and grew.

Grigor led him through a maze of tunnels, some of which looked to be centuries old. Some of the tunnels opened into well-organized living quarters, with proper lights, rooms like dormitories, niches for worship, mess halls, and many rooms for training. There were cells down there, too, and as they walked past, Vox could hear the wretched whimpering of female voices.

He paused. "What's that?"

Grigor turned and regarded the line of cells with heavy-lidded eyes. "Breeding pens."

"Who are those women?"

"They are not women," sneered Grigor. "They are cows. If they are lucky, if God favors them, they will bear a Upierczi son."

"If they don't?"

"Then they are less than useless to us."

He spat on the floor and turned to continue down the long corridor.

Vox lingered for a moment. One voice, a very young voice, suddenly screamed with the absolute and immediate horror of someone who was being brutally used and who knew, with absolute certainty, that no one would ever come to rescue her. It made Vox feel sick. He tried to tell himself that it was the chemo upsetting his stomach. If it accomplished nothing else, the lie at least kept him from vomiting.

He hurried to catch up to Grigor.

After another quarter mile, Vox stopped again, this time to peer at a piece of broken mosaic on a cracked wall. When Grigor saw him staring at it, the pale man said, "That is Darius the Great being crowned. It was placed there on the first anniversary of the Persian king's death. This wall was made four hundred and eighty-five years before the birth of Jesus Christ."

Vox turned and looked at the open mouths of tunnels and side corridors. "These tunnels are that old?"

"Some are," agreed Grigor. "Some are older still; and we have tunnels like these in many cities."

"You dug these holes?'

"The Upierczi did much of it, but your kind made many of them," murmured Grigor, still caressing the stonework. His eyelids drifted shut. "Do you know how the Upierczi came to be the slaves of the *Ordo Ruber*?"

"I . . . know the version I was told by the Scriptor's grandfather. About Sir Guy going looking for . . . *your* kind."

Grigor leaned his cheek against the stone wall. "Father Nicodemus sent Sir Guy out to find Upierczi anywhere he could. In Turkey and Russia, England and Romania. Many places. There were rumors of us, of course, and most rumors were false. They said that we were the corpses of the dead risen from graves to haunt and prey upon the living." He laughed and then shook his head. "We were not a race then. We were an aberration, an abomination. Freaks who were born to live in shadows, always hungry, always on the point of starvation, driven to mad acts of violence merely to survive. It is no different with any creature God has made—in the direst moment need overwhelms control."

"That hasn't changed," said Vox.

Grigor nodded. "Your people feared us, and that is to be understood. The Church, however, denounced us as demons, as children of Satan. Knights and warrior priests and anyone who could raise a sword on behalf of the Church were empowered to kill us, to hunt us to extinction." He sighed. "Think of that life. To be alone, and to believe that there is no one like you. No one who shares your nature, no one who *understands* your hungers. No one who loves you."

"Love?" said Vox quietly. "They make a lot about that in movies. *Dracula* and *Twilight* and all that shit. I don't suppose you get to the multiplex very often, but that's a kind of a theme out there. They think you are all about eternal love and romance. But I heard those women in the cells. Didn't sound like love songs to me."

Grigor turned away and looked deep into the shadows, and Vox wondered how much the man could see that he could not. Without immediately commenting on Vox's statement, Grigor continued his story.

"When Sir Guy died, his son and successor, along with Father Nicodemus, created the Red Knights. A new order of chivalry, of knights errant given authority by the Church to prosecute a campaign against faithlessness. But that was in name only. They called us knights, and we call ourselves knights, but that is not who and what we are."

"Then what are you?"

"Assassins. We were created to be the Order's answer to the Tariqa's *fida'i*. We were chess pieces. We were a sword, a knife, a gun. No different. Tools of war."

"You're more than that," said Vox.

"Yes," said Grigor and it was the first word he'd spoken that had real passion. "We made true knights of ourselves. We became in fact what they said we were in name only. We became a true order of chivalry. We became a society. A people."

"You still live in tunnels, Grigor."

"Because we choose to. It is our world, within but apart from the world above. We have thousands of miles of tunnels. We come and go and no one knows we are here. Archaeologists and miners sometimes find the tunnels, but we collapse connecting tunnels, and we are experts at disguising our private tunnels. We are not found unless we choose to be found."

"That's pretty fucking impressive."

Grigor gave a half smile. "It's necessary. We know that we could never integrate into the world above. We can play dress up and 'pass' for one of you, but not on close inspection. And we are still hunted up there. The Inquisition was created by a papal bull to hunt us down. Us and other things that move in the dark, most of who are only fantasies concocted by fools. Father Nicodemus was able to use some aspects of the Inquisition so that he and the sitting Scriptor could find true Upierczi. Find and recruit us; but to the Church at large we were monsters and therefore evil; and they still hunt us. We do not fear any man in single combat, or any two or three men. But the Inquisitors did not come at us in small numbers. They sent armies against us. They sent special teams—the Sabbatarians, the Brotherhood of the Holy Sepulcher, and many others over the years. Some—most—of those groups are long gone. Died out or killed by us or disbanded by changes in Church policies. Only the Inquisitors remain, and after a long silence they've become active again."

"Yeah," said Vox, "I know about one of them. The Sabbatarians. The Seven Kings ran into them a couple of times. I even used them once in a while for some wetworks stuff, but I broke off my ties with them. Idealistic trash. They're still around, though, and they're formidable in numbers."

"In the same way locusts are."

"There are a lot of them," said Vox, and Grigor nodded.

"Over the years we—with the help of Father Nicodemus—have managed to weaken their effectiveness by feeding them lies about who and what we are. About our strengths and weaknesses."

"Disinformation," Vox supplied. "Stakes, crosses, sunlight, that sort of shit?"

"Yes."

"Nicodemus is a tricky bastard. What about garlic?"

Grigor did not answer.

Vox said, "I heard a rumor that some other group is gunning for you too. Arklight?"

Grigor hissed like a snake. "Whores and daughters of whores."

"Maybe," said Vox grudgingly. "Whores with high-powered sniper rifles, though.

With a black-nailed finger, Grigor pointed into the darkness in the direction of the wretched weeping. "They were our whores once. There is not one of them who has not screamed for us."

"Charming," murmured Vox. A wave of nausea swept through him and he stopped to steady himself on a wall. "When do we start the treatments? I'm losing a lot of ground here."

The King of Thorns smiled.

"The treatment will make you scream," he murmured.

"Then I'll fucking scream," snarled Vox.

The word "scream" echoed through the endless darkness.

A challenge. A promise.

Chapter Twenty-Five

Homa Hotel

51 Khodami Street, Vanak Square

Tehran, Iran

June 15, 9:06 a.m.

The sniper's name was not Violin.

But it would do. For Joseph Ledger and for this crisis, it would do. The name meant something to her from a long time ago. Back when *she* meant something to herself. When she had a life instead of a mission.

Violin.

Even the sound of it in her mind was bittersweet. A memory of a girl who laughed freely and who thought that all the monsters in the world were in storybooks. Back before her eyes were opened.

Violin. She had liked the way Ledger had repeated it. He had truly tasted the name, the way a sensualist would. That intrigued her. She already knew that he was a passionate man, that was clear from the profiles Oracle had read to her. Ledger was a sensuous man, and a tragic one. He wore death and grief like garments.

And Violin understood that very well.

What she did not understand was why she had lingered to watch him, or worse yet, why she had called him. It felt correct while she was dialing, and yet in every way open to her analytical mind it was wrong. A tactical and strategic error and a clear break with Arklight protocol. Mother would be furious.

No, she corrected herself, Mother *will* be furious. The call was now part of her phone log, which meant that it was part of the mission file. Lilith would never overlook it.

"Oracle," she said aloud.

The screen on her small computer lit up with its smiling Mona Lisa.

"Oracle welcomes you."

"I want to enter a new code name."

"Voice recognition is active. What code name would you like to enter?"

"Violin."

"Is this for file or field use?"

"Field use. It will be my call sign for this mission. Enable."

"May I inquire as to why you have changed your code name? Has your cover been compromised?"

"My cover is intact. The change is to . . . maintain high security standards."

"Thank you. Call sign 'Violin' is enabled. All appropriate field teams will receive a coded memo. How may I help you, Violin?"

"I need to speak to my mother. Right now."

Chapter Twenty-Six

Tehran, Iran
One Year Ago

Hugo Vox sat in his car and wept.

He had never felt pain like this before. Not during chemo or radiation. Not even the cancer hurt this bad. Upier 531 was a lot more than gene therapy. Vox knew about gene therapy and it didn't hurt beyond the simple injections.

He felt like every cell in his body was tearing itself apart.

The car was soundproof, so his screams bounced off the windows and the leather seats and smashed into him like fists. He punched the steering wheel and dashboard.

Tears ran down his face.

"God!" he begged. "Please, God . . ."

But God had never once answered his prayers, even when Vox still believed.

Vox felt his mind fracture, felt pieces fall away. A fever burned through him and his skin was as hot as if he sat in a furnace. The sweat ran down so heavily that he felt like he was melting.

What had he done?

How could he have thought that this was going to save him, because now he was sure it was killing him.

Not only gene therapy.

Grigor's pet mad scientist, Dr. Hasbrouck, had given him three injections of something else. Three syringes with long needles. Syringes filled with fluid the color of blood.

No, not just the *color* of blood.

Upier 531.

Blood of the damned. Blood of the monsters who tunneled like pale moles in the bowels of the earth.

Blood of vampires.

Hasbrouck had strapped Vox down for those injections. Bound his wrists and legs and chest. And then he had raised one gleaming syringe above him. A bead of blood gleamed on the needlepoint.

"This may hurt a little," Hasbrouck had said with a sadistic chuckle. And then he had plunged the needle into his chest.

Into his heart.

Vox had screamed. Oh, how he had screamed.

The pain was so far beyond his understanding that he had no adjectives to describe it. He felt the alien blood as it entered him.

It shrieked its way into his heart, into his blood, throughout his body.

Vox did not pass out until the second needle. Hasbrouck, courteous man that he was, splashed cold water in Vox's face before he gave him the third injection.

"You really should pay attention to this," said the doctor. "It's not every day that someone makes you immortal. Have a little respect."

The third needle was the worst of all, because every inch of Vox's skin tried to recoil from it. Like a torture victim who knows that his last inch of unburned flesh is next to feel the Inquisitor's touch.

Vox passed out again.

And woke up behind the wheel in his own car.

The pain came and went. Discovering that he was still alive was little comfort. He put his face in his hands and sobbed.

A voice said, "Stop it. You embarrass me."

Vox's head shot up and he jerked sideways in his seat. A scream bubbled inside his throat, but it died on his tongue.

"How the fuck did you get in here?"

Father Nicodemus smiled. "What does it matter?"

Vox stared in mingled horror, doubt, and fascination at the old priest. It had been years since he'd seen him, but the cleric had not changed at all. Not a line, not a day.

"No, I guess not. But damn you're a spooky bastard. And, besides, I thought you said it was too dangerous for us to meet like this," Vox said, turning to glance through the tinted windows.

"No," said Nicodemus, "that isn't what I told you. I said it was dangerous for us to meet." He smiled. "Not at all the same thing."

A wave of agony swept over Vox and he recoiled from it as from a blow, shutting his eyes, hissing through clenched teeth. Through the haze of agony he heard Nicodemus speaking.

"Do you feel it?"

"Yes, I feel it, goddamn it. It fucking hurts!"

"No. Don't be a child, Hugo. Look through the pain. Look into its heart, see it for what it is."

Vox was panting like a dog, each breath a labor.

"Deep inside the pain something wonderful is happening."

"What?" gritted Vox.

The priest bent close and whispered to Vox, "You are becoming one of them."

Them.

"Please . . ." he begged.

Part Two
By the Rivers Dark

All warfare is based on deception.
Hence, when able to attack, we must seem unable;
when using our forces, we must seem inactive;
when we are near, we must make the enemy believe we are far away;
when far away, we must make him believe we are near.

—SUN TZU

Chapter Twenty-Seven

The Department of Military Sciences maintained eleven active field offices within the continental United States. The Baltimore field office was the seventh office to be established, and it occupied a warehouse once used by a terrorist cell to prepare for the launch of a global pandemic. Mr. Church had repurposed it and outfitted it with the very latest in anti- and counter-terrorism technologies. A staff of one hundred and sixty-three people worked at the Warehouse, including two full field teams, Alpha and Echo.

The TOC—Tactical Operations Center—was not as grand as the one at the main headquarters in the Hangar at Floyd Bennett Field in Brooklyn, but to Rudy Sanchez it was dazzling. The TOC was the heart of the Warehouse, a command center filled with computers and control consoles whose purpose Rudy could only guess at. He was a medical doctor and psychiatrist, but his knowledge of advanced tactical computer systems was nil. He was fine with that. Standing and watching as the technicians and officers worked gave him a chance to observe the staff under a variety of stressful conditions, and that was useful for him in his job as chief psychologist for the DMS.

At the moment, he stood with his finger hooked through the handle of a cup of coffee, watching as Circe O'Tree settled herself into the computer array that was restricted for her private use. The computers formed a three-quarter circle around a leather swivel chair, and there were plasma and holographic screens at various levels. Rudy appreciated the science fiction appearance because he knew two things about it. The first was that the presence of the most cutting-edge technology made Circe—and the other senior staff—feel powerful. They had virtually limitless research materials at their fingertips, all of it backed by the MindReader computer system. It shotgunned confidence into people like Circe. And that was the second thing Rudy knew about it: Mr. Church always provided the most sophisticated and exclusive equipment for that very reason. It was not the only reason he did that, but it was definitely there. A trait of a man who manipulated everyone around him in order to coax from them the highest possible levels of confidence, personal power, and mission excellence.

Rudy sipped his coffee. The coffee was first rate too. Everything here was, and that was part of Church's method. Treat everyone with the highest respect, provide them with things of quality, and demonstrably respect their opinions. The result was that the DMS staff tended to operate at a level of efficiency that was statistically freakish. Rudy felt it in himself, and he knew that Joe did too. Joe's track record of amazing field work owed as much to Church as it did to Joe's own exceptional nature.

He leaned a hip against the curved row of computers that surrounded Circe and watched her work. She logged on to the server and went through several levels of security in order to log into the MindReader network.

"I'm in," she announced and then patted the chair next to hers. "Have a seat. This might take some time . . . but don't touch anything."

"Wouldn't dream of it," said Rudy with a smile as he slid into the companion chair. He cupped his hands around his mug—which had the olive-drab Echo Team logo on it—and watched as Circe filled the screens with lists of data.

"What is all that?" asked Rudy.

"The materials from Joe's flash drive." She peered at it for a while, frowning and occasionally shaking her head. "Lot of junk here."

"Joe said that the agent swallowed it. Stomach acids and all that . . ."

But Circe said nothing. She chewed her lower lip as her eyes flicked over the information, and all the time her fingers were busy on the keys.

Weapons of mass destruction and the people who chose to use them were the core of her field of study, and that field had roots buried in history, religion, folklore, literature, psychology, and other fields. It was her particular genius that she could see connections between those disparate disciplines and then collate them into a cohesive profile. She worked in silence with an expression of ferocious interest on her lovely face.

Rudy studied it too, though much of the information was highly technical data on nuclear devices. Aside from that, he was not a field agent and despite the months he'd been with the DMS, he had yet to become inured to such words as "nukes" being thrown around as if they were a normal part of everyday life. It hurt him that this was a part of his life, and more so that it was part of the lives of the people he cared about.

Then suddenly everything seemed to jolt to a stop. While Circe was opening a file filled with random surveillance photos, one image hit them both like punches to the heart.

A big man, dressed in expensive clothes, stood with his head bowed in conversation with a smaller and much younger man. The image was labeled "Hugo Vox and unknown companion."

Vox.

"God," murmured Circe in a small, hurt voice.

Rudy reached out to take Circe's hand.

"No," she said. "I'm okay."

It was a lie, though, and they both knew it. Rudy knew it better than anyone. Whenever Vox's name came up, Circe's lovely face took on a haggard look, like a prisoner who had been too long away from sunlight and clean air. Aside from the damage Vox and the Seven Kings had done to the world, and the betrayal of Church, he had also been like an uncle to Circe. She had worked for him at his counterterrorism training facility, Terror Town, for years. It was Vox, rather than her own estranged father, to whom Circe went with personal and career problems. Rudy knew that the hurt and betrayal she felt would take years to heal, if it ever did.

Circe pounded the arms of her chair. "Goddamn it, Rudy! It's not fair."

"I know, *querida*. We all feel betrayed." He gave her hand a gentle squeeze. "You most of all."

"Me and Dad." She said this very quietly so that no one else in the TOC could hear. Even so, it made Rudy feel odd.

Dad.

Even now, after months of being a part of Circe's life, Rudy still had a hard time connecting the austere and mysterious Mr. Church with anyone's father. Let alone a "Dad." Joe privately referred to Church as Daddy Darth, a phrase that would assuredly not play well with the man himself.

Circe sniffed and wiped a tear from the corner of one eye. Rudy picked up her hand and kissed it.

"I hate like all fuck to intrude on this chick-flick moment."

They looked up to see a woman's face smiling sourly at them from one of the holographic screens. Middle-aged, black, wearing chunky designer jewelry and a Caribbean-print dashiki. Her dreadlocks were threaded with gray, and she wore granny glasses perched on her blunt nose. When she spoke, however, her accent was pure Brooklyn. Aunt Sallie, Mr. Church's second in command.

"Don't fret, *Tía*," soothed Rudy, "you know my heart belongs only to you."

"Nice try," said Aunt Sallie, "but flattery won't get you a threesome."

"A-*hem*," growled Circe softly.

Laughing, Aunt Sallie said, "Okay, kids, let's have first impressions. Did you find anything?"

"This information is recovered from a damaged flash drive, right?" asked Circe. "This is everything?"

"Yes," agreed Aunt Sallie.

"Do we have the actual drive in hand?"

"Ledger's sending it."

"And we're absolutely sure this flash drive is genuine?"

"We're not sure of anything." Aunt Sallie's eyes narrowed. "What are you thinking, girl?"

"I hesitate to use the word 'bullshit,' but—"

"But it fits?" finished Auntie.

Circe's eyes were hard. "Yes."

Chapter Twenty-Eight

Homa Hotel
51 Khodami Street, Vanak Square
Tehran, Iran
June 15, 9:14 a.m.

Violin nibbled a callus on her thumb while she waited for her mother to call. Oracle had forwarded her urgent request, but Lilith was always handling urgent requests. Especially now that the Red Order was so aggressively active here in Tehran. The mosque bombing, the assassinations . . . so many things impacted Arklight.

When her phone rang Violin jumped and dropped her cell but she darted out a hand and caught it before it struck the floor. *Bad nerves, good reflexes*, she thought as she punched the button. *Story of my life.*

"Hello, Mother."

"I was in an important meeting, girl," growled Lilith. "There had better be a good reason."

No hello, no inquiry about her safety. Another part of the story of her life.

"I know you probably haven't had time to read my field report," began Violin, "but the mission was scrubbed."

"By you?"

"By the client." Violin waited for a reply, got none, so she took a breath and plunged in. "You were correct, Mother, Rasouli was looking to hire an independent hitter, but we were wrong about the target. Rasouli wasn't gunning for Charles LaRoque."

"Who was the target?"

"President Ahmadinejad."

"*What?*"

"It wasn't a kill. He wanted a near miss. Something to scare him and shake things up."

Iran was involved in a very discreet internal war between Ahmadinejad and Rasouli. In public they were friends, happy and smiling for the press, always shaking hands, clearly men with a shared agenda. In truth Ahmadinejad was losing favor and losing ground and was trying to repair his position by removing key political opponents. A near assassination might wipe the smug smile off of Ahmadinejad's face, and do so publicly. If the president showed fear—and there would be hundreds of press cameras to record every expression that crossed his face—the perceived weakness would greatly strengthen Rasouli's position.

Lilith grunted. "What do you infer from that?"

Her mother was not asking for advice or an opinion; this was a test. It was always like that with her.

"There are two clear possibilities," said Violin, who had been preparing her answer since Rasouli contacted her. "Both possibilities are tied to Rasouli's political aspirations and to the offer made to him by LaRoque."

"Tell me."

"The first is that Rasouli is going to accept the position of Murshid and sign the Holy Agreement with LaRoque and the Red Order. Ordering a hit on Ahmadinejad would be a demonstration of his commitment. Also, he's been very vocal in denouncing the mosque bombing and the spate of assassinations. By now he must know that the Red Order is behind all of that, and yet he hasn't said anything. That in itself could be a message to LaRoque and the Order that he can keep their secrets."

"And the other possibility?"

"If Rasouli is *not* going to sign the Agreement, then it's likely he was going to use the bungled assassination attempt to begin the process of exposing the Red Order to the world. He would need to do this in a big way—so big, in fact, that LaRoque would not dare to have him killed. Exposing the Order could be orchestrated into a rallying cry to unite all of Islam against the West. Pretty easily, too. It would emasculate European power in the Middle East, and by association irreparably damage the United States. And it would give religion itself a shot in the arm if Rasouli exposed who and moreover *what* the Red Knights are. The Catholic Church, the Upierczi, the Inquisition . . . that could spark a true jihad that would put Catholicism and probably all Christians in the crosshairs. Islam has never been truly unified against the west, but this could do just that."

Lilith made a small sound that might have held an ounce of approval. "Which scenario do you think is most likely?"

"I don't know," admitted Violin, though she hated to show uncertainty. "The first serves Rasouli directly, and his profile paints him as severely ambitious. The second would make him a hero of Islam, and although that would give him more power, it would tie him more securely to the ayatollahs. Rasouli would be a hero of the faith, and he'd have to live that role. His psych profile, however, suggests that his personal faith is more political than actual. He's never a fundamentalist unless the cameras are rolling." She took a breath. "We need more information before we can decide how he's playing this."

"Yes."

"We do have *some* new information that might give us a fresh perspective," continued Violin. "When Rasouli scrubbed the hit on Ahmadinejad, he offered me a bonus to provide security for a meeting with an American agent."

She told her mother about the meeting in the coffee shop and about trailing Captain Ledger to his hotel.

Lilith was silent for a while and Violin could almost hear the wheels turning. It had taken Arklight seventeen months of careful work to get the right credentials in place for Violin's team of shooters to be considered "first choice" for quiet political hits. It meant actually doing some hits, though luckily none of them had been saints. Far from it.

"I . . . ran a search with Oracle on Ledger," ventured Violin. "In case he was a traitor or a suspected agent of the Red Order."

"And—?"

"He works for St. Germaine."

She heard a sound that sounded like a gasp; but that was impossible. Mother was far too controlled, too cold, to have such a human reaction.

"Mother—?" she prompted gently.

"Follow Ledger," barked Lilith. "Find out what Rasouli gave him and what he knows. I don't care how you do it, you find out."

Before Violin could say another word the line went dead.

Violin stared at the device for several seconds, totally confused by her mother's reaction. She set the phone down as gingerly as if it were a sleeping scorpion. Then she bent to her sniper scope and studied Joseph Ledger with intensified interest.

Chapter Twenty-Nine

The Warehouse
Baltimore, Maryland
June 15, 1:05 a.m. EST

"Why is it bullshit?" demanded Aunt Sallie.

"Let's conference in Bug," said Circe, and a moment later the bespectacled young man was peering at them from a screen next to the one showing Aunt Sallie.

"Here's the problem," began Circe. "I've done extensive work on damaged and partial documents. If you look at the history of recovered writings, from cartouches on Egyptian stelae, the Dead Sea scrolls, to things like this flash drive, the information gaps are random. They're determined by chance, by exposure to elements, and other factors."

Bug nodded agreement, and Rudy could tell that he was already on the same page as Circe.

Auntie peered over her glasses. "That's not what you're seeing here? So what am I missing?"

"It's the inventory," answered Circe. "We have two clear JPEGS of nuclear devices and several other 'damaged' image files. That gives us the type of device and establishes that they are already in place. We have field notes from an operative with a Geiger counter. Not a tape or digital recording of the counter, but personal observation notes that look like they were transferred from a phone text message. We have a list of targets, which is naturally compelling but also weirdly precise, considering that Rasouli has no verifiable 'source' for any of this. There's more, but that's my first impression."

"Wow," said Rudy. "You got all that by looking at this for twenty minutes? You always impress me, my dear."

"No," interrupted Circe, "that's just it, this is too fast. Too easy. It's like we're being handed too much too soon." Again, Bug was nodding along with everything she said.

Rudy frowned. "Isn't that was Rasouli was trying to do?"

"Yes," conceded Circe, "and I might have been less suspicious if the drive was intact. What troubles me is the fact that the drive was damaged and yet there are a lot of very key pieces here."

"Exactamundo," agreed Bug.

"It doesn't make sense, though" Circe said, then quickly corrected herself. "No—it *does* make sense, but only if the person placing those files on the drive *knew* that the drive would be damaged."

"Yup."

"No, that's wrong, too," murmured Aunt Sallie. "Damage from moisture is random. Does this mean that the files were added after the flash drive was removed during the autopsy?"

"I don't think so," said Bug. "In fact I'm pretty sure that's not the case."

Rudy asked, "Admittedly I don't know what I'm talking about, so forgive me if this is a foolish question, but . . . we can't actually be certain that the drive was really swallowed by Rasouli's agent, can we? So, could the moisture damage have been deliberate?"

Bug grinned so hard his face looked ready to explode. "Bingo!"

"Okay, boy genius," said Aunt Sallie, "tell us."

"I could do it," said Bug. "In fact I'm really, really, really sure that some-one else who is almost as smart as me did exactly that."

"Almost as smart?"

Bug sniffed. "If I did it, no one would ever have figured it out."

"Arrogance is a serious personality flaw," said Rudy, but he was smil-ing.

"The whole package here is a little too cute," said Bug. "Either Rasouli thinks we're pretty dumb, which isn't likely; or he thinks we're really smart. I'm going with that, because layer after layer he's giving us useful stuff, but stuff only we'd figure out. I mean, I'd buy the whole 'this was damaged' business if there were more bits of useless junk, but there's hardly any of that. Almost everything we have is useful in some way."

"Which is statistically improbable," added Circe.

"Why the subterfuge?" mused Rudy. "If the drive was deliberately damaged, should we infer that Rasouli is double-crossing us in some way?"

"Possibly," said Bug. "At the same time, I don't think he knows enough. By fragmenting the data he has, it tells us a lot while at the same time *possibly* disguising all that he doesn't know."

"Why go to such lengths?" asked Rudy. "He reached out to us for our help."

"Politics," suggested Aunt Sallie. "He's an ambitious little bastard. Maybe he found a way of strengthening his position within Iran, or maybe within Islam, while still removing a possible threat to his country. The less specific he is with us, the easier it could be to spin the actual outcome in his favor."

"That's cynical," Rudy said.

"Hell, we do it all the time. Spin control is the second most important tool of statecraft, and probably the third most important weapon of war after big guns and strong allies."

"It's also devious," added Rudy. "Very much the Hugo Vox model."

Circe sighed. "Yes."

"Do we trust the information?" asked Auntie. "*Can* we trust it?"

"Do we have a choice?" muttered Circe.

Chapter Thirty

I kept expecting the woman to call back, but she didn't.

Violin.

I went into the bathroom to pack my toiletries. Ghost came and sat in the doorway, watching me in case I happened to discover a beef bone in my shaving kit.

As I puttered around, I tried to make some sense of the pieces of the mystery I had, but it was like trying to assemble one picture with pieces from four different puzzles. There was the hikers thing. That's why I was here in Iran. There was no intention or even possibility of any interaction with the Iranian government. I don't think I had ever spoken Rasouli's name aloud before today; until now it was only a name in news stories and in a handful of CIA field reports that crossed my desk.

Before Rasouli, there was not even a whisper of rogue nukes. I mean, sure, everyone knows about Iran's nuclear project—which is not even a "leaked" secret. Iran was behind the first press stories. They wanted the fear of it to give them leverage. What the general public didn't know was that their program was about eighteen months ahead of the timetable predicted in the press, and that the whole thing had been kicked off with technology sold to them, and overseen, by the Russians. The Cold War was far from over—it simply had a new mailing address.

The CIA analysts were convinced to a high degree of confidence that Iran already had nuclear bombs. Maybe ten of them. But those bombs would be much smaller than the unit in the photo. They would be tactical nukes built into warheads. It was a scary fact of political life, and it's why the United States did absolutely nothing in direct support of the various waves of antigovernment unrest. And, it's why they let the hikers rot for a year. If it wasn't for the danger posed by leverage on Senator McHale, Echo Team would never have crossed the border.

So . . . okay, look at that. The hikers were collateral in the nukes thing; but the nuke in the picture isn't an Iranian nuke. It was probably of Russian manufacture, in whole or part, but the Russians were sharing a sleeping bag with Iran and if Rasouli wasn't lying, then this bomb was positioned as a threat *against* Iran.

"So whose nukes are they?" I asked Ghost.

He wagged his tail because that's what dogs do. They're too polite to interrupt.

Blowing up the Mideast oil field was a pointless act of destruction. Where was the advantage? How did that make a political statement useful to anyone involved in either the oil wars or the religious pissing contest?

And Violin? Who and what was she?

The fact that Rasouli knew Hugo Vox made all of my math fuzzy. This whole thing could be a Seven Kings beach party, in which case trying to sort through the lies to find the truth would be like trying to pick fly shit out of pepper.

I sighed. I had way too many questions and so far . . . not one single answer.

Ghost suddenly turned at a sound and then trotted into the other room. I didn't hear a knock, but Mr. Church's asset was due any minute. Maybe Ghost heard him on the stairs.

I reached for a clean shirt and was pulling it on when I suddenly heard two sounds that chilled me.

The first thing I heard was Ghost letting out a single savage bark of warning.

Then I heard a sharp yelp of pain. The sound was instantly cut off.

Chapter Thirty-One

Golden Oasis Hotel
Tehran, Iran
June 15, 9:53 a.m.

I came out of the bathroom at a dead run and slammed into a figure in dark clothes and a hood.

We rebounded from one another, and for a weird moment I thought it was a ninja and that I was in a very bad movie. Then I saw that his clothes were ordinary black pants and a baggy shirt, and his mask was a simple balaclava.

The eyes that glared at me through the opening in the mask were weird, though. Really weird. They were a luminous red—like a white rat's eyes—with long slitted pupils like a snake's. Obviously contact lenses, and probably for the dual purpose of disguising his looks and trying to spook his opponent. If I was the kind of guy to stand there and gawp at him, I'd be dead.

Ghost lay twitching on the rug by the front door. Two metal fléchettes were buried in his pelt and electricity coursed into him through silver wires that trailed up to a Taser the man held at arm's length. The attacker spun and tried to pistol-whip me with the Taser.

I ducked the swing, came up fast from the crouch and smacked him over the ear with an open palm. It's a useful blow that hurts like hell and jolts the balance, but if he was hurt, it didn't show; and his balance didn't suffer at all. He reacted by dropping the Taser and punching me in the ribs hard enough to lift my feet an inch off the floor. He tried to combine it with an overhand hammerblow, but I chopped it aside with my elbow. My ribs were white hot with pain, but I let that simply stoke the fury that had been burning in me since Rasouli ruined my morning. I wanted to hurt something that would scream, so I pivoted and drove at him with a flurry of precise strikes and nasty low kicks.

He matched me like we'd rehearsed this, blocking and parrying, slipping and evading every single strike; and he foot-jammed all my kicks. Then he found a hole in my attack, ducked in low and fast and drove a two-knuckle punch into my solar plexus. It missed the xiphoid by an inch as I turned away from it, but another white hot flare of pain exploded in my torso.

The punch almost dropped me. That one glancing blow was so immensely powerful that it sent me reeling halfway across the room.

That gave him a bigger hole, and he launched himself at me, snapping out with a vicious front kick that I barely evaded by turning and dropping into a three-point crouch. He landed and pivoted and his second kick was a side thrust that missed my knee by half an inch and shattered the heavy wooden leg of the desk chair. This guy was slimmer and shorter than me, but damn if he wasn't strong.

I hooked my fingers around the slatted backrest of the chair and swept it off the floor, catching him solidly on the shoulder. The blow knocked him against the wall, but he rebounded and shattered the chair with a backward sweep of his arm. I threw an arm up to protect my eyes from the splinters; but even as I did that I did a backward kick and caught him in the stomach with my heel. I put a lot of torque in that kick and it should have knocked him out and given stomach cramps to his whole family back home.

All he did was grunt.

I mean . . . holy shit. A full-grown silverback gorilla couldn't have stayed on his feet after a kick like that. My kick did exactly jack squat.

Well, not entirely true. It made him mad. And it was no fun to discover that up till now he hadn't actually been trying to kill me. The Taser and his first selection of attacks were meant to disable. Now he was pissed, and he drove at me, stabbing at my eyes with his fingertips and trying to crush my throat with the stiffened webbing between index finger and thumb. The vicious prick fought like I did—only he was a lot stronger and a whole lot faster.

And I am really frigging fast.

So I changed the game and barreled straight at him, wrapped my arms around his thighs and picked him up to drive him right into the cheap wooden dresser which exploded into a shower of splinters, socks, and underwear. We crashed down onto the floor and I tried to slam his head into the broken base of the dresser, but he kicked up between my legs, catching me on the butt and knocked me headfirst into the wall. I got my elbow up in time to save my skull, but it left my side open and he punched straight up and caught me in the gut.

As I staggered away from that, he kicked out with both feet and sent me flying back onto the bed. He was up before I finished landing and he pounced on me. The force trampolined us off the mattress and down on the far side between the bed and wall. The attacker put a knee on my chest and cocked his fist for another of those pile-driver punches of his, but I grabbed the edge of the night table and jerked it down into the path of the punch. His fist hit the table, and for the first time he reacted. He yanked back his fist and cursed.

Not in Persian. Not in any Middle Eastern language. It sounded Italian but wasn't, and though I couldn't quite understand it, his words seemed strangely familiar. It was like trying to understand Portuguese when all you knew how to speak was high-school Spanish.

In the split second while he flexed his injured hand I saw a few inches of bare skin in a gap between his glove and his sleeve. There was a small tattoo, less than an inch long. It was shaped like a cross but made from a longsword standing vertical with a horizontal dagger as the guard. That image overlaid a red circle the color of a drop of blood. A word was written above it, arching over the image, but it wasn't in English and I didn't recognize the alphabet.

No time to ponder that now. I pulled my knees sharply up and then kicked him in the chest with both heels. He flew backward onto the bed and fell off on the other side. I scrambled up and flipped the twin mattress on top of him, then threw myself on top of it like a kid doing a cannonball into a pool.

That tore another grunt from him. Louder, filled with more pain.

I liked that effect, so I jumped up and down a few more times.

But on the third drop he shoved up on the mattress and my body landed on a slant. I fell one way and the force sent him the other way.

We got to our feet three yards apart, our backs to opposite walls. We were both panting now, though even with the pounding I'd just given him he looked fresher than I did. The bastard.

"Where is it?" he said, this time in heavily accented English. His voice was low and raspy. A mean, nasty voice.

I knew what he wanted. I figured that much out when we started this dance.

"Fuck you," I said. Actually, what I said was "*Vaffanculo, testa di cazzo.*" Even if he was speaking some weird regional dialect of Italian I was pretty sure he'd catch my meaning.

He did, and as expected he didn't much like it.

His red eyes flared with murderous rage and rushed me. I tried to stall him with a kick, but he swatted my foot aside, grabbed me by the shirt, and threw me across the room. I crashed into the wall hard enough to knock the cheap paintings from the wall; then I crashed down on the floor.

You see guys in movies do that—pick someone up and throw them across the room. That's the movies. In the real world, it can't be done. Not with someone my size. Not fifteen feet through the air so that I hit the wall at head height. It is not physically possible for a human being to do that.

My brain kept telling me that as I crashed to the floor in a heap.

I rolled onto my hands and knees and spat blood onto the floor. There was a piece of tooth there too. Fireworks exploded in my eyes and my head felt like it was cracked in forty places.

"Where is it?" he demanded again as he stalked toward me. Then he did something weird—even when added to the other weird stuff that was going on. Ghost was sprawled on the floor between us, and when the man suddenly realized that he was about to step on Ghost's tail, he jerked his whole body sideways to avoid contact. A small, guttural cry escaped his throat as he did so. He rattled off something in that weird language, touched his heart, and drew a line with his fingers above his eyes. It had the same ritual feel as Catholics crossing themselves, though I'd never seen this gesture before. The Cop part of my mind wanted to make sense of the gesture and the man's strange aversion to touching Ghost, but the Warrior was running the show, even though he wasn't doing a great job of it, and that anomaly got buried under the need to survive the moment.

I tried to get up, but too many things hurt.

"What is on the flash drive the Murshid gave you?"

"The what?"

"The Tariqa," he bellowed. "The Saracen! Where it is? Where is the flash drive?"

"I shoved it up your ass—why don't you go look for it."

He kicked me in the side and I barely managed to tuck my elbow against my side to save my ribs. Even so, the kick knocked me against the wall and the impact ignited more starbursts in my head.

"Who are you working for?" he said. His anger made his eyes seem to catch fire. "Are you Rasouli's dog or are you working for that whore?"

"No," I groaned as I fought to get to my knees, "your mother hasn't called me."

He tried for another kick, but I was ready and I rolled away from it and got shakily to my feet.

"It's *her*, isn't it?" he said, his voice heavy with contempt. He spat out another word, loading it with bile. "Arklight!"

I had no idea who or what that was, and now didn't seem like a good time to ask. Running seemed like the best option, but my legs were rubbery and the room was doing a tilt-a-whirl around me.

Ski mask snarled at me. "Tell me or I will cut off your balls."

"What the fuck is it with you guys?" I demanded. "How come every psycho in the Middle East has a grudge against my nutsack?"

I think he actually smiled, though all I could see was the crinkle around his crimson eyes. Then he rushed at me so fast that his body seemed to blur, hands reaching to grab. I tried to parry him, but he slapped my hands away, clamped his fingers around my throat and picked me up. And I mean all the way up so that I hung suspended with my feet inches from the floor.

Again, for a guy his size and a guy my size, this simply was not possible.

He bent close so that those unnatural eyes were inches from mine. His hands were as cold as ice.

"Last chance," he sneered. "Where is the flash drive?"

"Fuck you. Where are the nukes?"

He paused for a moment, and I could see that I'd both hit a nerve and said the wrong thing.

"You know . . ." he breathed. Then his red eyes flared with rage that was ten times hotter than before. "Listen to me, you piece of shit—you have no idea what you are interfering with here. Give me the flash drive, tell me exactly who you've told, and I will end this quickly for you."

"Or," I choked out, "you could go piss up a rope."

His eyes grew hotter still. "I am doing *God's* work, and if you don't tell me what I want to know I will rip your throat out and drink your life."

Okay, I never heard that one before.

Not in real life.

I had a couple of witty comebacks for him. Stuff about his mother and livestock. But I thought that I was losing my audience. So instead I kneed him in the nuts as hard as I could. I put all of my pain and rage and fear into it. The impact canted him sharply forward, so I grabbed his head and clamped my teeth on his nose and tried my absolute best to bite it off. Blood exploded through the fabric of his mask, splashing against my face as cartilage collapsed between my teeth.

He screamed—so high and shrill that it hurt my ears. Then he started thrashing and tried to pull his head back from my teeth, but I wasn't about to let go. I growled at him, clenched harder, and whipped my head back and forth like a dog. Hot blood gushed into my mouth.

His screams hit the ultrasonic. He flung me away from him and staggered back, pawing at his ruined face with both hands. I slammed into the wall again and dropped hard to the floorboards on knees and palms. The blood in my mouth was hot and tasted of salt. I gagged and spat it out. Part of his nose and the lower half of his mask flopped onto the floor.

Screw fair play. Screw the rules.

The man reeled and thrashed, slamming into one wall and then the other, keening in a high-pitched wail of inarticulate agony. His mask hung in dripping shreds. Most of his nose was gone. His mouth and chin were slick with dark blood.

I got shakily to my feet, sick and dazed. I figured I had him now if I could manage one more really good hit. Maybe break his neck, or crush his hyoid bone.

Then the son of a bitch wheeled toward me and hissed. His lips peeled back as he bared his teeth.

Suddenly the whole world froze and in that fragment of time I stared at his mouth.

At his teeth.

Good God.

His teeth were all filed to razor-sharp points. Like the teeth of a shark. But the canines—something was wrong with them. Really goddamn wrong. They weren't just sharp, they were too long. Way too fucking long. Like the fangs of a dog. Or a wolf.

Or—

No. My mind refused to make that connection. It was insane and the day was already out of control.

And then the sharp-toothed, no-nose freakazoid son of a bitch pulled us right back into the real world.

He reached into a pocket and produced a gun.

Nothing weird or alien. Totally ordinary.

He had me and we both knew it.

So I let out a scream that was louder than his and I drove into him at full speed and force. It was a big, meaty impact that knocked blood from his face so hard it spattered the walls and ceiling. The gun went flying over my shoulder. Even then he tried to step out of it, but I had him and together we crashed through the glass door and all the way to the wrought-iron balcony. We hit the railing five flights above the empty street. There was glass and curtains and broken pieces of wood-framing everywhere, and even with all that we kept jabbing and punching at each other. Those jagged teeth bit the air, snapping at my face, my throat.

I shoved him back and then smashed him across the mouth with my elbow, exploding half his teeth over the rail and down into the street five stories below.

And *still* he fought.

Despite all of the injuries, the torn face, he spun me around and started bending me backward over the rail. I could feel my spine bending too far and too fast even while I wailed on him, smashing ribs and eyebrows and knocking more teeth out of his mouth.

Then suddenly his head jerked away from me like he'd been pulled by a rope. I heard a *crack* as his neck snapped, and saw a geyser of blood and brain matter splash against the shattered window frame, painting the floor and overturned mattress.

His body spun away back into the room, and he collapsed down onto the ruined bed like a puppet whose strings had been cut.

I never heard the shot that killed him. But I threw myself into the room and dove behind the bed.

Had the shooter been aiming for him?

Or had they tried to shoot me and missed?

Chapter Thirty-Two

Golden Oasis Hotel

Tehran, Iran

June 15, 9:46 a.m.

I lay there, panting like a marathon runner five feet from the finish line. Everything hurt, every inch of skin, every muscle, every nerve. I was drenched in sweat and blood, but I remained motionless, trying to hear an echo from a distant shooter.

But there was nothing. No sound except my own labored breaths.

The dead goon's pistol lay on the box spring, but it was in direct line of sight from the window. I had no gun, no weapons in the hotel room. Why should I? After all, I was a tourist on vacation here in Tehran. All of my tactical gear was slag on the street outside the police station.

I tried to melt into the floorboards, waiting for the next shot, for the next round to punch a hole through the wall and through my body.

My attacker lay in a twisted sprawl. The shot had taken him in the left temple and the exit wound had blown most of his head off. A big damn bullet, traveling at three thousand feet per second.

I waited.

Nothing.

I waited some more.

More nothing.

Across the room, Ghost chuffed and twitched. His ribs rose and fell as he fought to swim back to consciousness.

The memory of the dead man's teeth kept lunging out of the shadows in my mind, trying to eat away at what sanity I had left.

Gradually I decided I was waiting for something that wasn't going to happen. The shooter was almost certainly gone by now, not after a kill. Not in a security-obsessed country like this one. The shooter was in the wind. I had to get out of this room, though. Couldn't risk going outside yet. The basement had a nice, quiet laundry room. Good place to lay low for a few minutes at least until Ghost was able to travel.

The Warrior part of my personality was howling for blood; but the Cop part of my brain was analyzing what just happened. Or at least as much as was possible with a body that felt like it had been thrown down an elevator shaft and a head full of loud noises and thorns.

I grabbed the corner of the box spring and pulled it toward me until it tipped, sending the pistol sliding into my hand. I shoved it into my waistband at the small of my back. Then I wormed my way across the floor to the shooter. I had to risk reaching into the sniper's line of fire to grab the guy's foot, but I darted my hand out, clamped my fingers around his ankle and dragged him away from the window.

It was a wasted effort. I searched his pockets and got nothing. No jewelry, no scars or marks. All I got for my efforts was a better look at the tattoo, which told me nothing more than it had when I first spotted it. I pulled up his sleeve and used the camera in my cell to take a photo of it. It was written in an alphabet that was unknown to me, which was odd because I'm a student of languages. I speak a lot of them and can recognize a lot more. This wasn't anything I'd ever seen.

The dead man's mouth hung open and I could see his remaining front teeth. I took photos of them, too. Inside my chest my heart skipped a couple of beats. At close range those sharp shark teeth did not look like they'd been filed down. They looked like they'd grown in that way. I tried to pull one of the fangs loose, hoping that it was a fake. Some kind of combat denture. Something cosmetic. After three tries I yanked my hand back and wiped it on the rug.

I will rip your throat out and drink your life.

Hearing someone say that was bad enough, but people in my trade tend to talk all kinds of over-the-top trash. Fine. However, having someone with *fangs* say it is a whole different thing. You didn't just shake that off. Even though I knew—*knew*—there had to be a rational explanation, no matter how exotic the science, it still hit me harder than it should have. It was so weird, so real that it awakened an atavistic dread that took me all the way back to the cave. Like I was some grunting Neanderthal huddling by a meager fire while outside strange and unnameable sounds came out of the midnight darkness.

My inner voices—Cop, Warrior, and Civilized Man—were all silent. Afraid to speak to me, unable to tell me what to do.

"Joe Ledger," I told myself, "you have *got* to get the hell out of Dodge."

I said it aloud because I needed to hear my own voice sounding nice and normal. It didn't. I sounded scared and shaken and that didn't help a goddamn bit.

I got to my feet and fell right down on my ass again, and the sound provoked a weak *woof* from Ghost. His eyes were still closed, though.

Next time I tried to get up I did it slowly. My hands were shaking and they were ice cold.

Making sure to stay away from the window, I bent and dragged Ghost out into the hall and kicked the door shut. None of the other doors on my floor opened, which was the plan. When our local contacts had picked this hotel for Echo Team they'd rented all the rooms just to leave them empty. Most of the floor below me was empty too. No witnesses, no curious faces peering out from between cracked doors. I doubt anyone knew about what had just happened except the sniper, me, and whoever sent the son of Dracula in there.

There was nothing in the room that I needed more than I needed to get gone. My cell was in my pocket, but now was not the time to make a call. Besides, I think my hands were shaking too badly even to hit speed dial.

It took Ghost another minute to wake up and two more before he could stand. As soon as he was on all fours, we crept down the back steps to the laundry room. I wanted to clean us both up and get myself together before we went looking for a safe house.

Ghost had his tail between his legs and in my way so did I.

Chapter Thirty-Three

Hotel Vier Jahreszeiten Kempinski
Munich, Germany
June 15, 9:54 a.m.

The young man sat on the edge of the bed and stared at the pistol he had just finished loading. It was a slim, lightweight .22. Easily concealed, simple to operate. He had used guns like this for years. He had killed with them. Men and women. Many of them.

He even knew most of their names.

The fact that he did not know all of their names was like a nail in his head. The floor around the bed was littered with crumpled up sheets of paper on which lists of names had been scribbled. On the first few sheets, the names that he could remember were written in a neat, flowing script. On the more recent ones they were scrawled in haphazard fashion. More than once the tip of his pen had gouged into the notepad, cutting fresh pages like blades on flesh.

The young man knew about that, too. He had used knives more than once.

Even a garrote.

The most recent page lay crumpled on the floor between his bare feet. Beside it lay yesterday's bottle of Scotch. Today's was in splinters at the base of the wall where it had been thrown.

There were other bottles too. The room was a disaster, the trash can the only place uncluttered by discards. It stood empty, like a statement, by the open refrigerator door. Inside the fridge, a week's worth of leftovers had become worlds for new life forms, and the odor was appalling.

The young man did not care.

"Dr. Sirois!" he shouted suddenly, remembering another name. With fevered hands he began his list again. Seventy-*eight* names now. Seventy-eight.

He wrote them as carefully as trembling fingers would allow. As neatly as his mind would allow, but by the time he was halfway done the list even he couldn't read most of what he'd written. He'd lost count somewhere in the forties and tore the page from the pad, crushed it in his fist, and hurled it as far as he could.

Then he screamed.

"*Seventy-eight, you sodding freak!*"

Seventy-eight was too much. He knew that. Too many deaths. Too many murders. Far too many to atone for. There was no way anyone could be forgiven for that many deaths. A saint would burn for half as many, and he knew that he was far, far from that kind of grace.

Seventy-eight. Too many.

But not enough. There were more. He could remember them. He could remember the trigger-pulls, the plunge of blades. But why couldn't he remember their names?

He screamed again, an inarticulate plea to a God he knew would not spit on him.

When the phone rang, his screams died in the humid air of his hotel room. There was a ghost of an echo, and then silence.

Until the second ring.

The young man stared at the phone.

Not the hotel phone, which had been silent since he checked in three weeks ago.

Not at his personal cell phone, which lay smashed on the floor under the shoe he had used to destroy it.

No, this was the other cell. A bright purple one with a ruggedized rubber shell. The one he had picked up a hundred times, ready to make a call, ready to beg for forgiveness, but which he had put down each time.

The phone kept ringing.

It had not rung for weeks. Not since he had left the private villa that sat in the shade of the Kolakchal Mountain, Jamshidiyeh Park in Tehran. Not since he had been caught reading the encrypted computer files. Hacking those files had taken months. Reading them had broken his heart. Being caught reading them had resulted in a terrible fight. Shouts, hard words, and a single punch—the hardest the young man had ever thrown—that left the owner of those files dazed and bleeding on the floor. The words that man had said as the young man backed away from the horror of what he had just done—those words had opened up a fissure in his mind. They had broken something that the young man knew could not be mended.

Maybe not even by God Himself.

The purple phone kept ringing.

On the eleventh ring, he answered it. He did not speak, did not say hello, did not ask who was calling. There was only one person who could possibly have this number.

"Toys," whispered Hugo Vox. "C'mon, kid . . . say something for Christ's sake."

Toys bent forward as quickly and sharply as if he had been punched in the stomach.

"Toys!" begged Vox. "Are you *there?*"

Into the phone he said, "No."

And he disconnected the call.

Chapter Thirty-Four

Private Villa Near Jamshidiyeh Park

Tehran, Iran

June 15, 9:59 a.m.

Hugo Vox drew in a ragged breath and let it out through his nostrils, feeling his whole body deflate.

That single word.

No.

Vox stared at the coded cell phone on his desk. It lay beside a bottle of Scotch and a tumbler that was nearly empty. Vox snatched up the glass and drained the last of the Scotch, shivering as the ice rattled against his teeth.

He refilled the glass, drank half of it, set it down.

His sleeve was still rolled up and he looked at the injection mark, then touched the others beneath his shirt. They still hurt, but other things hurt worse.

"You miserable backstabbing little fuck," he said aloud. The house, however, was empty. Toys had been gone a month now, and Vox knew that he would never be back. On the computer monitor in front of him was the log-in screen of the bank to which he'd wired the billion he'd given to Toys after the Seven Kings fell apart. One hundredth of the assets Vox had in over seven hundred global markets, banks, and trusts. When Toys had left him, Vox had been determined to switch all but a penny out of it. That would have made a statement, sent a message.

So far he hadn't done it, even though he logged in to the banking site as often as six or seven times a day.

The fact that he could not yet do it irritated the shit out of him.

"You goddamn Judas," he growled. It was far from the first time he'd said that.

What troubled Vox most was his own reaction to Toys's betrayal. He should have been doing an Irish jig instead of sulking. Toys had found exactly what Vox had wanted him to find. Upier 531, the Upierczi, the Holy Agreement. All of it, exactly as planned. Vox still could not understand why Toys had reacted so . . . *weirdly*. This was exactly the sort of thing Toys had been involved with his whole adult life, first as Sebastian Gault's personal assistant and since then as Vox's protégé and unofficially adopted son. This was Toys's fucking heritage. All he had to do was join him for this last little bit of fun and the kid would have access to the other ninety-nine billion dollars.

How could anyone piss on that?

He closed his eyes and remembered the fight they'd had.

Vox had been in the kitchen at their villa, removing cardboard containers of takeout food from a cloth bag and placing them on the table. Humming to himself, happy with the way things were going with Grigor, and with that numb-nuts Charlie LaRoque. When he heard Toys open the cellar door, he looked up and smiled.

But the smile died on his lips.

"What the fuck—?"

Toys stood swaying in the doorway, his eyes red-rimmed, cheeks streaked with old and new tears. A pistol hanging limply from his hand, the barrel pointed at the floor.

"Hey, kiddo," Vox began, "what's—?"

Toys tossed a ring of keys onto the counter. Duplicates for the keys to Vox's office and the cabinet with his computer files. Vox shrugged; he'd known that Toys had made dupes. There were faint smudges of wax on two of the keys from where Toys had made impressions for copying.

"So what?" he asked.

"Upier 531."

Vox removed a container of rice from the bag. He glanced from Toys to the pistol and back again. "Yeah."

"Why?"

"Why do you *think*? What kind of question is that? You think I *want* to die?" demanded Vox. "You think I'd let myself rot if there was a way out?"

"That's not what I'm asking," said Toys. "You know it isn't."

"What do you think it's about? What's it ever about? You went into my banking records, right? You saw the deposits and the transfers. Christ, is this about the split? Are you turning on me over your share?"

"It's not about the money."

"The fuck it's not about the money, you little shithead," Vox fired back. "Okay, so I promised you a hundred billion when I died, and I'm not giving you a hundred billion 'cause I'm not fucking dying. Those injections are giving me a new shot, kiddo, and I'm fucking taking it—and I'm keeping the money I earned because now I'm going to have a chance at spending it. So, boo hoo, I'm a bad man. Are you trying to tell me you can't live off of *one* billion? Are you standing there and telling me that? You wouldn't have a fucking dime if it weren't for me. I treated you like my own *son*, you ungrateful shit. I'm giving you a *billion fucking dollars*, though. Who else ever gave anyone that kind of cash? It's already transferred to your account."

"It's not about the money," Toys repeated, his face growing red. "It's about where it's coming from."

Vox barked out a harsh laugh. "Oh, please, do not even go there." He paused and shook his head. "Look, don't think I don't know that you've been getting all moody and guilty lately. Ever since Gault died you've been watching way too many televangelists. It's creepy and it's silly, but I figured if it works for you, then who am I to tell you how to whitewash your soul. It's your money now, and a billion dollars buys a lot of forgiveness."

In two quick strides Toys closed the distance between them and struck Vox across the mouth. Not with the pistol. He used his open hand, a single whipcrack of a slap that spun Vox violently around and sent him crashing into the table. It tipped under his weight and Vox fell amid a torrent of exploding cartons of food and cutlery. He landed heavily, his face and chest splattered with hot soup and rice and cooked lamb. Vox screamed and slapped at his skin. But before he could recover, Toys bent down and shoved the barrel of the pistol hard against Vox's temple.

"Shut your mouth," whispered Toys in an icy hiss. "So help me God, Hugo, if you say one more word I will kill you."

Vox groaned and pawed at his mouth. His lip was pulped and bleeding and he stared at the red smear on the back of his hand. Despite Toys's warning, Vox growled, "If you want all of it then take it and fuck you. The bank codes are in—"

"I *have* the bank codes," snarled Toys, "but I don't want your sodding money. Piss on you and every penny of it. Keep it and choke on it."

Vox turned his head, ignoring the presence of the gun, and he glared up at Toys. "Then what do you fucking want?" When Toys did not speak, Vox chuckled. "Well goddamn," he said wonderingly, "I can see it in your eyes, boy, you really have lost your fucking mind and found Jesus. Ho-lee shit. I thought it was a scam. I thought you were running some kind of schuck, or maybe going through some kind of spring cleaning of the soul. Shit, I thought it was a frigging phase and—"

"A 'phase'?" echoed Toys softly.

"Of course," snapped Vox, "and that's what it damn well is. You're feeling some dumbass Catholic guilt because I filled your head with a bunch of bullshit about Judas last year when I was trying to get you away from that dickhead Gault. There was a point to all that, kiddo, and I thought you understood it. What, did you think I was proselytizing? I was trying to get you to understand about necessary sacrifice and how sometimes we all have to make a hard choice. Was I wrong about you? Are you too fucking stupid to understand that?"

"No," murmured Toys, "I understood you perfectly."

He cocked the hammer of the pistol, and it was the loudest sound Vox ever heard.

"Listen to me, Hugo," Toys said, so very softly. "Try to understand.

Try, for once, to listen objectively. Don't filter it through your own agenda. Just this once. Can you do that?"

Vox cleared his throat. His face and back hurt. The food was trickling down inside his clothes. "Yeah, sure, kiddo. Say your piece."

Toys leaned so close that his voice was a hot breeze on Vox's ear. "You lied to me, Hugo."

"Fuck it, kid, I lie to every—"

"Shhhh. Don't say anything. Just listen." The barrel of the gun slid along the line of Vox's cheek. "I never wanted your money. You thought I did because that's all you're capable of thinking. I almost pity you. Even Sebastian wasn't like that. At least he could love something. Amirah . . . your mother. Sebastian loved her. But you, Hugo? You don't love anything. I doubt you ever have."

Vox started to say something, to protest that statement, but Toys leaned toward him, forehead to forehead, the pistol now touching the point of Vox's chin.

"Please," begged Toys, "please don't say anything. Don't say that you love me. I've heard that. You said it a thousand times. That you love me like a son. Don't let me hear you say those words. I can do more than kill you. I will if you say that."

Vox said nothing.

"I'm not like you, Hugo. I'm not like Sebastian, either. I'm not strong in the same way . . . but I'm not weak in the same way, either. I didn't know that before. I thought I was weak, I thought I was broken. A broken toy. Quaint, I know. Corny. But it isn't the way things are, and I didn't know that until I read the files. I could have forgiven you about the money. After all, it's not even your money to give. It's all stolen, it's all blood money, and I have enough blood on my hands as it is. I could have forgiven you about Upier 531. A gene therapy that could cure your cancer? Something that could make you live for years? Maybe forever? That's wonderful, Hugo. That's magic, even if it's unproven. I could forgive any risk you'd take to change that."

Tears welled in Toys's eyes and fell on Vox's cheek.

"But the price you were willing to pay. Good Christ, Hugo. All those people? What is it with you? What was it with Sebastian and the Seven Kings? Are people unreal to you? Do you think they're simply bit-part players in your personal drama? No—don't say anything. I know the answer. That's exactly what you, and what people like you, think. No one else is real, no one else matters. Only you, your power, your profit, and whatever pieces of the world you can steal."

He sniffed, but the tears still fell. Vox was frozen to stillness.

"Hugo . . . you think that I'm like a son to you. Or, you thought so. When you found out you were dying I was the only way for you to become immortal. Fathers do that with their sons. That's what you thought you were going to leave behind. Me—a clone of you, someone to carry on the things you've done your whole life. More murders, more plots and plans. More chaos. When you looked at me, that's what you saw."

Toys pressed the pistol harder against Vox's chin.

"How could you hate anyone so much that you would want them to be like you?"

A last tear rolled from Toys's eye and fell, striking Vox on the lips.

Toys straightened and stepped back, his arm out, gun pointed, the barrel trembling but only slightly.

"You are a monster, Hugo," murmured Toys. "I'm not."

Vox sat up and wiped away the salty tear on his lips. He sneered at Toys. "Yeah? Then what the fuck are you?"

The answer was there in the young man's eyes for Vox to read. The hand holding the pistol stopped trembling, the black eye of the barrel stared without pity.

Then Toys dropped the pistol onto the tile floor.

"I'm damned," he said.

Without another word, he turned and walked through the house and out the front door.

Vox refilled his glass and drank.

He stared at the bank account log-in on the screen, seeing a smeared version of it through the hot tears in his eyes.

Beneath his skin he could feel the changes, feel the tissues moving and adapting.

He drank the Scotch.

"Fuck you," he said aloud.

And reached for the bottle.

Chapter Thirty-Five

The president of the United States was ten feet tall.

Even seated behind his desk in the Oval Office he was a giant, towering over Mr. Church, who stood with his hands clasped behind his back. The giant plasma screen in the Hangar conference room had flawless fidelity and except for the disparate scale, the president might have been there in the room.

"I wish I had more encouraging news, Mr. President," said Church. "However, we are still assessing the intelligence brought to us by Captain Ledger."

"I have to admit that I'm disappointed. I expected more. I expected to hear that you'd at least confirmed the location of all seven of the devices."

"When I learn to perform actual magic, Mr. President, I will make sure you receive the memo."

The president said nothing. With anyone else from the president of Russia to his own chief of staff he would have fired back a retort and fried them. Instead, he cleared his throat.

After a moment, Church said, "We have, in fact, established probable locations on four of the devices. There is a high probability that the one in Rasouli's photo is located in or near the Aghajari oil refinery in Iran. There is a slightly lower but still actionable probability that the other three are at the Beiji oil refinery in Iraq, the Abqaiq in Saudi Arabia, and the Toot oil field in Pakistan. DMS teams are en route to those locations. When and if we get locations on the other three I want to do a coordinated and simultaneous soft infiltration of all seven. We should get the best JSOC teams in the air."

The Joint Special Operations Command included many of the nation's elite teams, including Delta and the SEALs.

"What about the device here in the States?"

"We need to remain at our highest state of readiness without doing anything that sends a signal. Not to our allies, not to our enemies, and not to the world press. At this point we don't know if there is a device on U.S. soil, and if there is we have no idea where it *might* be. It could be a red herring, or it could be real, we don't know. So far there are no hints on Rasouli's drive beyond a possibility of our unknown enemies targeting oil fields."

"We have a lot of oil fields, Deacon."

"I am all too aware of that, Mr. President."

The president sighed and rubbed his tired eyes. "I want to hang Vox's head on the Capitol building spire."

"Get in line," said Church dryly. "But as much as we both want to see that happen, we don't know if Vox is our enemy in this particular game."

"He steered Rasouli toward Ledger."

"Yes, which means that our only source of information about a potentially catastrophic situation came about because of that."

"I hope you're not suggesting that Vox has had a change of heart and now wants to help us avoid an act of terrorism. You couldn't sell that on a soap opera."

"I believe you know my take on Hugo's patriotism."

"Then what is his role in this?"

"He is a trickster and manipulator. If he delivered a workable cure for cancer I would look for an angle. If he's helping us then he has a way to profit from that."

"Enemy of my enemy?" suggested the president. Church shrugged.

"Unknown. Now that we know the scope of his treachery as the head of the Seven Kings, we know that he has more friends in the Middle East than he has here. Iran would be in that family."

"So . . . he could be helping Rasouli," ventured the president. "If this is a real threat to Iran's oil fields, then Vox could be using us to help an ally."

"Yes. That's likely, but it doesn't mean that it's Hugo's only motive."

"I'm putting a lot of trust in you and MindReader, Deacon. We have to find those nukes. We can't allow a single device to detonate."

"We may not have a choice, Mr. President. I believe that it would be prudent to begin working on how to manage a crisis based on a variety of worst-case scenarios."

"I just had that conversation with State. No matter where a bomb goes off it creates a different political nightmare. At this point it's impossible to determine which worst-case scenario is actually the worst. On one side there's the risk to civilian populations, on another the risk of contamination to the oil fields is considerable. And the political fallout, pun intended, could cripple us in the region."

"I wish Captain Ledger had been able to record that conversation. We'd be able to haul Iran before NATO and the world and hang them out to dry for consorting with Vox. They would have to back down on their nuclear program—"

"Which would be nice," interrupted Church, "but it would still leave us with seven possible nukes in place, and no one to blame."

"We can blame Vox and the Seven Kings."

"We could," said Church dubiously, "but we would be guessing. That might sharpen focus or distract it entirely. Guesswork doesn't put our true enemy in the crosshairs."

The president looked at his watch. "I'm heading to the Situation Room now. We'll conference you in. Two minutes."

"I'll be here," said Church.

Chapter Thirty-Six

The Kingdom of Shadows
Beneath the Sands
June 15, 10:01 a.m.

The King of Thorns stretched out a pale hand to accept the cell phone offered by his fourth son. Grigor's fingernails, thick and dark, curled around the slender phone, trapping it in his palm like a tiny mouse caught by a spider. He was familiar with phones, but he did not care for them. All they possessed was sound. No smell, no taste. With a small sneer of distaste he put the phone to his ear.

"Yes."

"Grigor," said Charles LaRoque, "Your knight failed."

"Failed?"

"Yes, and I am very disappointed," said LaRoque in a waspish tone. "I was led to believe that the knights were more capable than this. A simple hit on a single target. Perhaps I should have hired someone who understands his profession."

Grigor's fingers tightened on the phone. Cracks jagged their way through the plastic cover.

"How did it happen?"

"Who cares how it happened? It happened. He failed. You failed, Grigor, because you chose the knight. You chose someone who apparently could not complete a simple mission, and now we have a potentially catastrophic situation. His body is still at the target site."

"I—" began Grigor, but the Scriptor cut him off.

"Don't humiliate yourself with excuses, Grigor. Clean it up and complete the assignment. Do not disappoint me again, I'm warning you."

The line went dead and Grigor lowered the phone from his ear. He regarded it with hooded eyes as if by looking at the device he could see the weak, doughy face of the new Scriptor. His white fingers curled around the phone until they formed a fist. There was a screech of protesting metal and plastic, and then Grigor opened his hand to let the mangled pieces fall.

Silence washed through the darkness for several moments.

"Nothing ever changes, does it?" asked Hugo Vox.

Grigor turned. Vox stood at the foot of the dais, a glass of Scotch in his hand. In the year since he had first met the former King of Fear, Vox had dwindled from a bombastic fat man to a ghost. His flesh was as loose as his clothes, and there were dark circles under his eyes.

"You heard everything?"

Vox nodded. "Charlie's old man treated you like dog shit and so did his grandfather. How the fuck did you put up with it this long?"

A grunt was Grigor's only reply.

"Are you going to do what LaRoque wants?" asked Vox.

"Yes," said Grigor.

The American nodded. "Because you want to, not because you have to, though. Am I right?"

Grigor gave that a single nod.

"Good," said the American. "That works for us."

Grigor made a slight gesture and one of his aides came hurrying out of the shadows. Grigor spoke to him in the language of the Red Order—a language Vox had learned well enough over the last year to catch the gist of Grigor's orders. The aide bowed and scuttled away.

"It will be so delicious to hang him by the heels and let his blood rain down. I would not even drink it. I would let it pool upon the ground and then piss in it."

"I like the way you think," said Vox, "but we need him alive for a little while longer. Him and Rasouli."

"Why? All we need now are the codes."

He gestured to a small device that lay on a brass table beside his throne. It was a converted satellite phone that had been rebuilt with Vox's own scrambler technology.

"Everything's in motion, Grigor," assured Vox. "A little more patience, a couple of tweaks, and then you can start your revolution and crack the pillars of heaven."

The King of Thorns glared with red hatred into the shadows. "I wonder sometimes if I can trust you, Hugo."

"You can definitely—" Vox suddenly doubled over as a ferocious coughing fit tore through him. He spat out the whiskey and reeled, catching himself on a stone wall as the coughs racked his wasted frame. The coughing fit lasted a whole minute during which Grigor did nothing except observe with a faint smile of amusement on his lips.

Vox tore a handkerchief from his pocket and pressed it to his mouth as the last deep coughs shook him. When he removed it the center of the cloth was stained with a few drops of blood. The scent of it perfumed the air.

"God," he wheezed. "Goddamn it . . ."

Grigor traced the contours of his own mouth with the tip of a black fingernail.

"What does it feel like to be so weak? To be sick?"

Vox glared up at him from beneath knitted brows. "Fuck you."

The King of Thorns laughed.

"You'd better step up the goddamn treatments," rasped Vox, "because that scrambler isn't worth shit without the access code, and without that scrambler you and your bloodsucking freak show of a race are going to remain slaves for the rest of time. So wipe that shit-eating smile off your face and find out where that asshole Dr. Hasbrouck is. I need my shots."

The smile on Grigor's face faded only a little as the echoes of Vox's words bounced off the cold stone walls of the caverns. "The doctor says that you'd never survive the last round of treatments."

"You better pray he's wrong, Grigor." Vox spat onto the floor. The sputum was dark with blood. "If I die then all your dreams die with me."

Chapter Thirty-Seven

Golden Oasis Hotel
Tehran, Iran
June 15, 10:02 a.m.

Ghost and I made it down to the hotel's basement laundry without being seen by anyone. I opened the back door and listened for commotion or sirens. There were none. I was right—no one had heard the fight and the shot was either silenced or fired from a great distance. It felt a little weird to me, even after everything I've done, that such a traumatic and dramatic moment could go unnoticed by people a couple of floors away. It makes you wonder about all of the ghastly things that happen every day all around us.

There were so many things about what had just occurred that I didn't know where to begin thinking about them. No—that wasn't true. The goon with the fangs knew about the flash drive, and he seemed pretty damned stunned when I mentioned the nukes. I wasn't sure how to interpret that. Did it mean that he knew what was on the flash drive but didn't think either Rasouli had told me or that I'd had a chance to check the drive's contents? Or was the nuke thing a big surprise to him?

Or did I not yet know enough to ask myself the right question?

Yes, muttered the Cop in my head.

The Warrior was still freaked out about the goon with the fangs. When you spend most of your life training in martial arts, military technique, and the specialized skills of special ops as I have, you come to accept that combat in all of its forms is a science. It's largely mathematical. If you hit someone in a specific part of the body at a precise angle and with sufficient force there is a predictable response, give or take some necessary variables. The same applies for a wide range of things, from lifting a barbell full of weights to shooting a pistol at a target. For some of this stuff there are thousands of years of trial and error as well as data collection to support what we know. Not what we guess but what we know. When you separate it all from sports or esoteric pursuits, combat is a science. I've dedicated my life to that science; if I have a church then that's it.

However, what I just experienced did not make sense according to anything I knew or believed.

I will rip your throat out and drink your life. The killer's voice kept whispering that to me.

I pulled out my cell and called Church.

"Go," he said.

"Boss, I am having a really, really bad day," I said.

"Are you talking about the devices?"

"Not directly."

"I'm on with the president. Do you need immediate assistance or can you wait ten?"

"I can wait ten," I said, "but not eleven."

"Understood." Church disconnected.

I sighed. In a very odd and childish way I felt snubbed by Church. I recognized it as a human overreaction to great fear mingled with physical injury. I needed Mommy or Daddy to kiss the boo-boo and tell me everything's all right. So, yeah, I'm immature at times. Just like everyone else.

I found a cracked bowl and filled it with clean water for Ghost. While he drank, I tried to assess my current situation. It was like inventorying a Kansas trailer park after tornado season. I hurt in so many places I stopped counting. My arms throbbed from blocking his punches and kicks, let alone those spots where his shots had actually landed. When I pulled up my shirt I saw huge red bruises forming; the intensity of color a clear indication of the amount of tissue damage he'd inflicted. Last time I had bruises like that was when I'd taken a pair of heavy-caliber rifle rounds in my vest; the Kevlar had kept me alive but the psi of the impacts had to go somewhere.

Ghost looked up from his bowl, water dripping from his snout. I doubt Shepherds could identify bruises by sight, but his sensitive nose could probably smell the blood seeping through the damaged muscle tissue.

He *whuffed* and began drinking again.

"Whuff," I agreed.

I dearly wanted to curl into a fetal position on my couch and sleep until November. Alternately, six shots of Jim Beam and a gallon of beer would work well as comfort food; but I was deep in Indian country, and there were hard miles to go before I had any kind of comfort.

"If you'd gone to the damn FBI academy you could have been politely arresting people between afternoons on the golf course," I reminded myself. All of my inner voices told me to shut the fuck up.

The coin-operated washers and dryers were full but no one was down there. I jammed the cellar door shut, then I turned on the faucet in the laundry sink and held my head under the cold water for almost a minute. The water that sluiced over my scalp ran red for almost half that time. The cold knocked the pain level down a few notches though, and I could feel my brain reluctantly starting to clear.

My phone rang. Church was early. Sputtering and pawing water out of my eyes, I pulled my phone and punched the button.

"Yeah, boss?"

"Hello," she said. "How many brownie points do I have now?"

Chapter Thirty-Eight

Golden Oasis Hotel
Tehran, Iran
June 15, 10:04 a.m.

"Ah . . . shit," I said into the phone.

Violin laughed.

"That was you?" I asked.

Instead of answering she asked, "How badly are you hurt?"

"Why do you care?"

"*How badly are you hurt?*"

I sighed. "Somewhere between trampled by a soccer mob and found dead in a ditch, but . . . I'll live. What's it to you, anyway?"

Violin took a beat before answering, and even then she didn't answer the question. "You're lucky."

I clicked the button to initiate the trace. Not that I thought it was worth the effort, but what the hell. "Lucky? In what way?"

"The knight should have killed you."

"'Knight'? What's that supposed to mean?"

Another pause. "I don't know if I should be telling you this."

"Will it keep me alive?"

"Maybe."

"Then tell me, for Christ's sake. That son of a bitch nearly tore my head off. You should have seen him. You should have seen his frigging *teeth*."

"I have—"

"He had *fangs* for— Wait, *what*?"

"I have seen his teeth," said Violin. "Not that same knight, of course, but I've seen their teeth."

"When? How?"

"It doesn't matter. What matters is that you should not have seen him at all."

"Meaning that I shouldn't have and still be alive? Like that?"

"Like that, yes."

I was quiet for a moment, thinking it through. "What are they?"

She took her time before answering. "I don't know for sure, Joseph."

"I think you're lying to me. And what's with the 'Joseph'? Why so formal?"

"I like 'Joseph' better than 'Joe.' 'Joseph' is more dignified, more serious than a 'Joe.'"

"I have to warn you," I said, "I'm more of a 'Joe' personality type."

"We'll see."

"Wait, rewind a second. You called that guy a knight. Knight of what? Round Table? Columbus?"

"No," she said. "I can't tell you that without approval."

"Whose approval?"

She didn't answer.

"You're wasting my time, girl," I said. "I'm going to hang up now and get my ass out of here."

"You can't," she warned. "The knight was dropped off by a car and it keeps circling the block."

"You're still watching my hotel?" I asked, not sure if that was a comfort or another layer of worry to stack on top of everything else.

"Yes, and if you go outside they'll see you. The best thing you can do right now is wait."

"I don't want to be here when the cops arrive."

"I'm monitoring the police channels. No one has reported a thing."

Which is what I expected, but didn't say so. "What if they send in another of these knights? Or a whole team of them?"

"I don't think they will. Its broad daylight and they won't risk a full-out raid, and they won't risk a room-by-room search. Especially since they can't know what happened to the knight who attacked you. They'll circle for a while and then they'll break off and fall back to wait for fresh intelligence."

"You seem to know a lot about them."

"We know enough."

"We?" I asked again. "Who's team are you on? Mossad, MI6?"

"No."

"AISE?" I asked. With her accent she could easily be with the Agenzia Informazioni e Sicurezza Esterna, Italy's version of the CIA.

"No, and stop trying to guess," she said. "You won't."

Impasse.

"What *can* you tell me?" I asked, fighting to keep the exasperation out of my voice. "If you're on my side, Violin, then help me out. What am I facing here? That bastard had incredible strength and fangs. Tell me something that makes sense of that."

"The knights are extremely dangerous. That's all I'm prepared to say right now. Just be glad you're alive."

"I'm always glad I'm alive. I leap out of bed singing Disney songs. But look, I know a little bit about genetics and I can't see how gene therapy accounts for his strength. He threw me all over the place and he simply did not have the mass for it. That guy was spooky strong."

Again she evaded the question. "Be glad he didn't bite you."

"I'm also always glad when people don't bite me." I checked the trace. It was still running but it was clearly getting nowhere. According to the meter the call was coming from Antarctica, which I somehow doubted. "If I tell you what the knight said to me, will you tell me what he meant?"

"I don't know if I can."

"Let's try. The knight asked me to give him what Rasouli gave me."

"What *did* Rasouli give you?"

"Indigestion and a feeling like my right hand will never be clean again."

"You won't tell me?"

"Maybe later. My question is, why was the knight looking for that. Or, better yet, who sent the knight?"

"I'm not sure, because it doesn't make much sense for the knight to be working against Rasouli."

"Do they work *for* him?"

"No. They work for his allies. That's why it doesn't make sense."

But as she said that her words slowed as if she was suddenly thinking that it did make sense. When I tried to get her to explain, she stonewalled me again. So I came at her from a different angle. "I think he told me your name. Maybe it's a last name or a call sign, or maybe it's your organization."

"He didn't know my real name."

"Well, I'm just telling you what the knight told me."

"What name did he say?" she asked cautiously.

I said, "Arklight."

She gasped, very high and sharp, and then she took a long time before she spoke. "That's not my name."

"Then who—?"

She hung up.

"Damn it."

It was so frustrating because I wanted more information. I wanted to know about that freak that shook my cookie bag back at the hotel. What the hell *was* he? How could anyone be that strong? Nothing I know could explain what just happened.

That really and truly scared me. It kept the adrenaline pumping through my system, and my hands still shook.

Ghost whined and rubbed against my leg. His eyes were glassy.

I stripped off my bloody shirt, opened a dryer that had about half-finished its cycle, and stole a white long-sleeved shirt that was damp and a bit too small. The buttons gapped but I could get it closed. My jeans were bloodstained, but there's just enough of an artsy-cum-punk crowd in the capital to suggest that the red splotches were some kind of statement. Yeah, that statement was "Holy shit, I'm still alive."

My hair was still dyed black from the police station raid, and I finger-combed it straight back and pulled on a painter's cap I found that looked like it was a thousand years old. I rolled up my bloody shirt and wrapped it in a bath towel that I also stole from the dryer.

My phone rang again. Her.

"They're gone," she said. "It's safe."

And she hung up again.

I looked at Ghost. "Women, y'know?"

He *whuffed*.

Then I opened the back door, saw that the street was clear, and we went out.

Chapter Thirty-Nine

On the Streets

Tehran, Iran

June 15, 10:34 a.m.

I cut through the streets in a random pattern. I used glass storefront windows to check behind me and across the street. I went into stores and out the back, I cut through alleys. If there was a tail I did not see it.

My cell rang and when I saw who it was I ducked into an alley to answer the call. Bug doesn't speak Persian.

"About frigging time," I growled into the phone.

"Hello to you, too, man," said Bug.

"What the hell have you been doing? Playing *Halo*?"

"No—though the new version of *Halo* is pretty badass. They got this one level that—"

"My whole body is a lethal weapon, you know," I said. "I know more ways to kill you than you know how to die. Are you aware of that?"

"Yeah, yeah, yeah, I promise I'll faint when I take my coffee break. I wanted to get back to you on those books you had me look up. Are you sure you have the correct titles?"

"It's word of mouth from an unreliable source."

"I know, Rasouli. King Dickhead of all the world."

"That's the one."

"The thing is, I can't see how the *Saladin Codex* can be connected to the nukes or anything related to nuclear science."

"Why not?"

"Well, it's a math book that was written in the twelfth century based on an even older book, and I'm no physicist, but I'm pretty sure the whole nuke thing came later than that."

"Shit."

"And," added Bug, "it's not even a good math book."

"Meaning?"

"It's a rewrite of a classic book called *Al-Kitāb al-mukhtaṣar fī hīsāb al-ğabr wa'l-muqābala*."

Bug murdered the pronunciation, but I could make out what he meant. "The Compendious Book on Calculation by Completion and Balancing," I translated.

"Right. It was written by some dude named Muhammad ibn Mūsā al-Khwārizmī, who was a noted mathematician of his time. Apparently *'al-ğabr'* is the original word for algebra, which is what the book is about. One of the earliest books on the subject, or maybe *the* earliest book on the subject."

"Algebra," I mused. "Physics is all about math, isn't it? Physics and nuclear technology are kissing cousins . . ."

"Well—sure, but this is pretty basic stuff. Nothing that gives us direct insight into nuclear science. I mean, c'mon, I learned this stuff in tenth grade."

"Okay, what about the *Saladin Codex*?"

"That was written in 1191 by someone named Ibrahim al-Asiri. He was a diplomat who worked for Saladin."

"Rasouli mentioned Saladin," I said, and explained what he'd said.

"Huh," grunted Bug, unimpressed. "Anyway, al-Asiri was also a mathematician, but apparently not a great one. His book attempted to refute some of the theories from the earlier work. No one was buying it, though, because algebra isn't a theory. Math is math."

"Tell that to my tax attorney," I muttered. "How's this help us?"

"That's what I'm saying, Joe, I don't see how it does. Al-Asiri's book was largely discredited. At most it's a footnote in the history of math."

"If it was dismissed, then why is it even a footnote?"

"Discredited," Bug corrected, "not dismissed. And it was only that particular book that was discredited, not the author. Al-Asiri was a very important man from a very, very important family. He was second cousin to Saladin and was involved in many of Saladin's most historically significant treaties during the Crusades."

"Saladin's name keeps coming up in this. Rasouli made a point of mentioning it, so maybe there's a clue there," I mused. "What about the word 'Saracen,' I know that relates, but how exactly?"

Bug tapped some keys. "Easy one. During the time of the Crusades the Europeans called all Muslims Saracens. Later that changed to Mohammadan and then Muslim. Purely a European word choice."

"Okay. What about the other one? The *Book of Shadows?*"

"Yeah," said Bug slowly, "that's where we go out of the blue and into the black. And by black I mean magic. Or, maybe it's white magic. What do I know from magic?"

"Magic?"

"Uh-huh. the *Book of Shadows* is the book of spells for witchcraft."

"You're shitting me."

"Serious as a heart attack, Joe. What the hell are you into over there? I mean . . . is the DMS suddenly at war with the forces of darkness?"

I thought about the freak with the fangs.

"Right now, Bug, I'd believe just about anything. Look—keep digging and get back to me with anything you find."

I hung up and lingered in the alley for a moment wondering if Bug's information moved me forward toward understanding or pulled a bag over my head.

"Witches. What do you think?" I asked Ghost.

He lifted his leg and peed on the wall.

"That's what I figured," I said.

We kept moving.

Chapter Forty

The Warehouse
Baltimore, Maryland
June 15, 1:48 a.m. EST

"Hey! I got something," cried Bug as his image popped onto a view screen. His face glowed with excitement.

After signing off with Aunt Sallie, Circe had buried herself in the material from the flash drive, and Rudy had followed her in, picking up the thread of her logic and working with her on the psychological aspects of the case. They looked up from the semicircle of data screens.

"We're in the middle of something, Bug—" Circe, began, but Bug overrode her.

"I've been tearing apart the documents on the flash drive," he said. "At first there didn't seem to be anything more than what we already had, but on a whim I matched the volume of data we've downloaded against the drive's storage potential and there was a discrepancy."

Rudy frowned. "Because some of the files were supposedly destroyed by moisture after Rasouli's agent swallowed the drive, correct?"

Bug gave him a pitying stare. "Silly mortal. 'Destroyed' is a relative term. Or, maybe it's a term people who are a lot less super-genius smart than me use."

"Bug," warned Circe quietly.

"Yeah, yeah, okay. There's more stuff on the drive than was openly indexed, and I'm *not* talking about real or faked damaged files. I'm talking about stuff that was coded to react like damaged files."

"You lost me," admitted Rudy.

"A file name is nothing but a piece of computer language. Zeros and ones, but arranged to create a readable name. When you give a file a name the computer writes that name in computer language, but here someone deliberately coded a few files so that their names appear as 'read error' warnings. That way they get hidden among the errors from the damage."

"Devious," Rudy agreed. "How many hidden files are there and what is in them?"

"There are ten files in two separate subfolders. One was marked BOS/ SC, and I don't think I have to go too far out on a limb to presume what that stands for."

"You lost me again," said Rudy.

"It was part of the verbal intel Ledger got from Rasouli," explained Bug. "Rasouli made oblique references to two books, the *Book of Shadows* and the *Saladin Codex*. BOS/SC. Anyway, when I cracked the files I expected to find complete texts or abstracts, but instead I got nine scanned images saved as pdfs. Very low-res and muddy. The other file is weird. All I could find was a Word doc with two words written in English. 'Fuzzy math.' That's it. I'm running some additional cleanup and deep extraction programs to see if there are other hidden layers, but so far, bubkes."

"Fuzzy math?" asked Rudy.

Circe grunted. "The Codex is supposed to be questionable commentary on an exact science, right? That says 'fuzzy math' to me. Could be some code hidden there. You get anything from the Codex, Bug?"

"Not so far. We don't actually have a copy of the *Codex,* so I can't check to see if there's anything buried in the text."

"Damn. Who has one?"

Bug made a face. "There is exactly one copy and it's in the National Museum in Tehran."

"Crap," said Circe. "Any full or partial scans online?"

"Not that I've found, but searching all foreign-language databases will take a little longer."

"What about the other one?" asked Rudy. "The *Book of Shadows.* Surely I've heard of that somewhere . . ."

Circe nodded. "It's the book of spells used in Wicca."

"Oh, for God's sake," complained Rudy, flapping a hand. "Really? We've done zombies, clones, and mutants, now the DMS is squaring off against black magic?"

"Don't laugh," said Circe with surprising heat. "And stop being so Catholic for a minute. Wicca isn't devil worship or black magic. That was all medieval propaganda created to suppress the rise of education among women. And even the concept of 'black' magic is completely unconnected to the modern Wicca, which is earthcentric and practiced according to positive energy and harmony with nature."

Rudy held up his hands, palms out. "Mea culpa."

Circe gave him a *harrumph.* "The modern practice is built mostly on a set of traditions created by Gerald Gardner, who first introduced the *Book of Shadows* to the initiates of his landmark Bricket Wood coven in the 1950s. It eventually became the central text for most of the other branches of the faith, including Alexandrianism and Mohsianism. But . . . I do have to admit that I don't see how it could possibly relate at all to nuclear bombs."

"I don't think it does," said Bug, "and the Gardner book probably isn't the *Book of Shadows* involved in this case. Rasouli didn't say anything to

Joe about witches. Here, let me put the pdfs up and you tell me if this is Wiccan stuff or not." He loaded an Adobe program and then opened the nine pdf files, throwing them onto nine smaller screens. Each file was a low-resolution scan of a single page from what looked like an ancient manuscript. Rudy bent forward and frowned at it. There were green and brown paintings of exotic plants that he did not recognize and line after line of writing in a language Rudy could not identify. Two of the pages were only text, and one was a complex diagram of the sun, with a face in the center and writing running in circles around the drawing.

"What language is that?" Rudy asked.

"I don't know," said Bug. "I just found these, and I wanted to show you before I started the recognition software. And the images are very low-res, so some of it might be hard to—"

Circe gasped. "My God!"

Rudy and Bug stared at her.

"I know what that is," she said.

Chapter Forty-One

Barrier Safe House
Tehran, Iran
June 15, 10:39 a.m.

The good news was that between the CIA, the DMS, and a few other alphabet agencies, we had safe houses and equipment drops all over Tehran. One agency spook I knew told me that he could hardly walk down the street without seeing someone from the "family."

"Invisible network my ass," he added.

So, I went to the closest haven. When Echo Team had first arrived in Tehran we spent half a day at a safe house run by Barrier. It was staffed by two agents, a father and son. The father, Fariel, looked old enough to have been a school chum of Xerxes. His son, Cyrus, was a schoolteacher and probably the most boring person I've ever met. The kind of guy who speaks in a nasal monotone and can only talk about what he saw on TV.

Right now, though? I could use normal and boring. That house also had plenty of weapons and equipment. Rearming would go a long way toward chasing off the shakes. If I'd had a good fighting knife this morning then the encounter in my hotel room would have been a whole lot shorter and more satisfying.

At least I think it would have.

The Barrier safe house was a one-stop, two-room little pillbox near a bus stop. Lots of people coming and going all the time, lots of strangers. Good place to hide, right there in the open.

I knocked. There was no special trick. I didn't have to knock three times then two then wait and knock four times. That was the movies. I knocked, and they answered.

Except that's not exactly what happened.

As the locked clicked open and the door swung inward, Ghost stiffened and gave a sharp *woof.* Even dazed as he was he knew that something was wrong.

I pushed inside, driving whoever was behind the door in and back. I kicked the door shut as the man fell. I pulled the pistol and dropped into a combat crouch.

The man who lay on the floor staring up at me was Cyrus, the son of the man who ran the safe house. He looked up at me with eyes that were wild with fear and pain.

He was covered with blood, head to toe.

Ghost growled, but he was still trembling and looked ready to collapse.

I squatted near him and whispered in Persian. "How many are there?"

He tried to speak but only blood bubbled from between his lips. Cyrus gestured wildly toward the doorway at the end of the short foyer.

I was already in motion, running with quick, small steps, the pistol held in front of me, mouth set and hard. At the end of the foyer I crouched and did a fast look around the corner.

The living room was a study in crimson.

I eased around the corner.

Nothing moved.

But it was not empty. A man—Fariel Omidi—hung on the wall. Big carpenter nails had been driven savagely through his wrists and hands and feet. He had been crucified.

His head hung low, and from the damage I saw there was no way he could still be alive. No way in hell.

Ghost whined from the foyer but I waved him to stillness.

I could see through the living room into the eat-in kitchen. The back door was open to the sunlight. The door to the bathroom stood ajar and I crabbed sideways and wheeled around to cover the interior space. Toilet, sink, and tub. All bloody, all empty.

Every cabinet and storage trunk had been torn open. All of the weapons and equipment were gone. Even the trapdoor beside the fridge had been ripped from its hinges. The boxes of grenades, shape charges, detonators, and other explosives were gone.

At the back door I peered into the alley. There were two bloody footprints and then tire tracks in the dirt.

This was all past tense. I lowered my gun and pulled the door shut, engaged the locks and propped a chair under the handle. Then I grabbed a bunch of dish towels and raced back to the entrance foyer.

Cyrus was still alive, but only just. I gingerly peeled back the shreds of his clothes to see how bad he was hurt, and I was sorry I did it. Everything had been done to him. Cuts and punctures. The bruised and ravaged marks of tools, probably pliers. Big burned patches. Maybe a portable propane burner. That and more.

I was amazed he was still alive.

I sponged blood from his nose and mouth and rolled some of the towels to place under his head. God only knows how Cyrus had managed to stay on his feet long enough to answer the door. Hope, maybe? If so, it was one more crushing disappointment on the worst day of his life. Cyrus was shivering with shock. I rushed back to the living room for a throw rug and draped it over him. The rug was bloody, too, but that didn't seem important.

"Hey, buddy," I said gently. "Can you understand me?"

His mouth worked for a moment and he made only mewling sounds, but he nodded ever so slightly.

"Who did this to you?"

He shook his head.

"How many were there? How big a team?"

Cyrus managed to raise his hand a few inches. He held up a single finger.

"One?" I asked. "You're saying that one man did this."

He shook his head but held up the single finger again. I tried to get him to explain. It wasn't one team, it seemed. It was one, but he objected to my choice of "man" or even "woman."

Cyrus tried hard to speak, but each time it came out as a meaningless wet mumble. And then with crushing and horrible realization I understood why.

They had cut out his tongue.

I closed my eyes for a moment and tried hard not to scream. Ghost whined from the living room doorway.

When I opened my eyes I saw Cyrus looking at me. He was slipping past the point where pain mattered to him, and he knew it. We both knew it.

"Listen to me, Cyrus," I said, dabbing cold sweat from his forehead, "I want to be straight with you, okay?"

He began to cry, knowing what I was going to say; but he nodded.

"You're hurt bad. Very bad. I—I can call for an ambulance, but . . ." I let it trail off. I was feeling too cowardly to put it into words. Cyrus reached out with his swollen, bloody hand and did something that broke my heart. He patted my thigh. He was taking me off the hook from having to tell him that he was dying.

I took his hand and held it.

"I'll find whoever did this," I promised him. "So help me God, I will find them."

He smiled with his ruined mouth. A small thing.

Cyrus touched one finger to his bloody chest and then slowly drew something on the floor. He used the pad of his finger to make a crimson dot, and then overlaid it with the symbol of the cross.

He looked from it to me and tried once more to speak the name of his killer. No—not a name. A word, a description. Two toneless syllables formed by a mouth that could not even speak that word.

Monster.

It was a horrible word, but it was no surprise to me. All this damage, all of the signs of physical power and rage—doors torn from their hinges, these men brutalized. I wonder if Cyrus and his father had stared into glaring red eyes as they were torn apart. A knight had done this, and if there was a better example of a monster hunting the streets of this country, I couldn't imagine it.

Cyrus sighed and his hand dropped away. I sat with him while all that had made up this little man evaporated into the red darkness. I hadn't liked him when I'd met him yesterday. A boring little guy who hadn't much liked me either. But now that was different. He would live in my heart and head forever. Cyrus Omidi. A victim of the very old war that defines the Middle East? Or a victim of something new?

I spoke his name aloud seven times. Don't ask me why. It felt like something I had to do.

I got to my feet and walked into the living room.

Fariel Omidi was past helping. There was nothing I could do for him. But I said his name seven times, too.

While I stood there, my phone rang.

"Captain," Church said, "sorry it's taken so long to get back to you. Give me a sit rep."

Chapter Forty-Two

Barrier Safe House
Tehran, Iran
June 15, 10:46 a.m.

I turned away from the dead man and stared at the floor. Ghost came and lay at my feet.

"I don't know where to begin," I said into the phone.

"Tell me," said Church.

So, I told him. About Violin. About the Red Knight in my hotel room. About the dead men whose pain seemed to scream through the air around me. I don't remember exactly what I said, but Church cut right through my words.

"Are you injured?" he demanded. "Do you need immediate medical attention?"

I paused. "No. No, I'm good."

"Are you in shock?"

"I—" I began and then stopped, realizing why he was asking that. My mind replayed the last few things I'd said and there was a rising hysterical note to my voice. The room was too bright, the colors too vivid. And the smell . . .

I took a long, deep breath and let it out slowly.

"I'm good," I assured him. "Been a bad day."

"For all of us, Captain."

We gave that a moment.

"You are going to need to get out of that location," he said.

"I know."

"Don't go to another Barrier safe house. The Company has one close to you."

"Soon as we're done I'm out of here," I assured him.

"The woman," Church said, shifting back to my report. "Violin. Give me a read on her."

"Hard to say exactly. She's a voice on the phone and she's probably lying to me."

"Then give me guesswork and suppositions."

I thought about it. "She sounds young. Late twenties. Her base accent is Italian, though she could be any nationality or race with an accent picked up by familiarity. She's a trained sniper. She's for hire. The people who hired her are connected to Vox, which is how Rasouli hired her. No idea whose side she's on, though she doesn't seem to like Rasouli. And she's tied up with someone or something called Arklight."

"Arklight," he said, repeating the name slowly, seeming to appreciate it. "Interesting."

"You've heard of it?"

"Yes. Did she confirm that she was part of Arklight?"

"No, when I asked her about it she hung up on me. Why? What's Arklight?"

He didn't answer.

"Yo! How about a little help for the guy standing in a room full of dead people?"

"Captain," said Church, "to tell you anything useful about Arklight would mean betraying a confidence."

"I don't care."

"It could also put you in danger." He paused. "And, yes, I know how absurd that sounds, given the circumstances."

"You think?"

"I need to make a call about this. In the short term, I have had dealings with Arklight in the past. Most of the time those dealings were harmonious.

Working together against a shared threat, that sort of thing. But they are not allies. There are no standing nonaggression agreements between us."

"Can you try to vague that up a bit more? I almost understood it."

He changed the subject. "The man who attacked you at the hotel, you said that he was winning the fight? Assess that. Are we talking about superior combat skill or something else?"

"We were pretty well matched for skill and technique. It'd be hard to put a label on his fighting style, but he wasn't trying anything on me that he hadn't done a lot of times before. Everything was very smooth, very efficient."

Church grunted his understanding. At a certain level, when you're fighting to kill rather than trying to win a belt or a tournament, all style is stripped away in favor of a selection of techniques that are the most practical and effective at the moment. Experts who engage in these kinds of fights usually rely on a small percentage of the skills they've learned; skills that they know they can use, and which they can use without thinking about it. At that level a kick is a kick is a kick; a punch is a punch.

"What about enhancements?" Church asked.

"I don't know. Nothing obvious, no exoskeletons or combat suit with joint servos. Nothing like that. He was faster and stronger, but the weird thing is that he didn't have the bulk for it. This was way beyond the limits of 'wiry strength.'"

"In the absence of the sniper, would he have won the fight?"

"Coin toss," I admitted. "We were hurting each other, so I guess it would have come down to who wanted it more. I tend to want it quite a lot."

"Fair enough."

"On the other hand, let's not rule out enhancement. Something chemical, maybe."

"I wonder what Dr. Hu would find in a blood test. I don't suppose you collected any—?"

"I didn't take a cheek swab or get him to pee in a cup for me, but I have plenty of his blood on my clothes."

"I'll arrange a pickup." He paused. "The attacker . . . gauge his strength. Use Bunny as a yardstick."

"Twice as strong. Easily," I said. "I know that sounds ridiculous, but that knight was a bull and—"

"Wait," Church cut in sharply. "You just called the attacker a 'knight.' What did you mean by that? You didn't mention that earlier."

"Oh," I said, and realized that he was right. When I'd blown through the story the first time I had called the attacker "the goon." So I backed up and explained what Violin had told me.

There was a long silence on the phone.

"Describe the symbol Cyrus Omidi drew on the floor."

"I can show it to you. The knight had it tattooed on his arm. I took a picture." I fiddled with the phone and sent the e-mail.

I heard Church hitting keys to open the e-mail.

When he spoke again his voice was tight and urgent. "Captain, listen to me very carefully. Get out of that house right now."

"Why—what's wrong?"

"Violin was correct. That was a Red Knight you faced in your hotel and another one who killed the Omidis. That means Arklight *is* involved. Get out of that house immediately and call me from the CIA safe house."

"Why—"

"*Go!*"

Chapter Forty-Three

The Hangar
Floyd Bennett Field, Brooklyn
June 15, 2:25 a.m. EST

Mr. Church set the phone down and stared at it. His hands were balled into fists on top of his desk blotter.

Then he snatched the phone up again and punched a speed dial.

"Yo," said Aunt Sallie after two rings.

"Auntie, the situation in Iran has just gotten significantly worse."

"We're hunting nukes, Deke, how much fucking worse can it—?"

"Captain Ledger is being hunted by Red Knights."

There was a stunned silence on the phone, and then Aunt Sallie whispered, "Oh my God!"

Chapter Forty-Four

"Wait," said Bug, "what?"

"Those pages," said Circe. "I recognize them. They're from an ancient codex called the Voynich manuscript. I'm sure of it."

"I don't think so," said Bug dubiously. "Rasouli seemed to think this was the *Book of Shadows*."

Circe shook her head. "You're wrong, Bug. That's the Voynich manuscript."

"What is the Voynich manuscript?" asked Rudy. "I've never heard of it."

"It's an old ciphertext," Circe said as she accessed a browser and went to one of the university research sites she subscribed to. In a few seconds a screen came up with THE VOYNICH MANUSCRIPT MYSTERY in bold letters. She went through the directory and pulled up several scans of individual pages. The pages were crammed with writing in a language none of them knew.

Bug whistled.

"Well I'll be damned," murmured Rudy.

Circe pulled up more pages, and some of these had pictures. Plants, naked women, celestial diagrams. The drawings were primitive, but they were orderly—even if the sense of order was elusive. Then she found one that matched a page from Rasouli's files.

"See? I was right," Circe said triumphantly. In a few minutes she matched seven of the nine pages, but then she frowned as she ran through every single page of the manuscript. "Wait . . . did I miss them?"

"No," said Bug. "The last two pages from Rasouli's file aren't in the Voynich thingee."

"Slow down," begged Rudy. "What *is* this?"

Circe took a breath. "The Voynich manuscript is a mysterious book that dates back to the fifteenth century. Radio carbon dating put it somewhere between 1404 to 1438 C.E., and from the materials used it's believed that it was created in northern Italy, which was a very important and wealthy part of Europe at the time."

"Who wrote this book?" asked Rudy.

"That's just it," said Circe, "no one knows who wrote it or why. It's named after Wilfrid Voynich, a rare-book dealer from New York who discovered the book in 1912 during a buying trip to Villa Mondragone, near Rome. It was in a trunkful of rare texts. Voynich spent the rest of his life trying to decipher the language, but he never did. In fact no one ever has."

"Maybe it's a fake language," suggested Rudy.

"Doubtful," said Bug, peering at it. "It's too orderly."

"Can we suppose for a moment that the two remaining pages from Rasouli's file are from the other book, the *Book of Shadows?*" suggested Rudy. "If so, they're clearly written in the same language. Maybe it's a secret language, reserved for use by members of a society."

"Sure," Circe agreed. "That's the consensus of scholars of the book, but it is an incredibly complex language. In all there are one hundred and seventy thousand distinct glyphs, or written elements. About thirty of these glyphs are used repeatedly throughout the manuscript."

"An alphabet?" said Bug.

"Probably, but no one has cracked it."

"Where is the book now?" asked Rudy. "And can we get it?"

"It's at Yale, in the Beinecke Rare Book and Manuscript Library, but there's no reason to get it. There are hundreds of Web sites devoted to the manuscript. Every page of it, including the covers, is available online."

Bug reached up to tap one of the pages on the screen. "Wait, isn't that a signature? I can almost read it. Jacob something something."

"Jacobus de Tepenecz," said Circe. "He wasn't the author, though. More likely he owned it for a while. De Tepenecz was a seventeenth-century physician and an expert in medical plants. In 1608 he was summoned to Prague to treat Emperor Rudolf II who was suffering from severe depression and melancholia. Because of his success with the emperor, de Tepenecz was appointed Imperial Chief Distiller. Scholars believe that he was given the Voynich manuscript as either payment or as a gift by Rudolf, who was a collector of occult books and manuscripts of arcane sciences. The ownership of the book has a lot of gaps in it. We do know that when Voynich purchased it he found a letter tucked between its pages that had been written in 1665 by Dr. Johannes Marcus Marci of Bohemia, and in that letter Dr. Marci claimed that the book was written by Roger Bacon."

"Who was—?" prompted Rudy.

"He was a Franciscan friar, philosopher, and alchemist in the thirteenth century. His nickname was 'Doctor Mirabilis'—'wonderful teacher.' But . . . Bacon was likely born around 1220 C.E. He died in 1294, more than a century before the book was written."

"Unless he really could do miracles," said Bug, but they ignored him.

"What's in the manuscript?" asked Rudy. "I see plants and diagrams . . ."

"That's just it," answered Circe, "on the surface the book appears to be a codex of herbology. But here's the kicker, while some of the plants in the book are recognizable, there are some plants that are either so badly drawn that they're unrecognizable, or they are plants that are currently unknown to science. Aside from the herbal drawings, there are others, including a number of cosmological diagrams, some of them with suns, moons, and stars, suggestive of astronomy or astrology. There are the twelve zodiacal symbols, and each of these has thirty female figures arranged in two or more concentric bands. Most of the females are at least partly naked, and each holds what appears to be a labeled star or is shown with the star attached by what could be a tether or cord of some kind to either arm." She took a breath. "And there are sections that show small naked women bathing in pools or tubs connected by an elaborate network of pipes, some of them clearly shaped like body organs. Some of the women wear crowns. Some pages look like complex formulae, but for what is anyone's guess. In short, we don't know what the book is about or why it was written."

Rudy said, "You called it a ciphertext rather than a codetext. What's the difference? I thought a cipher was another name for code."

Circe shook her head. "A cipher is the result of encryption performed on plaintext using an algorithm. It's mathematical. A code is simply a method used to transform a message into an obscured form. Like letter transposition or word-swapping. You decipher a code with a codebook that has the letters, words, or phrases that match the coded message. A cipher is much more complex, and it's often the word people should be using when describing something that has been encrypted."

"I knew that," Bug said quietly.

"I didn't," said Rudy, "and I have no idea what you just said. What I want to know is what the Voynich manuscript is and how it relates to seven nuclear bombs."

Circe blew out her cheeks. "Scholars have spent the last century trying to decipher the manuscript. How that relates, or how it helps . . . is anyone's guess."

Rudy stood and bent closer to the screens showing the two mystery pages. He looked back and forth between them, and then studied the Voynich pages. He grunted.

"What?" asked Circe.

"Well . . . I'm no handwriting expert," he said slowly, "but I don't think these other pages were written by the same person."

Chapter Forty-Five

On the Run
Tehran, Iran
June 15, 10:59 a.m.

Mr. Church said run, so I ran.

When Church is so rattled by something that he freaks at me on the phone, then my own scare-o-meter starts burying the needle. I ran like a son of a bitch and put a lot of gone between me and the death house.

Three blocks away I cut down an alley behind an abandoned house. Once I was sure that the place was completely deserted, I broke in. Ghost was too weak to do much running, so I left him in the kitchen and quickly cleared the whole house. Six empty rooms, lots of junk, some bugs, a dead rat, and nothing else.

There was no water, so we couldn't stay long, but I needed more information from Church. He answered my call right away.

"Are you somewhere safe?"

I explained my location.

"Very well. I'm retasking a satellite to try and track you. Echo Team is six hours out, and I've alerted Barrier as to the hit on their house."

"Good," I said, "so now tell me why I ran away like a six-year-old from a party clown. Who the hell are these Red Knights?"

"They are trained killers. Very, very tough."

"Yeah, well so am I."

"Captain Ledger," he said quietly, "take your ego out of gear for a moment and look at this objectively, I—"

"I *am* looking at it objectively," I cut in, "but your lack of confidence is starting to piss me off."

"Get over it," he said quietly and waited for another smart-mouth comment from me. I said nothing. After a moment, he continued. "The Red Knights are members of a brotherhood of assassins that emerged during the later Crusades. Over the centuries they have been tied to acts of murder, sabotage, and destruction that by today's standards would be classified as terrorism. Very little is known about them, and much of what is recorded is questionable. History distorts reliable intel; and, much like the ninja of Japan, the knights themselves contributed to, edited, and distorted their own mythology."

"Gosh, where have I heard that before? Oh, yeah . . . your friend Hugo Vox. Are we saying that this is all his scheme?"

"Unknown."

"Who runs these knights?"

"Also unknown, though there are unsubstantiated rumors of a group called the Red Order, but so far we haven't been able to put together a file on them. It's even possible Red Order and Red Knights are interchangeable terms; that's to be determined."

"Okay," I said dubiously, "so why haven't I heard of these Red Knights? If they're political it sounds like something we should be handling. What do we know about them?"

"About their organization? Next to nothing. About operatives like the one you encountered? We know bits and pieces, and none of it is good. Do not underestimate them and don't waste time with a database search on them. The DMS has not crossed paths with them before this." He paused. "*I* have."

"Crossed paths or crossed swords?" I asked.

He didn't answer that.

"Did anyone tell you to run away?"

"Captain—"

"Tell me why I just ran away, Church. Sure, the knight at the hotel blindsided me and I had some trouble. I was unarmed then. Different story now; and now I'm going to be expecting the next one to be stronger and faster than the average psycho asshole with fangs. And, speaking of which, what's with those goddamn fangs? Do they hire freaks? Are they implants of some kind, or is this some gene therapy bullshit?"

"We don't have time for a full briefing right now," Church said. "Continue on to the CIA safe house and when you are safe and settled we'll have a longer conversation. In the short term, I want you to be sensible of the degree of threat these knights represent. If you encounter another one, or even suspect that you are facing one of them, do not hesitate and do not give them a single chance. Escape if you can, and if that is not an option, do not allow yourself to be drawn into another hand-to-hand confrontation."

"Because—?"

"Because it is unlikely you would survive it."

"Kiss my ass. I was starting to *win* that fight."

"From what you told me, Captain, the knight wanted information from you," replied Church. "That opened a window of opportunity for you. If you are unfortunate enough to encounter another Red Knight, he's likely to be less chatty. My recommendation stands: don't engage them. The odds are not in your favor."

"Gee, Coach, thanks for the vote of confidence."

Mr. Church snorted. "You got lucky at the hotel, Captain. Don't bank on your new girlfriend being on hand to save you next time."

I will rip your throat out and drink your life.

"Jesus," I said, "what are you trying to do here? Scare the hell out of me?"

"If that's what it takes to drive the point home," said Church. "You haven't faced anything like this before. If you encounter another Red Knight, I want you to avoid contact and flee, or failing that, to terminate him immediately and with extreme prejudice."

I bit down on a few of the things I would have liked to say to him.

"Sure," I said.

"I'm serious, Captain."

"Don't worry, if I see another scary bad man I'll run away screaming like a nine-year-old girl."

He sighed. "See that you do. Call me from the safe house."

The line went dead.

I looked at the phone. "Kiss my ass," I said again.

But his words had made cold sweat break out all over my body.

Interlude One

Near the City of Acre

May 17, 1191 C.E.

A cold wind blew out of the desert, stirring the thousands of banners and flags that rose like a forest of silk above the camp. Hundreds of cooking fires set the night ablaze and the air was filled with laughter and songs and conversation. The fragile quiet of the night-time desert recoiled back from this rude intrusion, and overhead the stars seemed to turn shyly away from the firelight below.

Sir Guy LaRoque sat astride his horse and watched as his king, Philip II, walked toward the command tent with a phalanx of advisors around him. The whole camp was on fire with excitement. The kings of Europe were coming to the Crusade. Philip was there first, as was only right, bringing eight thousand men in one hundred ships and enough provisions to mount a countersiege against Saladin. By June, Richard the Lionheart of England would be here, and more crusaders would flood into the Holy Land in his wake. After a weary siege and inconclusive battles, the tide was turning.

The energy crackled like lightning in the air, and Sir Guy smiled. This was how it should be. This was what served God. Still smiling, Sir Guy tugged on the reins to turn his horse away from the camp, kicked it into a light canter, and set out into the darkest part of the surrounding desert. The standard-bearer, an old and trusted family servant, spurred his mount and followed. They rode in the general direction of the coast, but once there were hills between them and the camp, Sir Guy turned his horse away from the smell of salt water and headed toward the deep desert. A half an hour's easy gallop brought them to an outcrop of rock that rose like a cathedral from the shifting sands. Sir Guy stopped on a ridge and ordered his companion to unfurl the white flag.

After a full minute, a small light appeared at the base of the tall rock. A lamp was unshielded for a moment and then covered again. Sir Guy waited until this action was performed again, and again.

"Stay here," he told his servant. "Stay alert and sober."

With that, Sir Guy dismounted and walked down the sloping sand toward the rock. When he was ten yards away he called out in perfect Arabic.

"*As-salāmu 'alaykum.*"

"*Wa-laikum as-salâm,*" replied a voice from within the featureless shadows at the foot of the rock. There was movement and the lamp was once more unshielded, revealing in its glow the thin and ascetic face of a bearded Saracen. Sir Guy went forward to meet the other man and they shook hands warmly.

"Come, my friend," said the Saracen, "I have food and a warm fire inside."

Together they passed beyond the tapestry and entered a cave which cut nearly to the heart of the towering rock. Inside, the cave was comfortable, furnished with a rug for the floor, pillows, a low brass tray piled high with cooked meats and dried fruits, and a tall pitcher of clean water.

"You look well, Ibrahim," said Sir Guy as he warmed his hands over the flame.

Ibrahim al-Asiri was a tall thin man with a hawk nose that had been broken and badly set, giving him a villainous look that was at odds with his role as diplomat and counselor to Salāh-ed-Dīn Ayyūbi. Like Sir Guy, his counterpart in the politics of the wars here in the Holy Land, Ibrahim was a scholar, but, unlike the Frenchman, the Arab was also a mathematician of some note and the author of complex books on engineering, geometry, and algebra.

While they ate, the two men picked up the thread of a conversation that had occupied them over many previous secret meetings.

"I am taking the matter to a priest," said Sir Guy. "One of the Hospitallers of my order. An old friend of the family. He is a wise and subtle man, and I think he will see the logic of our plan."

Ibrahim frowned. "What will happen if he does not agree with us? What will he do?"

"Do?" laughed Sir Guy. "He would denounce me and I would be lucky to escape being publically whipped to death. My lands and fortune would be seized and I would be excommunicated." The Frenchman waved a hand at the expression of alarm on Ibrahim's face. "No, no, my friend, that's what could happen, but I do not think that it *will* happen. I know this man."

"So far," Ibrahim said, "this has all been nothing but an intellectual exercise, a discourse of a philosophical nature. Once you speak to this priest, it becomes something else."

"I know. With the first words I say to the priest it becomes treason and heresy."

They thought about that for several moments, each of them staring through the flickering fire at the future.

"We could turn back," suggested Ibrahim. "Now, I mean. We could finish our meal and you could ride back to your camp and I to mine, and we could never speak of this again."

"We could," agreed Sir Guy.

"If we do not, then we are irrevocably set on a course that will wash the world in blood and pain and destruction from now until the ending of time."

"Yes."

"We must be sure."

"I am sure," said Sir Guy. "If you were not a heathen of a Saracen then we would drink wine together to seal the bargain."

"And if you were not an infidel deserving of a jackal's death we would spit on our palms and shake upon it."

They smiled at each other.

"Let us do this, then," proposed Sir Guy. He sat forward and took a knife and held the edge of the blade in the heat of the fire. The steel grew hot very quickly. "Since flame and steel and blood are the things with which we will prove our allegiance to God and with which we will preserve His holy name here on earth, then let it be with flame and steel and blood that we seal our agreement."

"Our Holy Agreement," corrected Ibrahim.

Their eyes met across the flame.

"Our Holy Agreement," said Sir Guy.

He removed the smoking blade from the fire and opened his left hand. "The Crusades and the armies of the church are the right hand of God. We will be His left hand."

He cocked an amused eye at Ibrahim, "And don't tell me that your left is the hand you wipe your ass with, for I know that. No one will look there for proof of your fealty. And every time I see it I'll laugh."

"You are a whore's son and the grandson of a leper," replied Ibrahim, but he was laughing aloud as he said it.

Their laughter and smiles ebbed away as the edge of the blade turned from flat gray to a hellish red gold.

"Swear it, my brother," said Ibrahim, nodding to the blade.

"I swear to defend the church, and to preserve it, and insure that it will endure forever. By my heart, by my hand, by my honor, and by my blood I so swear." He set his teeth and pressed the flat of the blade into his palm. The glowing blade melted his flesh with a hiss and a curl of smoke. Sir Guy growled out in agony and then turned his cry into a ferocious prayer. "By God I swear!"

Gasping, gray-faced, he pulled the knife away and handed it to Ibrahim, then slumped back against the pillows. Ibrahim held the blade in the flames until the fading glow flared again. Then he, too, swore by his faith and on his God as he burned his promise into his skin. Then he dropped the knife into the heart of the fire where it would eventually melt into nothingness.

The smell of burning meat filled the tent.

The faces of the two diplomats were greasy with sweat.

Ibrahim held out his burned hand to his friend. "The left hand of God," he said.

Sir Guy grunted and leaned forward, reaching out to clasp hand to hand.

"The left hand of God."

They shook and it seemed to them that all around them the world itself trembled.

Chapter Forty-Six

"I say we pull him," growled Aunt Sallie. She flung herself into the leather guest chair across the desk from Mr. Church. "Pull him now before he screws everything up."

"Why?" asked Church. He sat back, his elbows on the arms of his chair, fingers steepled, eyes unreadable behind the tinted lenses of his glasses. "Beyond your general dislike of Ledger."

"He can't handle the knights and you damn well know it."

"He survived one encounter."

"Because some psycho bitch with a sniper rifle bailed him out. Pure luck."

"Ledger *is* lucky, Auntie. You have to admit that."

She snorted. "He may be, but the people around him sure as shit aren't."

"That's not entirely fair."

"Isn't it? Grace Courtland? Marty Hanler? Sergeant Faraday? I could keep going."

"How are any of those his fault?"

"Come on, Deke, we both know his history. Everyone who's ever been close to him has gotten killed or hurt."

"Again, that's not a fair assessment." Church took a Nilla wafer and pushed the plate across the desk. Aunt Sallie took one and snapped off a piece with her sharp white teeth; then she pointed the other half at Church. "If we're being fair here . . . then you tell me how it's fair to leave him in play? You actually *like* that ass clown. Do you want to see him torn apart?"

"No."

"Do you remember what happened in Stuttgart? In Florence? In—"

"I remember, Auntie."

"No, I think you need to refresh your mind on what happened, Deke. The knights are tougher than they ever were. Someone or something has amped them up. They tore apart an entire Mossad team. Sixteen trained agents. Dead. *Drained*. Is that what you want to do here? Feed your boy Ledger to those *things*?"

"Of course not. The Mossad team had no idea what they were up against."

"Does Ledger?" snapped Aunt Sallie, her eyes blazing.

They regarded each other across Church's broad desk. Aunt Sallie cocked an eyebrow.

"That sniper chick," she said.

"Violin? What about her?"

"She's with Arklight, isn't she?"

"Possibly."

" 'Possibly,' my ass. The number of woman snipers is pretty small, and the number of those who work the Middle East is a lot smaller. You do realize that she fits a certain profile."

"Yes," he said, "that has occurred to me."

"Does that mean you're going to call the Mothers?"

"Do you think I should?"

"If one of their gals is involved in this thing, I think you damn well better. I mean . . . who knows the knights better than Lilith and her secret society of psycho bitches?"

Despite everything, Church smiled. "I may actually tell her you said that."

Aunt Sallie shrugged. "I've called her worse things over the years." She leaned forward, forearms resting on her knees.

Church pressed a button on his phone. "Gus? Pack a go-bag and meet me on the roof. The situation in Iran is going south on us."

As he sat back, he caught Aunt Sallie's cocked eyebrow.

"You going over there to hold Ledger's hand?"

"Hardly. I want to have a face-to-face with Lilith."

"Wear armor."

They regarded each other for a moment, sharing without word all of the implications that were unfolding before them.

"Have you told Ledger?" asked Aunt Sallie quietly. "Have you told him what he's really facing over there?"

Mr. Church's eyes were flat and dead behind his tinted lenses.

"No," he said. "He's scared enough as it is."

Chapter Forty-Seven

The call with Church did not exactly have the effect I was looking for. I wanted support, some fresh intel, and a clear direction. Instead he tried to scare the crap out of me—and maybe succeeded more than I'd ever let him know.

I sat on the floor of the deserted living room and checked Ghost again. He was not severely injured, but he probably needed at least a full day to shake off that Taser. So far I hadn't given him ten minutes.

When I got to my feet and clicked my tongue for him to follow, he looked at me with huge eyes filled with equal parts hurt and disgust.

"Don't look at me like that," I told him. "We're fugitives. No rest for the weary. Miles to go before we sleep, and all that."

Nothing.

"Cobbler wouldn't sissy out on me." Cobbler was my aging house cat. He and Ghost had failed to bond. Spectacularly.

As Ghost finally hauled himself to all fours he gave me a look that could have chiseled my name on a tombstone.

I smoothed my clothes and ran my fingers through my hair, but I knew I still looked like crap. We slipped out the door and began heading toward the CIA safe house.

Even with a clean face and shirt, I looked like a street person, and I had a limping dog with blood on his fur. Not exactly the definition of non-descript, but as I walked I muttered to myself, reciting snatches of popular Persian songs and occasionally twitching my face and shoulder muscles. Even here, where suspicious characters are often questioned, no one likes to initiate contact with a disheveled man who is speaking to himself while twitching. People tend to pointedly ignore you, which is what I wanted. When anyone came too close I asked them for money, which usually guarantees that they quicken their steps while pleading poverty. A few threw blessings at me, which, hey . . . I took, all things considering. Twice people gave me money.

It's a weird world.

Ghost and I kept moving.

Interlude Two

Jaffa, The Holy Land
September 1191 C.E.

Sir Guy LaRoque waited while the little priest read through the document. They stood in a shaded courtyard of the Jerusalem hospital that was the local headquarters of the Knights Hospitaller. No other of the knights were around. Their only company was a sun-drowsy wasp that drifted through the shadows under the fig trees.

Finally the priest smiled as he sharpened his gaze on Sir Guy.

"Have you considered the consequences of what you are asking of me?"

Sir Guy half bowed. "I have. But weighed against what we stand to gain, now and in future years, I—"

The priest held up a hand to halt a repeat of the argument.

"You come here, to a sanctified and sacred hospital dedicated to the treatment of those wounded in God's own Crusade, and ask me, a priest, to willingly break the seal of the confessional."

"No, Father, that is not what I ask. To break the seal would be to share with another person that which was said to God through you, the confessor. I do not want to know the secrets of my brother crusaders. I would not ask such a thing. I ask only that you consider what you have heard, and to balance it against what needs to be done to protect our holy church. I ask that these insights guide you in the selection of men—righteous Christian men—who will join with us in this *new* crusade."

"You propose a crusade of secrets and lies."

"They are only lies if you disagree with our viewpoint. We have discussed this many times, Father, and each time you *did* agree with me. Do you say now that you lied before? Or has fear stolen away your faith in your own opinion?"

The priest turned, not quickly, not in anger, but slowly and with a calculated deliberation that was far more threatening. As he did so, his eyes seemed to change and Sir Guy nearly took a backward step. The color seemed to shift from gray to a swirl of greens and browns. It was certainly a result of the priest's movement through the sunlight and shadow, but it was momentarily unnerving.

"Softly now," said the priest, "for there are snares and nettles in the grass around your feet. Do not let ill-chosen words lead you to take a painful misstep."

Sir Guy placed a hand over his heart and bowed again. A deeper bow this time, held longer, the demonstration of apology and humility. "Have I offended, Father, then I am truly sorry. Before God and your holiness, I beg forgiveness for rude and rash words, poorly chosen and hastily spoken."

He felt a touch on his head. The priest's thin fingers caressed the brown curls that twisted out from under the silk cap.

"Peace, my son," murmured the priest. "Look at me."

Sir Guy slowly straightened, almost afraid to see that unnatural swirl of colors in the cleric's eyes, but what he saw was the same golden brown he had known for years.

"Thank you, Father."

"My son . . . this undertaking . . . it is with the consent and cooperation of the infidel and heretic Ibrahim al-Asiri? Cousin and private advisor to Saladin, enemy of God? You have made a preliminary bargain with a representative of the Antichrist on earth?"

"He is a Saracen, to be sure, but——"

"Yes or no, my friend?" asked the priest. "Did you enter into an agreement with Ibrahim al-Asiri?"

"I did. In the name of God and for my love of the Church, I did."

The priest took his hand and patted it. "I just wanted you to say it aloud. Plain and not couched in the twisted language of diplomacy which, I must admit, often sounds like the mutterings of the devil. Tell me the truth, Sir Guy, for much hangs on it. If I were to say no——if I threatened to do the terrible things that we both know I *can* do and indeed *should* do to a man who has brought this to me and asked of me what you have asked——would you be willing to kill me?"

Sir Guy said nothing.

"Speak now or I *will* call the guards."

"Yes," croaked the diplomat, though he knew that he could never do such a thing. He could kill an uncle or brother before he killed a priest.

"Then tell me one more thing. If you escaped; if you fled this hospital and the city, if you took a boat to Spain or some other port, if you changed your name and lived forever in hiding . . . would you still want this plan of yours to go forward? Does the substance of this agreement matter more to you than titles, land, wealth, or your own name? Does this agreement matter more to you than your own life?"

"Yes," Sir Guy said again. His throat felt like it was filled with shards of broken pottery.

The priest stepped closer, his face as severe as one of the saints of antiquity. "If I were to call my guards in here and have them strike you down and cut off your head and scatter the worthless pieces of your body to the vultures . . . would you even then want this agreement to move forward?"

Tears broke from Sir Guy's eyes and he buckled slowly to his knees. He drew his sword and let it clatter to the flagstones. His dagger clanged as he dropped that across the sword. Sir Guy bowed his head.

"Yes," he said in a voice that was filled with passion but without hope.

The tears dropped from his face onto the toe of the priest's shoe. A moment later the priest raised his foot and touched the tearstained toe to the tip of the dagger. It lay almost parallel to the sword, but the priest nudged it slowly until it sat crosswise so that the dagger formed the bar of a cross. Or the hilt of a sword. How often Sir Guy had noticed how similar cross and sword were to one another.

"Look at me."

Sir Guy raised his eyes and saw that the priest was smiling. It was not a nice smile. It was like looking at a snake smile, and as his seamed faced wrinkled with the smile, the priest's eyes once more seemed to be as much green as brown. Like the mottled skin of a toad.

"Swear to me, Guy LaRoque, knight of the Sacred Order of Hospitallers. Swear that you will live according to this agreement, now and for all of the days of your life. Swear that you will do everything in your power—everything that your faith and your imagination and your will demands—to insure that the substance of this agreement comes to pass. Swear that to me, now, on your knees, before God."

Sir Guy bent forward and caught a fold of the priest's robe and kissed the hem. "I swear," he said, the words as much a vow as a plea. "I swear before God, to the end of the world and the redemption of my sinner's soul . . . I swear."

"Then rise, Sir Guy LaRoque, knight of the holy Hospital of Jerusalem, protector of the Holy Land, soldier of God. I bless you and sanctify this Holy Agreement and all of its precious secrets. I bless it and God blesses it. Amen."

Sir Guy wept and kissed the priest's hem again before he climbed to his feet. "Thank you, Father. Thank you!"

The priest waved away the gratitude and the tears.

"What do you call this crusade of yours—of *ours*—my son?"

"In truth I have not yet thought of a fitting title. Ibrahim has already given his order a special name. The Tariqa. It is the Sufi word for 'the path.' He will be its first Murshid, its first guide along that path."

The old priest nodded. "We will have to do the same, for you know that you cannot use the name of the Sacred Order of Hospitallers for this cause."

"I confess that I've come up dry on that and—"

"*Ordo Ruber*," said the priest.

"Father?"

"The Red Order. We are born in the blood of Christ, are we not? And it is the blood of sacrifices and martyrs that shall sanctify our cause."

Sir Guy murmured the name, feeling how the words and all of their many possible meanings fit in his mouth. "Yes," he said. "That is perfect. The Red Order."

They stopped in the archway, both of them bathed in purple shadows. Sir Guy's heart was swelling with love and gratitude. He took the priest's hand, bent and kissed the blood red ruby of his ring.

"Thank you," he said. "I thank you with all my heart, Father Nicodemus."

Chapter Forty-Eight

Aunt Sallie and Church were still in his office when the phone rang with an overseas call. "Well, well," he said and showed the display to Aunt Sallie.

Auntie smiled like a happy cat in a canary store. "This should be interesting as all hell."

Church activated the scrambler and speaker.

Without preamble, Lilith demanded, "Have you talked to your agent, Ledger, today?"

"Yes."

"Do you know that he met with Jalil Rasouli?"

"Yes."

"Is he on or off the leash?"

"He has my trust."

"Okay. Good to know, I suppose," she said. Her tone was icy and scalpel sharp. "Word is that Rasouli gave something to Ledger. Care to tell me what it was?"

"Why do you need to know?"

"Because I think Rasouli is playing a game."

"And that would be different from his normal behavior in what way?"

"Don't try to be cute," Lilith said tersely. "Do you know that the new Scriptor of the Red Order is trying to recruit Rasouli as the new Murshid of the Tariqa?"

Church cocked an eyebrow at Aunt Sallie. She shook her head and began tapping keys on the MindReader interface.

"I was not aware of that," admitted Church. "Until today the Order has been off the radar since Baghdad. I am rather surprised to learn that they are active again."

"They never really stopped. The new Scriptor—Charles, the last of the LaRoques—took over after we took his father off the board."

"So that *was* you."

Lilith ignored that. "The Order slowed down for a bit until they could build a list of candidates for a new Murshid. Rasouli's been on the top of that list for a couple of years now."

Aunt Sallie signaled to Church to look at the information on her monitor. Church nodded.

"It's my understanding that Charles LaRoque has been treated for a variety of personality disorders since boyhood," said Church. "Paranoid schizophrenia, bipolar disorder, psychosis. A handful of others. How is he able to run an organization as sophisticated as the Order?"

"The priest."

"Priest?"

"The priest," she said again, emphasizing the word.

"Lilith, you never mentioned a priest to me. Let's remember that I've asked you many times for a complete history of the Red Order and each time you've refused. Actually, each time you never responded at all. So, again I ask, which priest? Who is he?"

There was a pause and when Lilith spoke again her tone changed. Less harsh, more cautious. "When Sir Guy LaRoque founded the Red Order he did so with the blessing of a priest from the Knights Hospitaller. Ever since then, each Scriptor has had a priest as his spiritual advisor."

"And the current priest is part of the Order? And he is managing Charles LaRoque even though the young man is mentally unstable? That suggests that it is the priest who is the de facto head of the Red Order."

"Yes."

"Who is this priest?"

"Arklight has been trying to figure that out for a long time," said Lilith. "There are some anomalies in his file."

"Such as?"

"Such as the fact that when we compare a four-month-old surveillance photo of him it is a perfect match to a photo from 1936 that was part of some church records recovered after the Second World War."

"There are a number of ways to doctor a—"

"And both photos match paintings hanging in churches in northern Italy. One from 1897 and one from 1633."

Aunt Sallie mouthed the words "Oh shit."

"We also have reliable visual confirmation from an agent in Baghdad that the current priest died in the bombing along with Charles's grandfather and the Tariqa council."

"What are you saying?"

"I'm not saying anything, St. Germaine."

"I prefer 'Church' these days. Or 'Deacon,' that still works. I don't really have a connection to 'St. Germaine' anymore. I'm sure we're both adult enough to understand why."

"Why not for once simply use your real name?" groused Lilith.

Church's voice was very cold. "Do you really want to open that door? There are other skeletons in the same closet."

Eventually Lilith said, "No."

"Will you give me the name of the current priest? And the names of any of the others you know to have been associated with the Red Order?"

"You still don't get it," said Lilith. "There is only one name."

"They . . . all adopt the same name?"

"That's one theory."

Church cocked his eyebrow at Aunt Sallie, who parked a haunch on the edge of the table and stared at him over the lenses of her granny glasses.

"Give me the name."

Lilith said, "Father Nicodemus."

Chapter Forty-Nine

On the Streets
Tehran, Iran
June 15, 11:22 a.m.

Ghost and I walked quickly through five or six streets lined with houses that had been left to crumble beneath the relentless Iranian sun. I saw a single sign with a notice about rezoning and impending construction, but it was at least five years old. The only life we encountered there were starving dogs who fled from Ghost's warning growls, and a single vulture who sat on a telephone pole that had long ago been stripped of its wires. The vulture's ugly, naked head swiveled slowly on its scrawny neck, watching us as we walked past.

"Don't get any ideas," I warned the scavenger, and gave him an evil squint that entirely failed to impress him.

A few blocks later we reentered a residential quarter where people still lived, though even here there was a sense of life fading to dust. I knew from my travels that the typical meal in an Iranian home was unleavened bread and lentils. That's it. Animal protein was a rarity. I wanted to sneer about it and speculate on how often the ayatollahs had lamb or chicken; but I'm from Baltimore. I've seen American poverty at its worst, and as the richest nation on earth we're the last ones who should throw stones about allowing poverty and starvation within our own borders.

There were a handful of cars, mostly junkers that were held together by rust and need. But one car caught my eye. It was also beat up but it didn't labor to make it down the block; and I saw it three times. Twice on streets that paralleled the one I was on, and once idling at a light a block ahead. My route may have been random, but I paid close attention to cars and people; and one of the tricks is looking down a cross street when you reach a corner to see what cars are moving along at your pace a block or two over.

Spotting the same car three times could have been a coincidence. Kim Kardashian's boobs could be real, too, and that's about as likely.

When I got to the next block, I cut through an alley, running only as fast as Ghost could manage. At the end of the alley, I went through a couple of backyards and then a side yard which took me back to the street just as the little sedan drove past. I was in deep shadows and the driver was looking slowly side to side to check the faces of pedestrians on a moderately busy market street.

The driver was a woman.

I could not tell much because she wore a chador, but her eyes were intelligent, intense and, except for heavy makeup, they did not look even remotely Middle Eastern. Northern Italian at best.

"Violin," I said, and I knew that I was right. My own Sniping Beauty. And as I murmured her name she turned in my direction, but I was in shadows and the traffic gave her no room to stop.

She could not have heard me. No way.

I opened my cell phone and called Bug, giving him the make, model, and license plate number of Violin's car.

"Whoa!" Bug said as soon as he ran it. "This is really weird. I got a screen pop-up that says all inquiries for this plate number are to be directed internally. Here, I mean. The DMS. The pop-up is initialed *D*."

D. For Deacon.

Church.

"Put him on the line," I demanded.

"I can't," said Bug, "he's on a conference call with somebody overseas. Don't know who and he's marked his line for 'no intrusion.'"

"Then make goddamn sure I'm his next call," I growled, and hung up.

Violin's car was gone by the time I stepped out of the alley with Ghost lumbering along beside me. A few people threw me annoyed looks. Iran had weird rules about dogs on the street. I ignored them.

As we picked our way through the crowds of shoppers, I kept one eye on the cars, watching to see if Violin circled back. Then I froze. Another car drifted along, and the driver, much like Violin, was looking side to side to scan the pedestrians. It wasn't my guardian angel. It was a man, and when he turned my way I saw a gaunt face and red rat eyes staring through the glass.

A Red Knight.

Christ.

I darted out of the flow of traffic and stood in the dense shadows under the broad awning of a big vegetable stand. The car rolled along, and the head moved back and forth, and I held my breath. Then it was gone in the long flow of traffic that vanished into the heat haze. He hadn't spotted me.

"Sheeez," I breathed.

I was becoming increasingly paranoid. It felt like there was nowhere to go, no place, not even a street corner, where I could catch my breath. It was getting hard to catch my breath and that had nothing to do with the relentless heat.

The vegetable seller glanced at me and offered a handful of figs. I shook my head, and with a word to Ghost, turned and headed a different way. We needed to get off the street right now. The CIA safe house was close.

We kept our heads down and melted into the crowd.

Interlude Three

Sir Guy LaRoque and Father Nicodemus sat at the end of a long rectangular table made from a massive and ornate wooden door that had once hung in a Jewish temple. The temple was now in ashes, its treasures parceled out among the priests and senior knights of the Hospitallers.

There were a dozen seats at the table. Nine knights sat there, and the rest were minor priests of Nicodemus's choosing. Each of them had sworn the same oaths, each had sealed their oaths with the tip of a heated knife blade.

Without looking up, Nicodemus said, "Do you know this story, Sir Guy? The binding of Isaac?"

The Frenchman hedged. "Perhaps not as well as I should—"

Nicodemus waved away the excuse with a gentle movement of his hand. "There are valuable lessons in the Bible's older books." He tapped the carving of Abraham with a long fingernail. "This one in particular. Abraham, a holy man, was commanded by God to bring his son to Mount Moriah, and there to build a sacrificial altar and sacrifice Isaac upon it. Abraham did as he was told. He built the altar and bound his son to it, drew his knife, and was ready—despite his breaking heart—to kill Isaac to prove his devotion to God. However, before the knife could plunge down, an angel appeared and stayed his hand, directing him to sacrifice a nearby ram instead."

As he spoke the men seated around the table grew quiet so they could hear the story. A few stood to better see the carving. Nicodemus nodded approval.

"The whole drama," he continued, "had been staged to force Abraham to prove beyond question his steadfast devotion to God."

Two of the priests murmured "Amen," which was picked up and echoed by the knights. However Nicodemus's next words silenced them. "Or so Abraham *told* everyone."

He looked at the men, each in turn, and the molten gold color of his eyes seemed to swirl with shadows. "Personally, I have sometimes doubted whether the story was fairly reported. After all, except for the boy, who was traumatized and confused, there were no credible witnesses." No one said a word. No one dared. "The power of the story is immeasurable. Because of it Abraham became the father of the Israelites, the father of us all in many ways. He became a leader whose right to lead was bestowed upon him by God. *Directly* by God. And why? Because of the power of his devotion, a devotion so steadfast that he would have slaughtered his own son."

The others nodded but said nothing.

"As I sat waiting for our brotherhood to gather," continued the priest, "I pondered this story, as I have oftentimes pondered it. We know firsthand that the histories being written about our Crusades are often at odds with the facts, but seldom at odds with the truth." He paused, eyes intense. "With the most useful version of the truth."

A wealthy knight halfway down the table said, "Surely, Father, there is only one truth. Everything else is . . ."

His voice trailed off as Nicodemus leaned forward. "Doesn't that depend on who is telling that truth, and who is listening?" Nicodemus allowed them to ponder that. "I have long ago accepted that history of *any* kind may be only a version told to suit the listener and serve the teller. Like the story of Abraham and Isaac. While we can understand and fully appreciate the effect of this story upon all of the generations that followed, we liberated thinkers are now *called* to look at the actual events. We can wonder what Abraham's true feelings were for Isaac. He could as easily have despised the boy. Or found him bland and uninteresting. Or, if—as some church scholars insist—Isaac was a grown man in his thirties at the time of the sacrifice, then the whole event might have been concocted by father and son. Certainly the result was that their line became *the* bloodline of the Jews. To tell you the truth, I rather like the idea that it was an agreement between them. It shows high intelligence and careful planning and demonstrates, to us in particular, the power that can be harvested from such courses."

"But you say that it might all be a lie," insisted the youngest man at the table, a priest who was the brother of a powerful knight.

"Yes," agreed Nicodemus, "a lie, but a lie with a purpose. A lie that guided the course of a nation, shaped the future of a people. A lie that, through the blood and history of the Jews, allowed for Christianity and Islam to be born into this world."

Sir Guy tapped the table with his forefinger. "Yes!" he said emphatically. "And there are two things that are most important about that lie. First, is that it *was* a lie. That is crucial to know. And the second thing is that no one else knows that it's a lie. Even you, Father Nicodemus, cannot and do not know that it was a lie. If proof ever existed it was either hidden away or erased, which is a very good thing to do with such dangerous truths."

The men agreed and a few beat their fists.

Nicodemus smiled his approval.

"And what dangerous and important truths rest with us," he said softly. "Tell me, my brothers . . . how will we write them into the pages of history?"

Chapter Fifty

The Hangar
Floyd Bennett Field, Brooklyn
June 15, 2:55 a.m. EST

"Nicodemus?" repeated Church. "That's very interesting. Is that a first or last name?"

"It's all we have," said Lilith. The speakers on Church's phone were of the best quality, and it sounded like Lilith was in the room with them.

"There have been priests named Nicodemus associated with the Red Order for eight hundred years?"

"Yes."

"And as far as you can determine they all look similar?"

"Disturbingly so."

Church glanced at Aunt Sallie, who nodded.

"Lilith, I just e-mailed you an image file. Take a look at it and let me know if this man is similar in appearance to the priest currently working with LaRoque."

"Opening it now," said Lilith. She made a sharp, disgusted sound. "Yes, that's him. Damn it, if you already know about him why are you grilling me on—"

"We did not know about the priest," interrupted Church. "This photo is from a supermax prison in Pennsylvania, here in the States."

"This man was in prison?"

"Yes. He was arrested at the scene of a multiple murder in Willow Grove, Pennsylvania and later convicted of the murders. The case was built on strong circumstantial evidence but there were no other suspects and he offered no defense."

"This looks exactly like the priest. Exactly. What is his name?"

"Nicodemus."

"When was this? When was he arrested?"

"1996."

"When was he released?"

"Lilith," said Church slowly, "he was not released. He was incarcerated at Graterford Prison until December of last year, at which point he apparently escaped."

"Then it can't be the same man. We have pictures of him from just before the air strike on the presidential palace in Baghdad on March 19, 2003. That's when the old Murshid and the Tariqa high council were killed, along with the current Scriptor's grandfather. So, your man would have been in prison."

"Yes," said Church softly. "Odd, isn't it." He did not phrase it as a question.

"One of us is working with bad intel," growled Lilith, "and I really doubt it's us. Arklight isn't—"

"Please," cut in Church. "No need to sell me on Arklight's capabilities. But there's something more about the prisoner Nicodemus. He was involved in the Seven Kings affair last year. The bombings and other attacks that were part of the Ten Plagues Initiative."

"Hugo Vox?"

"Yes."

"Mother of God."

"Yes."

"Vox knew most of the men who were killed in the Baghdad bombing. He's known the LaRoques all his life."

"I—didn't know that," admitted Church.

Lilith snorted. "You need better sources."

"The DMS often relies on the goodwill of its allies and the exchange of crucial intelligence. Tell, me . . . how is Oracle working out for you?"

The only reply from Lilith was a stony silence.

Aunt Sallie mouthed the words, "Stop dicking around and play the card."

Church sighed and nodded. "Lilith, when I gave you the Oracle system it was with the understanding that it be used to help your cause, and to provide occasional support for my operations."

"That was long before you built the DMS. I have no standing agreement with the Americans."

"You have an agreement with me," Church said quietly. "And with Aunt Sallie."

"Is she listening?" demanded Lilith.

"Yes."

"Bitch."

Aunt Sallie grinned, but said nothing.

"This conversation has made it abundantly clear," said Church, "that you have information that is likely crucial to one of our ongoing operations. I have never used MindReader to intrude into Oracle, and I would prefer not to."

The threat hung in the air.

"No. You tell me what's going on. Why is your man Ledger taking meetings with Jalil Rasouli."

"I want your word that this will be a fair and free exchange, Lilith. No games, okay?"

Instead of answering the question, Lilith said, "The shooter tracking Captain Ledger is my daughter."

Church sat back in his chair and closed his eyes for a moment.

"You put her in the field?"

"Of *course* I put her in the field. That's what she has trained for."

"Have you told her?" asked Church. "Does she know who her father is?"

Lilith took a moment, and when she spoke her voice was bitter. "She knows. Telling her was the cruelest thing I have ever done." She paused. "But I don't need to tell you about breaking a daughter's heart, do I?"

Church sighed again. "That's unkind, Lilith. I do what I do to protect Circe from who and what I am."

"So, she doesn't know who her father is?"

"She knows enough," said Church. "I don't see any benefit in doing her any additional harm."

Lilith snorted. "And now she works for you. Do your people know that she's your daughter?"

"Only those who need to know," he said. "And that topic is closed."

"Very well," said Lilith. "Now tell me about Ledger and Rasouli. What was on that flash drive?"

Church told her.

Chapter Fifty-One

Kingdom of Shadows
Under the Sand
June 15, 11:29 a.m.

"Your son is dead, Father," said Albion, the eleventh of Grigor's sons. "My brother is dead."

Those were the words that still burned in Grigor's mind.

Your son is dead.

Delos. The sixth of his sons to be born without genetic flaw. The sixth to receive Dr. Hasbrouck's genetic therapy.

Delos. Grigor's pride. One of his most trusted warriors. One of the elite even among the Red Knights.

His son.

His son was dead.

Grigor's rage was a terrible thing, but it was not evident. The storms that broke and howled were not physical things, they could not be felt or seen. There was no outward sign of it. Not unless someone could look into the bottomless crimson depths of his eyes.

Even though he wanted so badly to shriek out his fury, to burst listening ears with his cries, he sat in stillness.

LaRoque had made him send one of his sons to his death.

A knight.

One of the *pure* ones.

He sat on his throne there in the bottomless darkness and as the waves of pain washed over him, he endured them. *Welcomed* them. Let them feed the awful fires that burned in his heart. And there, deep down in his personal darkness, those flames grew hotter and more terrible still.

Interlude Four

On the Pilgrims' Road

The Holy Land

November 1191 C.E.

The three monks pushed the pilgrims toward the rock wall as the riders swept down the hill toward them. The ancient fort was little more than fragments of walls and an overgrown courtyard filled with palm trees whose trunks had burst upward through cracked flagstones. It was poor cover, but it was better than standing out here on the sand, waiting for the Saracens to sweep down and slaughter them.

Most of the pilgrims ran, their prayers strangled from their throats by fear. A few of the more devout wavered, caught between their belief that God would protect them and the fear that He might not chose to do so today. One old man stood his ground and held a cross up and out toward the approaching riders as if that was a shield that could turn any sword. His white beard fluttered in the hot wind.

"Go, *go!*" yelled Brother Julius, pushing his shoulder. The old man twisted away from the monk.

"No! I shall not move one inch from the path to Holy Jerusalem, and neither devils nor demons nor the swords of the infidels will—"

His words were struck to silence as a crossbow bolt buried itself to the fletching in his throat. The old pilgrim staggered backward a step, touching his fingers to the line of hot blood that ran down his chest. The sheer impossibility of his own death, of his mortality in the presence of God's grace here on the pilgrims' road, tethered him for a moment to life. His mouth formed the word "No." But the only sound that issued from his throat was the wet gurgle.

The old man sagged to his knees and his head slumped forward but he did not fall over, and Brother Julius marveled at the horror and beauty of it all: the devout traveler ending his pilgrimage in a posture of supplication.

More quarrels hissed through the air and Brother Julius wheeled as the caravan horses began to scream when the steel-headed missiles tore into their flesh. One reared high and lashed out, striking a nun on the cheek and snapping her neck with a dry-stick crack.

Brother Julius ran then. The other pilgrims were clambering over the ruins of the old fort as arrows struck sparks from the broken stone. The riders—a dozen Saracens in billowing desert cloaks—rode toward them like the horsemen of Saint John. They yipped and yelled and laughed as they fired their last volley of quarrels and then they hooked their crossbows over their saddle horns and drew their swords with a rippling wave of silver.

Brother Julius tried to leap over a fallen pear tree, and the skeletal fingers of a branch snagged the hem of his robe. The cloth caught fast and Julius fell flat on his face with a *whooomph*! Sand puffed up, filling his nose and mouth. He rolled onto his side, gagging and coughing.

Behind him he heard shrill screams and the sound of pain-filled voices pleading to God even as sword blades cut into them. Brother Julius closed his eyes and tried to mutter a prayer between fits of coughing. Soon the screams stopped but the dull-wet sound of steel on flesh continued for almost a full minute.

Then there was silence.

Brother Julius tried to crawl away, but he heard the crunch of a foot on the sand beside his head and he looked up into the face of one of the killers. The man had dark eyes and black hair that fluttered in the breeze. He had a thin mustache and a spiked beard on the point of his chin. He was not smiling; instead a look of sadness was painted over his features. And his face . . . there was something terribly wrong about his face.

"Make your peace with God," said the killer.

The clothes were Saracen, as were the armor and fittings. Even the decorations on the horse that stood nickering behind him were of Saracen make. But the man spoke in French.

"W—why . . . why are you doing this?" demanded the monk. "I don't understand. For the love of God—*why?*"

The killer raised his sword. "It is for the love of God that we do this. And may God have mercy on all our souls."

The sword flashed downward and Brother Julius felt himself detaching from the heat and the sand and his own flesh. He felt himself falling into darkness, into mystery.

The swordsman placed a foot on the monk's chest and pulled, tearing his blade free from where it had wedged deep in the bone. Then he dropped the weapon on the sand by the monk.

He turned and looked at his companions. Two of them were busy with the task of cutting off the heads of the pilgrims. They were laughing as they worked, tossing the heads like children playing with toys.

"Stop it!" growled the swordsman, and the men froze in place, their smiles disintegrating from their faces, their eyes instantly ashamed. He plucked at his robe with disgust. "Do you wear these and then forget who you are?"

Then two men glanced at each other, and then bowed deeply to the swordsman.

"Forgive foolish sinners, brother," said one.

The other, too ashamed to speak, merely nodded.

The swordsman walked over to them and placed his hands on their shoulders. The other warriors sat on their horses, chins buried on their chests, looking troubled and sad and weary.

"My brothers," said the swordsman, "battle is like strong wine even to the best of us. We become drunk on it, and we must guard against that. When we are done, I invite you all to join me in prayers to God in which we will ask for forgiveness of our sins and guidance for all things to come."

The men nodded. The swordsman turned to the men on the horses. They too nodded.

"Then let us be about our task with the reverence to which it is due."

No one spoke, but they nodded again and set to work.

Without laughter or games they collected the heads of the pilgrims and stacked them into a mound in the middle of the pilgrims' road. Another caravan of the faithful was due along this path in less than half a day. They set the head of Brother Julius atop the pile. They placed a ring of hands around the mound, and in each hand they placed a holy cross. Then the men formed a circle around the mound and fished for the fittings of their codpieces. Without meeting each other's eyes, they pulled out their penises and urinated on the mound, on the hands, and even on the crosses.

Last of all, the swordsman used a sharp stick to write a curse against all crusaders in the hard-packed dirt by the ruins. He concluded it with a description of how Pope Innocent III sodomized young boys and sheep. It was a filthy description, but it looked almost elegant when written in the flowing Arabic script.

The swordsman was weeping as he flung the stick away from him as if it was covered in offal. He stripped off his Saracen robes and folded them into a tight bundle before shoving them roughly into a saddle bag. He stood for a moment letting the wind dry the sweat-heavy dark brown hooded cape with a white cross embroidered on the left shoulder. The cross was not the plain outline of long post and short crosspiece, but was instead made to look like a dagger laid across a longsword, with both overlaying a red circle. The other men also shed their disguises to stand revealed. They stood in a circle around the devastation they had caused, and each of them bowed their heads in prayer.

"God forgive us," murmured the swordsman, leading the prayer. "And God grant that the pilgrims see and understand what they *must* understand."

"Amen," said each of the gathered men, and they said it gravely and with honesty.

With that, Sir Guy LaRoque turned away and walked with a heavy heart toward his horse. The trustworthy men of the Red Order of the Knights Hospitaller followed.

It had begun.

Chapter Fifty-Two

The big screen above Circe's MindReader console flashed white and then was filled by the bland face of Mr. Church. Rudy saw Circe's posture immediately stiffen and the muscles at the corners of her jaw tightened. He wondered if Church noticed it too. And if so, did he care.

"Let's jump right in," said Church. "Aunt Sallie tells me that you have problems with the content of the drive. Tell me."

"First," interrupted Rudy, "Is Joe okay?"

"He says so," said Church.

"Yes, but *is* he?"

"I haven't had time to personally give him a physical, Dr. Sanchez."

Rudy held his ground. "I expect a more complete answer as soon as possible."

"Noted," Church said with a small twitch of his mouth.

"What do we know about the nukes?" said Circe.

Church smiled faintly. "Based on the photos Rasouli provided, they appear to be Teller–Ulams. We're running extensive searches through intelligence agencies in thirty countries to see if we can get a line on who might have built them."

"Can't a person simply go online and download instructions for making them?" asked Rudy.

"You watch too many movies, Doctor. These are sophisticated and complex machines, and it takes a great deal of skill, the proper equipment, and genuine experts to do it right. From the photos it's clear that the casings are commercially manufactured, or rather were during the Cold War. These casings are late 1980s, and less than five hundred of this design were made."

"Five hundred?" echoed Rudy.

"A conservative estimate places the number of active nukes in the world at eight thousand," said Circe.

"That estimate is very conservative," said Church. "We know who bought this model openly or through standard military appropriations. We have decades of intelligence and, in some cases, mutual sharing of information. My guess is that we will find that most or all of those devices will be accounted for: still active, mothballed, or dismantled and the parts tracked. The problem is complicated by the fact that fifty-six of these devices were in the Republic of Kazakhstan, and after it became separated from Russia, we have not been able to verify the location or disposition of a third of those devices. This has become a typical, though increasingly frightening, state of affairs since the end of the Cold War."

"There's a second problem," added Circe. "Most of the superpowers have many more devices than have ever appeared on inventories, because they do not want them counted. Nuclear arms limitations agreements, as well intentioned as they are, have driven some countries into policies of secrecy that are truly frightening."

"So what does that mean for us?" asked Rudy. "In this case, I mean?"

"It should give us a few leads but we can't count on it taking us directly to a source," replied Circe. "Or to a buyer, if these things are black market items."

"Exactly." Church selected a Nilla wafer but did not take a bite. "This might—and I do mean *might*—help us eventually find the source of the bombs, but I'm not optimistic about that leading us to where all of the bombs currently are. We still only have probable locations on the first four. That kind of ferret work is time-consuming, and I doubt we have that kind of time. In the short term I am positioning our teams to move in and attempt to seize control of them and de-arm them."

The word "attempt" hung in the air like a bad smell.

"And if we can't?" asked Rudy.

"I have a number of experts working on developing various practical scenarios for how this could play out, including, unfortunately, a worst-case scenario."

"Worst-case meaning what?" asked Rudy. "Tell me that your concern is the human population of the region and not the oil fields."

Church said nothing, and his eyes were invisible behind his tinted glasses, but Rudy felt the impact of his stare.

"*Lo siento*," Rudy said, and placed his hand over his heart and half bowed.

Church shook his head to erase the gaffe from the conversation. He turned to focus on Circe. "How are you coming along with a list of potential instigators?"

She sighed and shook her head. "We simply don't have enough information to go on. We need to know more than we do or we're shooting in the dark."

"I agree," said Church, nodding. "Now give me what you have."

Circe told him about the concerns she and Bug had with the "damage" to the flash drive.

"I think we can all agree that Rasouli doctored it," Church said with a cold little smile. "What else?"

"The *Book of Shadows* and the *Saladin Codex*," said Rudy. "We've made some progress there." They told him about the Voynich manuscript.

"Yes," Church said, nodding. "I've heard of it. Have you been able to determine what it is, though? Voynich or the *Book of Shadows*?"

"Not so far," admitted Circe. "I've been going through the research done at Yale, at U of P, and elsewhere, but it's all theories. No one has cracked it yet."

"And those two extra pages?"

Circe shrugged. "Dead end, so far."

"What about the other book, the *Saladin Codex*? It's my understanding that it's an annotation and attempted refutation of *Al-Kitāb al-mukhtaṣar fī hīsāb al-ğabr wa'l-muqābala*. Does that suggest anything?"

Circe nodded, translating the name slowly, tasting the words. "'The Compendious Book on Calculation by Completion and Balancing.' Completion and balancing. Interesting."

"I thought so, too," said Church.

Rudy did not see the connection. "What does that suggest?"

"In terms of symbolism, it suggests a number of things," said Circe. "The desire for a return to order. Or, in different terms, to the 'correct' and precise way things should be. In the current Middle East situation, there are several clashing interpretations for the 'way things should be.' The Jews say the Holy Land is theirs, and they can make a good argument for it, from their perspective based on the length of time during which they occupied those lands, the whole 'chosen people' thing. Then there's the Christians who believe that the Holy Lands rightfully passed to them with the birth and, more significantly, the trial, execution, and resurrection of Jesus. Some groups actively believe that the Jews forfeited any rights to those lands when they brought Jesus to Pilate for trial." She took a breath. "And Islam, though a comparatively younger religion, believes that God specifically handed over the lease for those lands to them through Mohammed. Since there have been Arab peoples there for thousands of years, they, too, can make a good claim for possession."

"Not to mention the tensions ignited when the nation of Israel was founded," said Church. "And the deepening crisis when oil was discovered under the sands."

"Which brings in Europe and America," said Rudy.

"And Asia. China and Japan are major clients of OPEC."

"Balance," mused Rudy sourly. "What about completion?"

"In this context," said Church, "I find the word deeply troubling. It suggests an end to things. An endgame, perhaps."

"Nukes would accomplish that," said Circe.

"How?" asked Rudy. "Beyond simply blowing things up."

"You know the saying 'fire purifies'?" asked Circe. "If the oil fields were destroyed and the land laid waste by radiation, there could be no further conflict over there."

"What are we discussing here?" asked Rudy with a crooked smile. "A doomsday cult?"

Circe wasn't smiling.

"*Madre de Dios*," breathed Rudy.

Chapter Fifty-Three

CIA Safe House #11
Tehran, Iran
June 15, 12:29 p.m.

Once we were past the markets, the streets became empty and quiet. No human or car traffic. No sign of Violin, no sign of the Red Knight, but I didn't like the vibe. The atmosphere was supercharged with tension. I knew that a lot of it was nerves. This whole thing was freaking me out. Truly and deeply.

Haven lay right up the street, though, and I was already starting to breathe easier.

The best safe houses were run by the CIA. They'd been at this longer and they spent a lot of time developing teams to run and oversee the locations. The one Ghost and I headed to was at the fringe of a garment district, with an open lot on one side and a hardware store that was closed on the other. A "For Sale" sign was hung in the window of the store, and I suspected the Company owned that as well.

The safe house was occupied by husband and wife agents. They were a real married couple recruited years ago. Taraneh and Arastoo Mouradipour. Midthirties. His cover was a textile salesman, and she was floor manager for a small factory that made children's clothes.

Ghost and I walked past the house twice, once from across the street heading west, then on the same side as the house going east. Everything looked normal and quiet. A ten-year-old blue Paykan was parked outside, its paint job faded by sand and heat, several rust spots coated with primer. The only other vehicles in the area were a pair of white vans parked in the lot of a telephone installation company a few blocks away.

We walked all the way around the block and then cut down the alley that led to the open lot. I walked along the side of the house. Back door and side windows were intact. Everything looked calm, which is exactly what I wanted to see. Calm sounded pretty good to me. I needed a bath, food, a first aid kit and a chance to make a private call to Church. There was so much I needed to tell him.

When we reached the front of the house I went to the door and knocked.

Ghost, who was still sluggish, flopped down on the step and looked like he was about to go to sleep. I was getting worried about him. There was no way to tell how much damage the Taser had done, but Ghost was definitely not himself; his senses were clearly dulled and his energy almost bottomed out.

There was no immediate answer. I knocked again.

The protocol was to knock no more than three times. After that you walk away and try another safe house. I didn't want to walk into another house filled with blood and death, so I was willing to split if this didn't play out. The next closest was a convenience store half a mile from here.

However, I doubted Ghost had that much energy in him. I could sympathize. That goon in the hotel had really rung my chimes and now that the adrenaline was wearing off I could feel it.

I was about to knock a final time when I heard the lock click. The door opened a half inch and I saw a woman's eye peer at me through the crack.

"Yes?" she asked.

"May I speak with Mr. Pourali?"

That was the current code, and it changed every few days.

"Who is calling?" she asked, right on cue.

"Mr. Hosseini."

"Please come in," she said, stepping back and pulling open the door.

I clicked my tongue for Ghost, who jerked awake and scrambled to his feet. He followed me inside.

"Thank you," I said to the woman as she closed the door.

Ghost froze in place and let out a single sharp bark of warning, which was two seconds too late.

The woman produced a small black automatic from under her robes and pointed it at my face.

Chapter Fifty-Four

CIA Safe House #11
Tehran, Iran
June 15, 12:35 p.m.

"Inside or I'll kill you where you stand," she snapped, and she said it in English. Not good English, but good enough.

Ghost was trembling, caught between the impulses of his instincts and his training. I was pack leader and I hadn't given the command to hit.

"January," I said. It was today's clarification code word. If this was all a big mistake then the code word would dial everything back to normal.

She said, "Shut up."

Not the code reply I was hoping for.

I heard a floorboard creak behind me, and Ghost growled in time to warn me . . . but not in time to protect himself. As I whirled two men rushed at me through the doorway to the living room. They were not Red Knights, but that was the only consolation. The first threw a handful of powder in my face, blinding and gagging me; the other hurled a weighted metal-mesh net over Ghost. On another day, Ghost would have dodged the net and torn the man's throat out, but the Taser had blunted all of his edge. Ghost cringed, caught in fear and indecision, and the net slapped down around him. He howled in anger, thrashing and twisting to get away from it, but his struggles only wrapped the thing around him. He tripped over it and crashed to the floor.

I saw this through a haze of powder.

I tried to paw the stuff out of my eyes. It was cloying and thick, but it didn't seem like poison and it didn't actually hurt. Then the guy who threw it stepped in and planted a mother of a punch into my solar plexus. The sucker punch slammed all of the air out of my lungs and dropped me to my knees. I honked and wheezed and gasped like a salmon on a river bank. The pain was enormous but the lack of air was ten times worse. I could not breathe.

"Shoot him!" barked one of the men, and I felt the cold barrel of the gun jab me in the back of the neck.

"Say the word, Victor . . ." growled the woman. She had a low, nasty voice. She wanted to pull that trigger.

"No!" cried the other man—who I assumed was Victor—and there was the sharp sound of flesh on flesh as he slapped the woman's hand away. "We have to be sure."

They weren't speaking Persian. They spoke broken English and it sounded like each of them had a different native accent, but I was in no condition to analyze it.

Ghost whined and barked, but he couldn't come to my rescue. Between the net and the Taser, he was done. I was on my hands and knees, blinking and gagging, my whole body heaving with silent convulsions.

The first man bent close to me. "You can see it, Victor! Look how he reacts. The powder is already doing its work."

As I fought to control my traumatized diaphragm I struggled to process what they were saying.

The stuff they threw in my face definitely wasn't poison or some kind of knockout drug. From the smell I think it was *garlic*. Regular, fine-grain, powdered garlic. Not exactly the kind of thing the bad guys usually throw. What was their follow-up? Tomato sauce and a bay leaf?

I managed to suck in a tiny bit of air with a sound like a deflating bag-pipe.

"Let me kill him, Victor," begged the woman. "For God, for the cause . . ."

"No! And point that damn gun somewhere else before you shoot one of us."

Fingers knotted in my hair and then my head was jerked backward. The motion, violent as it was, helped open my airway and I gasped in a huge gulp of air like a swimmer coming up after staying underwater a minute too long.

The man named Victor—obviously the leader—touched the tip of something sharp and heavy under my chin and shifted around so that he could study my face. All I could see was a bleary version of his face. Heavy Slavic features and a thick moustache.

"I . . . don't know . . . who you are . . ." I wheezed, "but you got the . . . wrong guy."

"Shut up," he snapped. I could see beads of sweat popping out on his brow and running down his cheeks. It wasn't hot in the room—he was scared. Of me? Or of who he thought I was? He said to his companions, "Nadja, cover him. Be careful with that gun, but if he moves . . . blow his head off."

The woman, Nadja, shifted around and pointed the pistol at me in a two-hand grip.

"Iñigo, be ready with the hammer."

Hammer? Christ, that scared me more than the gun. A gun would at least be quick.

Victor squatted down and leaned so close to me I could smell his breath. It reeked of garlic and tobacco. I wanted to make a joke, something about being mugged by a cooking class, but somehow I didn't think I had the audience for it. I held my tongue and tried to regulate my breathing.

"He doesn't look like one of them. His eyes are blue."

"Then he's wearing contact lenses," Nadja fired back. "Peel them off, you'll see."

The second man, Iñigo, still held my hair, so I was unable to move away as Victor placed his rough fingertips on my face. Thumb below my left eye, two fingers on my eyebrow, and then he slowly spread them apart, widening my eye. His other hand held the weapon against the soft underside of my chin. I did not know what they intended to do—blind me, stab me, shoot me, or pummel me with a hammer, but they were poised and tense and ready. And I was still recovering from the body blow. I was in deep shit and I could feel sweat greasing my own face.

Victor leaned even closer, and now I could feel the heat of his breath on my cheek and my eye.

"No," he said slowly, dragging the word out in apparent surprise. "No, he is not wearing contacts."

"Oh, you're a blind fool, Victor," snarled the woman. "Let me do it—"

"Hush!" Victor growled and the woman faltered.

Iñigo kicked me in the hip. "Cut an eye out and take a closer look. He's one of *them*."

"Hush!" ordered Victor. He repeated the eye-widening procedure with my right eye, frowning as he did so. "See? He is not a knight."

Ah, I thought, and I realized what he was looking for. My guardian angel sniper called the killer at the hotel a knight, and that goon with the fangs had worn weird contact lenses. As soon as I thought that I realized that it was wrong. The knight would have been wearing the horror-show contact lenses over his real eyes. Victor and the others were checking my eyes to see if my normal eyes were color contacts over . . .

My mind stalled at that.

Over *what*? Did they think that the knights really had blazing red eyes with slitted pupils? Or . . . was that really true of the knights?

If so . . .

I will rip your throat out and drink your life.

Holy shit. What the hell was I into here?

Church had warned me that I got off lucky when I fought the knight.

"Please," I said, my voice strained because they had my head pulled back so far, "I'm not who you think I am."

Victor's frown turned into an ugly scowl. "Oh yes? And what do we think you are?"

"I have no idea . . . but whatever it is, you're wrong. Why don't we talk about this?"

"Victor, don't listen to him," warned Nadja. "He will try to control your mind."

I expected Victor to rebuke her for the silliness of that comment, but instead I saw doubt and fear insinuate their way onto his features. He pulled his hand back and forked the sign of the evil eye at me and fired off a fragment of prayer, "O Lord, protect with Your right hand those who trust in Your name. Deliver them from the evil one, and grant them everlasting joy."

Then he used his thumb to peel back my upper lip so he could examine my teeth. The others bent to look as well. Iñigo grunted.

"No," stated Victor, "he's human enough."

Human?

"Absolutely," I agreed, though with his fingers in my mouth it came out as "Ahzoluly."

Then Victor turned his head and looked at Ghost, who lay helpless and panting in the net. "And see—he comes with a fetch dog."

Iñigo's grip on my hair eased a bit. "I don't understand this. They said that he was a knight."

"I know," said Victor, licking his thick lips. "But when have you ever seen a knight in the presence of a fetch dog? I mean . . . how *could* that even happen?"

The others said nothing.

Victor straightened. "Krystos will be here any minute. He'll know what's happening. He'll get to the truth."

I really didn't like the way Victor said that. I doubt I was supposed to like it; and it seemed to me that the bad situation I was in was about to get a whole hell of a lot worse.

Whoever this Krystos was, I didn't want to meet him on my knees.

I had Iñigo to my right side holding my hair—though not as tightly as before. Nadja was behind him, aiming past his shoulder at my temple. Victor squatted in front of me, one hand still on my lip and the other holding some kind of spike under my chin. And Krystos and who knew how many others were on their way.

None of the odds were in my favor, and Lady Sniper was nowhere to be seen. I was outnumbered and outgunned; I had no weapons. Why should today be any different?

It was die—or go for it.

I went for it.

Chapter Fifty-Five

I wasn't nice about it, either.

With a bellow of pure rage, I kicked back with all my strength and caught Iñigo in the crotch. He flew backward, arms whipping wide, and his left forearm smashed Nadja across the nose and mouth. She screamed and her finger jerked the trigger, firing a bullet that punched a hole in the wall a foot from Victor's head. Nadja and Iñigo fell together in a screeching tangle of arms and legs. The moment Iñigo's hand released my hair, I darted my mouth forward and bit down hard on Victor's fingers. Bones crunched and he howled in agony. As he jerked his hand away, the spike cut me laterally across the underside of the chin, but then it clattered from his hand.

All of this took place inside one hot second.

I launched myself off the floor at Victor, but my foot slid in the coating of garlic powder they'd thrown at me. My reaching hands missed him by an inch as he backpedaled toward the entrance to the living room.

"*Monstrul!*" he bellowed as he scrabbled inside his coat. I thought he was going for a gun, but he produced a second spike and a second item, a rubber-headed mallet. And a detached part of my brain realized that it wasn't an ordinary spike. It was a piece of polished hardwood that had been lathed down to a deadly point. He raised both items as he dropped into a crouch to meet my charge.

The son of a bitch was going to fight me with a hammer and wooden stake.

This would have been a great time for a flag on the play so we could all sit down and take a moment to find the thread of sanity we'd obviously lost. I mean, seriously—a fucking stake?

"*Monstrul!*" he cried again. "*Monstrul!*"

It was a Romanian word. It means pretty much what you think it means.

He chopped at my chest with the stake while raising the hammer high for a big downward strike.

I slap-parried the hand holding the stake and smashed his nose with a straight jab; the blow knocked his head back, chin high, to expose his throat. I sidestepped and smashed him hard across the Adam's apple with the edge of my wrist. I could feel the cartilage collapse into rubble. Victor's shouts imploded into a whistling wheeze as he tried to find breath that would never be his again.

As he sagged to his knees I tore the stake out of his hand. Now I had a weapon.

Iñigo and Nadja were still disentangling themselves from each other in the cramped hallway. But suddenly I heard voices yelling from outside.

The kitchen door banged open and I heard the yelling of the names of my dancing partners.

The cavalry had arrived. Theirs, not mine.

Two men crowded into the doorway. One man—a big bruiser with a handlebar mustache—had another hammer and stake in his hairy fists; the other was an Irish-looking guy with no jacket and a shoulder holster over a black T-shirt. He was reaching for his nine millimeter.

I was out of time.

Screw this. If I was going to go down, then I was going down hard.

I still had the stake, so I kicked Mustache Pete in the nuts and drove the stake into Irish Bob's chest. It punched through his pectorals but jammed to a stop on the ribs, so I hammered it deep with the flat of my palm. I wasn't aiming for the heart—partly because that's protected by the sternum and partly because I wasn't as batshit crazy as these sons of bitches—but the spike sank to half its length in his left lung.

I let go of the stake and elbow-smashed him across the mouth which sent him sprawling into Mustache Pete, who seemed to be shaking off my kick too damn fast.

Incredibly the Irish guy wasn't dead. He snaked out a desperate hand and grabbed my sleeve as he fell and that jerked me forward off balance so that we slammed into Mustache Pete and the three of us fell together in a twisted, spinning comedy of flailing limbs.

My body was under the pile, with Irish Bob on top of me. The impact crushed us together and drove the stake all the way into him. He died on impact, his body going immediately slack with a terminal exhalation. Unfortunately, his sudden dead weight pinned me to the floor with Mustache

Pete half on top of us both. The combined weight of both men drove half the air out of my lungs. Irish Bob's holstered pistol was pinned between us, with my right hand twisted into the press at a painful angle. To make it worse, Mustache Pete was trying to stab me with the stake. He had no clear angle, but he kept chopping at me, mostly hitting his dead friend. His face was a mask of confusion, insanity, and horror, and as he chopped he continually whimpered a word I didn't know.

"Upier . . . Upier . . ."

I heard Iñigo's voice as he and Nadja tried to make sense of the melee on the floor.

"Mihai," shouted Nadja. "Move . . . move! Let me get a shot."

Mihai must have been Mustache Pete—and he ignored Nadja and kept stabbing at me with manic energy. It was a terrifying thing, and I had only one free hand to fend him off, but at the same time his body blocked Nadja's aim.

Out of the corner of my eye I saw Iñigo moving in at an angle. He bent and grabbed one of Irish Bob's ankles and started pulling him off of me. My legs were the only part of me that was free, so I kicked Iñigo in the kneecap. It wasn't the best angle, but, on the other hand, at most angles the knee is a pretty good target—strong as hell when it's bent and locked, fragile as a breadstick when it's straight. I caught him flat on the kneecap and his leg snapped with a gunshot *crack*.

His scream was ear-splitting—and then he collapsed right onto my other leg, and lay there twisting and screaming.

Shit.

Mihai rolled off of me and decided on a new plan. He crouched and sprang at me, holding the stake in both hands and plunging it down-ward with all his strength. There was nowhere I could go, no way I could avoid that deadly attack.

But Nadja chose that exact second to try to shoot me in the face. The timing was absolutely perfect. For me. Totally sucked for Mihai. I think he realized it, but by then he was already in the air and there was nothing he could do about it. Nadja's first bullet blew his jaw off, splashing my face and throat with hot blood.

Nadja screamed in panic, and, as many people inexperienced with guns often do, she kept pulling the trigger. Bullet after bullet chopped into Mihai and dug holes in the floor right next to my head. The impact warped the arc of Mihai's lunge, and he twisted as he went down, his shoulders and ruined face hitting the floor a foot from my cheek, his body flopping over so that he landed in a heap and did not move.

Nadja was still screaming when the slide locked back on the small automatic.

"Reload! Reload!" yelled Iñigo between shrieks of pain.

I heard a car screech to a stop in back. More people.

Iñigo shouted toward the sounds. "Krystos!"

Goddamn it.

Nadja fished in her clothes for a new magazine, dropped it, picked it up with trembling fingers. All the time she babbled to herself. "Oh merciful God . . . oh sweet savior . . ."

Iñigo was crawling toward me, or so I thought. Then I saw that Mihai's hammer and stake were right there. I squirmed and fought to get the dead weight off of me. Something hard jabbed me in the ribs and I realized that Irish Bob's pistol was there, caught between us.

As Nadja slapped the magazine into the pistol I gave a great heave and tore the nine millimeter from the clamshell holster. It was a hammerless Glock 17.

Beautiful.

I couldn't clear the body, though, so I buried the barrel against Irish Bob's love handle and fired. The bullet met no appreciable resistance as it punched a hole through the dead man and caught Nadja in the stomach. It stopped her as surely as if she'd hit a wall, but there were footsteps in the kitchen. I fired twice more, hitting her in the sternum and then in the chin as she sagged to her knees.

Iñigo actually stopped trying to stab me and stared with uncomprehending horror at Nadja.

With a growl I kicked my way out from under the bodies and put two rounds into him. Then I rolled onto my stomach as three figures rushed down the hall toward me. Two of them had guns in their hands, but they were pointing chest high, expecting a stand-up fight. From my prone position I emptied the rest of the magazine into them. The Glock carried seventeen rounds. I'd used three on Nadja and two on Iñigo. That gave me twelve bullets to cut these cocksuckers down.

They all went down.

One of them—the guy in front—died right there.

The other two took multiple hits. Arms and legs. I was dazed and hurt and my aim was screwed up, so they lived through it.

That was not going to be a lucky break for them.

Chapter Fifty-Six

CIA Safe House #11
Tehran, Iran
June 15, 12:41 p.m.

I scrambled to my feet and rushed the men in the hall. They were in a groaning heap and covered with blood. One of them tried to bring up his pistol, but I threw my own empty weapon at him, catching him in the face. While he was screaming, I broke his wrist and took the pistol from him. That jacked his screams up another notch. I wasn't in the mood for it, so I kicked him in the face until he stopped screaming, and then I dragged him by the hair into the living room.

The second survivor wasn't screaming, but he was conscious. Barely. He tried to crawl away, but his attempt was feeble. Once I disarmed him, I grabbed his ankle and pulled him out and dropped him next to his friend.

I had no cuffs and no rope. On the living room table was a big leather valise of the kind doctors used to carry. I fished in it and found various tools, more hammers and stakes, and a roll of duct tape. Nice. A thousand and one household uses.

I used a lot of it on the wrists and ankles of my two prisoners.

One of them—the guy who hadn't screamed—had a pretty bad wound high on his thigh. He tried to use his taped hands to staunch the blood flow, so I tore the headscarf off of the dead woman and made a compress of it, then bound it tightly with the tape. Not a great job, but good enough for now. He watched my eyes as I worked, and from his expression of despair I knew that *he* knew that this wasn't an act of kindness.

Patting the men down produced wallets with local driver's licenses. Even though I was never a cop in Iran I could tell that the IDs were phony. Even so, the name on the conscious guy's license was Krystos Gallikos. The other survivor was Constantin Enescu. A Greek and a Romanian. Add in the Russian broad, the Spanish Iñigo, Irish Bob, and whatever the hell Victor and Mihai were and we had a real League of Nations here.

"You speak English?" I asked Krystos.

He stared at me without apparent comprehension.

I simplified things. I put the barrel of his pistol against his forehead, then bent and whispered in his ear. "Don't fucking move."

He grasped the subtleties of my request and gave me an enthusiastic nod.

Constantin lay in a fetal ball, apparently unconscious.

Out in the hallway Ghost barked weakly. I shoved the gun into my waistband and hurried out to him. He was a mess, totally entangled in the flexible wire net. It took me a couple of minutes to extricate him, and his panicked flailing did not help. I soothed him and spoke quietly, but Ghost had been pushed past his limits. When he was free he crawled toward me and buried his head on my thighs. He let loose a stream of urine that pooled around him.

I bent and kissed his head and told him that he was a good, brave boy. He gave my face a few nervous licks and his body trembled as badly as if he were in an icebox.

In the enclosed hallway the mingled smells of urine, blood, and garlic made a strange, cloying miasma that was completely unpleasant. It felt like horror and defeat. I tried to coax Ghost to follow me, but he wouldn't; so I left him where he was for now.

Back in the living room I squatted in front of Krystos. His face was running with greasy sweat.

"I'll ask this again," I said, and I was mildly alarmed at how reasonable and calm my voice sounded. Given all that had just happened, this was not necessarily a good thing. "Do you understand English?"

He gave a stubborn shake of his head that allowed me to decide if he was saying no or telling me to go piss off. Behind me I heard a groan and whirled around. It was frigging Iñigo, still alive with two bullets in his chest cavity. Tough son of a bitch. He was crawling like a slug toward a pistol that lay on the floor a yard away. I went over and kicked the pistol under the couch.

Iñigo turned his head and glared up at me with total hatred. I stepped over and straddled his body, staring down at him from my full height. I looked from him to Krystos and back again.

"Who tipped you off about this place?" I asked him.

"Fuck you!" Iñigo growled and tried to spit at me.

"Wrong answer," I said and shot him in the head.

I made sure I was looking into Krystos's eyes when I did it. Sometimes you need to use visual aids to really make your point.

Krystos screamed and tried to crawl backward into the wallpaper. There is a difference between seeing death in combat and seeing an execution of someone you know. I lowered the pistol and walked back to Krystos and hunkered down in front of him.

"Okay," I said into an ugly silence. "Let's try this again. Do you understand English?"

Krystos whimpered and forked the sign of the evil eye at me with his bloody hands. I rang the barrel of the pistol off the top of his head. Not too hard, but hard enough.

"Last try," I suggested. "English?"

All at once the fight drained out of him. Maybe he finally grasped the fact that he was totally helpless and I owned his life. He kept staring at what was left of Iñigo's head. Without looking at me, he spoke in a tiny voice. "Y—yes. Some. A little."

"Good, now we're getting somewhere," I said with an approving smile. "Are there any more of you fucktards around here? Anyone else in the house?"

His eyes roved around to take stock of all the dead. He shook his head.

I placed the hot barrel against the knee of his undamaged leg. "Be real sure."

He whimpered as he cut a quick look toward the stairs and back. "No. My people . . . are all down here."

I didn't like the way he leaned on "my people" and knew that I was going to have to go upstairs. I sure as hell did not want to.

"Who sent you?"

"W—what?"

I said it slower. "Who. Sent. You?"

Now Krystos looked at me, and the expression that washed over his face was one of complete puzzlement. He said, "God."

His tone of voice suggested that he was surprised I didn't already know that.

"What's that supposed to mean?"

"God," he said again, shaking his head.

"You're saying that God sent you to kill me?"

He nodded.

"Do you even know who I am?"

He shook his head. "It does not matter. You are one of them. Upier!"

"Which is what, exactly?"

He shook his head in exasperation, apparently perplexed that I did not know what he was talking about.

"We'll come back to that," I said. "Why does 'God' want me dead?"

Krystos licked his lips and winced at the taste of his own blood. "To . . . stop."

"Stop what? Or who?"

"Evil. Big evil."

I was getting tired of this and it must have shown on my face because he immediately recoiled from me. "No! Please, no!"

"You're jerking me around, friend, and I'm not digging it. You can't be this stupid, so tell me what I want to know or we can up the ante on this game. Who are you people?"

"We are Sabbatarians. We are Sat . . . Sat . . ." and again he fished for the English version of a word but this time he came up with it. "The . . . Saturday People. Our . . . cell . . . was alerted. About you," he said, picking each word with care. "They said . . . you were working with . . . the *Ordo Ruber*. Against God. To . . . kill us all."

I sat back on my heels. "What in the wide blue fuck are you talking about? What are 'Saturday People'?"

Krystos touched his chest then nodded to the dead scattered around the room. "Saturday. All Saturday." He was trying to tell me something but he was clearly playing the wrong song for the wrong audience. His face twisted in fear and frustration. "They said . . . I mean . . . we believed . . . that there were no more . . . like you . . . no more Upierczi left. We thought you were all gone. Years ago. A hundred years. More."

"What do you mean 'like me'?"

He looked away, not wanting to say the word. I used the barrel of the pistol to make him face me again. I repeated my question. He thought about it and finally came up with a word that I did understand.

"*Vampir!*" he whispered.

Oh boy.

It was all so absurd that I almost smiled. Or, maybe I did. I felt my mouth do something ugly and twisted.

"Let me see if I have this straight. You jackasses think I'm a vampire?"

He cringed away from me, but he also nodded.

"Does that mean you think the Red Knights are vampires?"

Another nod.

I will rip your throat out and drink your life.

"Well, that's just fucking peachy, isn't it?" I said with a sigh.

There was a sound and we both turned to see Ghost, weak and trembling, standing in the doorway to the entrance hall. He started to come into the room, but I stopped him with a click of my tongue. Ghost sat down and studied Krystos with savage dog eyes.

A strange expression came over Krystos's face. He looked at me, confused. "Are you . . . *Stregoni benefici?*"

I tried to sort out the translation. "Beneficial witch?"

He gave his head a violent shake. "*Vampir,*" he insisted. "Church *vampir. Vampir* for God."

"Do I look like a fucking vampire, Einstein?" I snapped. Then I sat back on my heels and blew out my cheeks. "And . . . I can't believe I just asked that question."

Krystos continued to stare at me, but now there was a splinter of doubt in his eyes.

"Okay," I said, "here's the game plan. You are going to sit here and not move while I go check the rest of the house. My dog is going to watch you. You do *anything* to my dog, you even look at him crooked, and you're going to find that I'm a lot scarier than a vampire. Are we communicating here?"

Krystos cringed back and tried to melt into the wall. "No . . . !" he gasped. "No hurt. Never hurt white dog . . . fetch dog . . . *fetch!*"

I was getting more confused by the minute. "You want to play fetch with my dog? Really, you want to make a joke now? 'Cause I have to tell you, pal, it's not a great time to jerk my chain."

"No," he insisted, "*fetch* dog. Fetch!"

He searched my face for understanding and obviously found none because I had none to give. He turned his face toward the wall and began muttering prayers.

"You're less than useless," I told him as I got to my feet. "Stay there and shut up. Don't even think about trying to escape. You wouldn't get far and I'll kill you for trying."

He shook his head. Tears ran down his cheeks and dripped onto his shirt. A small part of me wanted to feel sorry for him, hurt and scared as he was, but the rest of me told that part to shut the fuck up.

The house was quiet. I checked the rest of the bodies. They were all dead.

I collected the weapons from the fearless vampire hunters. A couple of guns, some knives, and the hammers and stakes. I looked at those for a moment, still amazed that they were any part of my version of the real world. The stakes were eighteen inches long and lacquered to a high gloss. They hadn't been whittled, either; each one had been turned on a lathe by someone who understood woodworking. There was a long prayer carved into each one. The writing was tiny and I had to squint to read it, turning the stake in a circle to read the Latin that rolled around and around.

Sancte Michael Archangele, defende nos in proelio; contra nequitiam et insidias diaboli esto praesidium. Imperet illi Deus; supplices deprecamur: tuque, Princeps militiae Caelestis, Satanam aliosque spiritus malignos, qui ad perditionem animarum pervagantur in mundo, divina virtute in infernum detrude. Amen.

My Latin is only passable, but I could make out some of it: "Saint Michael the Archangel, defend us in the battle . . ." As far as I could make out it was a prayer against evil. It seemed to fit the agenda for Krystos and his crew, but it explained nothing.

"Joe, old son," I said aloud to myself, "you need to go the hell back to Baltimore. You need to take in an Orioles game, get drunk. Maybe get laid. Either way, you need to get your ass out of this freak show of a country."

How do you process something like this? I mean . . . these guys were actual vampire hunters. Or, to rephrase that, these total whack jobs were taking their shared delusion to an impressive level.

I found a second leather valise in the dining room. It was crammed with more stakes, pouches of garlic powder, jars of pure garlic oil, and bottles of water marked with a black cross. I opened the lid and sniffed. Far as I could tell it was only water. I looked at the cross again and then back to the babbling guy on the floor.

Holy water? I wondered. Well, why not? What the hell else would it be on a day like this? These jokers had the whole official vampire hunter kit.

Okay, I thought, *lots of fruitcakes in the world. People's beliefs are their own, yada yada.*

But why did they think I was a vampire?

Because they think you're a Red Knight, muttered my inner Cop. I thought about the knight. The eyes, the incredible speed and strength. The fangs.

I will rip your throat out and drink your life.

I'll buy a lot of weird shit. I mean, my job kind of depends on a belief in weird, but I'll only walk out onto that ledge as far as science will stretch. I'll do mad scientists and radical gene therapy. Been there, done that.

But . . . *vampires?*

"No fucking way," I said aloud. The echo of my words came back to sting me.

I didn't even know where to go with that speculation. I'm hunting rogue nukes in Iran. These guys are European vampire hunters. There's no couch for both of those things to sit side-by-side on.

"Shut up and check the house," I told myself.

The kitchen was empty, and I saw only two cars parked outside. No guards with them, but then I hadn't expected any. I'd check those later. There was no basement. When I came back into the living room I saw the guy with the leg wound slumped over and for a moment I thought he was dead, but I found a pulse in his throat. He'd simply passed out. Whether from blood loss, shock, or fear I couldn't tell and didn't much care.

At the foot of the stairs I stopped and cocked my head to listen. I was pretty sure that there was no one else here, but "pretty sure" is a damn poor excuse for certain knowledge. So I left Ghost in the hall, pulled the gun, and ran the stairs.

I found Taraneh and Arastoo Mouradipour in the bedroom.

Or, rather, I found what was left of them.

Interlude Five

"Come in," said the priest without turning. "You must be cold."

Sir Guy removed his cloak and drew near to the massive fire that blazed in the stone hearth. The priest's private study was deep within the bowels of the Krak des Chevaliers, and it was always winter down here.

"Draw near to my fire, my son."

Nicodemus always said it that way—"my fire"—and it always mildly unnerved Sir Guy, as if the priest ascribed some special meaning to those words that no one but he appreciated.

Nicodemus picked a poker and began jabbing at the burning logs, repositioning them. Each thrust of the metal rod sent up showers of glowing sparks and dropped the ghosts of ashes onto the stones. "Tell me, my friend, what news do you bring from the agreement?"

"I met with Ibrahim as you directed, Father," said Sir Guy, holding his hands out to the blaze to thaw his fingers. "He is ill, but still strong enough to work. We are nearly finished coding the books. I have four monks working now on the *Book of Shadows*, but Ibrahim does not seem to trust anyone else with what he is calling the *Saladin Codex*."

"He is very secretive," said Nicodemus, though his tone suggested admiration for that quality.

"However I fear for him," said Sir Guy. "His health fails and I believe that it is the work itself that assails him. It seems to be draining the life from him with every page."

"And what sickness do you suppose he has contracted from doing God's work?" asked the priest with asperity.

Sir Guy chose his words carefully. "Ibrahim and all of his Tariqa are very *religious*."

Nicodemus paused to cut him a quick look, then continued to poke at the fire. "Can that not be said of all of us, my son? Did not the two of you conceive this as an expression of your faith and concern for the future of our respective churches?"

"Yes, Father, but when I have doubts and fears about the spiritual *cost* of this, I have you to turn to. You *are* the church to me. Ibrahim has no such guide or refuge."

"Islam has *Istighfar*," countered Nicodemus. "It is one of the five pillars of that faith. The Tariqa confess their sins directly to God—not through man. Have you not heard your friend say '*astaghfirullah*'? 'I seek forgiveness from Allah?'"

"I understand that, Father, but when the Saracens pray for forgiveness they often cite specific sins that were made and the passages of their bible which speak of forgiveness of those sins. His struggle comes from the fact that we have essentially written new pages into the Koran and the Bible."

"Ah," said Nicodemus. "I see. Tell me then, what sins can he not find forgiveness for?"

"Murder of others of his own faith—"

"'Sacrifices,'" corrected the old man. "Murder is an act of hate. We do not hate those we kill. We love them, and in loving them we sacrifice them for the preservation of the church and the glory of God."

Sir Guy took a breath. "Of course, Father. Ibrahim is troubled by having to *sacrifice* those of great faith. Clerics. Their imams. His heart likewise rebels at the desecration of mosques."

"And yet, my son, this is the heart of our Agreement. We will each tend to our own flock and sacrifice our own lambs at the altars of God."

"Yes," said Sir Guy with passion, "and have you not seen how this also hurts our own people? I mean no insult by this, Father, but you do not go into the field with us. You do not see the wounds we open in the flesh of true believers. You do not hear their voices as they cry out to God for protection against monsters; and you do not hear the weeping of our knights in the night, in the dark. Many of our stoutest knights weep like children for the countless lives they've taken. Ibrahim is not the only one who fears for his sanity and his soul."

Nicodemus gave the fire a final jab and then turned, still holding the poker whose tip now glowed dark red. The blaze in his eyes was hotter still. "Is that what you've come here to tell me? Has everyone on both sides lost their nerve, then? I thought our knights were true soldiers of God. Are we to fold our tents so quickly, leaving so much sacred work unfinished?"

"No, Father. I proposed a solution to him that I believe will work to strengthen everyone's resolve."

Nicodemus narrowed his eyes. "What solution?"

"What we are doing now is all about, as you so rightly put it, *sacrifice*, and we have agreed that many sacrifices need to be made in order to inspire the people and remind them of their spiritual duty. We call it the Agreement, and we label each death as a sacrifice because we do not make war on each other. But what if it were otherwise? What I proposed to Ibrahim is a second Agreement that would permit a brand new kind of war. One that has never been fought upon the earth. One which would allow each side to feel the strength of holy purpose in their arm every time they draw a sword." He stepped closer to the fire and the old priest. "Father, I am saying that we turn our swords against the enemies of God."

"You are talking a holy war," growled Nicodemus, "and again I say that we already have that."

"We have an open war that is doing no one any lasting good. The Crusades have become a business venture to see who possesses the most land and the best trade routes, and for every enemy killed in the name of God there are a hundred slaughtered in the name of profit. I propose a limited war. A quiet war. A war fought in the shadows."

"Wars escalate. What would prevent this 'shadow war' from escalating into random killing, or killing for profit as we have now?"

"We would impose limits and restrictions. This would have to be managed carefully and regularly. Representatives from each side would have to meet regularly to agree on how many deaths would be allowed, how many castles or churches or mosques destroyed, and so on. And we would have to agree on the value of each death. Just as we now select our sacrifices for their importance to the masses, we would share that information with the other side, thereby transforming the process from self-sacrifice to mutually created martyrs."

Nicodemus pursed his lips and turned away, walking slowly and thoughtfully across the room to the shadowy wall and back again, passing Sir Guy and crossing to the opposite wall. Sir Guy stood in silence, watching the old priest as he paced. Five long minutes passed as Father Nicodemus thought it through, and his seamed face was etched with firelight and shadows. The priest stopped a few feet from the hearth and stared into it for another moment, and then nodded to himself.

"A war of shadows," he murmured as fire danced like devils in his eyes. "Yes. But your knights, skilled killers that they are, are too clumsy for the kind of killing you propose. This war would require stealth. Spies, who could steal into the strongholds of an enemy and kill them in their beds. *That* would strike fear into the hearts of the faithless and that would drive them back to God."

Sir Guy nodded. "Ibrahim said that he could make a deal with the *fida'i*, those Sufi killers who cause so much trouble for the Templars. The cult of assassins run by Hassan ibn Sabbah. Ibn Sabbah is a great friend of Ibrahim's. Would that we had their like in Europe. We will have to invent what we need. We will have to find a way to train candidates to become a new breed of warrior. Not knights but assassins like Ibn Sabbah's *fida'i*."

Nicodemus suddenly straightened and walked a few steps away. He stood staring into the shadows a long time and his body was so rigid with tension that Sir Guy dared not interrupt.

Finally, Nicodemus turned, but his face was in shadow.

"Do not be afraid, my son," murmured the priest. "God Himself speaks through me and He has whispered a word to me. The answer to what we need to wage our shadow war."

As Nicodemus stepped forward into the firelight Sir Guy gasped and took an involuntary step backward, for once again a strange and inexplicable change had come over the priest. His brown eyes swirled with colors—leprous yellows and greens, mushroom white, and the mottled brown of toad skin. Sir Guy touched the heavy silver cross that hung around his neck.

"What word?" asked Sir Guy with a dry throat.

The priest smiled, revealing crooked yellow teeth.

"Upierczi," he whispered.

Part Three
The Blood of Angels

Only be sure that thou eat not the blood:
for the blood is the life . . .
—DEUTERONOMY 12:23

Chapter Fifty-Seven

I sagged against the door frame.

"Ah . . . *Christ* . . ."

The Mouradipours had been stripped naked and tied to wooden chairs. On a nearby table were pliers, a hammer, matches, wire cutters, and other tools. Everything in the room was covered with blood and wrongness. They were both dead. I didn't need to search for pulses to figure that out. It would be nice to believe that they had died quickly and with some shred of dignity left, but that would be an absurd self-delusion. The team downstairs had torn information from them and then continued on to tear away their humanity. And the bastards had used burning matches to sear crosses over their hearts.

The Mouradipours were Muslim, so if it hadn't been for the stakes and garlic and all that vampire hunter bullshit I would have figured this for some kind of anti-Islamic statement.

And why kill the Mouradipours and then try to take me captive? Or, was capturing me a prelude to a trip up here to this makeshift torture chamber?

Probably.

Even so, why set up this hit at all? Just to get the flash drive? Or to keep its information out of someone else's hands? Hours had passed, surely they had to know that I would have passed along that information by now. What was the point of targeting me now?

And how many teams was I facing here?

The Red Knights were one faction, and they were top of the line. I would like to think that I would have won the fight in the hotel without

Violin's help, but I'm not sure I can say that with conviction. I can say without fear of contradiction that I have never faced anyone as fierce or capable as that knight.

On the other hand, the fearless vampire hunters—though clearly organized and violent—were Triple-A ball compared to the knight's major league status. Sure, the team downstairs was brutal, but they were absurdly clumsy. I'm pretty good in a fight, but I was unarmed when I stepped into the house, and I won this one too easily. They were not exactly amateurs, but they sure as hell weren't very high up on the professional food chain. If they hunted the Red Knights I wonder what the win-loss ratio was. If this was Vegas I'd bet the farm on the knights for a shutout.

Now, my friend the rat-bastard Rasouli was a third team.

Violin and whoever she worked for were a fourth.

Could I make an argument for any of them being the same team? Hard to say, because I had no idea who was lying to me and who was telling me the truth.

The knight clearly wanted the flash drive and had no love for Rasouli. That seemed obvious. Violin was willing to work with Rasouli to set up the meet this morning, but she *said* that she considered him to be a spitty place on the sidewalk. She knew about the knights. The knight knew about Arklight, and so did Violin, and she tried to scare the bejesus out of me by saying that my even knowing that name could be fatal. She also warned me away from the knights. The bastards downstairs knew about the knights but so far they hadn't mentioned anything about Rasouli, the flash drive, Arklight, the *Book of Shadows*, the *Saladin Codex*, or the nukes.

And on top of all that, were any of these teams the ones who planted the nukes?

If the nukes were even real.

My head was starting to spin. What would help me fill in the blanks?

I thought about Krystos and the Romanian guy. I looked at the dead bodies and the tools that had been used on them and some very ugly thoughts began forming in my head. The Civilized Man in my head cried out in protest. We didn't *do* that kind of thing. The Warrior was grinning and sharpening his knife. He was all for it. I looked to the Cop for the voice of reason, but he kept looking out of my eyes at the innocent couple who had been torn apart.

There was a clean sheet on the bed, and I pulled it off and covered the murdered couple. I don't know why: it wouldn't matter to them; it wouldn't make any of it better. I tried to tell myself that it was out of courtesy and respect, or a token act to afford them some measure of dignity even after this kind of death.

That sounded nice, but it was bullshit.

I couldn't bear to look at them. If I turned away I knew I'd still see them that way in my mind. If I covered them, then that would be my last memory of them. Or so I hoped. Any lingering regrets I might have had for shooting Iñigo drained away and left no trace.

I turned away and searched the upstairs for weapons and found nothing that provided any answers. So I stole one of Mr. Mouradipour's clean shirts from a hall closet. In the bathroom I washed the blood off my face and throat, ran fingers through my hair, and took a moment to look at the blue eyes in the mirror. They were filled with doubts and questions.

"What the hell is going on?" I asked the man in the mirror. He had no answers at all, so I went back downstairs.

I found Ghost standing in the living room staring at Krystos, who stared back as if mesmerized. I clicked my tongue and Ghost looked at me with a strange expression in his brown eyes. He was not trembling as much as before, and there was more wolf than shepherd in the look he gave me. Maybe it was the smell of fresh blood or the sight of wounded prey. Or maybe the stress had pushed him into a different head space.

"Ghost," I said, and for a moment he did nothing except stare.

I took a step toward him. It's a pack leader move, challenging and demanding. He would either back down or go for me.

"Down!" I ordered.

And, with only the slightest hesitation, he lay down. He didn't roll. I wasn't asking that of him. But he obeyed my order.

I squatted between Ghost and Krystos. I don't know if the Greek had participated in the horrors upstairs, or if he even knew about it, but he was part of this team. Apparently the leader of the team, and that put the whole thing on him as far as I was concerned. He could read those thoughts from my expression. He read other things too.

He began to cry.

Chapter Fifty-Eight

I stared at Krystos for a long time without speaking. Twenty, thirty seconds. It always feels longer when you're holding the low cards. He may have been a tough guy when he had a gun and a crew, but when it came to toughing it out with me, he was holding four low cards and a joker.

Silence and patience were my cards while I waited for him to break.

"P-please . . ." he said in a hoarse whisper. "For the love of God."

"Is that what you are, Krystos? A man of God? A true believer?"

"Yes."

"Your friends, too?"

He glanced around at the dead. "Yes."

"What's that mean exactly, being a 'man of God.' To you, I mean."

The word was a tough one for him but he came up with him. "Ordained."

I raised my eyebrows. "You're a minister?"

He shook his head. "Priest."

"Bullshit. What about going to hell for torture and murder?"

Krystos raised his bound wrists and nodded toward his left arm. "Sleeve," he said.

I pushed his sleeve up and there was tattoo of a cross with Latin words written in an arch above and below it. Above was

AD EXTIRPANDA

Below the cross

EXURGE D ET JUDICA CAUSAM TUAM

"What's that?"

"Permission," he said.

When I did not respond, he said something that I pretty much never expected to hear anywhere outside of a Dan Brown novel or an old episode of Monty Python.

"The Holy Inquisition."

Interlude Six

Fortress of Alamut

Alborz Mountains, Northern Iran.

June 1192 C.E.

Hassan ibn Sabbah sat on a couch that was draped in rich fabrics. Pillows littered the stairs of the dais on which the couch sat. Two warriors stood at the foot of the dais, naked swords laid across their naked arms, their faces as hard and unmoving as stone. The scent of hashish wafted through the chamber and out onto the breeze where it was whipped away high above the mountains.

A carpet lolled out like a great tongue, rippling down the stairs and stretching across the long reception chamber. Sewn into the fabric with delicate skill were fantastical battles. Eagles attacked dragons and tore them to pieces; desert djinn ripped the hearts from crusaders. It had been a gift from Ibn Sabbah's much missed old friend, the mathematician and poet Omar Khayyám. How Ibn Sabbah wished that his friend had lived to see this day. To see what Ibn Sabbah had accomplished.

He accepted a cup of juice from a servant who then bowed himself away from the dais, and as he sipped Ibn Sabbah studied the fifty men who stood in silent rows on either side of the runner carpet.

His *fida'i*.

His assassins.

His sacred killers. Guardians of the secret shared with him by his cousin, Ibrahim al-Asiri. Guardians, too, of the faith. Men who would be used to spill the blood of the infidel in the cleverest plan Sabbah had ever heard. Preserving the word of God through the spilling of blood.

A door at the far end of the chamber opened and Ibn Sabbah's chief advisor entered, followed by six bare-chested guards. Between each guard staggered a man in shackles. The prisoners were freshly washed and wore simple but clean clothes. Ibn Sabbah did not allow prisoners to be mistreated, and he absolutely forbade any unwashed person to enter this room or draw near to that precious carpet. The rows of assassins watched dispassionately as the prisoners were brought to the cleared space to the right of the dais and well away from the carpet. Ibn Sabbah nodded to his advisor who produced a key and unlocked the shackles.

Ibn Sabbah studied the three men. Two of them stared at the floor, terrified, confused, and lost. The third stared up at Ibn Sabbah with the defiance sometimes seen in the eyes of a man who is doomed but who wants to spit in death's eye. A brave man, which was doubly impressive because this man had seen other prisoners taken from the cells, day after day, and probably heard their screams. This man knew that none of those prisoners ever returned to the dungeons. *This one has heart*, Ibn Sabbah mused.

The advisor nodded to the guards who trotted over and laid their swords at the feet of the prisoners.

"Pick them up," ordered Ibn Sabbah.

Only the brave man raised his eyes to Ibn Sabbah. The man was a Sunni with a full beard and gray eyes. "Why? So you can snigger as fifty men cut us to pieces? I spit on such cowardice."

He made as if to do so, but Ibn Sabbah's voice stopped him.

"You have a chance to live," he said. "Do not squander it on an insult that you cannot take back."

Ibn Sabbah snapped his fingers and a single *fida'i* assassin stepped out of the line and padded silently to stand facing the prisoners. He carried no sword and had only a small curved dagger in his sash. The brave prisoner stood with lips pursed, but he did not spit. He eyed the assassin and then looked again at Ibn Sabbah.

"This is not a trick," said Ibn Sabbah. "I make you an offer. Take up those swords and face my man. If you kill or incapacitate him, then you may go free. I will give you each a camel and a pouch of gold coins. Before Allah I swear that I tell the truth."

The three Sunni prisoners shifted uneasily. The brave one continued to glare at Ibn Sabbah, though now there was doubt in his eyes.

"And if we fail to kill him?"

"Then he will assuredly kill you."

The brave Sunni nodded. "Which one of us fights him first?"

Ibn Sabbah smiled. "All three of you will fight him. Three men, three swords against my man and his knife. Surely even men such as you—thieves and pirates of the desert—could not call those unfair odds."

"Your word before Allah?" demanded the brave Sunni.

"May His wrath wither the flesh on my bones and make dust of my household."

The brave man grinned and fast as lightning he hooked his toe under the blade of the nearest sword and kicked it into the air, caught it like a magician, whirled and charged at the *fida'i*. The other men, even cowed as they were, bent and snatched up the weapons and joined in, knowing that God had granted them mercy when they believed their lives were over. The three of them charged toward the assassin, closing the few yards in a heartbeat, swords glittering as they struck.

And then the *fida'i* moved.

His body seemed to vanish like smoke as he dodged in and to one side with incredible speed. The dagger vanished from his sash as he ducked under the sword of the left-handed prisoner, a fat man with bullish shoulders. The assassin danced past him and turned. As he did blood erupted from the fat man's throat. Like a handful of rubies tossed into the wind, the drops of blood flew into the air and then spattered against the face and chest of the second prisoner, a tall man with the heavy forearms of a miller. The assassin pivoted and dropped low as the second man hacked at him with the sword.

"No!" cried the brave man, but it was too late. The miller was committed to the swing, and the assassin darted in and up; his blade opened a vertical line from crotch to breastbone. He stepped aside as the miller's entrails erupted from the wound and flopped wetly onto the floor. The miller gagged out a shocked denial as he sagged to his knees and toppled forward.

And now it was the *fida'i* and the last Sunni.

The Sunni was not a rash man. He had just witnessed two men fall in two seconds, men he had seen kill in desert raids. The sword in his hand felt heavy but its solidity was reassuring. And yet . . .

The *fida'i* did not rush him, but instead began circling, stalking with catlike silence. The Sunni suddenly lunged, cutting upward at an angle that almost always caught an opponent off guard. It was nearly impossible to evade the cut at that distance, and the Sunni was not slow. But the assassin fell backward onto the floor, and as the blade passed, he arched his body and flipped to his feet again like an acrobat. When the Sunni checked his swing and cut backward to take the man across the thighs, the assassin leapt into the air, spry as a monkey, and the blade missed his bare feet by an inch.

The assassin landed on the balls of his feet, balanced and ready. The Sunni pivoted and cut again and again and again, alternating long and short slashes; stabbing and chopping. He stamped forward and darted left and right, whipping the sword at the assassin at angles impossible to evade. But the blade never once touched him.

"Stand still you devil!" cried the Sunni as his frustration disintegrated into doubt. With each passing second he began to fear that he was indeed fighting a demon, some desert ghost who could not be harmed by human weapons.

Then behind him, the Sunni heard Ibn Sabbah speak.

"Stop toying with him."

For a fractured moment the Sunni thought that Ibn Sabbah had directed the comment at him; but then he saw the body language of the *fida'i* change. It was a subtle thing, a shift from acrobatic evasion to the attack posture of a hawk. With another blur of movement the assassin darted in under the Sunni's next swing, slipping past the blade with a hair's breadth to spare.

The Sunni felt the world freeze into a pinpoint of ice. He tried to speak, to ask what had happened, but his jaw would not move. There was a strange pressure under his chin, in his throat, and his brain felt wrong in ways the man could no longer identify. He heard a distant metallic sound and as an afterthought realized that he was no longer holding the sword. He saw the *fida'i* step back away from him, his hands equally empty. The Sunni reached up to touch his own throat and found the hard, cold edge of a blade there. That made no sense. How could a blade be in such an absurd place?

The room tilted as his knees gave way, and then the Sunni was falling, falling into the void with his jaws pinned shut so that he could not even speak the name of God.

The *fida'i* stood over him, his naked chest barely heaving to betray the effort he had just spent in the killing of these three men. On the floor, the

Sunni lay with the hilt of the dagger pressed up against his soft pallet and the very tip of the blade standing an inch above the top of the man's skull. The assassin glanced up at Ibn Sabbah, who nodded; then the assassin knelt and pulled his knife blade free.

Ibn Sabbah smiled down at the *fida'i* and waved him back to his place in line.

Yes, he thought, *Ibrahim will be so very pleased.*

Chapter Fifty-Nine

CIA Safe House #11
Tehran, Iran
June 15, 1:04 p.m.

I stared at Krystos. He would not meet my eyes.

My phone rang and I looked at the screen display. NO ID. I punched the button.

"Hello, Violin."

"Joseph, are you all right?"

"Now's not a good time."

"I—"

But I ended the call. I was confused enough and didn't need another cryptic conversation.

On the other hand, in a weird way some of this was starting to make sense, but the sense it made was badly warped, and I knew I was out of my depth. I told Ghost to watch the prisoners; then I walked into the kitchen to make a call. Church answered on the first ring.

I said, "Look, Boss, I know you're busy—I'm busier."

"Are you at the safe house?"

"Yes and no. I'm here, but it's no longer a safe house."

A slight pause, then he said, "I'm in video conference with Dr. Sanchez and Circe. I'll cycle you in. Okay, you're on speaker."

"Cowboy!" Rudy exclaimed. "How are—?"

"Not a social call, Rude. I'm going to give this to you fast."

They listened while I told him what had just happened. I heard Rudy curse and Circe gasp when I repeated the word "Upier." Everyone started asking questions before I even finished. I had to yell to get them to shut the hell up. "Hey, guys—I'm in a compromised safe house with dead bodies and two wounded prisoners. I'm calling for field support, not a panel discussion."

"Tell us what you need, Captain," barked Church.

"Sure. Let's start with this Upier stuff. Do we believe in vampires?" I asked. "The DMS, I mean."

"No," said Rudy and Circe.

Church did not answer.

"Boss," I prompted, "say something, 'cause you're scaring me here."

"We have to keep an open mind," said Church.

"Mother of God," said Rudy.

"What the hell does that mean?" I demanded. "Answer the question. Do we believe in vampires or not?"

"Yes," said Mr. Church.

Interlude Seven

The Leaping Stag
Newburgh, Yorkshire
January 30, 1193 C.E.

Sir Guy heard a scream as he stepped out of his room. The whole tavern was alive with shouts and yells and the stamping of boots as patrons and staff ran toward the front door.

"What is it?" demanded Sir Guy.

"It's little Mary!" cried one of the tavern boys. "They're bringing her in a cart!"

Sir Guy lingered for a moment, lips pursed, smoothing the wings of his mustache with two fingers. He heard a footfall and turned to see Brother Reynard, the little monk Father Nicodemus had sent to accompany him on this mission.

"You heard?" asked Sir Guy.

Brother Reynard nodded. "Is this what we came for?"

"Let's hope so."

They went downstairs and outside to join the crowd that was gathering around a rickety wooden cart pulled by a donkey. Sir Guy pushed his way through the throng. "Where is the reeve of this shire?"

A warty little man with a cheap sash of office was bent over the cart and looked up.

"I am, milord," he said, snatching his hat off his head and knuckling his forelock. "Faville is my name, sir."

Sir Guy removed a document from his pouch and held it up for inspection. The little man—chief constable of the district—could not read, but he was visibly impressed with all of the official-looking seals.

"I am here on orders from the Holy Father in Rome," lied Sir Guy. "His Holiness has heard of your troubles and sent me and this good monk here to help."

The reeve bobbed his head. "Thank you, milord. It is a great honor to have so distinguished a—"

"Let me see the body."

Sir Guy pushed past the reeve and stepped to the side of the cart. He pulled on his gloves and then raised the threadbare horse blanket that had been used to cover the body.

Beneath it lay a shepherd girl of no more than fifteen.

"This is 'ow we found 'er, milord," said Faville.

"God save us!" cried Brother Reynard, who peered past Sir Guy's elbow. "This is surely the devil's work."

Sir Guy could not argue. The girl had once been lovely, in the way that peasant girls can be before hard work and hard use made them old before their time. She had yellow hair that gleamed in the early sunlight, and pale blue eyes. Though she was but a girl her figure was womanly, with a premature heft of breast and good hips. But it was all ruined now. She lay naked and torn and frozen on a bed of straw.

Sir Guy shifted around to examine her face and neck. There was a small amount of blood on her throat, caked around the savage wounds, but otherwise the girl was not bathed in gore as might be expected from such injuries.

He cut a look at the reeve. "Did anyone clean her off?"

"No, your lordship," answered Faville. "This is 'ow she was. Stripped bare and bled white. Frozen stiff, too."

"What about the surroundings? How much blood was on the ground?"

The reeve shook his head and touched the cross around his neck. His eyes were shifty and frightened. "None to speak of, milord."

The crowd murmured. Sir Guy noted that although they were horrified, no one looked surprised.

"Her clothes?" he asked.

"Torn to rags and scattered among the bushes."

Sir Guy bent close and probed the wounds. As is so often the case, the legends had it wrong. Not a pair of clean punctures—that was a fantasy spun by bad poets and liars—but rather a ruin of flesh savaged by many sharp teeth.

It was exactly as Father Nicodemus had described it.

Sir Guy dropped the cloth and turned to the reeve, who was fidgeting and frightened.

"How many others have there been?"

Faville looked uncomfortable and Sir Guy knew that it was because he was the law in these parts and murders were occurring unchecked. "Six, milord."

"Where was the body found?"

Faville nodded toward the forest. "Near where the others were found, milord. She was in the fields up near the priory."

Sir Guy ordered the man to give him a precise set of directions. "And recall all of your scouts and officers. No one else is to go into those woods until Brother Reynard and I have run this fiend to ground."

"But . . . but, milord, at least let me send ten pikemen with you," stammered the reeve.

"What use are pikes against the devil?" said Sir Guy, which left the reeve nonplussed. "No, Brother Reynard and I are armed with special weapons blessed by the Holy Father himself. Stay here and see to this poor child."

Five minutes later he and the monk were galloping out of town.

When they eventually slowed their horses as they approached the scene of the murder, Brother Reynard asked, "'Special weapons'?"

Sir Guy grinned. "Peasants love a good story." He narrowed his eyes and studied the shadows under the trees. "Besides, in truth it is a weapon that we seek."

The monk's frown deepened. "Father Nicodemus sent us to find a monster."

The Frenchman shrugged. "For our purposes, it is the same thing."

Chapter Sixty

"Vampires . . ."

I repeated the word, trying to see how it fit in my mouth. It didn't. Not in this context.

"Wait," cut in Rudy, "are we talking actual monsters here?" I could only hear his voice, but I could imagine the way he'd look right now. Face tight, eyes dark and unblinking, his hand touching the middle of his tie, right over the spot where he wore a crucifix under his clothes.

"Dr. Sanchez," said Church, "I don't have the kind of answer you and Captain Ledger would like. Vampires exist, yes."

"Perhaps you misunderstand my question," said Rudy. "I'm asking if these vampires are—"

"Yes, Doctor, thank you for explaining the obvious to me," said Church coldly. "I do understand the question. Are we talking about supernatural monsters or something else? Frankly, I don't know. My tendency, as you well know, is to look for the scientific explanation."

"The *rational* answer," offered Rudy, but Church cut him off.

"Rational? You are a devout Catholic, Doctor. Is faith in an invisible God and invisible saints rational? Is it supernatural?"

"It's religion," replied Rudy. "It's faith. And it's not trying to kill my friend."

"Do you believe in ghosts, Doctor? That is, I believe, a requirement of Catholics, as it is of most religions. Ghosts, spirits, demons, all manner of creatures that cannot be quantified."

"*Yo!*" I shouted into the phone. "Can we save this for some time when I'm *not* standing in a house full of dead people?"

There was a brief silence, and Mr. Church said, "Quite right. To the point then. We have known for some time that the Red Knights either are, or pretend to be, some kind of vampire. We know that they are unusually strong and fast, which are qualities ascribed to most species of vampires in folklore. We know that they have unusual dentition, specifically they have sharp teeth and pronounced canines."

"Yup," I said. "I can testify to all of that. Fucker didn't turn into a bat, though."

"That's not part of the vampire legend," said Circe, joining the conversation after what I can only assume was a shocked silence. "There are a lot of legends of vampires transforming into different kinds of things. Mist and fog, swarms of flies, birds—mostly black ones—and even balls of light. But bats aren't on the list. It was made up for fiction."

I heard Rudy mutter. "I can't believe we are having this conversation."

"The knight I fought didn't transform into anything but dead meat after Violin put a bullet in his head. Maybe I watched the wrong movies, but I thought stakes were how you killed a vampire. Bullets in the head are zombies, and we've pretty much done zombies. And, I might add—they were the products of science, not black magic."

"The stakes are questionable," said Circe. "In most legends the vampire hunters use sharpened poles rather than stakes, and they don't kill the vampire. The stake was used to hold the vampire down, pinning it to the ground or to its coffin, so that the full Ritual of Exorcism could be performed."

"Dear God," said Rudy, "what's that?"

"They cut the vampire's head off, fill its mouth with garlic, turn it backward in the coffin, then drive iron nails into the arms and legs of the vampire and rebury it. Or cremate it."

"I'm here to tell you, Circe," I said, "a bullet in the brainpan does a spiffy job of dropping your modern-day vampire."

"I have found that a bullet in the brain works on *most* things," Church said dryly, and I couldn't argue with that.

"So, are we talking about something nonsupernatural?" asked Rudy. "If he could be shot and killed, doesn't that mean—?"

"It means we know how to kill it," said Church. "It doesn't mean that we understand its nature."

"Surely it's more likely that this is some kind of genetic aberration," insisted Rudy, "or at most an evolutionary sideline. We know that there were many kinds of human species evolving at once."

"It's very possible," agreed Church. "And it's the working premise I've maintained for many years. If these Upierczi are vampires, then we will want to ascertain whether that is a subspecies or separate species."

"Wait, roll back a sec. You said 'many years'?" I asked. "How long have you known about these Red Knights?"

He paused. "For quite a long time. I first encountered them in Europe, but that's a story that we don't have time for now, and it may not be relevant."

"Getting back to the whole 'stakes' thing," I said. "These jokers tried to use them on me." I described the general size and design. "Each one has the same thing written on it. It's Latin, so bear with me." I pulled the stake from my belt. "*Sancte Michael Archangele, defende nos in proelio; contra nequitiam et insidias diaboli esto praesidium—*"

"Ah," interrupted Circe, "it's the prayer to Saint Michael created by Pope Leo XIII in the late nineteenth century. The whole translation is, 'Saint Michael the Archangel, defend us in the battle, be our safeguard and protection against the wickedness and snares of the devil: May God rebuke him, we humbly pray; and do thou, O Prince of the heavenly host, by the power of God, thrust into hell Satan and all evil spirits who wander through the world seeking the ruin of souls. Amen.'" She paused. "An interesting choice, considering the scope of this situation."

"Interesting in what way?" Rudy asked, beating me to the question.

"The archangel Michael has a dual nature. His name is a symbol of humility before God and at the same time he is regarded as the field commander of the Army of God."

"Ah, so we're talking *militant* psycho vampire hunters," I said. "Groovy."

Church added, "Michael is also one of the very few angels venerated by Jews, Christians, and Muslims."

"Did Michael have problems with vampires? If so, I missed that in Sunday School."

"Not likely," answered Circe, "but as the leader of God's army he would naturally be the enemy of all evil. Going on the assumption that vampires are evil."

"The Red Knights get my vote for being evil. So are these vampire hunters," I reminded her. "Krystos and his asswipes tortured innocent people and were quite willing to kill me. Oh, and here's another thing to throw into the mix. Krystos said that he was with the Holy Inquisition. Even had their motto tattooed on his forearm."

234 | Jonathan Maberry

There was a silence.

"No," I said, "that wasn't a joke. Say something."

"How does one respond to that? I . . . thought that had been disbanded a couple of hundred years ago," said Rudy.

"Sure, and vampires were myths," I pointed out.

"Ah," he conceded.

"It's always good to keep an open mind," Church said quietly.

"Are we tracking any groups whose symbology includes a vampire motif?" I asked. "Some weird cult? Anything like that?"

"Only two," said Church. "The Red Knights and another group that may be the same as your Inquisitors."

"Let me guess . . . the Saturday People?"

"What?" asked Circe. "They're *Sabbatarians*?"

I said, "According to Krystos."

"Sabbatarians," she repeated, "are people born on Saturday."

"So what?" I asked. "So was my nephew. He doesn't run around stabbing people with pointy sticks."

"No, in folklore the Sabbatarians are monster hunters. The old beliefs come mostly from Greek legends, but it's found in other places, too. People born on the Sabbath are supposed to have special powers. They can see evil spirits and they are empowered by God to oppose supernatural evil."

"Were they connected with the Inquisition?"

"I can check, but I don't know. That's not to say they weren't. We're paving a lot of new ground here," Circe admitted. "I have a colleague, Jonatha Corbiel-Newton, she's probably the world's top scholar on vampire legends. I'll call her and pick her brain. Covertly, of course."

Rudy sighed. "Until five minutes ago I thought we were looking for nuclear weapons. Now we're hunting vampires."

"Yeah, about that," I said. "This is definitely one case, but don't ask me how they relate. We came into this wa-a-a-y too late to make sense of it without a guidebook."

"So it seems," said Church. "Here's the rest. Vox is definitely connected with this matter at several points. Some of that intel comes from a source connected to the woman, Violin. When you have more time I'll give you a more complete briefing, but for the short term, Violin is considered a friendly."

"She saved my life, so I've got some fuzzy bunny feelings for her."

"She is part of a deep-cover special ops group operating independently of any government. Their code name is Arklight. They have no political or national affiliation and very few friends. Their story is a long and very sad one. If the situation requires it I'll have Aunt Sallie give you a briefing. Their leader uses the code name Lilith. She's fierce, highly dangerous. Underestimate her at your peril." And then he filled me in on what he knew of the Red Order, the Scriptor, the Tariqa, the Murshid and, saving the best for last, he dropped the bomb about Nicodemus.

"That's it," I said. "I quit."

Church ignored me. "A lot of what we know is in bits and pieces. Let me make some calls and see if I can get more useful information. In the meantime, Captain, get what you can get out of Krystos, but don't take too long with it. You eliminated their team, but it doesn't mean they don't have backup. Unless Krystos has direct knowledge of the nukes, he is a distraction rather than a pathway to a solution. Find out what he knows and then get out of there. I'll call around and when I can verify a genuinely safe safe house, I'll text the information to you."

"Good. Before I go . . . where are we on the flash drive and the nukes?"

Circe and Rudy gave me the bullet points of what they'd found. Church wrapped it up by saying that field agents were working to verify the four known targets, and to remind me that Echo Team was already inside Iran and heading my way.

"First good news I've had all day," I said, and disconnected. I pocketed my phone and leaned against the wall for a moment.

"Vampires," I said aloud. There was no doubt in my mind that, as Rudy observed, this was probably some freak of genetics. I believed in God, but, contrary to what Mr. Church said, I didn't much believe in angels, demons, or monsters. Ghosts? Maybe. Vampires of the supernatural kind? Nope; and the word still didn't fit right in my mouth.

Chapter Sixty-One

When I came back to the living room, Ghost was standing over Krystos, growling right in the man's face. Krystos cringed back as far as he could but he was trapped by a hundred pounds of furious canine.

"Down," I snapped.

Ghost stopped growling but he held his ground, the hair standing stiff along his spine.

"Down!" I said again, but this time my tone was quiet. Ghost glared at me and uttered another low, threatening growl. There was no danger left anywhere else in the house. The growl was aimed at me.

"Down," I repeated a third time, and after another moment of hesitation he lowered himself to the ground, but all of his muscles were tensed as if he was about to spring. I deliberately turned my back on him, the way a confident pack leader would. At the moment I wasn't feeling all that confident. Dogs are smart, but when they're hurt and confused their thinking can get dangerously skewed. From Ghost's perspective, his pack leader was leading him into one painful situation after another.

Once more I squatted down in front of Krystos. I interrupted him in the middle of a prayer. His color was bad and he sat in a puddle of his own blood. I reached out and felt for Constantin's pulse. He didn't have one, and I felt a weird flash of irritation that he'd managed to duck out before we could have a meaningful chat.

Krystos watched me do it and read the news on my face. He closed his eyes for a moment and repeated the dead man's name several times. Greasy sweat ran in rivulets down Krystos's face.

I poked him on the forehead with a stiffened finger. "Pay attention, sparky."

"I am praying for the dead!" he snapped.

"Did you pray for the people upstairs?" I snarled.

He faltered. "Yes. I . . . I mean that the others would have done this."

"Before or after they tore out their fingernails?"

He looked at me with eyes that were glassy and bright. "They are the enemies of God!"

It was so hard not to yell back, to try and shout him down and make him understand that nobody's God orders something like this. I wanted to make my case; I wanted to knock some sense into him. But—really, what would be the point? How could I ever make someone like him budge from an entrenched stance that was hundreds of years in the making and backed by a papal order? This wasn't one of those debates where I could slide around to try to see things from his perspective. As the saying goes, that way lies madness.

The rage was hard to keep in its box, though. It burned in my mouth and in muscles, and it tingled like electricity in the dangerous tips of my fingers. When I trusted myself to speak normally, I asked, "Who told you I would be coming here?"

"I—I don't know," he said. "We got a call. My team was ordered to come here to do God's work and—"

"Who made the call?"

"I don't know."

I searched his face for the lie but I think he was too scared to pull any new stunts on me, and unfortunately that meant that he was probably no more than a grunt. A foot soldier in a war that was out of step with reality and with my real mission. The nukes.

"How many more of you are there?"

His mouth tightened with either pride or defiance. "Enough."

"Don't get cute with me."

"We are the Army of God," he declared. "We will never stop hunting. We will never cease in our war."

He said all that in awkward, broken English, but I got the point. I wasn't impressed.

"All of this is because you want to rid the world of vampires?"

"No—not that. That is not our mission. We want to save the world from the Upierczi."

"Upierczi? That's another word for vampire, right? So, with all that's going on in the world—wars, poverty, religious intolerance, disease—you 'priests' spend your time and resources hunting vamps?"

"Yes."

"Why?" I demanded. "'Cause right now I'm thinking you psychopaths have done a lot more harm to the world. What makes you better than them?"

His face took on a contemptuous cast and with an imperious tone, he said, "We fight to save the world. They want to destroy it."

"And how do they plan to do that?"

"They want to blow it up."

I sat back on my heels and stared at him. Again he read my expression and he nodded.

"The Upierczi have hidden for centuries," he said. "Now they are in the light. Now they attack openly. They have great weapons. Why else do you think they would reveal themselves to the world?"

"What do you mean by 'great weapons'?"

"Great," he repeated, letting me take the obvious definition from that. *Oh shit.*

"How do you know this? Are you working for Rasouli?"

He looked blank.

"Hugo Vox?"

Krystos shook his head. "I do not know these names."

"Who sent you here?"

"A priest of our church. He will know what you have done here. He will call down the wrath of the Almighty on you."

His accent was atrocious but his message was clear enough; but I wasn't buying. I'm pretty sure I could handle myself against a priest.

"I'll take my chances," I told him, but he sneered.

"Father Nicodemus will lay waste to your world. He has promised this!"

That, I thought, was mighty damn interesting, and it made me wonder whose side Nicodemus was on. There was Nicodemus with the Seven Kings last year. Nicodemus with the Red Order, and now Nicodemus with the Sabbatarians who were clearly enemies of the knights employed by the Red Order.

Who in hell was Nicodemus?

I left the room once more to call this in to Church, but got Aunt Sallie.

"What the fuck are you still doing at that house?" she bellowed.

"Trading Pokémon cards with the vampire hunters."

"Why are you calling?"

When I told her about Nicodemus, Auntie shut up for a moment, then said, very grudgingly, "Good work. Now get out of there."

"I wish I could spend some more quality time with this clown to see what else I can get."

"If wishes were horses," she said.

"Yeah. Tell you what, Auntie, much as it sounds goofy to say out loud, I think we need to take a look at this from the vampire doomsday perspective. I'm starting to think that maybe the Red Knights have the nukes."

"We will, but I doubt whether your friend Krystos had that right. Circe and Dr. Sanchez have forwarded the idea of a doomsday cult."

"You don't buy it, though?"

"Do you?"

"No, but my logic is kind of goofy."

"Big surprise," she said. "Tell me."

I said, "Answer me something first. Circe dismissed the changing into bats stuff, and we know that bullets kill the knights, so that's two bits of folklore down the crapper. But, what do the reports you've collected about the Red Knights and real-world vampires say about immortality? That's supposed to be a real theme with vampires, right?"

"Nothing lives forever, but from what little we know about the Red Knights, they're supposed to be exceptionally long-lived. Not necessarily immortal, but with lifespans far exceeding ordinary humans."

"Okay, so they're immortal-ish. Enough so for the sake of argument, okay?"

"Okay."

"Then tell me why immortals would want to destroy the world. No way that makes sense."

Aunt Sallie grunted. "This isn't like you, Ledger. This is very clever thinking. Let me run it by Deacon and Dr. Hu. In the meantime, Deke wanted me to text you. We have a safe house location that has been triple verified. It's close to where you are now, and Echo Team will meet you there in a few hours. It's an apartment over a convenience store. Deacon knows the man who owns it."

"One of his 'friends in the industry'?"

"No, just an old friend. Jamsheed Mustapha is a good man. We've worked with him in the past. Good guy, so try not to get him killed."

I let that pass. "What about Krystos?"

Auntie said, "That's your call."

She disconnected.

I still had the phone in my hand when I went back into the living room. Krystos looked at me with mingled hope and dread, but his mouth continually repeated a prayer of deliverance.

"Well," I said, "turns out that it sucks to be you."

I shot him through the heart.

Chapter Sixty-Two

CIA Safe House #11
Tehran, Iran
June 15, 1:18 p.m.

The gunshot made Ghost bark again, but it was a single sound. Loud and shocked and angry.

I ignored him as I watched Krystos slide slowly onto his side, eyes emptying of light, mouth hanging slack with his last prayers unfinished.

None of the thoughts inside my head were pretty ones. However, when I looked inside for self-recrimination I came up dry. That's something I knew I should be worried about, and I was pretty sure that all of this was going to come back and bite me on the ass, at least in an emotional or psychological way. At the moment, though, I watched Krystos die and did not feel a single thing about it. Not for him or the six other Sabbatarians. They were ordained priests; they were official Holy Inquisitors acting on orders given by a pope centuries ago. They believed that what they were doing was right, that they were doing what they had to do to save the world.

From vampires.

Vampires with nukes.

I closed my eyes and imagined for a moment that I stood in a cool breeze that was scented with lilacs and honeysuckle and just a hint of salt water. I strained to hear the soft whisper of Grace speaking my name.

But there was nothing.

When I opened my eyes, though, it was only me and Ghost in a house filled with ugly death. Ghost looked at me and I couldn't meet his eyes. I hung my head and told myself that the stinging in my eyes was from the gunpowder.

Yeah.

Before we left the house I dropped the magazines from the two nine millimeters and swapped bullets until I had a full magazine in one and a half-filled mag in my pocket. I took Nadja's .25 popgun, too, and the valise that was filled with stakes, hammers, garlic, and holy water. Who knows, maybe I'd really need them.

Lingering in the doorway to the hall, I glanced down at the dead man and spat on the floor by his shoes.

"That's for Taraneh and Arastoo Mouradipour, you piece of shit," I said quietly. And although it was true, I felt a hollow place in my chest. I'd just shot an unarmed man, a man who was injured and bound, and I'd made a joke about it as I pulled the trigger. It made *me* feel like a piece of shit.

My phone rang again. No ID. I didn't answer. Instead I headed toward the door, clicking my tongue for Ghost. After a moment I heard nails clicking on the floorboards.

Ghost followed right at my heel.

We went out the back.

There were two cars out back. I debated taking one, but there was no time to do a proper search for trackers or other bugs, and I already had enough problems.

I did rummage around, though. I found half a chicken sandwich on flatbread and gave that to Ghost, who didn't even bother to sniff. He attacked it as if it was trying to escape. As he ate, he cut me some hard looks, letting me know that we still had some issues to work out.

The first car had nothing else in it.

In the second I found a locked briefcase under a blanket on the rear seat. The locks were good and the case was reinforced. No time to jimmy it now, so I decided to take that with me. I popped the trunk and stood staring for a ten count at a full-blown arsenal. Six AK-47s with bundles of magazines held together by heavy-duty rubber bands, two rocket-propelled grenade launchers, and a small duffle bag of 1980's-era Russian hand grenades. The underside of the trunk lid was rigged with slots for a dozen of the stakes and four hammers. These guys were serious about this. I took some party favors and slammed the trunk.

Ghost finished his sandwich and looked up for more.

"Sorry, kiddo, but that's all I have."

His look of disgust eloquently showed how deeply disappointed he was in me. Man's best friend indeed.

There was nothing else to find.

"Let's go," I said softly.

We did not exactly run, but we walked mighty damned briskly away from there.

Interlude Eight
Krak des Chevaliers
June 1203 C.E.

Sir Guy LaRoque stared at death.

And death, in its many forms, stared back at him. The big stone fireplace blazed and threw its dancing light across the floor, and yet the shadows of the vast hall were not chased back. Rather they recoiled like some dark serpent, ready to strike the unwary.

Monks had brought a chair for Sir Guy and helped him into it, lifting his legs onto cushions and tucking a rug around his spindly limbs. The knight felt empty, like a suit of clothes stuffed with straw and sticks. No longer a vital man, not yet a corpse. Tottering in the gloom of a cancer that was consuming him from the inside out.

The figure closest to him was both death and life in Sir Guy's mind. Father Nicodemus, wizened but unyielding. He had been old when Sir Guy was a boy, but the man had not changed. Not a line, not a day. In his cups, Sir Guy comforted himself with the thought that it was God's own grace that touched this man with a lighter hand, sparing him so that Nicodemus could serve heaven on earth. Sir Guy needed drink to believe it then, and now, sober and loitering at the edge of the grave, he knew that it was sophistry of the weakest kind. In truth, he did not know how to think about the old priest. To do so conjured dreams, and his nights were already troubled.

"You have done so very well, my son," murmured the priest. "You have served Almighty God with a fealty and a zeal unmatched by any in the Red Order."

Sir Guy said nothing. He had so little energy that breathing was a herculean task that required all of his powers. Father Nicodemus patted him on the shoulder and his slender fingers lingered to stroke the dying knight's neck where it was exposed above the soiled collar of the Hospitaller doublet. It was so strange a thing, a pretense of tenderness that felt like a violative caress.

Then the priest took a few steps forward and held his arms wide as if to embrace the other deathly figures who stood in silent stillness.

Three men. They stood in a row, shoulder to shoulder, like brothers. Hollow faces that gave them a starved appearance. Thin-lipped mouths like knife slashes. Three shapes that pretended to be men. Three creatures Sir Guy had brought here from different parts of Europe and Asia. From Newburgh, from the Carpathian Mountains, and from a destroyed town in Turkey. They shared no common language, no sameness of culture, no drop of familial blood. And yet they were cut like poisoned fruit from the same blighted tree. Slender, pale as wax, with dark hair and eyes that burned like red coals. And teeth. Christ Jesus and all His saints, those dreadful teeth. Even after all this time that was the thing that continued to haunt Sir Guy, awake or asleep. Teeth like dogs. Like wolves.

Nicodemus spoke a word and it hung burning in the air.

"Upierczi."

Three pairs of red eyes widened, filling with fear, filling with wonder.

"The children of shadows," Nicodemus said to them. "Yes—I know you. Born of cold wombs, shunned and hated. Slaves to a hunger that you have been told is an affront to God. Reviled and condemned. Excommunicated and driven out to hunt in the night."

Three pairs of red eyes studied him. It was the only thing about them that moved, shifting slowly to follow Nicodemus as he paced across the burning expanse of the fireplace.

"The Upierczi have been called monsters, sons of Judas. Pariah. Demons." He stopped and fixed them with his own stare and it was darker and more fell than theirs. "But that is not what you are. Not demons. Not creations of Satan or fiends from the pit."

244 | Jonathan Maberry

They watched him. Sir Guy watched them as they studied the priest. Now there was uncertainty on their faces.

"When Sir Guy asked you to come with him, he promised safety. He promised you a place where you would be free, and be protected. He extended the arm of the church to you, offering to bless and sanctify you, to forgive you your sins and let you walk once more in the light that shines from the face of Jesus Christ."

They watched. One of them bowed his head and began softly to weep tears of blood.

Father Nicodemus stalked over to him and used one clawlike finger to lift the creature's chin. "Listen to me, child of shadows," he murmured in a gentler tone than Sir Guy had ever heard him use. "The Lord God has not forgotten you. You have not fallen out of His favor. You have not been barred from the grace of heaven." He leaned close and licked the bloody tear from the weeping monster's cheek. "God *made* you!" he whispered. He reached out his hands to touch the other two creatures, tracing lines across their wax white cheeks. "God is all and He makes all things and He made you. Therefore you are God's creations. Whoever tells you otherwise is a heretic and will burn in hell."

The silent creatures said nothing.

"I *know* what you feel, my children," continued the priest. "I, of all who walk upon the earth, understand the fires that burn in your hearts and the need in the pit of your stomach. You kill because you cannot prevent yourself. A power greater than your own will compels you to hunt, to tear open the flesh of your prey, to bathe your face and lips and tongue in the heat of the blood. And afterward you revile yourself because this is against God. This is what you have been told. Yet what does Deuteronomy chapter twelve, verse twenty-three say? 'The blood is the life!' Did not Jesus shed his blood to redeem all? Does not His blood wash the world of its sins? Does the wine of communion not *become* blood as it touches the lips of each Christian?" He pulled them all closer still, and Sir Guy had to strain to hear. "You are not sinners, my children. You are merely lost. All your lives you have been seeking to understand why God would strike you with so heavy a hand and force you into a life of sin. I tell you now that God has not shaped you to be monsters or sinners. God has forged you into weapons."

They stared at him, and the room—perhaps the world—was utterly silent.

"You have been brought here to be the holy weapons of God on earth. Do you hunger? Then know why: you were *meant* to feast upon the blood of the pagan and the heretic and the infidel. Do you seek shelter in the darkness? Then understand this: the darkness is *yours*. Use it. Let it heal you and hide you. Become the darkness and let it become you."

He stepped back from them and signaled to one of his monks who came hurrying over with Sir Guy's sword laid ceremoniously across his folded arms. The monk knelt and offered the handle to Nicodemus, who drew it with a ringing rasp. The priest turned and held the sword aloft, letting firelight flicker along its wicked edge.

"This sword," he intoned, his voice deep and grave, "has drunk the blood of countless enemies of God. In the service of the king of France, in the cause of the Knights Hospitaller, and in the war of shadows we have fought with the Saracen and the Jew and other enemies of Christ."

He turned and offered it to Sir Guy. "My son, my friend, take your sword."

Sir Guy's trembling fingers closed around the handle of the weapon he had thought he would never hold again. The touch of it lent some power to his withered hand and he held it out toward the Upierczi. The tip dipped for a moment but it did not fall to the ground.

"Sir Guy, Grand Master and Scriptor of the Holy Red Order, defender of the faith, servant and soldier of God, I entreat you to bestow upon these sacred warriors the title and privileges of knights of *Ordo Ruber*."

Sir Guy flicked a surprised glance at Nicodemus. This was nothing they had ever agreed upon. This was unexpected and strange, and he knew that it was wrong.

And yet, Nicodemus stood there, eyes burning and mouth smiling.

"I . . ." began Sir Guy. But he could not endure that stare, that will. "Y-yes," he gasped. "Yes."

One by one the Upierczi came toward his chair and knelt before him, and one by one Sir Guy LaRoque touched their shoulders with the sword, blessing them in the name of Michael the Archangel.

When it was done, so was the last strength in Sir Guy's arm. Nicodemus took it from him and handed the sword to a monk, who bowed out of the chamber.

Nicodemus ran a fingernail along Sir Guy's cheek. "You have served me well for many years, my son."

Sir Guy looked wearily up into his face, and his heart seemed to freeze. The old priest stood with his back to the Upierczi so that only the knight could see him. The priest's eyes underwent that process of change which Sir Guy had seen before, the colors swirling and changing, but this time the process did not stop until all color was completely gone, leaving eyes with no color, no whites. Eyes that were totally black. And the face also changed. It was not the wrinkled countenance of a priest grown old in the service of his God and his church. This face was both younger and older, timeless, endless; and endlessly wrong. It was a mask of a bottomless corruption and deception. The nose was still long and hooked, but the nostrils were more like slits; the mouth was lipless and lined with scores of needle-sharp teeth. Even the skin was mottled to an ophidian texture like a diseased toad. Worst of all, Sir Guy *knew* this face. It was the face of all the evil in the world. The face of the trickster. The enemy of God.

He screamed.

Sir Guy screamed and screamed and screamed until spit and blood flew from his mouth.

The trickster laughed.

Then Father Nicodemus turned away, his face once more that of a wizened priest. He swept a hand toward the screaming man.

"My knights," he said softly, "my Red Knights. Sir Guy offers up his blood as a sacrament to seal our new covenant. Show respect for his sacrifice. Quick, while he still cries out for God's own mercy."

The Red Knights smiled with their jagged mouths. Their eyes were filled with tears and the light of joy as they rushed forward to partake of God's mercy.

Chapter Sixty-Three

Violin was on the move, getting closer to Joe Ledger, and finding terrible wreckage along the way. It annoyed and angered her that Ledger wasn't taking her calls, but it also frightened her.

Oracle provided her with the locations of likely safe houses where Ledger might go to ground. She had gone to the first one too late. All she found were Ledger's footprints in the blood of a living room awash with dreadful pain.

The Red Knights had left their signature on every inch of that small house.

Seeing the carnage, Violin had braced herself against the possibility that one of the mangled figures was Ledger, but neither was. An old man and his son. She could tell at least that much from their faces.

Standing in the living room, Violin considered pulling the old man down from the wall, but it would take more time than she had.

She ran out the back and got into the car she used while in Iran. The car appeared to be sedate and slow, but that was all exterior illusion. A much fiercer creature dwelt under the hood, and the suspension was rigged for high-speed pursuit and hairpin handling.

Even so, she stayed within legal limits as she navigated the traffic toward the second safe house. One run by the CIA. She passed it and saw nothing untoward. Around back there were two parked cars. She circled the block looking for backup and found it.

Violin parked her car in the shade thrown by a tall stuccoed warehouse. Across the street a pair of white vans sat in the shade. She recognized them. Not those specific vans, but the type. And she knew what they signified.

Sabbatarians.

Her lip curled in cold contempt. Those maniacs should have died out years ago along with their blasphemous Inquisition. It offended Violin to her core that they continued to prosper and had even found some private source of funding in recent years. Their numbers were growing and the threat they represented was no joke.

She accessed Oracle.

"Oracle welcomes you, Violin."

"Quick field update. Please mark this urgent and make sure my mother sees it right away."

"Noted. Please proceed."

Violin explained about the slaughter rendered by the Red Knights and the Sabbatarian strike team she was currently observing.

Instead of the placid computer voice responding to her update, a very similar but far more intimidating voice barked, "Do you have Captain Ledger under active surveillance?"

Violin froze and had to take a moment to find her own voice. She looked down at the small screen on her computer and saw a face that was as ageless and beautiful as it was stern and humorless. Black hair shot with snow white streaks, cat green eyes, a full-lipped mouth compressed into a stern line.

Lilith. Cold as the moon and equally remote. It was difficult enough speaking with Lilith on the phone, seeing her on the computer made Violin instantly feel like a naughty ten-year-old again.

"Hello, Mother," said Violin, her voice immediately small and contrite.

"Don't 'Mother' me. Answer the question, girl."

"No, Mother. Ledger went into the wind after leaving his hotel, though I think I know where he is."

One eyebrow arched high on Lilith's forehead. "You 'think'?"

"Yes, Mother."

"Why are you wasting time talking to me instead of verifying his location?"

"Because there is a Sabbatarian strike team positioned near—"

"Did I ask for an excuse as to why you can't accomplish a simple task?" Lilith's tone was subzero. Colder even than usual.

"No, Mother, I—"

"And are you about to apologize instead of taking appropriate and immediate action? Is that the end result of everything I've taught you?"

"No, Mother, it's just—"

"Do I need to send a trainee instead? Someone who understands how to follow a simple order?"

Violin took a deep, steadying breath. It was that or put her fist through the monitor's screen.

"No, Mother, but—"

"Then follow your orders," barked Lilith. "Rasouli gave Ledger a flash drive with information on where as many as seven nuclear bombs have been hidden. Four, at least, are in the Middle East. Find Ledger and get that drive. Is that order simple enough for you?"

"My God! Wait—how do you know what Rasouli gave—?"

"How do you *think*?" snapped her mother. "I used common sense and asked the right question of the right person."

Ah, so that's it, thought Violin. *Mother spoke with St. Germaine.*

No wonder she's so angry. On a secret level, Violin was pleased to see her mother discomfited.

"Mother, I'm trying to understand why the Order sent a knight after Ledger. How could they have known about the flash drive?"

"I . . . don't know," said Lilith, her anger dropping down several notches. "That's a good question, too."

"On the other hand, this seems to confirm one of my theories—that Rasouli is not planning on accepting the role of Murshid."

But the screen had already gone dark.

Violin clenched her teeth. She considered taking the computer outside and backing her car over it a few times. It might make her feel good. Instead, she turned off the engine and got out of the car.

She was dressed in a traditional Iranian chador and headscarf, which made her shapeless and faceless. The eye makeup she had applied would fool anyone. She took a net-covered cloth grocery sack from the back seat and began walking slowly across the street. Not directly toward the white vans, but at an angle so that she would have to pass them. They appeared deserted.

As she approached, she could hear the squawk of a walkie-talkie and the hushed voice of a man speaking awkward Persian with a European accent, though she could not make out the words. The man was inside the second van. From his tone, though, he sounded agitated, concerned. He kept repeating a word, or perhaps a name, and got no replies.

"*Krystos! Krystos!*"

Then the rear door of the van opened and four men stepped out. They were dressed in ordinary clothes, but they held their sports coats closed in the way men do when they are trying to conceal something. Violin had seen it a thousand times. It amused her.

She needed to be amused. It was that or let the memory of her conversation with her mother turn her into a screaming wreck.

The men saw her and paused. They said nothing to her but their eyes were on her as she walked past the van. They were only pretending to be Iranian, but their stares were frank and impudent by Muslim standards. Invasive and rude.

No way to treat a lady, she thought.

Violin let herself trip over a crack in the sidewalk. She stumbled and dropped the grocery bag. One of the men made a reflexive move to catch her.

And he died.

The other three men never saw the blade. All they were aware of was a flash of black cloth and the sparkle of sunlight on steel, and then the man who had reached to help the woman was sagging to his knees as a jet of impossibly bright red geysered from his throat. Violin gracefully sidestepped to avoid the spray.

The men were shocked, but they were professionals. Even without understanding what was happening they knew something was wrong, that this was an attack of some kind. They went for their guns.

And then Violin was among them.

Her chador flapped and popped like laundry on a clothesline. Her hands became a blur as she moved into the center of the group, a blade in each hand, her body twisting with a dancer's grace. The steel wove patterns of light around her. Rubies of blood filled the air and splashed along the side of the van and on the front of the building. One gun cleared its holster but the hand holding it was no longer attached to its owner's wrist.

The men had no time to scream.

Violin cut their faces and throats and mouths and eyes. She slashed tendons and muscle and bone and then she suddenly froze in the center of the storm of blood. The men collapsed around her, their many parts creating a grotesquely artistic pattern on the ground.

From the first cut to the last it took four seconds.

Violin stared dispassionately down at the carnage.

Four seconds.

Beneath her scarf her mouth twitched in disgust.

It should only have taken three.

She looked up and down the empty street, then opened the back door of the lead van and examined the interior. In the back, one side was given over to a large and clunky array of surveillance equipment that looked like it might have first seen service during the Cold War. The other side was a weapons rack, with pistols and automatic rifles in metal clips, rows of tapered stakes hanging in rings mounted to the inner wall, and a sack filled with pouches of garlic.

Violin sneered at the equipment.

"*Idiota.*"

She spat into the van and turned away. Then she ran for her car.

By the time she reached the safe house, though, Joe Ledger was gone.

She searched the house and read the complete story told by the dead. The tortured couple upstairs, the others, killed by stake and bullets.

Violin stood in the living room for a full minute, staring at the dead man who lay slumped by the wall, a bullet hole glistening red over his heart. She read that, too, and nodded her approval.

Then she went to the doorway and peered up and down the empty street.

Violin stepped back into the quiet, shadowy, bloody hallway. She pushed back her sleeve and tapped the face of her watch. The image of the clock vanished to be replaced with a blank screen. Violin pressed her thumb to it for a moment. When she removed it the screen glowed green for a moment. Violin tapped the small receiver bud she wore in her left ear.

"Oracle."

"*Oracle welcomes you, Violin.*"

"Addition to mission report. A full Sabbatarian hit team tried to ambush Joseph Ledger. I eliminated the backup squad. Ledger took out the main squad."

"*Status of Captain Ledger?*" asked the computer.

"Unknown. I need that list of probable safe houses and bolt-holes."

"*Processing.*"

While she waited, Violin smiled because Joseph Ledger was still alive, but her smile was fragile because she had lost his trail. Worse still—much worse, in fact—was that she was treading on very dangerous ground. She had saved Ledger from a Red Knight, but in her report she had filed it as a "righteous kill," Arklight phrasing for a necessary assassination. Killing a knight would never be questioned, not even by Lilith or the other Mothers.

This action, though, could possibly be construed as an act of war. Arklight was not currently at war with the Sabbatarians. This hit could not be labeled as "righteous." A clever and devious mind could make a convincing argument that it was an attempt to save Ledger's life. That put it into a different category entirely. That was blood obligation. That was sacred ground filled with thorns and deadfalls.

As she drove, Violin racked her brain—and her heart—for an answer to the question that she knew would be coming. She prayed for another of her "flashes," but aside from the brief one this morning, there was nothing. It infuriated her. What was God's plan in giving her a gift that was faulty, questionable, and distracting? The fact that the flash had happened at all was skewing her focus. Was she acting on behalf of her mission objectives, or was she trying to save the life of Joseph Ledger?

It should have been an easy question to answer. Everything she had ever done, everything she had ever learned, had been geared toward making the response automatic. The Mission was all.

All.

Violin gripped the wheel. The muscles in her jaw ached from clenching.

The Mission was all.

Right?

"God," she breathed. Mother was going to be so angry.

Chapter Sixty-Four

Mustapha's Daily Goods
Tehran, Iran
June 15, 3:01 p.m.

In my trade, confidence is built on a platform whose legs are made up of good intelligence, continuous training, proper equipment, and field support. I had a sick dog, a dead man's gun, a stolen briefcase, a vampire hunter's stake in my belt, and a cell phone; and I was walking down a street in Tehran less than a day after breaking three political prisoners out of jail. I was involved in several murders and had left sufficient physical evidence behind to convict me on enough charges to lock me up until I was a thousand years old. Or enough to have me put against a wall.

Oh, yeah, and there were seven rogue nukes and somehow vampires were tied up in that.

My life used to be a lot less complicated.

I didn't need a safe house so much as I needed a nice quiet place to have a nervous breakdown.

We headed to the place Church assured me was genuinely safe. Ghost walked more slowly with every block, the fatigue catching up to him again. I stopped to pet him a couple of times, but he barely wagged his tail. I couldn't tell if we were friends again or if the events of the day had driven some kind of wedge into our relationship. It's like that with humans, and it can be that way with animals too.

When we reached the convenience store we walked past it and cut through an alley to the back where there was a small door beside a Dumpster. The store was the only open business in a district of warehouses that had been closed during the local economic troubles. The nearest residential area was blocks away, but there was a graveyard nearby and frequent mourners formed the basis of the store's customers.

It was a very useful setup for a safe house.

A key was hidden behind a brick, tenth from the ground, fifth from the door. I unlocked the door and peered inside. No crowd of armed thugs was waiting to pounce on me, so I nudged Ghost inside with my shin, checked that the coast was clear, and hustled inside, pulling the door shut behind me. The door looked frail and rickety, but it moved heavily, hinting at a steel core hidden beneath layers of weathered wood.

Ghost and I found ourselves in a storeroom with wire shelves stocked with dry and canned goods. I peered around the corner and saw a beaded curtain beyond which was the store. A clerk—the owner, Jamsheed Mustapha, I presumed—stood behind a counter pouring dry lentils onto a scale while an old woman watched. I crept to the edge of the doorway to eavesdrop, hoping they weren't talking about the best way to sharpen stakes. They weren't. They were sharing their outrage about the mosque bombing, which I imagine was still the number one topic of conversation

254 | Jonathan Maberry

in the country. The clerk did not look at me, although he'd probably gotten some signal that the security door had been opened.

In the corner of the storeroom was a tiny bathroom permanently marked "Under Repair." I opened the door and again had to push Ghost inside. He was still sluggish and muzzy from the Taser and was recovering very slowly. Tasers are configured to knock out an adult male, not a hundred-pound dog. I'm lucky that son of a bitch hadn't killed *my* son of a bitch.

I shut the door and sat down on the closed toilet seat. The stall was immaculate, and when I placed my palm flat on the wall I could feel its solidity and sense the faintest tremble of well-concealed electronics. If this was a safe house approved by Church then it was very likely built with "securepod" technology, something one of Church's friends was bringing to market. An ultrasecure, ultrahardened capsule similar to the escape pod used on Air Force One. This one didn't go anywhere, but it would offer physical protection and a secure spot for making reports.

Ghost immediately flopped onto the floor and whimpered softly. I bent down and ran my hands over him, checking to make sure that the Taser shock and burn were the only injuries he had sustained.

"You okay, fur-monster?" I asked.

He gave me an "Are you frigging kidding me?" look, but even with that he managed a wag. Just one, but there it was.

"Don't know about you," I said, "but I kinda want to switch gears from running and hiding to chasing and maiming."

He curled a quarter inch of muzzle to show me one fang. Better than nothing.

I examined the briefcase and saw that the locks were even better than they'd first appeared, and small bulges on other side felt like the right size and shape for thermite charges. Force the locks and the case explodes into a white-hot fireball. Not the sort of thing I wanted to do with the case resting on my lap. I set it aside for the moment.

There was a small sink and I turned the spigot and let the water run until it was cold. Then I used some paper towels to wash my face and sponge the garlic out of my nose, trying not to feel as freaked as the situation warranted. Those sons of bitches had tried to stun me with garlic and drive a wooden stake through my heart. That's something none of the guys back at the DMS is going to story-top.

For the third—or was it the fourth?—time today the immediate rush of adrenaline was flushing itself out of my blood. That fight or flight juice certainly amps you up but when it leaves it tends to take a lot of other things with it. Electrolytes were the least of it. I felt as if I had no energy left at all; I doubted I could go two out of three falls with Betty White.

When I closed my eyes I saw Krystos's face, the way he looked at the moment I pulled the trigger. I'd made a joke as I killed him. Like I was a hero in some summer action flick. A cheap one-liner while I blasted the life from him.

I pulled out my phone and dialed a number.

Not Church this time.

The call was answered on the third ring.

"Cowboy?" asked Rudy.

"Hey."

Are you alright?"

"I'm at the safe house. The one Church sent me to. It's cool. The place is secure."

"I am very glad to hear that. What about you, Joe? Are you okay?"

"No," I said, and the word came out fractured. "No, man, I'm not. I just killed a man while he was praying."

Chapter Sixty-Five

Mustapha's Daily Goods
Tehran, Iran
June 15, 3:14 p.m.

Rudy and I talked for nearly ten minutes.

"Joe," he said when I'd finished telling him about Krystos, "what else could you have done?"

"Nothing," I snapped. "That's my damn point. What choice did I have except to kill them? I'm not saying that I was wrong, or that I did it wrong. But I made a joke while I was doing it. Jesus."

"I think we both know that your sense of humor is as much a weapon for you as your fists or your gun. It protects you. It keeps the pain at arm's length."

"Except when it doesn't."

256 | Jonathan Maberry

"Except then, yes," he conceded. "Tell me, though, does any defense work all the time?"

"Running away?"

"Joe . . ."

"I know, I know. I just can't seem to square this in my head."

"A long time ago," he said, "or what seems like a long time ago, when we joined the DMS, we talked about this. About how violence always leaves a mark. Only the immoral or mentally unbalanced can kill without taking some harm themselves."

"We both know where I stand on that score."

"You are psychologically unique, Joe," Rudy corrected, "as is everyone. You are the end result of the damage you received and the work you've done to understand it and adjust to its presence in your life."

"Doesn't address the morals issue."

"No, but it's connected. When you were thirteen you had the common moral worldview shared by people of your age, gender, ethnicity, nationality, and family environment. When you were fourteen your worldview was knocked askew and you suffered intense physical and emotional trauma. As a result your morality underwent an adjustment. As you entered into a study of martial arts and learned to control your rage while developing dangerous combat skills, you began to understand that there were times and circumstances under which you would be willing to do harm to others. You knew then that if you ever confronted the teens who raped Helen and nearly killed you, that you could do great harm to them without suffering emotional harm from the act. This is not an irrational view given your history. Then, when you entered the military, your worldview was adjusted for you during basic and advanced training. You adopted the soldier's view of violence, and had you gone into battle I have no doubt that you could have fought and killed without feeling that you were committing immoral acts."

"It's not as simple as that."

"Of course it isn't. I'm generalizing here to make a point," he said. "After the army you entered the police academy. You learned another version of the worldview and adopted a new attitude toward when violence might be appropriate. And there was an adjustment of that when you became a detective and began working on the counterterrorist unit. The step into the DMS was an extraordinary one, Joe. Massive. The very first day you were in multiple firefights. Each time you have had to adjust your emotions and your worldview to allow for the reality of more and different kinds of killing. I know that with each step we have had to take a little time to explore what this is doing to you. And you know the warning I've given you several times."

"I know."

It was the kind of warning he, as a psychiatrist and a moral person, was honor-bound to give: be prepared for the day when you cannot do this anymore.

After Grace had been killed—after I'd tracked down her killer and torn him apart—I thought I'd reached my limit with this kind of work and this kind of life. Then the Seven Kings case blew up in my face and suddenly I was ankle deep in blood again. As much as I hated being a part of that fight, I discovered the ugly truth that it defined me. Not the killing. No, not that. It was the fight itself. It never seemed to be over and until it was, how could I, in good conscience, lay down my gun and let the innocent fend for themselves? How could I do that and not go crazy myself? Church had been a warrior in this far longer than anyone else I knew. During the Kings thing he tried to explain it to me. He said, "The darkness is all around us. Very few people have the courage to light a candle against it. We hold a candle against the darkness. Like the unknown and unseen enemy we fight, people like you and me—we *are* the darkness. In some ways we are more like the things we're fighting than the people we're protecting. We are part of the darkness. Granted our motives are better—from our perspective—but we wait in the darkness for our unseen enemy to make a move against those innocents with the candles. And by that light, we take aim."

I repeated those words to Rudy.

"I remember you telling me this. And I remember when you decided that this was, in fact, who you were."

"Sure, and that's all very noble, very grand, but can I say that I'm that kind of warrior and measure it against cracking a joke while I shoot a bound prisoner who's praying for mercy from God?"

Rudy began to answer, but there was a discreet tap on the door.

"I have to go, Rude."

"Joe—we need to finish this conversation."

"Yeah," I said. "I know."

I hung up, got to my feet, and pulled my gun from my waistband.

Chapter Sixty-Six

Mustapha's Daily Goods

Tehran, Iran

June 15, 3:19 p.m.

I opened the door a quarter inch. Enough to see a single eye peering in at me. If that eye was red or even reddish I was going to put a bullet through it.

"Are you okay in there, my friend? Do you need assistance?"

They were the kinds of question anyone would ask, but the exact phrasing was a prearranged code. I opened the door a few inches, pistol out of sight. Ghost stuck his nose into the crack and began cataloging everything he could about the man outside.

"I'm just a little tired from the trip," I said, using the proper response to the coded questions.

"Perhaps I can help," he said.

I opened the door and the store clerk's eyes darted first to Ghost, then to my lowered gun and finally to me. No shock or surprise registered on his face.

"I am Jamsheed Mustapha," he said.

I didn't give my name, and he didn't ask.

Jamsheed was about fifty but he wasn't carrying it well. His posture was bad and his face was deeply lined. Stress lines, not laugh lines. "The store is locked," he said, "and I've engaged the jammers. No one is listening and no one knows you're here."

"Works for me," I said as I eased the hammer down on the pistol and returned it to my waistband. Jamsheed backed away to allow me to step outside. Ghost remained right where he was, cued to do so by a small finger signal I gave him. He would watch and wait and stay alert until I signaled him to stand down.

"As-salāmu 'alaykum," I said.

"Wa-laikum as-salâm," said Jamsheed and offered me his hand. We shook. He had frail bones but managed to give a firm shake. He did a second, longer appraisal, taking in the ill-fitting shirt, bloodstains, my battered face, the works.

"You are hurt? I have a first aid kit in my apartment. We'll get you cleaned up. I have clothes, too. There will be some in your size." He paused. "Have you spoken to the *Mujtahid?*"

I nodded. *Mujtahid* was the Arabic word for "scholar," but it was also one of the many code names for Mr. Church. I relaxed even more at that name and gave the stand-down signal to Ghost, who immediately flopped down and appeared to lapse into a canine coma. Apparently he *was* faking his combat readiness.

"Is there something wrong with your dog?" asked Jamsheed.

I explained about the Taser and the net. Jamsheed asked me to wait, and he went into the store and came back with a plastic bowl, two bottles of water, and a bag of high-protein dog biscuits. He handed everything to me. It was clear that he knew enough about military-trained dogs to not try to give the food and water to Ghost directly. I thanked him. Jamsheed earned a whole lot of points from me for that kindness. I knelt and emptied one bottle into the bowl, tore open the bag of biscuits, and laid six of them in a row. Ghost pried open an eye, flexed his nostrils, and wagged his tail. He got shakily to his feet and set-to with a will, lapping up the water and then suddenly going hog wild on the biscuits, his usual daintiness forgotten for the moment.

"Are the police looking for you?" asked Jamsheed.

I shook my head. "They're looking for someone, but no one has my description."

"That simplifies this. You look like you could use some food and drink as well, my friend."

"At this point, I'd even go for one of the dog biscuits."

Ghost shot me a "don't even think about it" look and moved to stand between me and his food.

"My team is coming for me," I said. "Can I stay here for a few hours and wait?"

"Of course, of course, as long as you need." He didn't ask for details, and I had no idea what information Church told him. Jamsheed seemed to be taking all of this in stride. He took me by the arm and led me through a small door into his apartment. It was cramped, but very clean and decorated with gorgeous framed photographs of children, animals, landscapes, and buildings.

"Your work?" I asked.

He nodded. "A hobby. I hope to retire from this *work* and concentrate on photography." He leaned on the word "work."

"You have an incredible eye," I said, and I wasn't joking. Each of the pictures was a small masterpiece of composition. Not just a flower, but an angle that showed light caressing the striations on a delicate petal in a way that cast it as an alien landscape. Not merely a photo of a child with a kitten, but a glimpse into the wonder in that child's eyes and the trust in the body language of the kitten. Each piece was a statement filled with visual poetry that betrayed a deep understanding of the connection between the physical world and the spiritual. "These are really quite beautiful."

He made a modest sound of dismissal.

"No," I said, crossing to stand in front of one picture in particular, "you have the gift."

Jamsheed came and stood next to me, trying to see the picture through my eyes—a foreigner, a soldier, a non-Muslim, a stranger. The image that caught me, that riveted me, was of a chain-link fence beyond which a group of kids played soccer in a deserted parking lot. Beyond the skill of the composition, the story it told struck me to the heart. A bunch of kids totally absorbed in their game. At that distance and with a gentle softening of the focus, he made the children nonspecific. It no longer mattered if they were preteens or teens, if they were boys or girls, or if they were Muslim or Christian. What mattered, what shone through, was that they were innocent and at peace with the fun they were having. That picture might have been taken anywhere. England or Uruguay, Alabama or here in Iran. There were so many lessons implied in the simple grace of those children, and it had been perfectly captured by this man's camera.

He waited out my long silence, then asked, "What does it say to you?"

"Lots," I said. "But I guess . . . two things most of all."

"Oh?"

"Everybody has kids," I said, "and everybody loves their kids."

Jamsheed touched the edge of the frame near the image of a little girl who was no more than a happy blur as she ran after a ball. "Yes."

"And . . . this is why we do what we do."

I turned to him and saw a mix of thoughtful expressions play across his face. "It's funny," he said, "but I would have thought you would say something like, 'this is why we fight.' "

"I know. That occurred to me," I admitted, "but it isn't the right way to say it. I'm not in this business to fight. Seeing these pictures . . . I don't think you are, either. It's not about the conflict. It's about what it preserves and what it allows."

Jamsheed nodded and went over to a tiny kitchenette and began filling a teapot with water. "I once knew a Sufi who said that anyone who goes to war is crazy. But . . . I don't think he was exactly correct. I believe it is more accurate to say that anyone who *wants* to go to war is crazy."

"That says it," I agreed.

He put the kettle on the burner, then fetched a first aid kit and helped me clean and dress my wounds. He had to pick some window glass and wood splinters out of my scalp and back from when I had crashed out of my hotel room and onto the balcony while waltzing with the knight.

"You have a lot of scars already," he said as he worked, "so these should blend in."

"Hazards of the job."

"Mm."

I caught Jamsheed sniffing a few times as he worked, and it took me a moment to make the connection.

"Garlic," I said.

"Yes." He didn't ask, though he clearly wanted to.

"Long, weird story. Probably best if I don't share."

He nodded. "Yes. I understand."

"Do you do field work?" I asked.

"Not anymore." He considered for a moment and then unbuttoned the top two buttons of his shirt and pulled the cloth apart to reveal two scars. Bullet holes. "Souvenirs of an adventurous youth."

I noticed that he had other scars. More than his share. Around his eyes, around his fingernails. He'd been beaten and very likely tortured at some point. He noticed me looking and offered the smallest of shrugs, but he didn't comment.

When he was done picking out the last of the splinters, he showed me the bathroom and even turned on the shower for me. Before I closed the bathroom door, I asked, "Why don't you retire? The world needs more artists."

He shrugged. "The time isn't right yet."

It was a simple statement, but a sad one, and it stayed with me while I showered, dried, and changed into clean clothes. Jamsheed was a lot smaller than me, but he was well stocked. When I came out of the bathroom I found several choices of clothes in extra-large. I dressed in khakis and a white dress shirt. Jamsheed also left me a makeup kit and a hot cup of tea. I sipped the tea as I touched up the dye job Khalid had given me before we rescued the hikers. My tan only needed a mild olive tint. Jamsheed didn't have brown contact lenses, but there were plenty of blue-eyed people in the Middle East.

When I came out, Jamsheed inspected the work and nodded approval. Ghost had come in from the storeroom and lay sprawled in front of an oscillating fan, twitching every now and then as he dreamed.

Jamsheed set out plates of food and we ate a lunch of *chelo kabab*— steamed saffron basmati rice and grilled chunks of goat, accompanied by pomegranate soup. He apologized for it being leftovers, but I didn't care. It was delicious and I cleaned my plate. When Ghost woke up and saw that my plate was empty, he looked truly wounded. However, Jamsheed fetched a bowl of leftover *khoresht beh*, a lamb stew thick with rice and vegetables. Ghost nearly fell on him and wept. Jamsheed watched with some amusement as Ghost attacked the food.

Jamsheed was not a talkative man. Perhaps it was because he did not want to know anything about who I was or why I was in Iran. He may have been our local contact, but it did not change the fact that he was Iranian. I wondered what conflicts warred inside his artist's mind. What was it about his government that made him want to side with people like Church? I'd met a few people like him before, and they ranged from traitors whose souls could be bought to idealists who believed that change for their country was necessary.

Then I saw him cutting quick looks at me and twice he opened his mouth to say something then changed his mind. I set my fork down.

"What is it?" I asked.

Jamsheed furrowed his brow. "The incident last night. The young Americans."

I waited.

"Was that you? Is that why you're here?"

I sat back and dabbed my mouth with a napkin.

Jamsheed looked uneasy. "I know, I know—I shouldn't be asking such questions."

"Then why are you?"

He got up and walked over to the picture of the children playing soccer. He stared at it for a long time. "We are a warlike people. I don't mean just us Iranians. I mean all people. Humans. The veneer of civilization is very thin."

"At times," I said. "Not always."

He conceded with only a small nod. "No, not always. But too often it is true. War is a disease and we are all infected. And, like carriers, we pass it along to our children." He touched the picture. "Sometimes, we even *involve* our children. That is against God. No matter what faith you are, no matter how devoutly you pray, it is an affront to God."

"Yes it is," I said.

He turned to me. "Not everyone in my country's government is corrupt. Not everyone is in love with war. There are good people here."

I nodded. "I know that. I can say the same about my government, or any government. There are always heroes and villains. And there are people who do bad things because they think it's right. Depends on the viewpoint they've come to believe in. Some are misled, some come from a tradition of intolerance. Look how long it took my country to free its slaves and give everyone the vote. As far as I know, no one country holds the patent on moral perfection."

Jamsheed sighed. "This was not the first time my government kidnapped young people and called them spies. Ever since we began our nuclear program, it has become unofficial *policy* to use these kinds of tactics. It gets into the world press, and even though we are condemned for it, there is just enough room for doubt to stall the process of releasing them. It is . . ." He fished for a word, waving his hand as if he could snatch it out of the air. The word he came up with was "dishonorable."

"Yes it damn well is."

"To use *children* is . . ." He wanted another word, a worse word. But what word was really adequate?

We looked into each other's eyes for a long time. There were all kinds of things being said without either of us having to say another word. Eventually, though, I did say one word.

"Evil."

He nodded. "Yes," he said softly. "It is the worst face of evil."

Chapter Sixty-Seven

The Warehouse
Baltimore, Maryland
June 15, 6:55 a.m. EST

"Hey, docs!" Bug called. Circe and Rudy glanced up and saw him waving to them on the big monitor.

"What have you got?" asked Circe.

"Weird, weird stuff," he said, tapping the main screen on which were dozens of overlapping windows and text boxes. "I've been going through the field notes and even with most of the stuff corrupted there are hundreds of pages of stuff. I had MindReader index the words, and I hit a few I didn't know. One in particular came up and I tried to translate it from Arabic or Persian, but it's neither of those languages. Turns out its Russian."

Rudy bent close to turn and make sense of the data on Bug's screen, but there was too much that he didn't know. "What's the word?"

"Upierczi."

"That's the same word Joe heard from the Greek man, Krystos," said Rudy.

Circe nodded. "Right. It's the Russian word for vampires."

"Ouch," breathed Rudy. "Joe won't like that."

"What's the context, Bug?"

Bug grinned. "That's the part he *really* won't like. According to Rasouli's field agent, the Upierczi are high on the list of groups suspected of having planted the bombs."

They looked at each other for several moments.

"Okay," said Bug, "I found this stuff out, I forwarded it to the Big Boss,

Auntie, and Joe, but I have no idea where to *go* with it, if you know what I mean."

"I do," admitted Rudy. "We can all say the word 'vampire,' and speculate about whether they are real or not, but that doesn't connect us to the actual phenomenon. There are people involved in this case who other people believe to be vampires. The point is, what do *we* believe?"

"We can't begin to answer that, Rudy," said Circe. She chewed her lip for a moment. "I think we need an expert."

"Who?" mused Bug. "Stephen King?"

"Close enough." Circe looked at the wall clock. "God, it's almost seven in the morning. Have we really been here all night?"

Very quickly, Rudy said, "At least last night ended well."

Even though Bug could not hear the comment, Circe turned away to hide her flushed cheeks. She dug her cell phone out of her purse and searched for the number of Professor Jonathan Corbiel-Newton.

"This is her day off. She always sleeps in on Sundays." Circe murmured as she listened to the rings. "She's going to kill me."

Rudy snorted. "She'll get over it. Maybe Mr. Church will bring her inside his 'circle of trust' as the permanent DMS vampire expert."

"Don't joke."

"I'm not," he said.

Interlude Nine

Jerusalem
March 3, 1229 C.E.

"It is as cold as the grave in here."

The young nun, Sister Sophia, scolded the old priest with her disapproving stare as she hustled around the room to pull closed the shutters and draw the heavy drapes.

Father Esteban, a hawk-nosed man of seventy, raised his head from the letter he was writing and watched her with mingled annoyance and amusement.

As Sister Sophia wheeled on him with a fierce scowl. "And look at you! By the blessed virgin you are positively blue with cold. What could you be thinking to let yourself get into such a state?"

"I'm sorry," said the priest, his voice thick with fatigue, "I have been very busy."

"You'll be less busy if you get sick again, Father Esteban. You know what the doctor advised." Sister Sophia was many years younger than the priest and ostensibly his servant during his retreat; however, Father Esteban knew that he had no authority in her presence. Not unless there was a third person present, at which point she would play the role of the dutiful bride of Christ and pad around him with quiet deference. But that was all an act. Sister Sophia had been charged by her mother superior—a harpy of mythic ferocity—to nurse Esteban back to health and prevent him from doing exactly what he had just done: work himself to the point of exhaustion while ignoring the needs of the body.

Father Esteban muttered some apologies as he accepted a cup of hot wine. He sipped the wine and peered through the steam to the last lines he had written. The report was the latest in a series of such missives he had prepared for the Holy Father in Rome. Reports on the murders of pilgrims on the road to Jerusalem, of churches burned, of nuns raped and sodomized. Saracens at their worst. From eyewitness accounts to blasphemous passages of the Koran written in feces or blood upon church walls. Two months ago the tone of his letters had changed, and these recent letters included accounts of retaliation by Knights Hospitaller and other remnants of the crusaders. Retribution was swift and it was brutal. Mosques were burned. Families of suspected Saracen raiders were tortured and put to the sword. Imam were skinned alive or burned at the stake. Father Esteban did not approve of such harsh actions, but he understood their purpose. To respond in kind and with greater ferocity to show that the children of God were not lambs for the sacrifice of heathens. After his most recent journey to collect reports, his latest letter had yet another flavor.

> *The last week has been without incident. The pilgrim road is now under the protection of the Knights Hospitaller and the senior knight, Sir Guy LaRoque, assures me that the Saracens have been dissuaded from further attacks upon the children of God. However, I remain unconvinced that the threat has so easily been resolved after . . .*

There was a clang behind him and he flinched as he realized what it was. Sister Sophia had raised the metal cover of his dinner tray and then slammed it down again as she saw the uneaten dinner.

"Holy Mary, Mother of God . . ."

If it had been anyone else, Father Esteban would have admonished her for swearing, but he knew better. It was more than his peace of mind—and perhaps his life—was worth to duel with Sophia when she held the moral high ground.

Before Sister Sophia could get to full gallop, however, there was a sharp sound at the window.

"What was that?" asked the young nun, her voice suddenly hushed.

"Perhaps a bird flew into the shutters," suggested Father Esteban.

"Perhaps," said Sister Sophia dubiously, and she took a reflexive step forward as if to stand between Father Esteban and harm.

They listened for several moments, but all they heard from outside was the fierce desert wind blowing across the endless wastes.

"A bird, then," conceded Sister Sophia, though she did not open the window to confirm this. Both of them had heard the stories about this desert. About the jinni and other unholy demons who haunted the Arabian sands. Lost souls who lured travelers to oases and then feasted on them, flesh and bone.

Then the sound came again. A blow upon the casement, sharp and hard.

The nun crossed herself.

Father Esteban did not. Though a priest and investigator for the church, he privately regarded himself as a political cleric rather than a man of deep faith. It was not true to say that he had entirely lost his faith, because he had never entirely had it. He was the youngest son of his family and, as was traditional among the nobility, after his oldest brother began to manage the estates and his middle brother went to war, Esteban had gone into the priesthood. It had been expected of him, and gainsaying the policies of a thousand years of tradition and the iron will of his widowed mother had been impossible options.

Father Esteban slid his hand under a sheaf of old parchments to touch the handle of the thin-bladed knife he used to cut the tapes on official documents. It was not much, but it was better than prayer, at least in his experience.

Sister Sophia crept to the window and leaned an ear toward the drapes, listening. Her right fist was clutched so tightly around her rosary that her knuckles were white and her lips moved in a soundless prayer to the Virgin.

They waited. A minute. Two.

Five.

Silence was all they heard. Father Esteban let out a breath and uncurled his fingers from the knife.

Finally the nun began to relax, her cramped attitude of listening yielding first to conditional relief and then to rueful humor as she caught the eye of the priest.

"And here, look at us, cringing at sounds like children sent to bed on a moonless night. What a picture we are."

Suddenly there was a tremendous crash as the shutters exploded inward, tearing the drapes from their rings and showering the nun with a storm of jagged splinters. The fierce impact staggered Sister Sophia, but she did not fall. Instead something dark lashed out and clamped around her throat, catching her, lifting her to her toes, choking off her screams. A bulky figure stepped through the shattered window, its face covered in a dark red mask, its body hidden beneath a cloak the color of old blood.

"Sophia!" screamed Father Esteban as he leapt to his feet and stared in uncomprehending horror at what he was seeing. The masked intruder held the nun with one hand. Sister Sophia twisted and writhed in the grip, beating at the hand with her small fist; and then the man did the impossible—he lifted the nun even higher until her toes barely touched the floor, and then higher still so that she hung inches above the stone.

With a cry of horror, Father Esteban snatched up the dagger he had just set down and rushed across the room, tottering on feet whose circulation had not fully returned.

The nun tried to scream a warning, or perhaps a plea, but she could force no sound at all past the stricture in her throat. Her pale face had flushed red and was now turning a violent purple.

"Let her go!" bellowed Esteban, and he drove the blade of the knife toward the chest of the figure cloaked in drapes and darkness. But the figure hissed at him like a jungle cat and flung the writhing nun at him with unnatural force. Father Esteban had no chance to dodge and he took her weight full in the chest; then they were falling in a shrieking sprawl of arms and legs. Father Esteban crashed to the stone floor and Sister Sophia's weight landed hip first onto his chest with a sound like breaking sticks. Pain exploded in Father Esteban's chest, and his eyes filled with sparks of white fire.

The nun sagged down, unconscious. Esteban struggled to push her off of him, to see the attacker, to draw in a single breath of air. The slender dagger was still clutched in one hand but it was useless to him.

Then, without warning, the weight was gone. The intruder was there, his fists knotted in the nun's black habit, and without even a grunt of effort he tore the black cloth apart to reveal the white undergarments; then he slashed and ripped these until the naked and innocent flesh of the nun was revealed. It was a horrible transgression, and Father Esteban bellowed in outrage and fury, but the intruder ignored him as he studied the young breasts and clean limbs of the nearly naked woman. The intruder smiled and nodded.

"Yes, she will do very well" he said, and pushed her roughly aside.

The hulking black figure then turned slowly toward the priest. His red robes swirled in the stiff breeze that blew in through the destroyed window. There was no mark, no symbol or badge on any of his garments, and they covered him entirely except for a narrow opening through which two intensely unnatural eyes glared. They were fierce and strange, their irises as blood red as his clothes.

Like the eyes of a rat.

Like the eyes of a demon.

"God!" cried the priest, the word torn from him, from the deep well in which the last of his faith dwelled. He stabbed at the attacker, lunging with his failing strength to try to plunge the needle tip of the dagger into one of those inhuman eyes. But the man—the *thing*, for it could not possibly be a man—caught the priest's wrist. Then, with an almost casual jerk, he snapped Father Esteban's wrist as easily as if the bones were late winter icicles.

Red hot agony erupted in the priest's arm and he screamed.

He screamed in pain and in fury and in outrage at this attack, and at all that it meant. He knew who and what this man had to be. A Saracen, one of the *Hashashin* come to murder him, come to silence the voice of the Holy Church.

But he, Father Esteban, was wrong about that, as he was wrong about so many things; and for him, clarity and understanding came far too late.

The intruder released his grip on the priest's shattered wrist and reached up to his mask, pulling the red cloth slowly away. Revealing his face.

Not a Saracen face.

The skin was pale, the features narrow, the lips thin. A European face.

But not that either.

When the intruder smiled, Father Esteban knew with all certainty that this man did not belong to any country. He did not belong to this world. Thin, colorless lips peeled back to reveal teeth that were yellow and crooked. And wrong.

So wrong.

Each was tapered to a point as needle-sharp as Esteban's dagger. Not filed the way some of the African cannibals do. No . . . Father Esteban knew that these teeth, as unnatural as they were, were completely natural to this man.

This *creature*.

"For the love of God!" cried the priest, his terror and shock greater than the pain in his chest and wrist.

The thing bent closer to him and Esteban could smell the rancid-meat stink of its breath.

"Yes, Father," said the monster. "All things are done for the love of God."

That awful mouth stretched open as the red-eyed thing lunged at him.

There was a moment of white-hot pain, and then the colors drained out of the world and took sound and feeling with them, leaving Father Esteban floating in a sea of nothingness. As the darkness wrapped its cloak around him, a single word echoed in his mind, pulsing slowly with the fading beats of his heart.

Vampiro.

Chapter Sixty-Eight

My cell vibrated in my pocket. I pulled it and looked at the code on the screen. Mr. Church. Jamsheed excused himself and went out to his store so I could take the call.

I doubted it was good news.

"I heard from Bug," Church said. "He's located a device here in the States."

"Where?"

"Louisiana."

Bang. There it was.

Chapter Sixty-Nine

"Christ," I said. "Tell me."

"Bug initiated a MindReader search of cargo ships, oil tankers, fishing fleets, and other craft capable of carrying a large, shielded device. Back-tracking through ports where cargo could be quietly shifted from one craft to another. These are routes and transfers that would not ring bells on any standard-security computers, so we got lucky."

"Now give me the bad news."

"It's on an oil rig in the Gulf of Mexico a few miles off the coast of New Orleans. We confirmed the presence of a nuclear signature with a flyover. Low levels, which means it is likely shielded, probably not a danger to the staff aboard the rig, but too high to be anything other than what it is. I have two of our people doing a soft infil right now under cover of a random inspection of blowout preventers. The rig is about due for a check, so we caught that break."

"Shit."

272 | Jonathan Maberry

"I borrowed SEAL Team Six to work a coordinated operation with Riptide Team out of Miami. Aunt Sallie will coordinate it from the TOC at the Hangar."

"When do they hit it?"

"The president is making that decision now."

"Who's stalling, him or you?"

"Me. I talked him out of giving an immediate go-order. We now know that the devices exist, and that the U.S. is on the list. I don't want to hit one and have that serve as a signal for our enemies to trigger the other devices."

"No joke. During my interrogation with Krystos, he said the Sabbatarians were trying to prevent the Red Knights from destroying the world, and he wasn't talking about a global suckfest. His crew think that these Upierczi freaks are the ones with the nukes."

"Aunt Sallie told me that you forwarded a theory along those lines," he said, "so I've arranged for Dr. Hu to join us. I'm conferencing him in now."

"Swell," I said.

"I heard that," said Hu.

"It was an expression of great joy," I said. "I've missed you and longed to hear your voice."

"Eat me."

Church sighed heavily, which effectively silenced the sniping war.

The only person at the DMS who disliked me more than Aunt Sallie was Dr. William Hu, the head of Church's vast science and research department. Hu was a couple miles beyond brilliant, and he had what would have been a fun pop-culture sensibility if it wasn't for the fact that he was a totally amoral asshole. If there was a plague totally unknown to science that was killing thousands of people an hour, Hu was as happy as a kid on Christmas morning because he had a new toy to play with. By comparison, Hu made Dr. Frankenstein look like Jonas Salk. Granted, Bug had some weird detachments from the real world, too, but Bug had a heart. I'd need a full autopsy of Hu before I believed he did, and I'd pay for that procedure right now.

For his part, Hu once described me as a "muscle-headed mouth breather."

"Doctor," began Church in a rather more commanding voice than usual, "I would like you to give Captain Ledger some useful feedback on his theories."

I heard Hu quietly mumble the word "theories." "Sure," he said.

"First up, what the hell are the Upierczi? Are they vampires?"

"I'd need to dissect one," Hu said, sounding jazzed at the thought, "so I can only speculate on whether the model of the traditional vampire is medically possible. It isn't. Not as Hollywood shows it. Therianthropy is—"

"Whoa—what?"

"Therianthropy," he said, pronouncing it slowly for those of us on the short bus. "From the Greek *therion*, meaning 'beast' and *anthropos*, meaning 'human.' Creatures who can change their form. Also known as 'shapeshifting,' but it's mythology, not science. Refers to creatures that could change shape from animal to human, or human to animal."

"Like vampires turning into bats."

"And werewolves, which would be subclassified as lycanthropes. Folklore's filled with crap like that. You got cynanthropy, which is transforming into a dog, ailuranthropy, turning into a cat, yada, yada, yada. There is no evidence of any credible kind that humans can transform."

"What about sunlight?"

"Possibly. Photophobia is a fear of sunlight and a morbid fear of it is called heliophobia, but Auntie said that your 'theory' was that these Upierczi have increased resistance to radiation. That would contradict a fear of sunlight unless the fear was purely psychological and not physiological."

"Isn't that likely here?" I asked. "If we're going to talk about vampires of any kind existing, even if they're just faking it somehow, then they are going to have to be aware of the myths and legends."

"Okay," he agreed grudgingly, "there are a couple of takes on that. Either the Upierczi are some kind of vampire, in which case their unusual nature inspired some of the legends about what we popularly think about vampires. Storytellers, campfire tales, and fiction writers filled in the rest."

"Or, maybe the Upierczi deliberately provided their own disinformation campaign," I suggested.

"Maybe," he said, but I knew I'd scored a point.

"Could a human subspecies have a greater tolerance for radiation?" I asked.

"Sure. Not to the point where they can juggle isotopes, but we've seen a pretty big range. Some of the exposure studies after Chernobyl and Fukushima show that."

"Enough for them to live in a postnuclear environment?"

"That would depend on where the nukes detonate, both in relation to prevailing wind and ocean currents and to actual proximity to the highest concentrations. When Chernobyl melted down everyone thought that the area around it would be a total dead zone, but we saw plant growth return much more quickly, and also the return of animals and birds. Nature loves to adapt. Now . . . another factor in species survival would be the number of nukes. If the Upierczi live anywhere near one of the blast zones, it's doubtful they would be able to withstand the doses. However, if they are removed from the blast zones, it would be up to their unique biology as to how soon they could reinhabit those areas." He paused. "We're looking for seven nukes worldwide? That would not pose a lasting threat even to the normal human population."

"It wouldn't?"

"Well, I mean a bunch of people would be toast. Worst-case scenario from the five we already know of, including New Orleans, would be maybe fifty million dead from the blasts, maybe two hundred million dead in two to forty years from cancers. That's nothing matched against the six and three quarter billion who wouldn't die."

"That's 'nothing'?"

"Try thinking big picture once in a while," said Hu smugly.

"Are you—"I began, my voice rising.

"Don't start," warned Church. "We don't have the time for it."

I bit down on the things I wanted to say to Hu, and he was probably grinning at the other end of the phone, thinking that he'd just scored by having me yelled at by the teacher.

"What if the Upierczi stay underground?" asked Church.

"What do you mean?" I asked. "In graves or—"

"In tunnels. We have some intelligence that they live, or at least *lived*, in tunnels."

"Well," mused Hu, "rock and dirt are great insulators as long as they aren't part of a contaminated water table or underground river."

"In deserts?" I asked.

"Pretty good place to be. Again, though, they'd have to be away from water or, if Rasouli's intel is right, away from the oil sands."

"New topic," I said. "Physiology. The Red Knight I fought was faster and stronger than me. Not just a little, either. What's the upper range of human potential?"

"Impossible to say," answered Hu, "because it depends on too many factors. Muscle density, bone density, and overall cellular structure. We keep pushing back the limits for fastest and strongest all the time, and I'm not just talking steroids. Every Olympic Games you have new world records set. There are going to be some extreme limits, of course. Human bones and muscle will never allow someone to bench-press a ton or outrun a sports car, but there is a whole lot of wiggle room; and that's before we get into gene therapy. Remember the Berserkers from the Jakoby thing. They were big men who received DNA from silverback gorillas. Granted, it caused other mutations and it was a long way from healthy for the subjects, but in the short term those men were much stronger than ordinary humans. Now, if we talk natural mutation in terms of physical potential, that will vary, and we've seen average guys who are surprisingly strong and bulky guys who don't have the strength to open a beer bottle. Like I said, I'd need to cut one of these guys to pin it down."

"I'll see what I can do," I said. "What can I use to fight them? Those Sabbatarian freaks had hammers, stakes, holy water, and garlic."

Hu snorted. "Forget holy water unless the Upierczi actually believe in it."

"Why would that make a difference?"

"It wouldn't, except psychologically," said Church. "They'd fear it or try to evade it, which might open up an opportunity for you."

"What about the stakes and hammers?"

"I expect," said Hu, "that would work on anybody. If you don't have a gun, a big pointed stick is worth a try."

"And garlic?"

"Hm. Might be something to that. I did a search through the literature, and, though garlic allergies aren't that common, there is plenty of documentation."

"Fatal allergies?" I asked hopefully.

"Not usually. Most garlic allergies are a form of contact dermatitis. Chefs get it once in a while when they get garlic oil or dust in a cut. They present with patterns of asymmetrical fissures on the affected fingertips, maybe some thickening and shedding of the outer skin layers. In really rare cases that can progress to second- or even third-degree burns. Actually it's a component of garlic, the chemical diallyl disulfide, or DADS, along with related compounds allyl propyl disulfide and allicin. You find all three in other plants in the genus Allium, too, like leeks and onions."

"So what do I do, ask the Red Knights to make me some garlic bread and hope they have an accident with a knife?"

Hu laughed despite himself. "If the Upierczi have a congenital allergy, that could be in our favor. It'd be better if you could get some dust or oil directly into their lungs or bloodstream. That's probably why the Sabbatarians threw garlic in your face. If you breathed it and you were a Upier, then you might go into anaphylaxis. Then they'd go all Buffy the Vampire Slayer on you and we wouldn't be having this conversation."

"Sorry to disappoint."

"Hope springs eternal," Hu said. "The kicker is that we don't know if garlic is a genuine allergen to them or if that's more disinformation. You're going to have to figure that out on the fly."

"Swell. Anything else you can tell me?"

"Nothing that isn't blind speculation. We don't have the data to do more than speculate."

"Thank you, Doctor," said Church, and he dropped Hu out of the conversation. "Any other thoughts, Captain?"

"Just one. What are the chances that the Iranian government is behind this whole thing? I know Rasouli gave me the flash drive, but I can see how he could be pulling a fast one: planting nukes in Iran and in the States and tipping us off so that we find them."

"To what end?"

"To whitewash their reputation. They discover a global threat and reach across political and religious differences to join with us in a joint operation that proves to the world that they're part of the solution and not the core of the problem."

"Why do so covertly?"

"Because if it goes wrong they can plausibly deny any involvement and probably dump it all on us. After all—we have the original flash drive now, and we have people operating inside their borders without permission. We flub it, they have proof; we don't flub it and we can both retroactively spin the story that this was all a hush-hush joint operation from the jump."

"Chasing Hugo Vox is turning you into a cynic, Captain."

"Hard to stay optimistic with a bunch of nukes ready to pop," I pointed out.

"I could accept that Rasouli is behind it, but not as an official representative of the Iranian government," mused Church. "They couldn't afford to come within a million miles of such a plan. It would do irreparable political harm to the sitting party."

"What about a move by an opposition party or a dissident group?"

He considered. "It would take enormous resources and would be ultimately self-defeating."

"Only if they pulled the trigger."

Church paused a little before he said, "Yes."

"Do we have an overall game plan yet?"

"If we can we locate the last two devices, then we go for a quarterback blitz."

"That'll be interesting."

"Won't it, though?"

I closed my eyes and prayed to the gods of war to cut us a break. What Church was suggesting was to have teams move against every target at exactly the same time. It was a strategist's worst-case scenario because if thousands of years of organized warfare have taught us anything it's that no major campaign ever goes off exactly according to plan. There are always snafus. And that word came into military parlance as a result. SNAFU. Situation normal all fucked up. Tells you all you need to know.

"And if we don't locate the other two?" I asked.

"Then we may have to try something riskier."

"Like taking out the five we know about in order to secure suspects who we can interrogate?"

278 | Jonathan Maberry

"Glad to see we're on the same page."

"It's not a good page, Boss. There are a lot of ways that can go wrong too."

"Yes."

"And only one way it can go right."

"Yes."

"Holy shit."

"Yes." He sighed. "I'll be landing in Kuwait in a bit. Hope to see you there by this time tomorrow."

I heard the faint *bing-bong* of the doorbell downstairs.

"I think the courier's here," I said, and disconnected.

Chapter Seventy

Private Villa Near Jamshidiyeh Park

Tehran, Iran

June 15, 6:52 p.m.

Hugo Vox was bent over the toilet, his stomach heaving and churning with nothing left to expel, when the phone began ringing. His private cell.

He clawed a towel off the bar and wiped his mouth and crawled out of the bathroom to the night table. Walking was an impossibility this soon after the dose kicked in. There was only enough time to drive home and swallow half a dozen aspirin before the first waves hit, and it was worse with each treatment. He joked to Grigor about the fact that the cure was going to kill him before it cured him. Now he wasn't sure it *was* a joke.

The thick sausages of his swollen fingers were clumsy on the buttons, but he finally hit the right one.

"What?" he demanded.

"Mr. Verrecchia?"

Ah. It was Father Belloq, East Asia regional coordinator for the Sabbatarians. That group knew Vox by his old family name, Verrecchia—a name his grandfather had changed at Ellis Island, but which Vox still used for certain operations. As far as Belloq was concerned, "Luigi Verrecchia" was a devoted and very rich Catholic who was serving God by covertly using a great deal of his wealth to fund the operations of the Inquisition. And that wasn't all that far from the truth, except in terms of motives. Vox couldn't care less about the church, or its God, but he found it useful to have a vicious little private army he could aim at his enemies. The Sabbatarians were everywhere, their ranks significantly expanded over the last fifteen years thanks to the millions Vox funneled into their numbered accounts. They were blind fanatics who were convinced they were making serious inroads into the fight against supernatural evil. In point of fact, they had contributed significantly to five of the most lucrative operations of the Seven Kings.

They had no real role in the chaos that Vox was building around the Red Order, the Tariqa, Iranian politics, and the mad plans of the King of Thorns; but that was the point. Vox loved adding random elements. It would drive Church and the DMS up a goddamn wall trying to figure out how the Sabbatarians factored in. Sure, there was the obvious vampire connection, but the Sabbatarians created the *wrong* connection. Chaos was a lovely, lovely thing.

Vox took a breath and adjusted his tone. "Yes, Father. Do you have something to report?"

"We have had a problem, sir."

"Tell me."

Belloq told him about the failed ambush of Joe Ledger.

"You lost the whole team?" growled Vox. His anger was only partly contrived. It would not have surprised Vox to hear that Ledger had taken out at least half the team; he knew Ledger was that good. But all of them?

"Every last man is in the arms of Jesus."

"Please, Father Belloq, this is madness," said Vox, mopping sweat from his face. His stomach felt like it was ready to explode, but there was nothing left it in. "What could possibly have happened to all those men?"

"There is only one possible explanation," said the priest with undisguised contempt. "Upierczi."

Vox faked a gasp and then waited a few seconds for Belloq to appreciate how disturbed he was by this news.

"Surely no single Red Knight could—"

"No, sir. We believe that the Upierczi are out in force. Sir . . . I'm afraid that the thing we were afraid of is about to happen."

"You mean . . . ?"

"Yes . . . it seems certain now that the Upierczi have obtained nuclear weapons."

Vox didn't have the energy for a cry of dismay, so he let a protracted silence convey the right amount of shock. When he thought enough time had passed, Vox said, "Are you *positive*?"

"Sir," said Belloq, "when you know the world of covert operations as well as I do, you understand that very little is certain. We operate on degrees of 'confidence' in a thing, and then we are forced to act. If we waited for absolute certainty it would be too late."

"Yes, yes," said Vox with feigned distress, "you are right, of course. I don't understand these things. It's just that . . . my God! Bombs? What would vampires want or need with such dreadful weapons?"

He heard Belloq sigh with exasperation. Good. That was the right reaction. He wanted the man to be impatient. Impatience was useful.

"Sir," said Belloq, "I've explained this a dozen times. The Red Order has lost control of the Upierczi. The Kingdom of Shadows is in open revolt and they are about to make war on the world of men. And the human traitors who work for the Upierczi have infiltrated every government, every level of industry and world trade. The launching of bombs will be the first wave . . . and I believe it will send a signal for a complete takeover of world governments and key industries."

"You think it will actually come to that? Humans helping monsters to conquer the world?"

"It *is* happening!" insisted the priest. "And we are running out of time. That list your chief of security provided . . . We need to act on that immediately. We need to cut off the Hydra's head before we are overwhelmed."

Vox almost laughed. The phrasing was so trite, so corny. Belloq might be a ruthless killer, but he was also a complete ham-bone. That was also useful.

"The list," Vox echoed, as if fretting over a dreadful decision. In truth the list was one he had prepared and added to while still in the good graces of Church and the president of the United States. It was his own version of a nuclear bomb, and once used it would do far more damage than the Teller–Ulams hidden throughout the Middle East. That list would blow a hole in the world and leave nothing but chaos behind.

A very, very profitable chaos.

"I'm sorry," Vox said contritely. "This is all beyond me, and it terri-
fies me."

"We're all scared," Belloq assured him. "But courage is defined by acting even in the presence of great fear. God needs us to be courageous.
God needs us to be the heroes in this battle against the forces of evil."

Forces of evil. Vox had to cover the phone while he laughed quietly. He
wished he could put that on a business card.

"Tell me what to do," he said after a moment.

"There is only one thing you *need* do, sir. You need to give me permission to use that list. I promised that we would do nothing without your
say-so. Mr. Verrecchia—now is the time. Search your heart, search your
faith . . . Ask yourself what God requires of you."

Vox was silent as he picked lint off his pajama bottoms, letting the
clock burn. Letting Belloq imagine the torment that "Verrecchia" must
be experiencing because of the consequences of this action. Many people
would die. Thousands of them. Men, women, and even children. No one
could be spared. It was the only way to protect the world from the vampire uprising.

Although he kept his voice grave, Vox was smiling as he said, "Let God's
will be done."

He disconnected and tossed the phone on the bed.

The sickness in his stomach was still there, but Vox realized that the
trembling in his legs and arms was less. Much less. Even though the side
effects hit him sooner and harder with each treatment of Upier 531, there
was no doubt at all that they were wearing off sooner. He rolled up his
sleeve and peeled off the bandage to examine the puncture marks.

There were none.

Vox pulled open his robe and pulled up his vomit-stained undershirt.

This time his gasp was genuine.

The big puncture wounds from the horse needles Dr. Hasbrouck used
on him were . . .

Well, shit, he thought. *They were gone.*

No. That wasn't the right way to think of it, he realized with a new and
dark delight.

They were *healed*.

He closed his eyes.

The treatments were working.

And with a jolt he realized that he hadn't had a coughing fit all day.

Hugo Vox smiled. If Father Belloq had been there to see that smile, the Sabbatarian would have screamed and grabbed for a hammer and a stake.

Chapter Seventy-One

The Hangar

Floyd Bennett Field, Brooklyn

June 15, 10:25 a.m. EST

Church's phone rang and he saw that it was Lilith again. He answered.

"Have you had a chance to look at the contents of the flash drive?" he asked.

"Yes."

"Your opinion?"

"It's contrived."

"That was Circe's take."

Lilith paused. "How is Circe?"

"She's well," said Church coldly, "but she is not a topic of conversation."

"You are a difficult person to like," she said.

"Many have said the same about you."

Neither of them spoke for a few seconds, and in that silence much was said.

Eventually Lilith returned to Church's original question. "Rasouli is feeding the Red Order to you."

"So it seems," agreed Church, "though I still don't know what the Red Order is. Not in full. I suspect you do."

"Actually," she said, "I don't. I know how they operate, I know some of the players, but there is something called the Holy Agreement, and I would give a lot to know what's in it. We believe that the Agreement was drafted and signed by Sir Guy LaRoque, the first Scriptor of the Red Order, and his counterpart, Ibrahim al-Asiri, who was, in turn, the first Murshid."

"Surely you have a guess about its content."

"Guesses are useless in the absence of verifiable information. We have a thousand theories, and some of them may be correct, but there's no me-ter that will let us know. It's fair to say that Rasouli's information does more harm than good to our speculations, because we can't factor nukes into any of our scenarios."

"We're building some theories along the lines of a doomsday cult. Does that make any sense based on your understanding of this matter?"

"Doomsday? No."

"What about a faction rising within the Order or the Tariqa with a bent toward mutually destructive tactics? Suicide bombers and big-ticket destruction are not unknown in these circles," he said.

"Maybe, but in their own way, both sides of the Agreement have tended more toward moderation than extremist acts."

"You view blowing up mosques and murdering nuns to be indicative of balance?"

"Yes," she said. "No other view makes much sense, not when you con-sider how long this has been going on."

"Interesting," he said thoughtfully, then changed the subject. "We are trying to make sense of Rasouli's mention of the *Book of Shadows*. My people are trying to decode the fragments of the book included on the drive."

"Good luck. We've been trying to decode that damned thing for—" She suddenly stopped and there was a heavy silence at the other end.

"Lilith?" prodded Church. "How exactly have you been trying to de-code the pages? Is there something you would like to tell me? Did you provide those pages to Rasouli? Is that what you started to say?"

"God, no. But . . ." Lilith cleared her throat. "We, um . . . we actually *have* a complete copy of the *Book of Shadows*. We've had it for some time."

"Have you?" Church said mildly. "And were you planning on telling me about it before or after the nukes detonated?"

Lilith said nothing.

"How long have you had the *Book*?"

"Well . . . give or take . . . seven years."

Church sighed. "This kind of obfuscation is exactly why counterter-rorism is a bureaucratic nightmare."

"Wait a damn minute," snapped Lilith. "You speak as if you had a right to it. Some of our people died to obtain this copy."

"So lay some flowers on their grave and move on from the dramatics," he fired back. "I've made my resources available to the Mothers and to Arklight on a number of occasions."

"Sure, but you never let us have access to MindReader. You keep that to yourself."

"Hardly the same thing."

"Well, it's water under the bridge, isn't it?" she fired back. "We have a copy of the *Book of Shadows*, and if you stop being such a prick I'll consider e-mailing you a high-res scan."

"Have you translated any of it?"

"No."

"In *seven years*?"

"Perhaps we may have accomplished something if we had Mind-Reader."

"Point taken. Send me the e-mail now and I will make sure that it is fed through MindReader. I further promise that I will share the results of that scan. All of it, unreservedly."

After a moment she said, "Thank you." And hung up. Forcefully.

Chapter Seventy-Two

Over Kuwaiti Airspace
June 15, 10:28 a.m. EST

Church pressed the intercom.

"Bug, I'm sending through a file. It's a complete scan of the *Book of Shadows*. The book is four hundred and thirty one pages of densely written and coded text. Run it through MindReader. Pattern recognition, decryption, the deciphering software, all of it. If you get anything, no matter how small it seems, contact me at once."

"You got it."

"Also, tell Circe and Dr. Sanchez that we have this. Let them have full access. Circe may want to compare it to the Voynich manuscript."

"Sure."

Chapter Seventy-Three

I went downstairs and out through the back to meet Abdul Jamar. Twilight brought the cool breezes and birdsong that are the rewards for anyone who survives the blistering heat of the day. I stayed in the shadows as a three-year-old Runna X12 pulled to the curb. I noted that the dome light was rigged not to come on as he opened the door.

Abdul was dumpy little man with face like a tired accountant and glasses with thick lenses. You'd never pick him out as a dissident operative working with the CIA to overthrow Ahmadinejad, which I suppose was the point.

He looked me up and down with apparent disinterest. "Cold for this time of year," he said.

"More like January," I agreed.

He sighed as if the simple exchange of code words was a burden and a pain in the ass. He glanced at Ghost, who was poking his head out past my thigh.

"Friendly dog?" Abdul asked, beginning to reach out for a quick pet.

"Not today," I said. Abdul whipped his hand back. He opened the trunk of his car and produced a zippered laptop case and a blue gym bag.

"For you," he said to me, keeping an eye on Ghost.

I took the items and handed him a plain white envelope that I had borrowed from Jamsheed. It was sealed and folded several times around the flash drive.

"For the pouch?" Abdul asked.

"Yes. I'm not joking when I say that you need to protect that with your life."

Abdul managed to look deeply unimpressed. Without another word he got back into his car and drove away. Charming guy.

I checked that the alley was empty and went back inside. Jamsheed was in his store, so I took my gear to the bedroom and locked the door. The briefcase and valise I'd taken from the vampire hunters were on the bed.

I told Ghost to guard the door and he did so by flopping down in front of it and falling asleep.

The laptop was a DMS tactical field computer. Ultrasophisticated, hardened against EMPs, rigged with 128-bit code scramblers, with a powerful satellite uplink. I turned it on and punched in the proper passwords.

The other bag included party favors. A Beretta 9mm with a Trinity sound suppressor and four extra magazines loaded with subsonic hollow points. A nylon shoulder rig was included with a fast-draw holster, and it had slots for two of the mags. A Rapid Response Folder, which is a nifty tactical knife that clipped on to my right pants pocket and hung out of sight. A snap of the wrist flicks out a 3.375-inch blade which, though short, allowed a fighter to cut and slash at full speed with no drag at all on the arm. There were four flash-bangs and four fragmentation grenades. And a Smith & Wesson Airweight Centennial, a hammerless .38 revolver in an ankle holster. As I unpacked it I could feel my body happily pumping out testosterone. If I ran into another Red Knight, it was going to be a substantially different encounter, no matter what Church or Violin thought about my chances. I felt like saying "Fuckin' A" or "Bring the pain," but I knew Ghost disapproved of that kind of rah-rah crap.

I strapped on the Airweight and clipped the RRF in place, then shrugged into the shoulder rig.

The computer case had a few extra goodies, including a new set of earbuds with a pocket-sized uplink booster. The receiver looked like a mole and affixed to the inside of my ear. The mike was a pale freckle on my upper lip. The technology is a couple of giant steps ahead of what's in all of the holiday catalogs for the covert-ops community. Mr. Church has a friend in the industry, and he always has the coolest stuff.

There was also a smaller zippered case containing a complete toolkit useful for everything from rewiring a toaster to, for example, de-arming a booby-trapped briefcase.

Back when I was a cop, we had specialists to come in and do this sort of thing. They were very brave men and women who had jobs I never envied. In the Rangers I had some basic bomb-handling courses, but it wasn't until I began working for the DMS that I learned how to do this sort of thing for real.

It did occur to me—now, I mean—that it would have been more practical to have searched the cars and then asked Krystos for the combination before I shot him. Can't unring a bell, though.

I took the toolkit and the briefcase into the bathroom and closed the door.

I removed a tiny electronics detector and ran it over the case. As expected, the locks were wired. The question now was whether they had a simple intrusion trigger or a dead-man's fail-safe. I ran the scanner over every inch of the case and matched the readings against the unit's stored records of over three thousand trigger variations. The reading was not one hundred percent, but it was weighted heavily toward the locks being simple antitheft. They'd blow if the wrong combination was entered too many times on the coded touch pad, or if the locks were tampered with.

However, when I ran the scanner over the front and back of the case there was no electronic signature. I smiled a larcenous little smile and set the case on the closed lid of the toilet seat and pulled my RRF. The blade flicked into place with hardly a sound, and I took a breath and then stabbed the case. Not all the way through, only enough to cut through the side, then I sawed a line through the leather and compressed cardboard. Nothing blew up.

"Amateurs," I sneered.

This sort of thing was typical of people who didn't quite grasp the philosophy of security. These are the kinds of people who will spend ten thousand dollars on security alarms and locks for every door and window on the first floor and completely ignore the windows on the second or third floor. Crooks count on that kind of thinking.

So do guys like me.

I cut a rectangular piece out of the center of the case, making sure to stay well clear of the locks and the trip wires; then I lifted out the panel and tossed it into the trash can. The resulting hole revealed several file folders and a few assorted items. A pack of cigarettes and a lighter. Passports for each of the people I'd killed at the CIA safe house, and IDs for four more men whom I had not seen.

I set those aside and removed the folders and flipped open the top one. There was a sheaf of documents held together with a clunky metal clip. I removed the clip and put it in my shirt pocket. The top sheet had an official seal that matched the tattoo on Krystos's arm. The seal of the Holy

Inquisition. The content of the letter and all of the attached papers were written in Greek. I can speak a little of the language, but I can't read a word of it.

It was a speed bump but not a dead end. The field computer had a detachable wand scanner. I ran it over every page in the top folder and set it aside. The second folder had more of the same, as did the third. It wasn't until I opened the fourth folder that I realized that I had found something that literally took my breath away.

Beneath the same sort of official-looking cover letter was a series of eight-by-ten glossy surveillance photos of me, Top, Bunny, Khalid, Lydia, and John Smith. On the back of each was a handwritten note in English that included a brief physical description and a summary of our military or police training.

I recognized the handwriting. I'd seen it a million times on reports from Terror Town and on evaluations of potential staff members being vetted for top secret clearance.

Hugo Vox.

"Shit," I said aloud.

There was more, and it was worse. Much worse. A thick sheaf of printed pages held together by a heavy binder clip. I stared at the information on the lists and felt an icy hand punch through my chest and close its fingers around my heart.

I dropped everything and called Church right away.

Interlude Ten

The Kingdom of Shadows
Beneath the Sands
April 1231 C.E.

Sister Sophia clutched at the tatters of her habit, pulling them to her to try to hide her nakedness. It was a hopeless task. Her clothes were little more than streamers of black and white. Grimed with dirt and filth, caked with blood.

A metal grate in the iron door clanged open and a pale hand shoved in a bundle wrapped in cloth and a leather pitcher. Immediately she could smell bread and cooked meat. The grate slammed shut and she listened to hear the soft footsteps fade into silence. Then Sophia sobbed and crawled across the floor toward the food and tore open the bundle. A small loaf of coarse black bread and a leg of something—she could not tell what animal it had come from. The meat was bloody raw inside and charred outside, but it was the first food they had given her in three days. She wept hysterically as she tore at it with her teeth.

After she'd eaten as much of the meat as she could stomach, she drank from the pitcher. The water was cold but it smelled of sulfur. Then she sagged back, once more trying to hide herself with her rags. It did not matter that there was no one there to see her uncovered skin. She was ashamed in the eyes of God. Ashamed for what she had become.

She closed her eyes and prayed to Mary, to Jesus, to the angels and saints. Not for rescue—Sister Sophia did not believe that she could be rescued. No, she prayed for death. If it were not a mortal sin she would have taken her own life, or at least tried. She contemplated smashing her head against the rocks, or taking her rags and making a rope of them.

But that would be suicide, and she would slide further down into the pit if she did that, her soul lost and unredeemable.

And . . . worse still, it would be murder.

She could not bear to touch her stomach, but she could feel it growing, day by day.

In the other cells along the hall, she could hear babies crying. She could hear the mothers. Some crying, others praying. A few cackling in nonsensical words, their minds broken by the horrors.

"Mother Mary," she prayed, "please . . ."

Inside her womb, her baby kicked.

It was sharp and sudden. Vicious. But what else would it be? How could she expect anything but that from a child of a monster?

Chapter Seventy-Four

Mustapha's Daily Goods
Tehran, Iran
June 15, 7:31 p.m.

"Go," said Church.

"I think Hugo Vox is working with the Sabbatarians."

"What makes you think so?"

"I opened the briefcase I took from Krystos and found some stuff. Two things in particular and you are not going to like them. The first is a directory of safe houses all through the Middle East. Nothing newer than January first, though, so it fits with what he might have known before he went into the wind."

"I figured as much. I sent out a network-wide warning after your 'adventures' today. The CIA has confirmed two other compromised locations, ditto for Barrier, and the Israelis lost one. Right now you're sitting in the only safe house in Iran that we know for sure was never on Hugo's radar. As bad as this is, it could be worse. Most of the houses are untouched, so staff was able to evac safely. We might be in the clear there and—"

"There's something else," I said. "Something a whole lot worse."

I could hear Church take a breath. After today he was probably wishing he could change his number. "Tell me."

I didn't actually want to tell him. It would be like dropping a hand grenade into his lap.

"I found a printed list. Fifteen pages of it. Names, social security numbers, home addresses, family members. The works."

"Who is on the list?"

"Everyone who works for the Department of Military Sciences," I said. "And their families. Rudy's on that list. My father and brother are on that list. And, Church—?" I said softly, "Circe is on that list, and it says that she's your daughter."

"God . . ." Church breathed. "Oh my God."

The silence became huge, filled with flying debris.

Church disconnected without another word.

Chapter Seventy-Five

Mustapha's Daily Goods
Tehran, Iran
June 15, 7:36 p.m.

I sat on the edge of the tub and stared at the list. My father. My brother and his wife. My nephew. My best friend. Everyone I cared about.

Hugo Vox. The desire to find and kill him was unbearable.

If I were in Vox's place I'd be hiding from Church. Vox seemed to be doing the opposite; he was on the offensive. But to what end? Pissing Church off even more than he already was would not seem to have a happy ending.

Vox loved chaos, but this seemed like something else. It was vindictive, it was needlessly cruel. What had happened to twist Vox into that kind of monster? Or was this another layer of the real Vox that we were only now seeing? If so, how deep did his corruption go? How deep could it go?

Those were questions I never wanted to get the answers to.

Fear crawled like ants under my skin. My hands were shaking so badly that I dropped the papers, which landed heavily on the corner with the chunky binder clip. It made an odd sound as it landed. Not the hollow metal sound you'd expect from a clip; this was a dull *thud*.

I snatched it up and peered at it. The clip was heavier than it needed to be to bind papers. I hadn't paid enough attention to that at first; now I did. I opened the spring-metal jaws and studied the inside. There was a tiny bead of plastic inside, painted the same color as the clip's body. I grabbed my scanner and ran it over the clip and the electronics detector pinged.

The little bead was a bug of some kind. But what kind?

Then I understood. It wasn't a listening device or another booby trap. It was a backup in case the papers in the briefcase were stolen.

It was a tracking device.

"Oh, shit," I said.

Two seconds later an explosion rocked the entire house.

Chapter Seventy-Six

Mustapha's Daily Goods
Tehran, Iran
June 15, 7:38 p.m.

The blast came from the back of the building and sounded like an entry charge. Someone—almost certainly the Sabbatarians—had blasted through the rear door.

Ghost leapt out of a dream and onto his feet. He gave a single startled bark and crouched by the closed door, eyes narrowed, ears straight up, fur bristling along his spine. I tore the Beretta out of my shoulder rig and whipped open the door.

Smoke billowed up the stairwell, and I heard Jamsheed yelling in protest for two seconds before his words were cut off by a meaty thud. No way to tell if he was dead or if they'd clubbed him down.

"Upstairs!" someone yelled in French. I heard someone reply with a German accent.

Definitely the Sabbatarians. Pricks.

My rage howled inside of me. The list of names burned in my mind, and I wanted to hurt these pricks. I wanted to hurt them so bad it was an actual physical ache in my chest.

But I did it smart. I backtracked to the bedroom and grabbed the grenades, shoved most of them into my pockets; but I pulled the pins on a couple of flash-bangs and dropped them down the stairwell. Then I wrapped one arm around Ghost's head and the other around my own and huddled down.

The blasts were massive in the small house, and harsh white light etched the slats on the stair rails and the edges of the framed photographs on all the walls.

Before the echo had a chance to fade I was up and running; Ghost was right with me. There were six of them with automatic weapons, two with hammers and stakes. Jamsheed lay on the floor; he had a vicious bruise above his right eyebrow and blood was pooled around his head. Several of the Sabbatarians were kneeling or bent over in pain; most of them were screaming.

"Hit! Hit! Hit!" I bellowed, and Ghost shook off his pain and weariness and became a white missile of furious bloodlust. He took the closest figure hard, teeth tearing into the man's inner thigh, high near his crotch. There was a sudden blast of red blood as Ghost's fangs slashed open the man's femoral artery.

I opened up with the Beretta, using double taps on everyone I saw, one to the chest to stall them, one to the head to blast them out of my life. My inner Warrior was screaming at me to kill them all.

One of the men turned toward me and even though he was dazed from the flash-bang, he opened up with an AK-47, the rounds chopping into the stairwell inches behind me. I closed to zero distance and put two into his face. As he fell his finger clutched around the trigger and hot rounds stitched a line up the wall and across the ceiling.

Ghost barked a warning and I turned in time to dodge away from a man raising a pistol with both hands. He shot where I had been and I shot where he was. The man staggered out of sight.

Behind me someone screamed in terrible pain as Ghost went for his throat. The scream ended with a wet gurgle.

There were five men down already and three on their feet. The flash-bangs had done their jobs in the confined space of the entry hall. These men were disoriented and, even though they were armed, they had no aim. I killed two of them before the slide locked back on my Beretta. The last guy didn't have a pistol, and he thought I was helpless with an empty gun, so he rushed me with the stake. I used the pistol to bash the stake aside and then I snapped his leg with a side-thrust kick. He screamed and twisted down to the floor, and I rechambered the kick and slammed my heel against his ear, flinging him onto his side.

I swapped out the magazine as I spun around. Everybody was down. Ghost stood over the second man he'd killed, and his muzzle was black with blood.

The back door was a charred ruin, hanging in splinters from a single twisted hinge, and I could see a black sedan parked outside. Around me were the dead and dying. My rage was still boiling, but my inner Cop voice was telling me to dial it down, to find someone with a pulse. To get some answers.

And then a figure stepped into the doorway.

Tall, lithe, dressed in a black chador. I pointed my gun at her. Ghost growled from deep in his chest.

She said, "Joseph—they're coming!"

Instantly a hail of bullets tore into the doorframe as Violin dove into the room.

Chapter Seventy-Seven

Mustapha's Daily Goods
Tehran, Iran
June 15, 7:42 p.m.

The bullets filled the air as Violin hit the floor, rolled over a dead man, grabbed him, and pulled him into a sitting position to serve as a shield.

Ghost looked to me for a command. To him she was another potential enemy, a danger to the pack. With a word I could order him to tear her apart or accept her into the pack.

"Home!" I snapped. It was the word that would change everything about how he would react to her. "Home" was code for "friend." Instantly Ghost's gaze shifted away from her and refocused on the barrage that continued to tear apart the doorway. He hunkered down behind the man whose throat he had torn out, bristling, muscles trembling as he waited for the command and the opportunity to fight.

Violin turned to me and tore away the chador that hid her face and body.

I don't know what I expected to see. Certainly not the "monster" she considered herself to be. She was beautiful, but not in the way that Circe is. Not curvy and elegant; she had none of the fineness of features that belonged on the covers of fashion magazines. Her features were sharper, more foxlike than feline, with intelligent eyes, sharply defined cheekbones, thin lips that were curled into a wicked combat smile, and a body like a dancer's. Small breasts, long limbs, superb tone. She wore black formfitting clothes with lots of pockets and cross belts for weapons. On a strap slung across her body was a compact Micro Tavor-21 Israeli bullpup assault rifle with an extended thirty-two-round magazine. Very sexy. She reminded me of Grace. Not in looks, but in her air of competence and lethal potential. It took a single microsecond to take all of this in.

"How many?" I yelled.

"Too many," she said. "Two full teams. Twenty at least."

"Christ."

"Maybe more in front."

We looked at each other in the way soldiers will on a battlefield, gauging each other's competence and skills. It was a lightning-fast conversation that would have been slowed down by words. She nodded to me and I nodded back.

The hail of bullets slowed and I heard men yelling orders. They were coming.

"Call it," I said.

"Front," said Violin.

"Back," I agreed.

She spun around and ran in a fast crouch toward the store; I pulled a grenade out of my pocket. Not a flash-bang this time. As shadows filled the destroyed doorway I pulled the pin and threw it.

"Ghost—*frag out!*"

Ghost flattened behind the corpse.

The grenade hit the floor right inside the door and took a short bounce just as the second wave of Sabbatarians rounded the corner. The frag exploded at waist height, blowing the men apart. There were terrible screams from the attackers who hadn't been in the direct blast radius. Men and women. Then gunfire.

I dove forward and slid chest-first to the doorway, my pistol out in front, and even before I stopped sliding I began firing. I emptied the second magazine into the mass of them, shooting for the center of any man-shaped shadow, firing the magazine dry as bullets tore through the air three feet above me. They couldn't see me through the smoke, and the confusion was too great for them to grasp that I was shooting from a prone position.

Ghost barked, wanting to be in the middle of this, but this was a gun-fight; there was no place for him.

Behind me the front door was blasted to splinters by heavy-caliber gunfire. A second later I heard the distinctive *pop-pop-pop* of the compact MTAR-21. And more screams.

Something came whistling through the air and struck the doorframe above my head; glass exploded and I was showered by splinters and a noxious-smelling liquid. Even with the intense stink of cordite in the air, I could identify the smell. Garlic oil.

Freaks.

They still thought they were fighting vampires. Suddenly I understood why they had sent so many. They were that afraid of the Red Knights. Maybe they'd found Krystos and his crew and thought that a Red Knight had taken out the whole team, so this time they sent two teams.

"Reloading!" I heard Violin yell.

I rolled onto my back and fired six shots downrange past where she crouched. I saw one figure fall and others scatter. As Violin slapped the magazine into place I heard feet crunch on glass, and I twisted out of the way as bullets chopped into the floor where I had been lying. I fired as I rolled away, sloppily but continually, and someone screamed.

But then several of them opened up at once and I had to throw myself behind the wall and curl into a ball to save my eyes from the glass and tile splinters that filled the air like a swarm of hornets.

Ghost kept barking, furious and frustrated.

Men began pouring into the building, running past me, unaware of the figure curled in the corner, hidden by smoke. They aimed their guns at the sound of the barks and I came up onto one knee and fired, hitting two of them and causing the others to skid to a stop. They realized their mistake and turned, but then Ghost hit them from the other side. He was among them like a white demon, and instantly it was all screams and blood. Guns were useless that close and already too late.

Beyond the melee I saw Violin rise up from behind the counter and kill three men in two seconds, her weapon switched to semiautomatic for accuracy and ammunition conservation. I'd only spotted two extra mags on her rig, and she had to be near the end of the second. I swapped out my own and slapped my last one into place; but as I came to my feet I pulled another fragmentation grenade and lobbed it outside. Just as it cleared the doorway there was a figure there and the grenade burst against the man's chest, tearing him apart but effectively screening the knot of shooters behind him. I faded to one side and fired, but even as I pulled the trigger I saw three men fall. One flew backward from my bullet, but two more dropped with that distinctive rag-doll sprawl of men who had taken headshots.

Then a voice yelled in my earbud.

"*No fire from the house. Friendlies on nine, twelve, and three.*"

I knew that voice.

Top.

I tapped my earbud and yelled. "Echo! Echo! Echo! Be advised, friendly taking fire in front of store. Friendly is female and inside."

Bunny said, "*Got it.*"

Immediately the street out front and the alley behind were torn apart by bullets fired from three separate positions. Men screamed and shouted. The Sabbatarians tried to return fire, but they were being ambushed by Echo Team, and that is a bad place to be.

"Violin!" I barked. "Cease fire. My team is outside. Hold your position."

There was no answer, and when I risked leaning out to look, her shooting position was empty. Ghost stood panting in the hallway, but beyond him there were only dead Sabbatarians and a floor littered with bullet casings and blood.

Then it was over.

The gunfire stopped. There were no more screams, no shouts. Just the sound of running feet as Echo Team swarmed into the store from both sides, weapons out, eyes blazing with anger.

"*Clear!*" called Khalid as he checked the small rooms downstairs. He and Lydia ran for the stairs and cleared the second floor. No one had tried to come in that way.

Bunny's monstrous form filled the front doorway, a combat shotgun in his hands.

"Hostiles are all down," he reported.

Top Sims helped me up off the floor. He looked me up and down. "I can't leave you on your own for five minutes without you getting into some shit, can I?"

Chapter Seventy-Eight

Mustapha's Daily Goods
Tehran, Iran
June 15, 7:49 p.m.

"Did you see her?" I demanded as Echo gathered around.

Bunny frowned. "See who, Boss?"

"The woman. Violin. She was fighting them from the store."

He shook his head. "Didn't see anybody but the bad guys. Lot of hostiles down out there. Saw a couple stiffs with their throats cut, too. Whoever she was, chick can fight. Who was she?"

"Long story." I hurried into the store and checked the bodies, and though one of them was female, it wasn't Violin. "Check everyone. Do we have anyone with a pulse?"

"Got one here," said Lydia, who was crouched over a slender figure. Jamsheed.

"He's one of ours," I said. "Khalid—?"

"On it." Everyone on Echo Team was a certified medic, but Khalid was an actual medical doctor with a specialty in traumatic injuries. He went to work on Jamsheed.

Top said, "This was a pretty noisy frat party, Cap'n. We're going to be ass deep in police real soon."

We listened for sirens but did not hear any yet. I wasn't certain how reassuring that was. Special Forces and military SWAT units don't roll with sirens.

"Who's watching the street?"

"John Smith and he's got night vision."

I tapped my earbud. "Cowboy to Chatterbox. What are you seeing?"

"Nothing."

He wasn't the most talkative guy on the team.

"Stay sharp. You see so much as an old lady with a shopping cart give a yell."

"K."

I turned to Khalid. "Talk to me."

He looked up from where he knelt by Jamsheed. I could read it on his face. "Blunt force trauma to the head resulting in a depressed fracture. Got some pretty severe damage to the cervical spine . . ." He let the rest hang.

I moved over and dropped to my knees by Jamsheed. His eyes were open, but they were bright and glassy with pain and one pupil was fully dilated, indicating a cerebral hemorrhage. Khalid's eyes bored into mine and he gave a tiny shake of his head. I took a cotton square from him and dabbed at the blood and sweat on Jamsheed's face.

Before I could say anything, Jamsheed spoke. His voice was hoarse, low. "You cannot stay here. The police . . ."

"I know, but we have to—"

"No, you don't," he interrupted. "You can't take me with you and still do what you have to do."

"You don't even know what we're here for."

He smiled faintly. "Does it matter? You work for the *Mujtahid*. He called me to say that I should trust you because *he* trusted you."

I didn't know what to say to that, so I nodded.

Jamsheed tried to lift his hand; I took it and his fingers curled as tightly around mine as he could manage. He looked into my eyes and saw the truth, but instead of panic I saw a peaceful expression settle over his face.

"I am so . . . tired . . . of war," he said, and that said a lot.

I thought of the photos he had on his walls and the gentle way he had touched the frame of the one with the playing children.

"The little girl—?" I asked.

His lips formed the word "yes." The hurt and loss was palpable.

"She'll be waiting for you, brother," I said.

He nodded and then hissed with the agony that it caused. When he opened his eyes he seemed farther away.

We regarded each other for a few moments, and then he squeezed my hand.

"*Ma'assalama,*" he said. Go in peace.

I returned his squeeze. "*Fi aman Allah.*"

Go with God.

Jamsheed died without another sound, a quiet man going silently into the shadows that stood between this ugly world of pain and the paradise he believed waited for him. I placed his hands on his chest and sat back, exhausted and defeated. Ghost came over and sniffed Jamsheed, then he whined and lay down as if in vigil.

From the storeroom behind me, Lydia snapped her fingers. "Got another live one."

My exhaustion shattered and fell away, and I turned, instantly hot and angry. Even Bunny took an involuntary step back from me when he saw my face. Top quickly closed in and knelt down, and I think he also saw my face and wanted to get between me and a hostile who was still conscious. The Sabbatarian was a young Spanish-looking man with a slab face and beefy shoulders. There was a ragged red hole on his right sleeve.

"Took one through the biceps," said Lydia. "Arm's busted above the elbow."

The Sabbatarian glared up at us with a mixture of anger, fear, and defiance.

"You got one chance, friend," I said through gritted teeth. "Cooperate with us and we'll provide protection and—"

But the Sabbatarian suddenly snapped his jaws shut and grimaced. I could hear something crunch.

"Ah, shit!" yelled Bunny. "Poison tooth. Fuck . . ."

It was over in five seconds. The bitter almond stink of cyanide rose from the man's mouth as his lips went slack and hung open. Bunny spun away and punched the wall hard enough to leave a hole the size of a softball.

"Spilled milk," said Top. "And we got to go."

"Boss," said John Smith in my earbud. "Six units coming hard from the center of town. Black SUVs. Five minutes."

"Copy that. We're out of here. Watch our backs and meet us at the end of the block in two."

"K."

I turned to the others; they'd all heard the same info from Smith. "What do we have for wheels?"

"White vegetable truck," said Bunny. "Two blocks east."

"Let's go. Lydia, my laptop's in the bedroom. Grab it. Khalid, you're on point. Let's move."

Less than two minutes later we were crammed into a vegetable truck that smelled of rotting cabbage and diesel oil, rolling through quiet streets, leaving another scene of bloody destruction far behind.

Chapter Seventy-Nine

Near Mustapha's Daily Goods
Tehran, Iran
June 15, 8:12 p.m.

"Oracle," said Violin.

"Oracle welcomes you, Violin."

"I need to talk to my mother. Now. Priority Alpha."

This order bypassed the computer's AI conversation functions and sent an urgent request to Lilith. It took seventeen nail-biting seconds before the screen changed to show a live streaming image of Violin's mother.

"Status report," said Lilith instead of a greeting.

"The Sabbatarians sent two full teams against Captain Ledger."

"Is he alive?"

"Yes." She explained what happened and braced herself for the scolding she knew would follow the admission of having stepped in to help the DMS agent.

"Good." Lilith frowned and her gaze turned inward as she sorted it through. After a few moments she demanded, "What about you? Are you unhurt?"

"Yes, Mother."

There was a slight softening of Lilith's stern mouth. "Good. You did the right thing."

The comment hit Violin like a punch; and Lilith caught her expression. "I . . ."

"Close your mouth, girl, before you swallow a fly."

Violin took a steadying breath and said, "What do you want me to do next?"

"What do *you* think you should do next?"

Several seconds flitted past as Violin thought it through. Then she told her mother.

Lilith's tolerant smile vanished entirely.

"What choice do we have?" asked Violin.

"None," said Lilith bitterly. "None at all."

Chapter Eighty

On the Road
Tehran, Iran
June 15, 9:17 p.m.

We drove for miles, killing time to make damn sure we weren't being followed. Tehran is a massive city, bigger and more densely populated than New York. We avoided main roads where security checkpoints would be more common and instead threaded our way through the poorer outskirts of the town.

"Let's find someplace quiet," I suggested. "We have a lot of catching up to do."

"Another safe house?" asked Lydia, who was driving.

"Not a chance."

Luckily there were plenty of abandoned buildings, and we found one with no squatters. It had once been a building-supply company but it looked like no one had set foot in it for decades. Lydia parked inside. We huddled inside the ruins of an office. Smith stood by the window and watched the access road that led from a little-traveled street to the loading bay.

"That guy back there," began Lydia. "The Iranian guy. Friend of yours?"

"We just met, but he was one of the good guys."

She nodded. They all did. At some later time we would talk about it. I'd want to tell them about the man and his kindness, about his photos, and the unspoken tragedy implied in those simple images. Such discussions are not for the battlefield. While they can strengthen us by connecting us to our shared humanity, to talk about it while we were still in danger was to invite in weakness. Everything in its place and time.

I straddled a crooked office chair that was missing its wheels. Bunny and Lydia sat cross-legged on the floor—near to each other, which is something they'd started doing a lot lately. Khalid sat on a crate and Top remained standing. John Smith was outside setting up an observation post and was listening in via the team channel.

Ghost flopped down in front of Bunny and Lydia and was getting his full share of petting.

"How much do you know?" I asked them.

Top spread his hands. "The big man was feeling unusually chatty today," he said. "Told me just about everything you and he talked about. Nukes, Rasouli, Arklight, your girlfriend with the sniper scope."

"Put laser sights on your nuts, huh?" asked Bunny. I ignored him.

"And he told us some weird shit about vampires."

"Right," I said, "and you met the fearless vampire hunters back at Jamsheed's."

Top ran a hand over his shaved head. "Cap'n, how much of this is happening and how much of this is Mr. Church having some kind of neurological incident?"

"It's all happening," I said, and gave it to them again from my side, filling in any details they might not have gotten from Church.

When I was done, my guys stared at me, at each other, and ultimately into the middle distance as seconds fell off the clock.

Top Sims was the first to speak. "Cap'n, I think I can speak for everyone when I say, what the fuck?"

"I hear you." I looked at their faces. "Ask your questions."

Lydia held up a hand. "Sir? Permission to return to reality."

"Denied," I said. "If I have to deal with this stuff then so do you."

"Permission to shoot myself?" she asked hopefully.

"Let me get back to you on that."

"Where the Christ do we start?" asked Bunny.

"Nukes," suggested Khalid. "We have to start there. But . . . that's problematic. I mean, do we have even a clue as to the players and their teams?"

"Lots of clues, but no idea where we stand with them," I said.

Khalid shook his head. "Where does Rasouli fit into this? How does it make sense that he brings this to us?"

I shrugged. "Don't know yet."

"Whatever it means, he seems to be the only one on our side," said Lydia. "Kind of makes me feel dirty."

"Good dirty or bad dirty?" asked Bunny, which earned him a hard elbow in the ribs.

"Okay," Top said slowly, "all of this is fascinating as shit, but who has the damn nukes?"

"We don't know," I admitted. "Though the Sabbatarians seem to think it's the Upierczi."

"Why the hell would vampires want nukes?" demanded Bunny. "I mean . . . they're fucking vampires, right?"

"Guess they want to blow something up," answered Top. "Same as anybody."

I told them about the conversation I'd had with Hu and Church about the Upierczi and my still-in-the-development-stage doomsday theory.

"Right," said Top, "Okay, I'm with Lydia now. I'd like to catch a cab back to the real world."

Bunny shot him a sour look. "Which real world would that be, old man? This time last year we were shooting zombies."

"Yeah," Top conceded. "Fuck me."

Chapter Eighty-One

"That doesn't answer the question of why these Upierczi want to blow up the oil fields," said Khalid.

"No it doesn't," I agreed. "So when we get one of these pointy-toothed bastards in a corner, I want him kneecapped and cuffed and then we're going to have a group therapy session with him, feel me?"

"Hooah," they agreed.

"If Rasouli knows about the nukes," asked Khalid, "isn't this something the State Department and NATO should be handling?"

I said, "We are not in a position of trust. Rasouli came to us on the sly, and he clearly didn't trust his own government."

"Swell."

Bunny leaned forward. "Look, I don't like to be the one to piss in the punchbowl here, Boss, but how come we're not all shouting the name Hugo Vox? I mean, vampires notwithstanding, does anyone really think that he's not the Big Bad Wolf here? He's already wanted by every law enforcement agency on the planet. Shouldn't outing him to the authorities as the main villain be a natural next step to finding and stopping the vamps from triggering five sonofabitching nukes?"

"Seven," corrected Khalid.

"Seven sonofabitching nukes. Jeez. My point is—"

"We can't do much about him for now," I said, "because we don't know his exact role and we don't know where he is."

Top gave me a shrewd look. "There's something else, ain't there? I can see it in your face, Cap'n, there's more to this."

"There's one more thing." They all came to point, eyes sharp and focused, waiting for me to drop the last bomb. "When I took out the first Sabbatarian team today I obtained a briefcase which had, among other things, materials that had to have come from Vox."

"What kind of materials?" asked Top.

"A list of all DMS staff as of the end of last year. And . . . the names and addresses of everyone's families."

If I'd dropped a flash-bang into the center of the room I couldn't have hit them harder. Top's eyes went wide and his lips parted in a silent O. He had an ex-wife back home, and a daughter who had lost both her legs in Baghdad when a mine blew up under her Bradley. It was the reason he joined the DMS, and now he was thousands of miles away from being able to stand between them and an unknown group of killers.

I held up my hands. "Church knows about this and he's taken steps. Everyone on that list is going to be taken into protective custody."

"Which won't mean shit if Vox is behind this," growled Top. "He had people wired into the cops, the FBI, everywhere. Probably still does."

"I know, but Church is on it."

Top looked at me with a stare so hard and cold that it felt like physical blows.

"We didn't start this war, Top," I said. "We have to count ourselves lucky that we found that list. It gives us a chance."

We sat in silence thinking about the possible consequences. If I hadn't found that list, if the Sabbatarians had been able to move on it, the resulting carnage and grief would have destroyed the DMS at its core. Even if we survived, the damage done to us would be like third-degree burns on our psyche. We'd never recover.

"Vox," said Top. Just the name, but it had so much meaning; he said so much with it.

"Vox," I agreed.

Lydia cleared her throat and glanced at me. "What exactly are we supposed to do when we find the weapons?"

It took effort to turn away from Top. "What would your guess be?"

She shrugged. "Locate and secure each nuke, de-arm the weapons, and have a meaningful conversation with anyone left who still has a pulse. Then go home and drink a gallon of tequila."

Everyone laughed. It was all forced, though. Even Top measured out half an inch of smile. "Now you know the game plan," I said.

Bunny asked, "Is there any kind of evacuation plan in case we drop the ball?"

306 | Jonathan Maberry

"Evacuate who, Farmboy?" snapped Top. "The entire Middle East? How exactly do we do that?"

I rubbed my eyes. "Okay, we're waiting for the go-order to hit the Aghajari oil refinery. It'll be a quiet infil. Locate and de-arm." I opened my tactical computer and called up the mission files uploaded by Bug. "First thing we have to do is study the layout of the refinery according to the blueprints Rasouli provided, matching them against satellite photos and intel from our own sources. I want six ways in and ten ways out."

"Hooah" said Top. No one else joined him.

"Then I want you to pair up and buddy-test each other on the wiring schematics of the Teller–Ulam bomb and its variations. Swap teams every half hour. Everybody knows what everybody else knows. We don't want surprises and missed cues when de-arming the nukes. Hooah?"

"Hooah." All of them said it this time.

"After that, everyone gets rack time."

"Sleepy soldiers are clumsy soldiers," said Khalid, then punctuated it by quietly going, "Ka-boooooooom."

"Hoo-fucking-ah," said Bunny.

Chapter Eighty-Two

Abandoned Warehouse
Outskirts of Tehran
June 16, 12:22 a.m.

While the others worked on their de-arming drills, I read through the vampire information Circe had obtained from Dr. Corbiel-Newton. Most of it was useless fairy-tale stuff or speculation without hope of verification. Some of it, though, was more practical, taking a look at the possibility of vampirism as a natural phenomenon. That was the same ground I had covered with Hu, but there were some things here that I found very interesting. Especially about garlic. In the movies, garlic simply repels a vampire, kind of like pepper spray, but it doesn't kill them. In a lot of the world's folklore, however, garlic was lethal to them, especially if introduced into the bloodstream or via a mucus membrane. In something called the "ritual of exorcism," fresh garlic was placed in the mouth of a vampire. In some cultures garlic paste was used on skin or clothes as a deterrent and could kill a vampire if one of them bit skin that was coated with it. Of course . . . that would require a vampire with a head cold who couldn't smell the damn garlic.

As I thought that, an idea skittered across my brain. It was there and gone. My three inner selves—the Cop, the Warrior, and the Civilized Man—all made grabs for it, but we came up dry.

So I went out and retrieved the Sabbatarians' valise from the back of the vegetable truck, and then laid out the contents. Hammers and stakes to one side. I doubted they would be useful. Ditto the vials of holy water. But the bags of garlic powder and the jars of garlic oil . . . even touching them coaxed that idea out of its hiding place in the shadows of my brain.

I held a bag of garlic powder in one hand and a jar of oil in the other.

It was the Cop who figured it all out.

But it made the Warrior smile and smile.

Chapter Eighty-Three

Abandoned Warehouse
Outskirts of Tehran
June 16, 1:34 a.m.

I needed to sleep, but I knew that wasn't going to happen. Instead I walked the perimeter of the warehouse to make sure it was secure. It was. We could not have been farther from the flow of life here in Tehran if we were on the moon. The night sky was immensely dark and littered with ten trillion cold points of light.

I fished a stick of gum out of a pocket and chewed it, enjoying the mint burn, glad to be rid of the lingering taste of garlic. Ghost came sleepily out of the warehouse and trudged along with me, pausing now and again to leave his mark on useful walls.

I called in for Church but was rerouted to Aunt Sallie. She listened to my report without much comment except to make a biting remark about my "letting" Jamsheed get killed.

"You're a charming lady," I said. "Anyone ever tell you that?"

"Eat me," she replied. "Church will be in touch when he wants you to know something. Until then, lay low and try not to get anyone else killed."

A crushing reply was poised on the tip of my tongue but she hung up on me.

Almost immediately the phone buzzed and I hit the button in hopes of flattening Aunt Sallie with my rejoinder.

"Hello, Joseph."

I smiled, "Hello, Violin."

She paused and I strained to hear if there was any background noise, anything that I could use to get a lead on where she was. But there was nothing. Ghost must have heard her voice and he actually wagged his tail. Dog's a little weird.

"Are you somewhere safe?"

"For now," I said, though that was only true in the physical sense. Everything inside my head felt like it was a junk pile of hand grenades without their pins and bottles of badly stored chemicals. "Thanks for the help today."

"I wish I could have warned you, but I found out where you were by following the Sabbatarians. There are teams of them all over Tehran."

"I'm surprised they can operate so freely."

"They can't. There have been a lot of arrests over the years, here and elsewhere. They are charged as spies. The church doesn't know about them and their own people disown them. Most of them die in prison."

"Pity," I said. "Are they really part of the Inquisition?"

"How did you—? Oh. You must have questioned some of them."

"Only one and he didn't know much."

"You're probably wrong about that. How hard did you try?"

Ouch, I thought. Ghost stood sniffing the wind as if trying to catch Violin's scent on the breeze. Something caught his attention and he wandered off into the shadows. Probably some interesting jackal poop. Ghost is a scatological connoisseur.

"Since I already know some of it," I said to Violin, "how about telling me more?"

"Yes," she said.

It took me a two-count to catch up to that. "What?"

"Yes," she said. "I think it's time to tell you what's going on."

"First—whoopee, and I mean that sincerely. Second, why the change of heart?"

"It's . . . complicated."

"That seems to be a theme lately. Care to elaborate?"

"I asked my mother." When I laughed, she said, "I'm not joking."

"Your mother. Lilith, right?"

"How—? Ah . . . Mr. Church told you. Good, that will make it easier. She's here in Tehran and she's asked me to bring you to her."

"When?"

"Now. Can you get away for an hour?"

"Maybe," I said dubiously. "Where are you?"

"Right behind you," she said.

Chapter Eighty-Four

Abandoned Warehouse
Outskirts of Tehran
June 16, 1:41 a.m.

I spun around and tore my pistol out of its holster.

She was ten feet away and she already had her gun out and up.

Ghost came pelting out of the darkness like a white bullet, but I gave him a hand signal and he stopped thirty feet from Violin's right flank, uttering a low growl that was full of promises. So much for wagging his tail. I guess that he didn't like being blindsided any more than I did.

"Drop it," I said.

"No," she said, "I don't think I will."

We stared at each other.

She smiled first. Small and tentative. Then I felt my mouth twitch.

"On two?" I said.

"Sure."

I counted it down and when I hit zero we both abruptly tilted our pistols to the sky and took our fingers off the triggers.

We stood there assessing each other, then lowered our guns. Neither of us reholstered them, though.

"Hello, Joseph," she said.

"Hello, Violin."

She was both similar and different to the image of her that I had constructed partly from memories distorted by the smoke and thunder of the gun battle at Jamsheed's and partly from how I'd imagined her since that first call yesterday morning. Lean, fox-faced, with erect posture and the slightly splay-footed stance you see in ballet dancers. The MTAR-21 assault rifle hung from its strap, and she held a Ruger Mark III .22 caliber pistol down at her side. In many ways she reminded me heartbreakingly of Grace, but she was also very different. Younger, taller, with an air of innocence about her—despite her profession—that Grace did not share. I wondered if they could have been friends.

"Come with me," she said. "Lilith is waiting."

"You call your mother by her first name?"

Violin shrugged.

"Is it a code name? Like Violin?"

"Nobody I know uses their real names," she said, and there was sadness in her eyes.

"I do."

She nodded. "And I find that so strange."

Chapter Eighty-Five

The Warehouse
Baltimore, Maryland
June 15, 5:15 p.m. EST

Rudy set the coffee cup down where Circe could see it, but she was too focused to notice or care. Her workstation monitors were filled with multi-screen images from the Voynich manuscript and the *Book of Shadows*. Images came and went as Circe, sitting rock-still except for the hand controlling the mouse and her darting eyes, studied the arcane pages.

The communicator gave a soft *bing-bong* and Bug's face replaced one of the screens. He was grinning.

"Hey, docs . . . I got some good news. Or, at least I think it's good news."

Circe looked up and Rudy could see the lines of stress and worry that were etched into her lovely face. That, and the desperate hope in her eyes, made his heart ache.

"What is it?" she asked.

"MindReader came through again. I had my buddy Aziz help me with some search arguments in a couple of different Persian dialects, and that gave us the edge we needed to slip through the security at the National Museum in Tehran. And guess what we found there?"

Circe's eyes came fully alive and she half rose from her chair.

"You *found* it?" she demanded.

"Yes, ma'am," beamed Bug. "I just uploaded it to the server. A complete copy of the *Saladin Codex*."

"Is it in the same ciphertext?" asked Rudy.

The question dialed up the wattage on Bug's grin. "Nope. There are fifty-four separate translations. Persian, Arabic, Pashtun, Farsi, and . . . wait for it, wait for it . . . English."

The change that came over Circe's face was miraculous. As Rudy watched he could see the weariness drop away, the stress burn itself to nothingness, revealing a refreshed intensity and a predatory glint that was startling and, he had to admit, a bit intimidating. For the first time he could see in her eyes the reflection of her father.

"Now we have a chance," said Circe fiercely. "Damn it, now we have a real chance."

"Let's just hope that there's some clue in there to help us crack the other books," observed Rudy and he was instantly sorry he said it because the newfound confidence in Circe's eyes diminished by half in the space of a heartbeat. He wanted to bang his head against the wall, but Circe set her jaw and almost sneered at the possibility of defeat.

"No, damn it," she growled. "We *are* going to crack this. We have to."

It broke Rudy's heart to hear her tack on those last three desperate words.

Chapter Eighty-Six

Arklight Camp
Outskirts of Tehran
June 16, 1:50 a.m.

Violin led me to another warehouse two blocks over. The rear loading doors were open and there were several cars and small panel trucks parked inside, out of sight. Ghost sniffed the air and growled, cutting inquiring looks at me. I signaled him to remain calm and alert. Having the signal seemed to calm him—dogs are always at their most content when the pack leader has things under control. Not that I actually did, but it was nice that my dog thought so.

There were twenty-five people in the warehouse, all women. The youngest was about Violin's age, the oldest was at least seventy. They all looked fit and trim, though, and they were all armed. The women stood in a loose circle around another woman who sat on an overturned packing crate. As we approached, the circle opened to allow us in. The eyes that turned toward me were in no way welcoming. There were no smiles, no acknowledging nods. Twenty-five sets of eyes assessed me as if I were a side of beef, and not a very fresh one.

"I brought him, mother," announced Violin. She peeled off from my side and went to stand by the seated woman. That gave me a chance to take a closer look at the woman I presumed was "Lilith." Each of these women looked powerful, but Lilith was different. She was magnificent, with a face that was cold and beautiful, like the death mask of an ancient queen. Sculpted cheekbones and a strong chin, straight nose and a high, clear brow. But her eyes were absolutely compelling. Endlessly deep and intelligent. And totally without mercy.

"These are the Mothers of the Fallen," said Violin. "And this is my mother, Lilith."

Ghost whined faintly and looked at me. It was pretty obvious that he was confused in the presence of what was perhaps a much more powerful pack leader.

"Captain Ledger," said Lilith. "My daughter has risked much to arrange this meeting."

I stopped about ten feet from where she sat. "So what's the drill? Do I bow and curtsy?"

"No," she said, "but you can mind your manners."

"Yeah, about that?" I said. "Kiss my ass."

Violin stiffened but before she—or anyone else—could say anything Lilith raised her hand slightly. It silenced all reaction, but I could feel all those eyes burning into me. The Mothers of the Fallen were not lining up to join the Joe Ledger fan club. That went both ways.

"Here's the thing," I said, "it's not that I have any specific disrespect for you—whoever the hell you are—or these fine ladies here. Or your daughter. It's just that I just had a real bitch of a day yesterday, and I'm tired, sore, and cranky. I've been chased, attacked by Sabbatarians and vampires, and people have been very mean to my dog."

Ghost woofed.

"And," I concluded, "your daughter put sniper scopes on me to force me into a meeting with Iran's biggest psychopath who told me that there are nuclear bombs planted all over the Middle East. One of those bombs is in the United States. My boss gave me the impression that you know more about what's going on, but so far you haven't told me shit. So, if you're looking for deference or civility, I'm fresh out. In fact, I'm wondering why the fuck you're wasting time with clandestine meetings, cryptic phone calls, and a lot of cloak and dagger bullshit."

Lilith smiled a little. Beautiful as she was, her smile was unpleasant. Kind of an *Ilsa, She Wolf of the SS* vibe.

"I won't apologize for the confusion, Captain," Lilith began. "Arklight is not in the habit of sharing information except under very limited circumstances. When my daughter was contacted by Rasouli yesterday she had no idea who you were. Once you provided your name, she was able to do a database search to come up with some background on you. We know about your military and police careers, and we know that you are an agent of the Department of Military Sciences. You work for St. Germaine."

"Who?"

"Mr. Church."

"What do *you* know of Mr. Church?"

"Almost certainly more than you do," she said.

"And we're back to the cryptic bullshit. You still haven't explained what the 'Mother of the Fallen' are, what Arklight is, and how you know anything about Mr. Church."

Lilith ignored that. "There have been times when Arklight's agenda has overlapped with his operations."

" 'Overlapped' is a slippery word. I don't know who you ladies are or what you stand for. Granted, Violin saved my bacon at the hotel when the Red Knight attacked me, and she stepped in during the Sabbatarian hit on one of our safe houses, so she gets a lot of Brownie points for that." I saw Violin look away to hide a smile. "But at the same time she's stalled me all day long, feeding me enigmatic bits and pieces of information. Plus there's that whole 'working for Rasouli' thing. Let's start with that, and I'd like some straight answers. No bullshit, no runaround."

"Watch your mouth," snapped a tall woman as she stepped up and laid a hand on the butt of a holstered pistol. She was a hatchet-faced broad who looked like she could go three rounds with Top *and* Bunny. Ghost growled, but I flicked my finger and he went silent but stayed hyperalert. "You will speak to Lilith with respect or—"

"Actually, sister," I interrupted, "I'll speak to her any goddamn way I want, and you will pretty much stand down and shut the fuck up."

I thought the woman was going to go for it. The others were equally tense, hands touching weapons.

But then a red dot appeared on the center on Lilith's forehead. Violin gasped. The women turned and stared in horror.

In my ear John Smith murmured, "Call it, boss."

Chapter Eighty-Seven

Arklight Camp
Outskirts of Tehran
June 16, 2:03 a.m.

Lilith reached her hand up and touched her forehead as if she could feel the negligible heat of the red dot. When she lowered her hand she even looked at her fingers as if there should be blood there. She nodded slowly, more to herself than to me. Then she raised her eyes to me and I suddenly felt the full impact of her stare.

"If you must shoot," she said, "then take your shot. You'll live long enough to see me fall, but not a second longer."

I had to admire her guts. I know from recent personal experience that it's not easy to play it cool with a laser sight on you. She was doing a better job of it than I did yesterday.

"Lilith," growled the woman who had fronted me, "I'll cover you and—"

Another red light appeared out of the shadows and glowed on the center of her chest. Then another and another, touching the women on either side of Lilith. And a last one, floating right between Violin's breasts.

"Let's be clear about this," I said calmly. "I give the word, you die. You make a move, you die. You fuck with me one second longer, you die. Screw with me, Lilith, and my team will pile up the bodies of these women and then I will ask you again. Is that clear enough or do I have to shoot your daughter to make my point?"

"You wouldn't do that," said Lilith, and Violin's eyes pleaded silently for me to agree.

Then a voice from the shadows said, "Yes, he would."

Ghost gave a single sharp bark of surprise and everyone turned to see a tall, blocky figure walk slowly out of the darkness. I don't know why I was surprised. Not after the day I had. Not considering who this was—but I was still slack-jawed.

In my earbud I heard Top say, "I swear I didn't see him, Cap'n. Came out of nowhere."

Yeah, I thought, *he tends to do that. Spooky bastard.*

Mr. Church wore a summer-weight white suit and dark tie. He carried no visible weapon and his eyes were hidden behind the lenses of his tinted glasses. He walked past me without a comment and stood in front of Lilith, but I noted that he chose an angle that did not block John Smith's line of sight.

I heard a ripple of murmured voices around me; most of them said the name, "St. Germaine."

Lilith got slowly to her feet and stood face to face with Church.

"You came," she said.

He smiled at her, and it may have been the only genuine and unguarded smile I have ever seen from him.

And then Mr. Church pulled Lilith to him and they embraced.

Let me tell you something, this wasn't the kind of hug the president gives a foreign dignitary, or the kind two football players share after a winning touchdown. No sir. This had familiarity in it that went all the way to the chromosomes, and there was serious heat there. I cut a look at Violin, who had one eyebrow arched as far as it would go. When she saw me looking she gave a tiny shake of her head.

In my earbud I heard Bunny say, "Wow."

Church released Lilith and stood back from her, and they both turned to face me.

"Please tell your team to stand down, Captain," said Church. "Bring then in."

The laser lights vanished at once. I tapped my earbud. "Hold your positions."

If Church was surprised or annoyed by that, he didn't show it.

"How did you know where we were?" I asked. "I only gave Aunt Sallie the coordinates of our warehouse."

"I was invited," said Church, nodding toward Lilith.

"Okay," I said, "I am now completely and thoroughly confused. Will someone please tell me what the *hell* is going on?"

"You aren't the only one who doesn't know exactly what's going on," said Church. "We know some things and Lilith and her people know some things. We have to hope that if we all put our puzzle pieces on the table it will add up to one clear picture."

"Thanks for giving me a heads up, Church," I complained. He ignored me.

Church looked at his watch. "What's the status of your team?"

"At the risk of sounding like a male stereotype," I said, "Echo Team is cocked, locked, and ready to rock."

"Good. I have transport on the way. We roll in one hour. And, yes, Captain, that means all teams are on active standby. On the president's order we will hit all five of the sites in one coordinated strike."

"What about the other two devices?"

Church paused and I could feel the eyes of everyone in the place burning into us. "We don't know where they are. We're going to have to run the play with what we have. If we're very lucky we may secure one or more of the people involved in this and see if we can encourage them to unburden their souls." It was said offhand, but the intent beneath the words was lethal.

"God help anyone who gets in our way, then," I said.

Church gave me a bleak stare. "I believe they will discover that God has abandoned them."

He turned toward Lilith.

"Now," he said.

Chapter Eighty-Eight

"It all started eight hundred years ago with Sir Guy LaRoque, emissary for Philip II of France," began Lilith. "He was a senior member of the Knights Hospitaller, which is a noble order dedicated to good works. However, Sir Guy created within the Hospitallers a second and very much more secret group which became known as the *Ordo Ruber*, the Red Order. The group was illegally sanctioned by Father Nicodemus, the senior Hospitaller priest in the Holy Land during the Third Crusade."

"Nicodemus," I echoed, and a chill raced up my spine.

"Sir Guy brought his plan to his counterpart," continued Lilith, "a man named Ibrahim al-Asiri, who was emissary for Saladin. These two men were much of a mind, and between them they shared the observation that it was remarkable that, during times of the severest strife between Christendom and Islam, people flocked to church in greater numbers and showed much greater fealty to God."

"No atheists in foxholes," I said, but caught a reproving look from Church. I mimed zipping my mouth shut.

"Exactly," agreed Lilith. "They likewise observed that in times of peace, people strayed from the house and the word of God. LaRoque and al-Asiri found this intolerable and feared that extended times of peace would lead inevitably to the decline of faith. Understand, Captain, these men were religious zealots as well as political manipulators. They were ambassadors and spokesmen for great leaders, and also advisors. They could see things from what they likely viewed as a big picture perspective, and indeed history has shown that religions rise and fall. Few endure. So, seeing that this was a trend, and knowing that the Crusades must necessarily end one day, these two men decided to dedicate themselves to a course of action that would ensure the eternal preservation of their churches. They drafted an agreement between them that there should always be tension and conflict between Christendom and Islam. Nothing fills a church, or indeed a mosque, more surely than the need to pray for the confusion and destruction of the enemy, especially when the enemy is the enemy of one's God." She paused and fixed me with a penetrating stare. "Sir Guy, with the help of Nicodemus, founded his Red Order to oversee this work. Ibrahim created the Tariqa—the Path—to do the same for Islam, and within months of signing the Holy Agreement, they began a campaign of selective murder, arson, and desecration. There has always been strife here in the Middle East—but this was the birth of a new kind of conflict."

I goggled at her. "You're talking about hate crimes."

"Yes, Captain, in a very real sense the Holy Agreement formed by the Red Order and the Tariqa was the beginning of terrorism as we know it. They invented hate crimes as we know that concept."

Even though I was standing still I suddenly felt like I was falling. "To get people *to go to church?*"

In my earbud I heard a low whistle. Probably Top.

Church murmured, "The road to hell is paved with good intentions."

Lilith nodded. "It's possible, I suppose, that Sir Guy and Ibrahim had the best intentions as they saw it, but it speaks to a very malecentric viewpoint that what a person can see or imagine is his by right to have."

My Y chromosome wanted me to protest, but anything I could say would be built on shaky ground. Lilith must have caught a look on my face and gave me a slice of a cool smile.

"These secret societies operate totally without the knowledge or sanction of the governing bodies of their religions," she continued. "Neither the Catholic Church nor the imams of Islam would tolerate such acts. They would decry them as blasphemous and heretical, which they most assuredly are, but not from the perspective of the Red Order and the Tariqa. Much like a shadow government will often act in opposition to, say, the Constitution of the United States or the Magna Carta, because they believe their vision, however illegal and unpopular, is the best course of action. It's sophistry, of course, and therefore self-justifying. The leader of the Red Order became known as the Scriptor out of respect for Sir Guy LaRoque drafting the original Holy Agreement. The leader of the Tariqa is known as the Murshid, or 'guide.'"

"How did something like this fly under the radar for eight hundred years?" I asked.

Her cold smile was gone. "You would be surprised and appalled to know how many dreadful things are unknown to the world at large. Your organization fights such things, as does Arklight."

Church nodded. "And assassinations are useful for more things than inspiring religious intolerance. Establish a pattern of swift and terrible retribution for the slightest act of betrayal and you can hide almost anything."

It was an ugly point, but I knew that he was right.

"At first the Holy Agreement between Sir Guy and Ibrahim dictated that each side should carry out actions only against their own people. It was believed that this would allow each side to control the effect. Of course when one of Sir Guy's knights murdered a pilgrim on the road to Jerusalem or burned a church, there was evidence planted to implicate the Muslims. Over time, however, men from both sides became sickened by committing atrocities against their own. Perhaps it was the last shred of conscience clinging to them, so it became necessary for the Holy Agreement to be amended to allow each side to commit murders and perpetrate the acts of desecration against the other side. These hits were strictly regulated and always agreed upon, but it was much easier for each side to strike with righteous fury at the *other* side. This became known as the Shadow War, and that has lasted all these centuries."

"Who did the actual killings, though?" I asked. "It isn't easy to pull something like this off over and over again, and suicide bombing is relatively recent."

"These aren't suicide attacks," she said as she sat down once again on the overturned crate. "The Tariqa perfected the model first. There was already a group of highly skilled killers operating in the Middle East, an order of Nizari Ismailis founded in 1080 during the First Crusade. You know about the *Hashashin*?"

I nodded.

"That Order of Assassins was so effective that they tipped the balance of power in the Shadow War. The Knights Hospitaller were skilled fighters, but they were battlefield warriors, not the kind of subtle and nimble assassin who could scale a wall or pass stealthily past picketed guards. The Red Order needed something as effective, but Europe had no precedent. Not even the Roman legions were useful as a model for assassins of such high quality and effectiveness." She paused and her face darkened. "This is where the story takes a darker turn."

"Darker?" I said, half smiling. "How much darker can it get?"

"Vampires," said Mr. Church.

"Ah shit," I sighed. "I was kind of hoping we wouldn't get back to that."

"This is the real world," said Lilith coldly, "and they are a part of it."

"Are they supernatural? 'Cause that seems to be the big question."

Violin moved to stand beside her mother. Her eyes looked haunted, and her mother touched her arm for a moment. Instead of reassuring her, the touch sparked an involuntary shiver. Lilith sighed.

"The Upierczi are monsters," said Lilith, "and as twisted as they seem, they are a part of nature."

"You know this for a fact?" asked Church, beating me to the punch.

Lilith nodded. "Arklight managed to obtain tissue samples from one—at a terrible cost, I might add. We did extensive testing. We ran a full metabolic panel—sodium, potassium, chloride, bicarbonate, BUN, magnesium, creatinine, and calcium. We did arterial blood gas to measure blood pH and bicarbonate levels. We did full blood count, Hematocrit, and MCV, ESR. We ran molecular profiles—protein electrophoresis, western blot, liver function. Everything. And we ran a full DNA. The Upierczi are genetically human, but they are not Homo sapiens and—"

"I hate like hell to interrupt this Discovery Channel episode, but can we get back to the actual point? The Red Order used the Upierczi as assassins. And—?"

Lilith nodded, accepting my rebuke. "The Upierczi are more than a match for the order of assassins, but their numbers have always been low. There were never many of them, thank God. They've tried to change that with breeding programs, however."

There was a murmur of deep disgust among the women.

"The Red Order began this process. Capturing women, keeping them in pens, encouraging the Upierczi to rape them over and over again until they conceived. Most of the children were stillborn. Some few survived, and of those three quarters were normal babies that showed no significant trace of the Upierczi traits. Others were hybrids—dhampyrs—but attempts to raise and train them as Upierczi met with complete failure for the Order. A few—a handful—were born as Upierczi, and they kept their blasphemous bloodline alive."

Lilith paused and wiped away a tear. Violin placed her hand on her mother's shoulder and gave it a squeeze, and Lilith reached up and briefly clasped her daughter's hand. I was clearly missing something here, and I wasn't sure I wanted to know what it was.

"For a long while the Upierczi tried another tactic. They kept the women who bore Upierczi children and forced them to produce child after child. This was not ultimately successful, so they tried another tactic. When a dhampyr was born, if it was female, she was kept and raised, and when she was old enough, she was raped and impregnated and forced to bear a child. This nearly always resulted in an Upierczi birth. For a while this seemed like the solution to their problems . . . but the vampires and their Red Order masters did not understand the nature of genetics. Not then, at least. Generation after generation of forced inbreeding did not expand the Upierczi—it nearly destroyed them. Children were born who were Upierczi, but who were mongoloid and severely retarded. Freakish births, a sharp rise in stillbirths. Lunacy, madness, a drop in physical abilities, reduced intelligence." She took a steadying breath. "For a while it seemed as if their own attempt to breed a master race was going to result in the death of the entire species."

"I met one of the knights," I said. "There was nothing genetically weak about him. What changed? What happened?"

"The science of genetics happened," said Mr. Church.

I looked at him.

"Gene therapy, artificial insemination, gene splicing. Rebreeding techniques. Science caught up to the needs of the Upierczi." He turned to Lilith. "Am I right?"

"Yes," she said, tears glistening in her eyes. "The Red Order hired the very best scientists. They spent tens of millions to fund radical genetic research and development. They created a 'rebirth' process in the 1980s, improving upon it every year. Not just new births, but therapy to fix genetic flaws in living members. Understand, Captain, the Upierczi are not immortal, but their lifespan is exceptionally long. Some are more than two centuries old. And there is one who is rumored to be three hundred and twenty years old. Grigor, the oldest and by far the most powerful of the Upierczi. He is the father of the new order of vampires. His genes—never tainted by inbreeding—became the alpha cell line in a course of gene therapy called Upier 531. It was developed by Dr. Dieter Hasbrouck.

Now, the new wave of Upierczi is stronger, faster, more durable—and many will live as long as Grigor. Hasbrouck did extensive gene therapy. He amped up the wound repair system so the knights heal much more quickly, and they have a greatly enhanced ultraviolet light repair system as well. I believe it was an attempt to make them better able to tolerate sunlight, which weakens them, but instead he gave them virtual immunity to cancer and a resistance to radiation. If these bombs go off, any Upierczi not in the direct blast radius might actually survive. That," she said, "is what we face."

"Jesus Christ," I breathed. My heart was pounding so hard that I wanted to scream. If Church hadn't been standing right beside me, nodding as Lilith spoke, I doubted I would believe it. But his presence—the absolute solidity of everything that he was—made it all doubly real. Too real.

I licked my lips. They were dry as dust.

"You . . . left something out," I said.

Lilith nodded, clearly expecting the question.

"You glossed right over the dhampyri. The hybrids. The ones who were forced to give birth to so many of the Upierczi. What happened to them?"

Lilith stared at me with bottomless dark eyes.

"I think you already know the answer to that, Captain Ledger."

"The Mothers of the Fallen," I breathed, and those words hurt my mouth. I swallowed a throatful of broken glass. "And . . . their children? The girls, the *dhampyri*? What happened to them?"

Violin had tears in her eyes, but her voice was fierce. "Our mothers escaped to save us."

"Some escaped," said Lilith sadly. "Most died. The rest . . . we dedicated ourselves to a single cause."

"To destroy the monsters. The Upierczi, Nicodemus, the Red Order. All of them."

I tried to say something. Anything.

All I could do was look into the eyes of these women. Lilith, Violin, each of them.

Violin stared at me, into me. So did Lilith. Looking for my reaction, for my true feelings.

But I simply could not speak.

Chapter Eighty-Nine
The Department of Military Sciences
Worldwide

The Warehouse, Baltimore, Maryland

For Rudy Sanchez it was like someone had driven a cold steel spike into his chest.

All of the display screens in the mobile computer center were filled with pages of ciphertext and meters showing progress on other sections of the two books. But the central display screen had a different image, a real-time feed from a button camera worn by Mr. Church. It was all there. The Mothers of the Fallen. Lilith and Violin. Joe.

The things Lilith said. The truths she shared.

Rudy wanted to close his eyes, but he couldn't. To continue watching and listening and understanding was far more than a job requirement, however. To turn away would be the worst kind of cowardice—the kind that refuses to hear the truth. The kind that refuses to care.

He touched the crucifix he wore beneath his shirt.

He barely felt the pain from the crushing, desperate grip Circe had on his other hand.

The Hangar, Floyd Bennett Field, Brooklyn

Aunt Sallie stood apart so she could study the faces of her staff as they watched and listened to Lilith. She saw shock and horror. She saw tears. She saw jaw-clenched rage. She watched to see if any of them turned away, or sneered privately, or smiled, because God help them if they did.

What she saw on the faces of her people, however, was what she thought she would see. What she needed to see.

No one was looking at her. They were unable to look away. So no one saw her nod her approval of them.

Echo Team, Outskirts of Tehran

Top Sims heard a small sound. A wet sniff, muffled and discreet. He cut a look sideways, expecting it to be Bunny. But he saw John Smith pull back from his sniper scope to wipe his eyes and nose. Top grunted softly to himself.

He had known Smith for almost a year, had been in every kind of fight with him, had fought to save the world alongside him, but he did not actually *know* him. The sniper's file was filled with data but no insight. His psych evals were by the numbers, describing a quiet man with an interior life he did not care to share. Not uncommon for someone raised in an orphanage and bounced around from one foster home to the next. No criminal record, though. No politics, no religion, and if he had opinions he never shared them. He was a blank, a question mark except in one regard: he was the best sniper currently serving in the U.S. military. The best by a good margin. He killed whatever he aimed at. He never pulled a trigger in a questionable situation; he was patient enough to wait for a clear target and an unshakable reason.

Seeing Bunny, Lydia, or Khalid cry would not have jolted Top. Not even surprised him. Bunny, for all his size and experience, was a softie who really did believe that the good guys won in the end. Lydia also had a lot of heart beneath the wisecracks and trash talk. And Khalid, the scholar of the team, was a deeply passionate man, very religious, strongly invested in social justice and ethics. They would cry. They were all probably fighting tears now.

But Smith? Smith never showed a thing. Not a goddamn thing. Not when he killed. Not when his comrades went down. Not when he took a bullet. He was the only person who showed less on his face than Mr. Church.

And yet this—what the woman Lilith was saying, what they were all finding out about the strange mission they were on—was turning dials on the man.

Smith must have sensed him watching and turned slightly toward Top. He touched his left thumb to the tear glistening in his eye then reached out and smeared the wetness along the barrel of his rifle. He said nothing, did nothing else. It was a statement and he let Top interpret according to his own understanding.

Top nodded.

Maybe he did understand.

Chapter Ninety

Abandoned Warehouse
Tehran, Iran
June 16, 2:32 a.m.

"Do you understand now?" asked Violin, her voice quiet in the pin-drop silence. "Why I had to be careful? Why I couldn't just—"

"Yes," I said hoarsely. "I understand." Though I wished I could tear that knowledge from my mind. I looked at Church. He nodded, his face uncharacteristically sad.

He patted me on the shoulder. "I knew a fraction of this," he said. "If I had known more . . . well, the Red Order and the Upierczi would have been more squarely on the DMS radar a long time ago."

"We're going to do something about this," I demanded. "Right?"

Church gave me a fraction of an arctic smile. "What would your guess be?"

In my earbud I heard several of my team softly growl, "Hooah."

Church turned to Lilith. "You should have told me this a long time ago," he said, but his tone was gentle.

"It wasn't your fight," she said.

Church grunted softly. "Of course it is."

Violin looked at me. "Joseph, you and your soldiers, you fight against madmen and terrorists to defend the world and a certain way of life, but your fight is a new one. There are older struggles."

"Yeah," I said bitterly. "Believe me when I tell you that you've made your point."

She nodded and gave me a small smile that seemed to hold a thousand different meanings. Grace had a smile like that, and for just a moment I thought I heard Grace's sweet voice whisper my name.

I closed my eyes for a moment. Then I inhaled through my nose and let

326 | Jonathan Maberry

out a big chestful of air. "Okay," I said, "I think I have almost all the players except one. Who or what is Arklight?"

"Arklight was formed as the militant arm of the Mothers," said Violin, and her eyes were fierce with pride. "Most of the field agents are their children."

"Dhampyri?" I asked, almost afraid to use the word.

Violin paused for a moment, then nodded. "We are dedicated to the destruction of the Holy Agreement, the Red Order, the Tariqa and the Upierczi. We are the children of monsters, and many of us are the mothers of monsters . . . but *we* are not monsters. In comic books and movies dhampyr have super powers. We don't. Though, there are some useful qualities, I suppose. A few 'gifts.' Perhaps 'side-effects' is more medically correct. From the Upierczi blood in our veins we have some physical advantages."

"Speed and strength?" I ventured.

"Some," said Violin, though she smiled when she said it, allowing me to infer what I could from that.

"What about the age thing. Are you immortal, too? Or—what passes for immortal?"

Lilith shrugged. "Some of us are pretty well-preserved for our ages."

And I saw a twinkle in her eye that made me wonder just how old she was. And . . . how old Violin was.

Church consulted his watch. "The president should be calling me any time now. We have to make some decisions, the first of which is whether we continue to work our separate and counter-productive agendas, or whether we combine our resources. The Red Order and the Upierczi are clearly tied to our hunt for the nukes. That makes it everyone's fight."

Lilith glanced around at the other Mothers. Some were stone-faced, a few still openly hostile, but most of them had predatory gleams in their eyes. Some of them even smiled. Kind of the way the big hunting cats smile. You don't want to see that smile coming at you out of the dark.

The older women in the group nodded to Lilith, one by one, and she in turn nodded to Church. Some of the tension seemed to go out of his big shoulders.

"Then let's go to work," he said.

Chapter Ninety-One

Hugo Vox punched the wall.

He punched it for two reasons. The simplest was that it was the handiest wall, right there next to his desk. The other reason was far less obvious, even to him. It was a reason rooted in fear and hope, and that reason had a name.

Upier 531.

The wall was smooth, with painted drywall over lath. In his youth, Vox could have put his fist through a wall like that all the way to the elbow. He'd done it in college and in at least two boardrooms. Since the cancer took hold, his rage had not manifested in outbursts of that kind. Energy was to be conserved, and he feared the frailty which had transformed him from a robust bear to a tottering old man with bones of matchwood.

All of that, though, was yesterday's news.

When he woke up after a midnight nap, his whole body was on fire. Not with pain . . . not the gnawing, destructive pain. No, this was something else entirely. This was a swollen pain, and expanded pain. When he'd gotten out of bed he'd actually yelled. Not from hurt, but from the sheer joy of having enough breath to do it.

Here in the office he'd spent the rest of the predawn hours working at his computer, his fingers flying over the keys. Playing. Twisting things for the sheer nasty joy of it. The fuck you fun of it. It felt like playing chess against an opponent who was bound and gagged. He moved all the pieces around on both sides. The Red Order, the Sabbatarians, the Tariqa, the Upierczi, Arklight. And Church.

As Vox thought about his old "friend," he felt his mouth begin to turn down into its usual frown, but the burn wouldn't let that happen. Instead his mouth twitched and rebelled and broke into a grin. A big, happy, malicious grin. The old bear's grin.

He launched himself from his chair and slammed his fist into the wall.

All the way to the elbow.

"Fuck yeah!" he roared, and with a grunt he tore his arm free. The splintered lath tried to claw at his skin, but even though it drew blood it could no more stop him than the cancer could. Not anymore.

Not any fucking more.

He roared again and laughed, and punched the wall again and again.

Then he poured a huge glass of Scotch, gulped it down, and flung himself back into his chair. The computer was still on and he scrolled through his list of names, considering each player and the general chaos in which they all floated. All of them searching for meaning, fighting for it, killing for it, dying for it.

And not one of them—not even Church—appreciating that chaos was its own end. Chaos was its own formless agenda.

"Fuck you, Deacon!" he bellowed and pounded his fist on the table hard enough to make his whiskey bottle dance.

His phone rang and he frowned at it.

There was no screen display at all. Not even one to tell him that it was a blocked call. Vox smiled and picked it up.

"Hello, Uncle."

"Hello, Nephew."

"I feel fucking great today."

"I know. It's good to have you back."

"Back? Hell, I was never like this before. I feel . . . I feel . . ."

"I know. It's delicious, isn't it?"

"Yes it goddamn well is."

The caller paused. "Are you ready?"

"Yeah."

"You know there's no going back?"

"Shit, don't try to scare me with burned bridges, Uncle. I'm ready to light the match."

They both laughed quietly about that. Vox, perhaps, laughed a little bit louder.

"Then let it all burn down," said Father Nicodemus.

Chapter Ninety-Two

We had a quick strategy session during which Lilith told Church that he could have Arklight teams to assist with the refinery raids. He accepted without hesitation. While they began working out the details, I moved outside, needing some space to process everything.

Violin found me in the shadows outside of the warehouse. We stood together looking at the stars. Then she said, "This must be so hard for you. So strange. You, an American soldier . . . fighting monsters."

"Since I joined the DMS last year, nothing has been normal. I'm not sure I even believe in that concept anymore."

"This is normal for me," she said. "This is all I've ever known. I was born into this world."

"I'm sorry."

"No. It is what it is. Perhaps someday I'll find another kind of normal."

"Maybe I can help you look."

"Maybe you could."

"About the Sabbatarians," I said. "You guys seem to hate each other worse than the Dodgers and the Giants. But you're both kind of on the same side, right? So what gives?"

" 'Same side'?" she snorted. "Hardly. They know that most of us were either breeding stock for the Upierczi or born from those forced matings. The Sabbatarians, in their great Christian mercy, consider us Satan's whores. The dhampyri doubly so."

"Jesus."

"They long ago named us enemies of God and marked us for extermination." She shrugged. "We have responded in kind."

"Then I'm glad we put a bunch of those assholes down."

Violin nodded but said nothing.

Above, the Milky Way pivoted around us.

"You know, one of the things that's eating at me here," I admitted, "is Nicodemus. Who the hell *is* he?"

A haunted look flashed through Violin's eyes. "As long as there has been a Red Order there has been a Father Nicodemus associated with it. My mother thinks it is the same man, but I don't believe that. I don't believe in ghosts or demons; I think it's part of the propaganda the Red Order has always used. Besides, it's probably a title passed down from one person to another, much in the same way that 'Scriptor' is passed down through the LaRoques."

"Don't priests sometimes take new names when they take holy orders?" I asked. "Biblical names?"

"Not as frequently these days," said Violin, "but yes."

I pulled my cell and called Bug and told him to hack the Vatican or whoever certifies priests. "If these Nicodemus guys are legitimate clerics," I told him, "then there should be records in the registry of holy orders. Find out."

I slipped the cell back into my pocket.

"Nicodemus is a strange man," said Violin. "I saw him a few times when I was a little girl down in the Shadow Kingdom." She cut me a look. "That's what they call it."

"Yes, very dramatic," I said sourly. "Can you give me a physical description of Nicodemus?" She did, and I felt my skin crawl. "Okay, that's a step over the line into weirdsville. That description exactly matches the inmate."

"What happened to him?" asked Violin.

"He disappeared."

"How did he escape?"

"I didn't say he escaped," I said. "He vanished from his cell. No evidence at all of a jailbreak. Security cameras went haywire, guards saw nothing, and then he dropped completely off the radar. I was there when it happened. Thoroughly creepy and borderline impossible the way it happened. But even so, it couldn't be the same man. Could it?"

Before she could reply Church appeared in the doorway and snapped his fingers for us, and we hurried over. Lilith was with him. "Circe," he said into the phone, "you're on speaker. Repeat what you just told me."

"When Rasouli gave the flash drive to Joe, he mentioned the *Book of Shadows*. When Lilith sent us her scan she included a note saying that Arklight believes that the *Book* is the secret history of the Red Order and the Holy Agreement. It's in ciphertext, however, and it's unreadable. Arklight had it for years and couldn't crack it. The same ciphertext is used in a book called the Voynich manuscript, which is in a library at Yale. We now have both complete texts, and the language is the same. With me so far?"

She didn't wait for an answer and instead plunged ahead.

"Rasouli also mentioned the *Saladin Codex*, which is a text on mathematics. MindReader pulled multiple translations of it and just finished a comparative analysis. The *Codex* is a work of minor importance and one with a number of flaws. Now, from a distance, we have two unreadable books and one that is readable but seems to be entirely unrelated to this matter."

"That's from a distance," I said. "How about close up?"

"Well . . . Rudy and I may have made a little progress," continued Circe. "First, you have to understand that ciphertext isn't a code. It's mathematical. However, even when using MindReader to analyze the *Codex* for a key to the cipher we came up dry. But here's the thing, and this changes everything . . . this is where the Voynich manuscript comes in."

I looked at Church and saw him stiffen. Lilith, too. You could feel the tension crackling all around us.

"We think the Voynich manuscript was *allowed* to be found by the Order. It puts it out there so that anyone can find it and read it. Every page is on the Net. They don't care if the average person finds it—it's gibberish to them. However, if you have that as a reference, and you have access to the other two books, then you can read them all."

"How do you know?" I asked.

"Because," said Circe, "we *found* the key to the cipher."

"*What?*" demanded Lilith, almost in a shriek.

"At least we think we've found it. Bug is programming it into MindReader right now. He says that we should have a full translation within hours."

Lilith shook her head. "We've spent years trying to make sense of it, and we have looked at the *Codex* as well. There is no key to the ciphertext."

"There is," insisted Circe, "and it's in the Voynich manuscript. Rudy figured it out. Or, he kicked off the line of thinking that's brought us to this point. He said that we're overthinking this. You see, if the *Book* is the history of the Agreement, then the Red Order and the Tariqa want their members to be able to read it. Otherwise . . . why write it down?"

"Makes sense," I said. "How does it help us, though?"

"Well, we backed up and looked at the issues of translation from the perspective of two ideologies, two cultures who are effectively at war on a permanent basis. They have different customs, different languages, different points of reference on virtually everything . . . except one. There is one area in which all advanced cultures can agree, language differences aside."

I had no idea where she was going with this, but Church and Lilith said it at the same time.

"Math."

"Math," agreed Circe. "The Voynich manuscript and the *Book of Shadows* are written in an invented language that has order and structure to it. Therefore it has mathematical predictability as long as anyone who tries to read it has a set of precise, immutable guidelines."

"Such as a ciphertext," I said.

"Yes. And the third book in our mix, the *Saladin Codex* is a book on understanding the science and functions of math."

Chapter Ninety-Three

Arklight Camp

Outskirts of Tehran

June 16, 3:15 a.m.

Circe was so excited that her voice bubbled out of the phone. "One of the reasons historians never paid much attention to the *Saladin Codex* is it was widely regarded as a well-intentioned and fundamentally flawed set of theories about math. The author was so well-respected that the book was given a place of honor in a museum, but it was an open secret that al-Asiri was no true mathematician. Certainly not by the exacting standards of the Muslim world, and let's remember that they invented algebra."

"Is the math in the *Codex* actually flawed?" I asked.

"Yes, but now we no longer think that al-Asiri made a mistake. We think that he made a very precise set of deliberately flawed computations. Thousands of them. And somewhere in those flawed numbers is the key to the ciphertext."

"How's the Voynich book play into it?" asked Church.

"There are celestial charts and drawings all through that book. We know that algebra and trigonometry are used in celestial charting and navigation. The connection seemed obvious, or so I thought. Anyway, I had Bug use MindReader to plot the positions of the celestial charts in the Voynich manuscript, but we got error after error because the diagrams are wrong. The astrological star patterns in the Voynich book aren't exactly in the right place. Scholars had dismissed this as the errors often found in old sky maps made before the invention of ultraprecise telescopes.

"Then Bug had the idea of trying those same calculations based on algebra and trigonometry as it appears in the *Codex*. Al-Asiri's calculations have long been decried as bad math. They aren't. They're brilliant math, but they're deliberately flawed math. When we charted the same astrological star patterns using al-Asiri's skewed mathematics, they matched *exactly* with the star patterns in the Voynich manuscript."

Church and Lilith looked stunned. So did many of the Mothers.

"Um," I said, "speaking on behalf of C students in math everywhere, what the hell are you talking about?"

"Joe," said Circe, "math *is* an exact science. However if you build a flaw into it, then the flaw becomes an exact flaw and every computation is exactly wrong in the same way."

"So what? How does that help us?"

"If you look at the errors, you have a key to understanding math from a certain perspective. You can actually use al-Asiri's errors to do proper calculations. That predictability and regularity is a cipher. It's a key to understanding anything else that is based on the same code. We began applying it to other drawings in the Voynich manuscript. A predictable mathematical sequence is one of the most common replacement ciphers. We applied it to English and got nowhere. We tried French as it was spoken in the twelfth century, and nothing. The same thing with Arabic and Persian. Nothing. Then we thought about commonalities. Charles La-Roque and Ibrahim al-Asiri were diplomats as well as deeply religious men. They were creating an agreement designed to preserve their churches, correct? So, in what language would these men write that agreement? We thought they might have written it in Hebrew, the original language of the Old Testament, but LaRoque was a Christian and al-Asiri was a Muslim, and Hebrew was the language of the Jews. Both men would probably have had some anti-Jewish sentiments. The Bible was often translated into Greek and Aramaic. And Aramaic was the language of diplomacy throughout the Middle East for a thousand years, and virtually all Middle

Eastern languages can be traced back to it; and the Aramaic alphabet was eventually adopted for writing the Hebrew language. Formerly, Hebrew had been written using an alphabet closer in form to that of Phoenician. Everything fit. We now know that Aramaic is the language used to write the Holy Agreement."

Lilith seemed unable to speak, but she finally croaked out a question. "And the cipher?"

"We hit one last hitch. MindReader was able to translate the first page of the *Book of Shadows*, which is mostly introductions of Sir Guy LaRoque and Ibrahim al-Asiri and their various titles and political affiliations. Typical diplomatic stuff and not of any use to us because we know who they were."

"Damn," growled Violin, and a wave of disappointment began sweeping through the Mothers and Echo Team.

But Circe was not done. "The code is devious; it changes incrementally. MindReader's pattern search figured this last part out. On the first page of the *Book of Shadows*, the mathematical error was exactly as described in the *Codex*. However, on the *second* page, the error is doubled, then tripled on the third page, and on and on until you get to page ten, then it resets to the first error. With that last piece, we can now calculate the rate of error and use those errors to create a key to crack the ciphertext." She took a breath. "The *Book of Shadows* and the Voynich Manuscript are ours."

"Good God," murmured Church. "This is brilliant work, Circe."

"Rudy and Bug did as much as I did," she said.

"I will thank you personally when I see you," he said. "Bug, how soon before MindReader deciphers both books?"

"Two hours. Because the books are handwritten, and by more than one person, it has to adjust to variations in the way the coded documents were phrased."

"Do what you can to speed that up. Call me when you find anything, and I do mean *anything*."

He disconnected the call and stood silent, his jaw tight, mind working. Lilith had the same inward-looking expression. Maybe we all did. No one said anything. This was massive news to Church and the Mothers, but I felt like I was on the fringes of it. Maybe it would help Arklight—with or without the help of the DMS—take down the Red Order and the Tariqa, but that seemed to be tomorrow's battle. I didn't see how the translation of old books was going to help us find nukes today.

Then Church's cell rang again. Everyone came to point like a pack of retrievers, but it wasn't Circe. Church listened for a moment and then said, "Very well."

He closed the phone and looked at me.

"That was the president," he said. "The word is given. The mission is a go."

Chapter Ninety-Four

Arklight Camp
Outskirts of Tehran
June 16, 3:23 a.m.

Church stepped out of the warehouse to make a series of phone calls to get this rolling; the first of which was to Aunt Sallie. She was in the big Tactical Operations Center at the Hangar, which made NORAD look like an Internet café.

Bug called us just as Church rejoined me.

"I ran down every priest who chose the name of Nicodemus," said Bug, "and either MindReader is having a senior moment or there is something mucho freaky about the Vatican database."

"Why?"

"Well, there is a pretty tightly managed registry of priests. Names, personal data, photographs, the works. This goes back pretty far, to the point where paper records were stored and later scanned; and back past that to written records. All scanned now into their systems. Worldwide there have been a couple of hundred priests who chose that name, and a few for whom that was their birth name. Now here's the kicker. About once every generation, call it twenty-five to thirty years, there is a record of another priest taking that name. Always from the same place, Verona in northern Italy. The thing is, we have dates of births and dates of deaths of each priest, but when I cross-referenced this with public records in Italy, they don't match. In fact, there are no records at all of any of those priests. Either these guys lied when they applied to priest school or whatever it's called, or there's a conspiracy to hide the true identities of these guys."

"Swell," I said. "Another mystery. 'Cause I was just thinking that I wasn't nearly confused enough."

"Then buckle up, Joe," said Bug, "because there's one more thing that popped up. I added Verona to the general pattern search for this case and guess whose grandfather was born there?"

"Just tell me, Bug."

"The family name is Verrecchia. But that's not the name he uses now."

"What's the name?"

"Vox."

"Wait—Hugo Vox's family comes from the same town as Nicodemus?"

"More than the same town, Joe. Half of the men who adopted Nicodemus as their priest names were born as Verrecchias. Nicodemus and Vox are from the same family."

Chapter Ninety-Five

Private Villa Near Jamshidiyeh Park
Tehran, Iran
June 16, 3:24 a.m.

Vox looked at his watch and smiled. Time to make the first of his calls.

He took several fast, panting breaths while he punched a speed dial. Charles LaRoque answered on the second ring.

"*Jesus, kid, you got to stop them*," said Vox, putting panic and urgency into his voice in exactly the right amounts.

"Stop who?"

"The Tariqa, who the fuck do you think I'm talking about. That whole thing with Rasouli and the flash drive? That was a smokescreen. It was bullshit to get the authorities looking in the wrong direction. And all the time he's working out a deal with your pet monsters to shove the Agreement right up your ass."

"What are you talking about?" LaRoque's voice was filled with genuine panic.

"I'm talking about doomsday, you stupid fuck. I warned you—*begged* you—not to tell Rasouli too much before he took the full oath. He's not the Murshid and never had any intention of being that. You know what he wants? He wants to put a lot of Christian heads on poles. He doesn't want to keep the Shadow War going. That's small potatoes for him. He's ramping up Iran to be a nuclear power. And he's got a really goddamn good chance of uniting all of Islam against the West. You Red Order clowns think you've been keeping the church alive? Rasouli is going to blow Christianity off the planet with a mushroom cloud and remake the world in the name of Allah."

"That's ridiculous, Hugo," said LaRoque with a forced laugh. "Even if Rasouli betrays us, he doesn't have that kind of power. Iran doesn't have nuclear weapons yet."

"Iran doesn't," Vox said, "but Rasouli does. He arranged to buy decommissioned devices from the black market. The same bombs you tried to buy before 9/11. *He has them*."

"Impossible. We never told him about—"

"He has an inside track to the whole Red Order. You have no secrets left, Charlie. Rasouli has you by the balls."

"No, you're wrong. No one in the Order would dare—"

"Don't you listen? I never said that a Hospitaller betrayed you. What I'm saying is that those bloodsucking dogs you *think* you have on the leash have been off the leash for a long damn time."

"What?" LaRoque asked, but now there was doubt in his voice.

"Yeah," said Vox. "Rasouli has made a deal with *your* devils."

Chapter Ninety-Six

Arklight Camp
Outskirts of Tehran
June 16, 3:27 a.m.

"Vox and Nicodemus are related," I said. "That's it, I'm going home."

I expected Church to looked rattled by the news, but he stood there, slowly nodding to himself.

"What?" I asked.

"Pieces are coming together."

"Making what kind of a picture?"

"I'm not entirely sure yet, but let me ask you this, Captain, do you feel that we're at war with the Red Order?"

I thought about it. "Actually, even though this thing is tied to them, I . . . I really don't see how. We're at war with someone."

"Are we?"

"The nukes."

"The nukes are in play, but we haven't yet cracked the logic of their placement. There have been no threats, no demands. Nothing in the case files on the Red Order suggests an anti-American agenda."

I thought about it. "Y'know, I kind of have the same feeling about Rasouli. I mean, he kicked this off by giving me the flash drive, but the drive itself is sketchy, and he's been totally off the radar since it began. Granted, that's not even a full day yet, but Rasouli feels like a day player. A walk on."

Church shook his head. "He's more important than that, otherwise the flash drive would have been sent anonymously through the mail. No, Rasouli and the Red Order are in this. I'm simply not convinced we're at war with them."

"They sent a Red Knight after me."

"Someone sent a knight after the drive. Not the same thing."

I grunted. "What about the Sabbatarians?"

"They're independents. They hunt the Upierczi, which means they don't work for the Red Order; and they are fiercely Catholic, which means that they aren't acting on behalf of Rasouli."

"The question, then, is who pointed them at me?"

"Captain—take yourself out of the equation. They were pointed at the knights, who were in turn pointed at the flash drive. You . . . got in the way."

"Ah. I guess the villains just aren't that into me."

He manfully refused to smile.

"Okay," I said, "I'm going to nominate Vox as the bad guy. Who else has 'criminal mastermind' on his business cards?"

"Vox alone?"

Interesting question. "Nicodemus?"

Church shrugged. He left to make a few more calls.

I saw Echo Team standing apart from the activity, looking like a biker gang that had crashed a women's empowerment meeting. I gestured for them to follow me to the far end of the warehouse.

"Good job tonight," I told them. "I was listening and I still never heard you on my six."

"Kinda the point," said Lydia. "Clumsy soldiers don't get Christmas bonuses."

We stood for a moment, each of us looking back at the cluster of Arklight women as they continued arming for war. I saw Violin sliding loaded magazines into slots on a bandolier. She saw me watching and gave me a brief nod that I returned. We turned away at the same moment.

"Top," I said, "get back to the other warehouse and get everything ready. Finish modifying our equipment, but don't use all the garlic. Church will have some kind of transport here soon. As soon I talk to the Big Man again I'll come back for a mission briefing. Everyone eat some food, hit the head, take your vitamins. Finish that special project I gave you earlier from those notes Circe got from that folklore professor. Looks like we're going to need it. We need to be ready to rock, and who knows how long this will take. Bring as much extra ammunition as you can carry."

"Boss," said Bunny, "what that woman said? That's all true, isn't it?"

"Yeah."

He shook his head. Bunny was no naïve kid, but this was all a long, long way from Southern California.

Khalid looked concerned. "There's a question we need to ask these women here," he said. "If garlic hurts the vampires, is it safe to use around the . . . um . . . what was the word?"

"Dhampyri."

"Yes."

"Good question. I'll ask. In the meantime, let's hustle."

"Hooah," they said, and I watched them vanish through the back door, silent as ghosts.

Chapter Ninety-Seven

Arklight Camp
Outskirts of Tehran
June 16, 3:43 a.m.

As I turned to go find Violin, I saw Church heading quickly toward me.

"We're hitting them all, Captain. A coordinated soft infiltration. Everyone is moving in at the same time. Four targets here in the Middle East and the one in Louisiana. I have every DMS and JSOC team not currently assigned to one of the targets on deck. Nuclear response teams are on high alert. We'll do whatever is possible to do, but we can't wait any longer."

Soft infiltrations meant stealth and nonlethal weapons. Doing just one required extensive planning and training. Doing five? I whistled. "You ever do anything like this before?"

"No one has. So, we get to write the playbook on it. Your team has to avoid a political incident as well as find the bomb."

"You want us to do this on tippy-toes?"

"Correct. You'll infil during this evening's shift change. Once you're in position, you'll begin an unobtrusive search for the device. Floor plans and construction blueprints for the refinery were on the flash drive, and Aunt Sallie has mapped out several likely areas for such a device to be hidden. Given its nature, and based upon the image from Rasouli's phone, we are looking at a basement or subbasement. The construction blueprints of the refinery and the current surveillance layout are close matches, but they're not exact. There are some postconstruction additions and some things that apparently were never built. Or at least that's the CIA's determination. Your map will have anomalies indicated by red dots. Don't trust the Company's report. When in doubt get eyes on those anomalies. Abdul will rendezvous with you here and deliver you to the site. He has a workable plan prepared."

"Already? How's that possible?"

"It's a repurposed plan. Abdul was working with the Company to set up an operation at one of the nuclear power plants. He delivers heavy mechanical parts to refineries and the nuclear plant—turbines, generators, transformers, air purification systems, and so on. There's a lot of overlap with the refineries and the nuclear station, and Abdul is well known. The refineries operate twenty-four hours a day, though at night the staff is reduced by about half. Nighttime deliveries are common. Heavy equipment is often delivered at night to be ready for installation by the larger morning shift, so this won't raise any eyebrows. Abdul has been ordered to scrap the other plan in favor of this."

"What's our confidence in the infil plan? Can Abdul get us in?"

"Almost certainly, though this operation might compromise him, which means that his usefulness in Iran will likely end. He won't be happy about it, and the CIA is definitely not happy about it, but I don't particularly care about their feelings, Captain, and neither should you."

"I don't. Mission comes first, and our mission has a shorter shelf life than theirs, so it sucks to be them. End of story." I paused. "What about the last two nukes?"

Church shook his head. "We're nowhere with them."

I stared at him. "Damn."

"Yes.

"When do we roll?"

"Abdul should be here in twenty minutes. Figure two hours to the re-finery, with a half an hour on either end for loading and unloading."

I looked at my watch. "We'll be hitting the place just shy of dawn. That doesn't leave us much time to prepare a mission plan."

"Figure it out on the fly."

"Rasouli could be lying about the number of sites," I pointed out. "There might only be five nukes. Or none."

"Or there could be twenty," said Church. "I'm aware of the risks; however, the overall threat increases the longer we let this play out. The president wants the sweep to focus on the known targets, regardless of additional intel."

"Yikes. There are a whole lot of ways this could go wrong."

"Yes, and very few ways to get everything right. And once this is all over there will be very angry people in several foreign governments, even among our allies. We're putting armed soldiers into play without seeking permission from *any* government. A lot of sovereignty rules are going to be bent or broken, and that's too bad. The State Department is working up several variations of a presidential response, no matter how this spins out. Best-case scenario is that we'll later claim to the world press that we were always working in concert with, and at the invitation of, these gov-ernments. If we find and de-arm the bombs, then those governments will have to stand by us publicly and agree that they invited us in as advisors."

"Armanihandjob, too?"

Church didn't respond. I was two for two with nobody laughing at that joke.

"We have to face the possibility that our enemies will detonate the re-maining two devices as soon as they know about the hits."

"Well, you're just a ray of sunshine," I said. "I so look forward to our little chats."

"If you want something cheerier, I hear that Best Buy is hiring." He cocked his head at me. "Until you determine that the device is, in fact, at the refinery, you will be operating under limited rules of engagement. Avoid conflict but don't get taken. If fired upon, you are not authorized to use lethal force. We are not at war with Iran."

"So don't start one," I said, "yeah, I get that. You're asking a lot from Tasers and beanbag rounds."

"This order comes from the president, not from me. However, make sure the nonlethal weapons aren't all you are carrying."

"Something else," I said. "Khalid brought up the question of whether these dhampyri are vulnerable to garlic?"

"It varies. I know that some of them have been killed by Sabbatarians who attacked them thinking they were Upierczi. In heavy doses garlic is fatal to them too. But it's not a matter of simply being around garlic. The garlic oil has to be introduced into the bloodstream, or in powder form into the lungs. They will be wearing ballistic shielding and each of them carries injectable epinephrine. Every soldier knows there are risks."

He held out his hand.

"Good hunting, Captain."

Chapter Ninety-Eight

Private Villa Near Jamshidiyeh Park
Tehran, Iran
June 16, 3:44 a.m.

After the call to LaRoque was finished, Vox was so charged with energy that he had to run around the house for several minutes just to calm down. His whole body seemed to be cranking out more energy than a nuclear power plant. He ran up and down the stairs twenty times. Finally, breathing heavily and bathed in sweat, he came back to his office and made the second call.

"It's the middle of the damn night, Hugo," Rasouli answered in an angry mumble. "This had better be important, or so help me."

"Shut up and listen," said Vox in a deep growl. "We have problems. The thing about using the phony flash drive to get the DMS to take out the Red Order—that worked like a charm. Church and his crew are ready to swat that psychopath LaRoque. You'll come out of it looking like a hero. Rah, rah, we can all celebrate the new president of Iran. *But*," Vox said, leaning heavily on the word, "there's a wrinkle and it's a big goddamn wrinkle. Those nukes are real. No, don't say anything. I know what I told you, but it turns out LaRoque is even crazier than I thought he was. He didn't just buy cases for them; turns out he had no intention of just using the photos as blackmail. No, this sick fuck bought real nukes from some black-market thugs in Kazakhstan."

"Beard of the prophet . . ."

"And there really *is* one under the Aghajari refinery."

The noise Rasouli made sounded to Vox like someone was choking a turkey. He jammed his mouth into the crook of his elbow to stifle a laugh. Then he took a breath and said, "Here's the kicker. That agent you met, Captain Ledger, he's going after the nuke. Yes, the one at Aghajari. And he's doing it with a full American Spec Ops team. Right now. Today or maybe tomorrow at the latest. If you're going to do something, you had better do it right goddamn now."

He hung up before Rasouli's head could explode. And because he couldn't hold back his own laughter a moment longer.

Chapter Ninety-Nine
Outskirts of Tehran
June 16, 3:52 a.m.

I left the warehouse and began walking back to where Echo Team was waiting. Ghost trotted along beside me. He was still a little off his game from the Taser and the fights yesterday, but he was coming back.

Before I was halfway there, I heard a familiar voice.

"Joseph!"

I turned and, despite everything, I smiled.

Ghost, the big furry flirt, wagged his tail.

Violin ran through the shadows to catch up then slowed to a stop five feet away. We looked at each other and my smile faltered. So did hers.

"Wow," I said, "you really know how to show a guy a good time. Best first date ever."

Violin laughed.

She had a good laugh. A genuine laugh, and given everything that I now knew about her I wondered how it was possible for her to have any trace of a sense of humor. It said a lot about the person she was. It was that indomitability of spirit that made me believe that women like her and her mother and the others would not only survive their own history but one day rise completely above it. I wanted to say that to her, but now was in every way not the right time.

"I don't know where to put all of this in my head," I admitted.

"I know," she said. "I'm sorry you have to."

Her voice was a little sad. She knelt down to pet Ghost, who immediately lost his damn mind and rolled on the ground like a puppy. So much for the impressive dignity of the military trained dog. She even found his happy spot that made him kick his leg.

"Over the years," Violin said as she stroked Ghost's thick fur, "different groups have deliberately clouded the public's perception about vampires. First it was the church, labeling them as actual satanic creatures. Then it was the Red Order, building a mystique around them so that they would be feared, but also misunderstood. The Order were the first ones to distort the powers and vulnerabilities of the Upierczi. Many of the classic writings about vampires were influenced by the Order. Leone Allacci, Reverend Sabine Baring-Gould, Dom Augustin Calmet, Reverend Montague Sommers, Walter Map, William of Newburgh, and even Bram Stoker either worked for the Order or were heavily influenced by them. It was more useful to have people believe that vampires were supernatural. Like the hate crimes the Order and the Tariqa committed, such beliefs drove people back to the protection of the church."

"It's disgusting," I said.

She nodded. "Over the centuries, though, even the Upierczi have come to believe some of it. Their leader, Grigor, believes himself to be a true immortal, a kind of dark angel. There have been Upierczi who have gone mad because they began believing that they were actually monsters. They collapsed in terror at the sight of the cross or the Eucharist. Propaganda is a powerful weapon."

"Yes, and that's the sort of thing Vox loves to play with. God help us all if he ever starts working directly with the Upierczi. It's bad enough he's screwing around with Rasouli and LaRoque."

"I agree. If he was with Grigor, we'd be doomed." She glanced down at Ghost. "Do you know why the knight who attacked you in your hotel room did not simply kill your dog?"

"I've wondered about it."

"The knights are afraid of white dogs. There are many legends about the magical powers of white dogs. Vampire hunters have used them for centuries to find the graves of vampires. A lot of cultures, especially the Greeks, have always believed that dogs can foresee evil. And of course there's the legend of the fetch dog."

"The what? I keep hearing that word. What is it?"

She looked up, surprised. "I thought you knew about that. The Sabbatarians of legend had magical powers and they traveled with a dog called a 'fetch' who lived wholly or partly in the spirit world. The fetch dog could sniff out evil, which the Sabbatarians would then dispatch using various magical means. A *white* fetch dog would be exponentially more powerful than any other kind. This legend has been heavily reinforced over the years by Sabbatarian hit teams bringing trained attack dogs with them. The Upierczi—even the ones who do not believe themselves to be evil—know of many cases where a fetch dog was used to kill one of their kind."

"So why didn't the knight kill Ghost?"

"Oh," she said, flexing her fingers in Ghost's fur, "they can't do that. Fetch dogs belong to God. They are to dogs what saints are to humans. To harm one is to incur the wrath of God and all his angels."

I smiled. "Great, now that Ghost's heard that he'll be insufferable."

Violin gave Ghost a final pat and stood up. The shadows around us seemed to create an opaque screen between us and the reality of what we were really facing. Or about to face.

"When this is over . . ." I said, and let it hang.

"Yes," she said. "When it's over." She looked away, her eyes filled with sadness.

"No," I said clumsily, "I meant when this thing tonight is over. Not the war. I don't want to wait until the end of the war to get to know you."

She took a tentative step toward me. And another. She was so beautiful, so powerful in the way that a woman can be powerful. I'd known her for less than a full day. Longest day of my life, but still less than a day. I wanted to know her for a lot of days, for years.

I looked into her eyes and saw—or thought I saw—my thoughts mirrored there. Can it be like that? Love at first sight is a romance novel myth. Isn't it?

Violin took another step toward me and I moved to meet her. She was tall, almost tall enough to look me straight in the eyes. She touched my cheek with one strong, soft hand.

"Joseph," she said and suddenly she was in my arms. I could feel the heat of her breath on my face as she went up onto her toes, and I bent toward her, our hearts hammering, mouths open.

Then panic instantly flashed through my brain and I pushed her away and staggered back, colliding with Ghost who gave a sharp startled bark.

"No!" I gasped, clapping a hand over my mouth.

Violin gaped at me for a horrible moment. Then her face twisted into a feral mask of fury. "I told you I was a monster," she hissed and she turned to run, but I darted out a hand and caught her arm. She surprised me, though, and wrenched her arm out of my hand.

"Stop!" I yelled.

She did, but her eyes were filled with hurt and anger.

"Listen to me," I said sharply. "It isn't about you. It's because I don't want to hurt you."

"No, you heard what I was and—"

"Violin—before I left the other warehouse I ate an entire bag of powdered garlic. That's why I've been chewing gum. If I kissed you now . . ."

She studied my face, looking for the lie, her whole body still tensed to run. And then a smile slowly blossomed on her face. It was like seeing the sun coming up over the mountains. It lit up her features and painted the night in brightness.

"Violin . . ." I said.

But she threw back her head and laughed, and then she walked away into the night.

In my earbud Top said, "Abdul's two minutes out, Cap'n. We're ready to roll."

"Copy that," I said with a sigh.

Ghost looked at me as if I was the biggest fool who ever walked on two legs. He was a great judge of character and I could find no fault with his opinion.

Feeling like an idiot, I turned and ran toward the warehouse where my team was waiting.

Chapter One Hundred

On the Road
Iran
June 16, 4:17 a.m.

The plan was for Abdul to take us to an auto repair yard ostensibly owned by his cousin but actually owned by the CIA. He wasn't happy to see us. He was seriously disgruntled about having a woman along on what he clearly regarded as a "man's mission." He said as much in various ways, making sure his comments were loud enough for Lydia to hear. Regruntling him wasn't high on my list of priorities. If we'd had a lot more time I might have put him in a room with Lydia so they could talk it out and come to some sort of meeting of the minds, though admittedly that would probably end with a meeting between her foot and his nuts. Détente would suffer.

We followed him in the vegetable truck. Even with what we were facing and everything that Lilith had told us—or maybe because of it—everyone was laughing during the trip. Mostly making fun of Bunny, though I finally got some mileage out of "Armanihandjob." Yeah, I know, juvenile . . . but as an icebreaker on the way to de-arm a nuke possibly planted by vampires, what do you want?

Abdul led us to the deserted auto repair yard and parked by the vehicle that he would use to drive us into the refinery compound: a clunker of a Chinese Foton diesel truck. It had room for two up front and a big flatbed in the back.

Lydia turned to Abdul. "Unless you got a cloak of invisibility, *cuate*, how are we—"

Abdul cut her off with a curt shake of his head and then pointed. "Of course not," he snapped irritably. He strode over to the closest box and opened it. True to its label there was a big hunk of machinery in there. Some kind of turbine. However, Abdul fiddled with a metal knob and the turbine suddenly opened with a hiss of hydraulics. It was a shell and inside was a tiny capsule with a bench. Bunny whistled, but Abdul gave him a sour look. "We made these to smuggle in a team of techs to the nuclear power station. To sabotage the centrifuges." He shook his head. "We spent *three years* developing this plan. Three. Now—*poof!*—it has to be scrapped."

Top smiled at him. "Did your station chief explain to you exactly what we're doing?"

Abdul shook his head. "I don't care. You Americans all think you're Austin Powers. It's all bullshit."

Top, still smiling, bent close and patted Abdul on the shoulder. "I'm really sorry to screw up your plans for recreational vandalism, my friend, but we're trying to keep your country from getting blown into orbit. So, if it's all the same to you, you can take your sour feelings and your little pouty face and go piss up a rope."

Abdul stared at him, uncertain how to react because Top's friendly and affable smile never even wavered. Then Abdul's eyes shifted away from Top and swept over the faces of the other members of Echo Team. He wasn't playing to a friendly crowd.

"Okay, okay, but this is bullshit," Abdul insisted. His expression suggested that he'd like Top and the rest of us to die in the desert and be eaten by vultures. Three years is a lot of time to invest in anything, but overall my nerves were running so high that, like Top, I managed not to give a shit. You know, the whole nukes thing.

I asked, "What's the plan to get us into the refinery?"

"These are valuable parts that have been back-ordered for months," said Abdul. "I have the actual parts here too, and I would have delivered them and waited until these parts were ordered for the nuclear plant." He waited for us to console him about his great loss, got no love, and continued. "We set it up that way so that when the team was ready we could show up virtually any time of day or night."

"Good."

We were out of earshot of the others and Abdul cut me a quick look. He ticked his chin in Top's direction. "Is what he said true?"

"Unfortunately."

He sighed and cursed some more, mostly to himself. Or to God. When he had the last shell open he waved the team over and began locking us into the metal capsules. It was uncomfortably like going into a coffin, but it would get us in. I tucked Ghost into one with a rawhide bone and fresh water. It wasn't the first time he'd done something like this, and he was trained for it, though he still contrived to give me an aggrieved look as I closed the door.

Because of space constraints, the cases had to be loaded after we were inside the capsules, so there was a lot of nauseous swaying as the chain hoist lifted us up and a heavy—and perhaps deliberate—thump as the crates were set down into the stake bed. The capsule allowed me to sit straight and move my arms and legs a bit. Standing and lying down were out of the question and after a while—and a few thousand jolts and bumps from the truck—my lower back was starting to sing a sad song. I figured Bunny had it worse than me. Kid was six foot seven, and Abdul had packed him into the crate like a magazine in a gun. Not a lot of rattle room.

We were radio silent, giving a bit of respect to Iran's military police. They were a long way from stupid. Between their own science and what they bought from China and North Korea, they had an impressive array of security sensors, backed by satellites, hidden detection bases, and a general sense of hostile paranoia.

The Foton had, apparently, no shocks or suspension worth mentioning, and I do believe that Abdul found every single goddamn pothole to drive over along the way. Helluva guy. I'd let him marry my sister, if I had one and didn't like her.

I spent the rest of the ride going over the de-arming sequences. I have to admit it, though . . . when the crate was opened and the air of the refinery, reeking of oil and sweat and heat, struck me full in the face, it was a relief.

The crate had begun to feel like a coffin.

Chapter One Hundred One

Aghajari Oil Refinery
Iran
June 16, 4:56 a.m.

The refinery was a crazy house of people. It seemed like thousands to me, running, yelling, pounding up and down metal staircases, moving pallets of fifty-five gallon drums. For them, it was just another day.

There were so many people, and our intel about the daily operations of the refinery were so good—thanks to the now deeply bitter Abdul—that we were able to vanish right into the human herd of petroleum workers. Bug, at Mr. Church's direction, had hacked into the operations computers here and inserted our work records, IDs, and other data. If someone didn't recognize us and went to check, they'd find out that we were either just transferred from another rig or had been there for a while but in another part of the massive Aghajari complex. No one took the risk of questioning security officers. Too many of the ordinary cops on rigs like this were actually members of Rasouli's secret police. This wasn't Stalinist Russia, but it wasn't tremendously far away from it, either.

Before we left the storage room where Abdul uncrated us, we synched up and ran through the game plan. We had miles of the refinery to cover. The photo of the nuke showed a poured concrete floor and rock walls, which meant that we didn't have to crawl around up in the pipes looking for it. However, there was a basement and four subbasements that included endless corridors, storerooms, offices, closets, and even staff quarters, as well as rooms dedicated to water, sewage, electricity, fire systems, alarms, and more. We divided the place into three sections, checked the function of our digital Geiger counters, tapped our earbuds to make sure everyone was on the team channel, and then went to work.

"Okay," I said as everyone crouched down, "combat call signs from here out. Everyone on coded channel one-eight. Warbride, Ghost, and I will do a sweep of the north half of the lower level. Dancing Duck, you and Chatterbox take the upper levels. Shouldn't take you long."

That was true enough. Although a bomb does more damage in an air burst—which could be approximated by mounting it high on the rig—the likelihood of it being there was small. It would be spotted and it wouldn't do as much damage to the oil, and the oil was a more likely target than a refinery stuck out in the middle of a desert. The upper-deck sweeps were necessary for certainty, though, even if they felt like time wasters.

"Sergeant Rock and Green Giant, sweep the lower levels. If either or both teams come up dry, then rendezvous with me down under. Rasouli's picture showed a cavern or underground chamber."

"What if we meet the fearless vampire hunters or those Red Knight goons?" asked Lydia.

"They're not Iranian nationals," I said. "No grace for them. So that means one person on each team has a nonlethal gun for diplomacy and the other has live rounds for deal-closing. Chatterbox, Sergeant Rock, and Warbride are the best shooters, so you get to play with the grown-up toys."

"Hooah," they acknowledged.

I unslung the bag I carried and opened it. We had used most of the garlic powder and oil according to Jonatha Corbiel-Newton's instructions, but there was some left. Everyone held their hands up and I filled their palms with powder.

Bunny's face was screwed up in distaste as he choked his down. "Never eating Italian food again," he complained. He washed it down with a mouthful of water. We'd been following this ritual for hours now, and I felt like my stomach was churning from all I'd swallowed. I passed around my pack of gum and everyone took a stick.

I used the last of the powder on Ghost, working it into his fur. He absolutely hated it, and it probably reduced his sense of smell by two-thirds, but I was the pack leader and he endured it. Pretty sure he was going to crap in my shoes first chance he got.

Before we broke the huddle I added a final note. "This is a shit job and we all know it. We're rolling on squeaky wheels here as far as intel goes and we know for a fact that we have more enemies than friends. Watch your asses, trust no one, and do not get taken."

"Yeah," said Warbride, "and don't take candy from strangers."

Everyone grinned, and it seemed for a moment as if they were all at peace with this. Maybe, I thought, it was the kind of warrior's calm that sometimes happens when soldiers know that they're walking into the valley of the shadow of death and that there's no real way out.

Chapter One Hundred Two

Private Villa Near Jamshidiyeh Park
Tehran, Iran
June 16, 5:00 a.m.

The last call was the kicker, and he was looking forward to this. It rang eight times before Grigor answered.

"There's been kind of a wrinkle," said Vox breathlessly. "This is urgent and you have to act right now. You need to get the triggers in place, and I mean right now."

"We don't have the—"

"I know, I know. Look, Grigor, you've played fair with me and I've been jerking you around. That was wrong, and I'm saying it to you right now. I was wrong and I apologize. I'm also sorry as hell about your son. I . . . lost my son recently, too. So I'm going to stop screwing around with you. I'll text you the password to activate the code scrambler."

Grigor said nothing, but Vox was sure he could hear the Upier's mind churning.

"Something's happened that made me realize that I've been screwing with the wrong guy here."

"What do you mean?"

"It's LaRoque . . . he *knows*."

"Knows what?"

"Everything. He knows about the bombs. He knows that the Upierczi are about to rise up. He knows everything."

"Impossible!"

"No it's not impossible. He's kept you in chains for eight hundred years—do you think he hasn't had you monitored? Especially since the rebirth? You're more of a threat to him than ever, and he knows it. Just as he knows that the Order isn't as strong as it used to be. The Agreement's in pieces, and you know as well as I do that Rasouli is never going to re-start the Shadow War. That fucker wants a true jihad. Guess who will be caught in the middle? Guess who LaRoque will use as cannon fodder to *force* a new Shadow War? Do you honestly think LaRoque or Nicodemus cares a wet fart about you?"

"So what?" sneered Grigor. "Let them come for us. Let them hunt us in the tunnels."

"Jesus, man, do you ever listen to yourself? Stop auditioning for the remake of *Dracula* and pay attention. LaRoque isn't going to come after you himself. He's too afraid of you. No, he's leaked information to the authorities. To the DMS, to that agent Ledger, the one who killed your son at the hotel. LaRoque will go into hiding while Special Forces teams come after you, and believe me they will hunt you through the tunnels, and there are a lot more of them than there are of you."

Grigor was silent, and Vox smiled to himself. Nice. Now it was time to play his final card. The one real kicker. The one that would take all the chips on the table.

"Grigor . . . there's one more thing."

"What?" demanded the King of Thorns.

"The American Spec Ops teams have allies in this. Allies who can help them find you and hunt you."

"Who? Those Sabbatarian fools? We laugh as we kill them—"

Vox said, "Arklight."

The sound Grigor made was somewhere between a snarl of animal hatred and a hunting scream. Vox leaned away from the phone, wincing. He thought he heard the name Lilith in there somewhere. Vox was sure he had never heard so much hatred directed at a single person before.

It made his groin throb.

"Give me that password," seethed Grigor. "I will show them a war like nothing they have ever seen. I will drown them in lakes of blood . . ."

Vox stopped listening to the tirade. He tapped in the password that would activate the code scrambler he had given Grigor. The scrambler, with its powerful satellite uplink that could send detonation codes to those lovely nuclear devices.

As soon as the password went through, Vox called up the file of all DMS personnel and their families and sent that too. What the hell. The Sabbatarians didn't seem to be getting the job done. Let Edward the Sparkly Vampire and his undead hordes tackle it. That sounded like a whole lot of fun. Maybe Grigor would be the one to finally tear Deacon's throat out. How sweet would that be?

Vox disconnected the call halfway through Grigor describing how he would crack his enemies' bones and suck out the marrow. Or something like that. Vox didn't care.

All of his cares were over.

Chapter One Hundred Three

Church had a complete tactical operations board in his Humvee. It was a new design, one that used flexible circuits for a display board that could be erected in curved panels to form a large semicircular arena. High-res images and holographic overlays created a three-dimensional model of the two theaters of operation. Louisiana and the Middle East, and this latter was subdivided into four separate locations: the Aghajari oil refinery in Iran, the Beiji oil refinery in Iraq, the Abqaiq in Saudi Arabia, and the Toot oilfield in Pakistan.

Small glowing dots indicated the transponder signals from the teams that were moving into position.

A central screen showed Aunt Sallie and the TOC at the Hangar. Church was an observer here, watching Auntie run the show.

"All teams on station," said Aunt Sallie, who was seated to his right at a gleaming command console. "WMD alarms and hot loop equipment stowed. OPs pulled in. All personnel report alert. Infil teams one through six report ready to move immediately. We are at REDCON-One. Waiting for the word."

Church sensed movement and saw Lilith standing by the opening to the little arena, and he waved her inside. She studied the display and nodded approval.

"You always did like your toys," she said with a faint smile.

"High technology used correctly allows for the greatest efficiency," he murmured as he tapped keys to bring up another smaller set of display windows. This showed the screens that Rudy, Bug, and Circe were looking at. He and Lilith leaned forward to study them.

"Is that the translation?" asked Lilith.

"Yes." He touched a button to open a line. "Circe, what do you have?"

"MindReader has decrypted four percent of the *Book* so far and about twice as much of the Voynich manuscript. Each one is different, and each is very disturbing in its own way."

"How so?"

"The first few pages of the *Book of Shadows* is the Holy Agreement, and it's what we expected. The Red Order and the Tariqa agree to work together to do 'what is necessary'—that's the phrasing they were apparently most comfortable with—in order to 'lead the people to faith and to fealty to God in all things,' yada yada. Essentially, it's an argument in favor of hate crimes. Or maybe we should call them 'faith crimes.' Something like that. The rest of it though . . . my God! It's a kind of history without commentary. It lists every single thing both sides have done to carry out the Agreement. If the whole book is like this, it will be the most complete confession of guilt ever recorded. Hundreds of thousands of deaths. More if you count wars that were started or extended because of the Holy Agreement. We even found a section that shows that the Order influenced Pope Clement V to disband and excommunicate the Knights Templar because the Red Order needed their fortune and resources to continue their private war. That will rewrite a lot of history books. Actually—this all will."

Church didn't comment. "Keep at it," was all he said. He muted the audio feed.

He turned to Lilith. "This is what you wanted," he said. "You can take this to the world court, to NATO, to any group of governments and they will start a new version of the Inquisition to hunt down anyone responsible, anyone still connected to the Order or the Tariqa."

Lilith stood with her hand to her throat, considering it. "It doesn't take down the Upierczi. Unless we can produce a body, no one will believe that they even exist."

"They are slaves of the Order," said Church. "Perhaps one of them will give the Upierczi up as part of a deal."

But she shook her head. "This is where you and I differ," she said. "You think Nicodemus is the power behind all of this. Nicodemus and now Vox. I don't."

"You think it's Grigor."

"I know it is. I can feel it in my bones, in my heart." She closed her eyes. "I lived in one of his cells for fourteen years. He took thirteen children from me. Ripped them from my womb, one after the other. I can't even count the number of times he raped me." Her eyes were as hard as fists. "I know what his dreams were. It may have been the LaRoques who brought in the scientists and paid to have Upier 531 developed—but it was Grigor who demanded it. Yes, he demanded it. He made the Order repair the bloodline of his kind. It fulfilled a dream he had. He talked about that dream incessantly. In the night, in the long dark when no one from the Order was down there in the tunnels. Grigor talked to himself, to his people, about the dreams of the Shadow Kingdom. I would lay there at night, naked, filthy, starving, chained to the wall with an iron collar around my ankle, listening to the echoes of his words whispering through the darkness. You call them slaves, but they see themselves as warriors. A race of warriors. The Red Order kept them in shackles through faith, and then when God would not save the Upierczi, science did. Do you think that lesson was lost on Grigor?"

"What's your point?"

"Look at it from Grigor's perspective. At first the Upierczi were a scattered race of genetic freaks, or at best a dying and failed offshoot of Homo sapiens. The Red Order found them and gave them purpose, but for centuries kept them in chains. They are called knights, but they are slaves and they know it. Over the centuries, despite the promises of the Order and their own prayers, the bloodline of the Upierczi has failed, become polluted. They've faded to the brink of extinction. God did not come even when the Red Order called on Him. Then science saved them. By taking the DNA of the greatest among them, Grigor, their race was reborn. Not in the image of God. Not by the grace of God. They were remade in the image of Grigor. When faith fails and science answers, where do you turn?"

Church said nothing.

"When you have lived as slaves for centuries and accepted your slavery because it was God's will, what happens when you stop believing that?"

Church said nothing.

"There is a war coming, Deacon, no doubt about it. But it's not about oil and it's not about politics. I've known you a long time and yet I don't know you at all. So I wonder how willing you are to fight this kind of war."

He stood up and walked to the entrance and looked out at the night for a long time. Far in the distance a night bird cried out in a voice that was as sad and desolate as all the pain in the world.

His cell phone rang. Mr. Church answered it and listened for a moment.

"I understand," he said. "Thank you, Mr. President."

He set his phone down and touched a button on the console. "Auntie, the word is given and it is 'go.'"

Aunt Sallie nodded and sent the command signal. "All dogs off the leash."

On the screen, the glowing dots began to move.

Church looked at Lilith. "A theory, however compelling, is not a target. If Arklight has any intel that you haven't shared, then now is the time. Give me a target, Lilith, and I'll show you what kind of war I am willing to wage against those monsters."

There was a soft *ping* and Church touched the button to unmute the computer center.

"Mr. Church," said Rudy, "we have something you need to see."

"Is it about the Red Order?"

"It's about the nukes," said Circe. "There aren't seven of them."

"Then how—"

"There are *eight*."

Chapter One Hundred Four

Aghajari Oil Refinery
Iran
June 16, 5:29 a.m.

We moved down a set of metal stairs that zigzagged along a steep wall, with Ghost's nails clicking behind me. I was dressed like a security guard, and Lydia was in her chador and carrying a clipboard with important looking papers on it. She made sure not to make eye contact with any of the men, and she walked a half pace behind me. The men who passed us did not avoid looking at her. I don't know how they were able to determine how good looking she was under the billowing black clothes—and Lydia was a hottie by any rational definition, a little bit of JLo but with a Michelle Rodriguez badass bad-girl sneer—but every single man who passed us gave her a thorough up and down.

At one point, when we were alone, she murmured, "I can't tell . . . are they undressing me with their eyes or wondering how I would look with another layer of clothes on?"

"Beats me, sister."

"I can't tell you how much I'd like to flash my boobs at them just to see them have total coronaries."

"I think they stone you for that here."

"Might be worth it."

I grinned and we kept going.

Although it's usually cold beneath the desert floor, it was hot as hell down here. Steam hissed up from vents like the whole place was going to blow—or that's how it looked to my frenzied imagination. When we passed refinery staff, they were going about their business as if it were just another day on the job, which to them it was. Actually, I guess for me it was too. Jesus, I need to get into a safer line of work. Lion taming, maybe; I heard the benefits package is good.

The farther down we went the more humid the air became, and the heavier the smell of raw oil and cooked petroleum. Two levels down I saw that the walls were lined with stretches of dark lichen and cobwebs.

"Are we at the center of the earth yet?" asked Lydia.

"Australia's a couple of floors down."

When we were at the base of the last stairwell, Lydia slid back her sleeve and tapped the keys of the PDA strapped to her wrist. We studied the map and compared it to our surroundings. The floors were marked with old painted lines color-coded for different destinations for routine maintenance. We followed one that rounded a snaking series of turns, passing dozens of small rooms with locked doors.

Lydia was a better lockpick than I was and she fished out a couple of pieces of flexible plastic and loided the locked rooms. Janitorial office, supply closets, bathrooms. Nothing of interest, so we kept moving.

Ghost, with his heightened senses, was drinking it all in, cataloging a thousand smells and their variations. He was trained to react to nitrites from explosives, to decomposing flesh, and to a few other key smells, but so far he wasn't giving me any of the signals that said he'd found anything. You can't train dogs to detect nuclear materials.

When we were in a stretch of empty corridor Lydia checked the PDA again, then looked at the walls and up at the low ceiling. "We're getting seriously deep here, Gaucho. We still have a signal?"

I tapped my earbud. "Talk to me, Dancing Duck."

Khalid said, "Checked all my unknowns off the list on levels eight and seven. Nothing. Laundry rooms and showers. Heading down a level."

His signal was almost buried under a hiss of static.

"Roger that," I said. "Sergeant Rock?"

"Nothing yet but we need to finish level two. Five more unknowns to put eyes on. Lots of foot traffic here. Slowing us down." His signal was even worse; he sounded like he was whispering at the bottom of a well.

"Copy. Your signal is weak and variable."

"Back atcha. What's your twenty, Cowboy?"

"We're rock bottom. No joy. Moving to zero point."

Zero point was the last spot where Abdul's spies had been able to penetrate and add to the map. Based on the original design plans of the refinery, there should be four hundred yards of corridor and several utility rooms there.

We rounded another bend and encountered two problems at the same time.

The corridor ended forty feet beyond the turn. Not in a closed door but in a flat brick wall. There were doors along the side of the corridor, however, and one stood ajar as four security officers stepped out into the hall.

They glanced at me and Lydia and Ghost.

The guards were all low-ranking patrol officers, the kind who were too far down on the pecking order to know if I was part of the staff or not. Unfortunately the other guy wore the bars of a major in the Iranian security forces. The top ranking officer in the whole refinery was a major with big eyes and buck teeth. He ignored Lydia—who was pretending to look at the floor—and pointed at me.

"You!" he said.

One word, but he said it in a way that we all knew was going to be trouble. Damn.

Chapter One Hundred Five

Arklight Camp
Outskirts of Tehran
June 16, 5:31 a.m.

Church put the call on speakerphone. Lilith bent to listen.

"Remember I told you that I thought this whole thing might be part of a doomsday cult?" asked Circe. "We all dismissed it because those kinds of cults are usually small and underfunded. Now I think I was right the first time."

"Tell me," said Church.

"When MindReader used the math code on the two anomalous pages Rasouli gave us, we think we found something. These are scans, of course, but from ultra-high-res analysis they don't appear to use the same materials as the other pages. Toomey down in handwriting analysis tells me they were written with a fine-point gel pen, not a quill, fountain pen, or brush, which Voynich and the *Book* are."

"This is modern?"

"This is recent. This is what we're looking for. Rasouli had it but apparently couldn't translate it. One page includes records of a purchase of eight nuclear devices. The five we're already targeting and *three* we can't locate. According to the records, the locations were picked by mutual agreement back in 1999, a year before the devices were purchased. The money was paid to black marketers in Kazakhstan in August 2001. The process of taking possession of them and delivering them to the refineries was slowed by everything that happened after 9/11. We also have the contact information for the black marketers, so we can target them whenever we want."

Bug cut in at this point. "Now it gets tricky, Boss, because some entries aren't in ciphertext—they're simple two letter abbreviations. Like a personal shorthand. We were able to identify five of them because we already know where those nukes are. The codes are B/I, A/S, T/P, and L/A. That has to be Beiji oil refinery in Iraq, the Abqaiq in Saudi Arabia, the Toot oilfield in Pakistan, and the Louisiana platform in America."

"What are the other three codes?"

"V/I, M/S, and J/I," said Circe. "We're running pattern analysis but so far we haven't figured it out."

Chapter One Hundred Six

Aghajari Oil Refinery
Iran
June 16, 5:44 a.m.

We were twenty feet away.

The major's hand strayed toward his holstered pistol. The other cops grabbed for the AK-47s slung from their shoulders.

I said, "Hit!"

Ghost went from a tense crouch to full speed in two steps. The buck-toothed major's gun cleared his holster but that was as far as it was ever going to go because Ghost hit him like a cannonball, catching the man on the meat of his forearm and using all of his canine weight and mass to slam the major back against the edge of the doorway. The major screamed and fell down and out of sight with Ghost atop him.

I can't run as fast as a shepherd, but I'm no slowpoke. I barreled right for the guards, all of whom made the mistake of taking half a second to gape in mingled horror and indecision. That was a half second too long.

When I was ten feet from them I threw myself into a rugby tackle that plucked two guys completely off their feet. They fell down and I body-surfed one of them for three yards. I heard Lydia's footfalls less than a yard behind me.

I hammered the rifle out of one guard's hand, smashed him across the mouth with an elbow, and rolled sideways off of him and whipped the same elbow around into a backward blow that caught the second officer in the nose.

From that angle I saw Lydia slide into the third guard like Rickey Henderson stealing second base. Her right foot caught him on the shin and chopped his leg out from under him. His body crashed down on hers, but as he landed she caught his shoulders and turned at the perfect moment, slamming him face down onto the hard floor.

I had most of my weight on the second cop, and I gave his nose a couple of extra pops while I axe-kicked the first guard into dreamland. Then I pivoted on my hip and hopped atop the second guard, who, despite three hits to the face, was still full of game. I straddled his chest and arms with my thighs, grabbed two sides of his shirt and cross-choked him. Do it wrong and the guy either dies of a fractured hyoid bone or struggles with you like they do in the movies. Do it right, using valve pressure on both carotid arteries and the cloth to cut off the airway, and your opponent goes sleepy-by in eight seconds. I did it right.

As soon as he sagged down, I released the pressure, flipped him over, and speed-cuffed him with his own handcuffs. I looked up to see Lydia whipping cuffs around the third guard. His face was a mass of blood, but he was still struggling feebly.

"Hold still, *cabrón*, or I'll break off something you don't want to lose."

"Get the other one. Wrist and ankles," I said, and left her to cuff the first cop. I was up and moving, skidding around the doorway into the office.

The major was down and he was bloody, but he wasn't dead. The pistol lay in the doorway and the arm that had grabbed for it was torn and bleeding—though still attached. Ghost was crouched down over the officer, his bloody fangs clamped around his throat. Not hard enough to kill or even break the skin, but hard enough to make a very clear point: lie still or die.

The officer had put up a struggle, though. Blood was smeared eight feet into the room, which meant that he was trying to drag himself away from Ghost even while the dog was chomping on him. I glanced past the major. There was a glass case with a fire ax on the wall by the door to a small bathroom. Ghost had shifted from a tug of war with the major's arm to a more effective hold on his throat only a few inches short of the wall with the ax. His teeth hadn't torn into the man's throat, but the pressure was there and the major was one bad decision away from dying.

He stopped and lay utterly still except for his heaving chest. The wounds on his arm must not have been as bad as they looked because they only bled sluggishly. Must have hurt like hell, though, because the officer's face was as white as milk.

I drew my pistol and put the barrel to his temple.

To Ghost, I said, "Off. Watch."

Ghost opened his jaws with great reluctance and moved to sit in the corner between the bathroom and a wall on which was a poster-sized copy of the same floor plan I had in my PDA. Ghost sat down where he and the major could have a meaningful visual encounter. Like me, Ghost had shaken off most of the ill effects of yesterday, and like me he was in no mood to get pushed around today.

Lydia appeared in the doorway with one of the rifles in her hands. Before she could speak I gave a quick shake of my head and then ticked my chin toward the door. She nodded and went outside without a word.

I knelt by the major. The officer was wide-eyed with fear, but he wasn't looking at me. He couldn't tear his eyes away from Ghost, who was, to be fair, looking smug and giving him the evil eye. I snapped my fingers in front of the major's eyes, and he flinched and shifted his gaze to me.

"Listen to me," I said in hushed Persian, but I gave my accent a tweak, putting just a hint of Russian in it. "This can go two ways, and I don't think I need to explain the bad way. If you play fair with me, I'll let you bandage your arm and I'll tie you up without further injury."

The major's lip curled back from his big horse teeth as he prepared to fire back a vicious comment, but Ghost warned him with a soft growl.

"We are not here to sabotage the refinery," I said. "I don't care if you believe that or not. It won't change anything. Someone else *is* here to sabotage the place. Listen closely to what I'm about to say next. They have planted a nuclear device in one of the subcellars. I am here to de-arm it because neither of us wants that device to detonate. Can we agree on that?"

"No! We do not have any weapons like that here. What stupidity is this?"

I put a little extra pressure on the gun barrel. "Be nice. If you know anything about that device, then now would be a good time to unburden your soul."

He started to shake his head, but the barrel wouldn't permit the movement. Instead he said, "No!"

"Take a second," I cautioned. "Think it through. It would be so unfortunate if I learned otherwise and had to come back here to discuss it with you."

"No," he said again. "Why would I plant a bomb in my own country? It is the Americans who—"

"Shhh," I soothed. "You don't want to debate politics with me right now, trust me on this. I'll ask it one more time: do you know anything about the device?"

"No. Of course not!" He spat the words at me. "I do not believe it."

If he was lying, then he was a pretty good actor.

"Very well. I'm going to step back and you can get up. Be smart about how you do that." I kept the gun on him, and the major sat up, wincing and hissing with pain. He clamped his left hand over the ragged wounds in his right forearm. I asked him to tell me where the first aid kit was and he nodded toward a box mounted to a wall.

"Bandage your arm. Do it quickly," I said and stepped back while he did so.

"I need to wash it," he said and started walking toward the bathroom. That fire ax would have been an easy grab for him.

I put the barrel of the gun in his ear. "Nice try. Clean it with alcohol or wrap it dirty."

He threw me ugly looks and aimed uglier looks at Ghost, who managed not to wilt and die under the lethal glare. The major opened the first aid kit and started angrily tearing open packaged alcohol swabs.

"Who are you?" he demanded.

"No one," I said. "I'm not even here."

"You are not Russian," he said, and then tried to prove it by rattling off a quick insult in that language. Something about my mother and a goat. In the same tongue I told him that his father dallied with little boys and ate pork during Ramadan. That shut him up and probably raised his blood pressure by too many points. He cut another look at the wall with the fire ax.

"Those are bad thoughts you're having, friend," I said.

He continued cleaning his wounds, though his eyes flicked to the wall over and over again.

My earbud buzzed and, through a burst of bad static, Khalid said he was two floors up. I touched the bud and, still in Russian, said to wait until further orders. Khalid doesn't speak a word of Russian, but it didn't matter. He was sharp enough not to spoil whatever play I was making. The major, however, looked somewhat mollified, if still alarmed and confused. And he kept shooting frightened looks at Ghost, who in turn occasionally licked at the blood on his muzzle. A nice effect.

When the major was done wrapping his arm, I took him into the adjoining bathroom and used his own metal handcuffs to chain him to the toilet pipes. Then I had Lydia stand guard as I dragged the other cops in and similarly secured them. It was a tight fit in the tiny bathroom cubicle. The place stank of old urine and fresh blood. The guards started coming around, but they were sick and dazed and hurt; they had no real fight left in them.

"If nothing goes boom," I said to them, "someone will be along to let you out. Hopefully that will be today. If you start yelling or try to escape, I will come back here and kill you. Tell me you understand."

The major answered for all of them. A short guttural grunt. Good enough.

I closed and locked the door and barricaded it with a desk.

"Come on," I said to Ghost, and went back out into the hall.

"Gaucho," Lydia said quietly, "I've been trying to raise the rest of the team but all I'm hearing is my own voice."

I tried my earbud. Nothing.

"Worry about it later," I said. "We still have a nuke to find before it blows us all into orbit."

She faked a coquettish grin. "Aww, you sure know how to sweet-talk a girl."

The clock inside my head said *tick-tock*.

Chapter One Hundred Seven

Aghajari Oil Refinery
Iran
June 16, 5:52 a.m.

But the hall wasn't telling us anything. It was a short run to a blank wall made from gray bricks. I pulled up the floor plans for this level and studied them. The original designs called for a corridor leading ten yards straight ahead and then a big square room forty yards per side. The plans had been to use the room for bulk storage and to build a heavy-duty elevator down from the loading bay. Technically this is where Abdul's machine parts should have been taken to be uncrated and then switched to other elevators to bring them where the parts were needed. But the chamber had been x-ed off of the blueprints in favor of a more practical ground-level storehouse that would allow parts to be rolled in from trucks by forklift. Less expensive and cumbersome than a subterranean storeroom.

Lydia pounded a fist on the wall and shook her head. "This doesn't make sense, Gaucho. I mean . . . it had to be expensive as hell—and time consuming—to cut a corridor this far into the rock just to put in a few extra storerooms and a security substation. And it would have cost even more to run plumbing, electricity, computer and phone lines, and everything else all the way the down here. Who does that without a reason?"

"No one does that," I agreed.

And yet there was no door hidden in the wall.

"Shall we go ask the major again?" she asked.

"It's that or go out for a beer."

Ghost wagged his tail. Booze hound. But as we approached the door, Ghost immediately started growling. The fur on his back stood up like the bristles on a wire brush, and he barked sharply at the closed bathroom door.

"*Cuidado*," snapped Lydia, bringing the rifle up.

I pulled open the door and we went in fast. The room was as we left it. Ghost ran straight to the desk that blocked the bathroom and his growls deepened. Something was pulling the wolf out from under the dog's facade.

"Cover me," I said as I grabbed the desk and hauled it out of the way. Lydia and Ghost moved to one side. I drew my gun and yanked the bathroom door open.

The soldiers we'd roughed up were where we had left them, except that they were dead. Their throats had been torn away and they lay in a lake of blood. The metal cuffs I'd used to secure the major were twisted out of shape as if someone had put them in a vise and applied a hell of a lot of leverage. Or an unnatural amount of physical strength.

And the major was gone.

Ghost snarled. Not at the dead men, but at the rear wall of the small cubicle. There were bloody handprints on the wood behind the toilet, and the back wall—actually my missing hidden door—stood ajar. I quieted Ghost with a gesture as I bent close to the opening. There was no sound, but a harsh, foul-smelling odor wafted out on a sluggish current of air. It wasn't the stink of petroleum or the sewage smell of methane, and it wasn't the garlic I'd swallowed. This was a stench that provoked the most primitive reactions in me so that in my head the Civilized Man cringed back, the Cop became aware and defensive, and the Warrior bared his teeth in fearful, vicious defiance.

It was the sick-sweet aroma of rotting meat.

The perfume of death.

Chapter One Hundred Eight

Violin tapped her earpiece. "Oracle."

"Oracle welcomes you, Violin."

"Patch me through to my mother."

Lilith came on the line in a few seconds. "Where are you?"

"I'm a mile from the Aghajari refinery."

"Good. The rest of the team is ten minutes out. Leave a trail of bread crumbs for them."

Violin patted her pockets to make sure that she had plenty of transponders. They were small and designed to look like discarded cigarette butts. All she had to do was crush the filter to activate the battery. All Arklight field teams had trackers.

"And, daughter?" said Lilith.

"Yes?"

"Be smart."

"You trained me well, Mother."

"I'm not talking about the mission. I trust you in combat. But you know nothing at all about men."

Violin hesitated. "What do you mean?"

"You're not a good liar, my love. I saw how you looked at Captain Ledger, and how he looked at you. I did not live my entire life in a cell. Don't let infatuation or any other feeling affect you. Not now, not tonight. Be the warrior you are."

"Yes, Mother."

"'Yes, Mother.' I wonder if you heard a word I said."

"I hear you, Mother. I'll be careful and I'll be smart."

"Good," said Lilith. "And there's one more thing . . ."

"Yes?"

"When you face the Upierczi . . . I know some of them are your brothers."

"Yes."

"They are not family to us, girl. They are monsters. Show them mercy and they will consume you."

In the darkness, Violin smiled. It was as cold as knife steel. "Mother—'mercy' was a lesson you never taught me."

She disconnected the call and melted into the shadows.

Chapter One Hundred Nine

Aghajari Oil Refinery
Iran
June 16, 5:57 a.m.

I backed away from the open door. "Listen, this is what we came for. Go upstairs until you get a signal and then get everyone down here."

Lydia eyed me dubiously. "What are you going to do?"

"I'm going to wait right here until you get back."

"C'mon, Gaucho . . . I was born at night but it wasn't *last* night."

"Just go. That's an order, Warbride. Clock's ticking so do it now."

She gave me the kind of look my mother gave me when she was really pissed, but she did as she was told. "Try to be alive when we get back," she snapped, and then with a swirl of black robes she was gone.

I stepped over the corpses and moved to the door once more, listening to the darkness. Nothing. I even tried the earbud once more. Same thing. I would like to think that the lack of signal was simple interference from the dense rock, but I wasn't actually stupid.

"Uh-oh," I said to Ghost. I said it like Scooby-Doo. "Rut-roh!' The joke didn't make either of us feel any better.

I debated getting the hell out of there, and if this mission was about anything else I would have. This was so phony they should have just painted the word "Trap" on the secret door. On the other hand, if I walked away now and the device was really here, then what was my next play? Buy a condolence card for the relatives of anyone who *used* to live in the Middle East? Not much of an option.

I licked my lips and used my toe to nudge the door open. I wasn't afraid of smaller explosives like Semtex. Ghost was trained to sniff them out and warn me. I glanced at him. He wasn't barking but he was shivering and his hair was standing out in all directions. Not as comforting as I would have liked. I clicked my tongue and he flinched. Then he shook his body like he was shaking off cold water and he looked up at me with troubled eyes. I wished he could talk because the information his senses were processing were probably going to be pretty crucial to my survival over the next few minutes. But only Lassie can explain complex predicaments with a bark; Ghost was merely a dog.

Letting the barrel and flashlight lead the way, I stepped out of the bloody bathroom and into a narrow passage with rough stone walls. The same kind of stone as the wall in the picture Rasouli showed me. Rough, gray white. A little whiter than the walls behind the metal stairs I'd climbed down. A different mineral composition this far down.

I moved down the hallway. Ghost, as silent as his name, was right behind me. The corridor turned and turned, making sharp rights and lefts and then tilted as it angled down deeper into the underbelly of the desert bedrock. The air moved past me, flowing up from below. The stink of death was still there.

I rounded the last turn and the hallway ended at an open doorway beyond which was a massive chamber. There were stacks of wooden crates in uneven rows, but this was clearly not a storeroom. I stood in a vast cavern whose ceiling was a mass of dripstone stalactites that hung like the fangs of an infinitely large dragon. Water dripped seventy feet to the concrete floor, where it pooled around broken stones, fallen rock, and the corpses of at least two dozen men.

They were piled into a mound, their bodies torn and slashed, their skin crawling with maggots and cockroaches and vermin that skittered away from my flashlight beam. The stench of all that rotting meat was dreadful.

I moved cautiously forward. All of the bodies were male, and some of them were naked. No way to tell if they were Iranian, but that was my guess. Many of them were tough-looking, well-muscled, in their twenties and thirties. From the uniforms of the clothed ones I could tell that they were refinery roughnecks and security people. Some of the naked ones probably were too; the killers had likely made them strip off their uniforms before the killing began. I wondered if one of the killers was wearing a major's uniform.

I shined the light over them, frowning more and more at each new detail I picked out. These bodies were at least a couple of days old. Did that mean that their killers had been fully infiltrated into the refinery for two days? If one of the dead men *was* the major, then his impostor could easily have ordered staff changes of any kind. Reassignments, replacements. It's not like Iran has union reps who can make protests or ask questions.

How deep did the infiltration go? And what was its purpose?

I walked around the mound of dead. The injuries were traumatic. Crushed skulls. Arms and legs torn out of their sockets. Throats savaged.

I took a step forward and my foot crunched down on something. I lifted my foot and looked at what I'd stepped on. Dentures. Big buck-toothed dentures. Or . . . maybe false teeth is a better word. The Hollywood kind that fit over regular teeth. Like the major's teeth.

"Oh, crap," I said, but I was only half surprised.

The major had been an Upier. Had to be. I replayed the fight in the security office. The major had gone down easily, but he'd gone down because Ghost attacked him. Ghost was a white dog—a fetch dog, as far as the Upierczi were concerned—and he was covered in garlic powder. Ghost had eaten some garlic too, and during the fight he'd bitten the major. Garlic was supposed to be fatal, but there might not have been enough of it in Ghost's saliva for a lethal dose. Instead it had probably weakened the Upier, but not enough to keep him from breaking out of the cuffs. Then he'd killed the other guards and fed on them. Disgusting as that sounds. What had that done for him? Probably like Popeye eating spinach.

As I looked at the corpses, I understood that there had to be a lot of Red Knights here at the refinery, and they'd just started their workday with an O-positive energy drink.

Ghost trembled beside me. I tore my gaze away from the corpses for a moment and looked at my dog. He was cross-trained for all sorts of things including searching for dead bodies, and he doesn't weigh moral or social implications. He shouldn't have been scared by this. Excited by blood and the evidence of slaughter, sure, that's hardwired into his animal brain. But not mass murder. And yet he was clearly terrified. His eyes were huge and rolling as if he was checking every possible line of escape at once, and drool dripped from the corners of his mouth. At the point where his body touched my leg I could feel his heart hammering away at dangerous speeds.

"Easy, boy," I said in a voice I hoped was soothing. Ghost glupped back some of the drool and looked up at me, though whether it was for reassurance that the pack leader would protect him or instructions on what to do next was anyone's guess. I stroked his side and patted his flank. He pressed more firmly against me. "It's okay, Ghost . . . it'll all be okay."

I was pretty damn sure I was lying to him. To both of us.

Then I tore myself away from the carnage and looked around the cavern. I shined my light and saw something dark on top of one of the crates and at closer inspection saw twenty sets of folded clothes. Not the missing uniforms, but almost certainly the clothes of the men who had taken them. Black pants, black shirts, black balaclavas.

"Oh . . . shit," I said aloud. Did that mean there were twenty Upierczi down here? Or were they up in the refinery? Up where my team was.

Shit.

I dropped the balaclava I was holding and directed the light into the cavern. It was so wide that the beam didn't reach the far side, and from the uneven walls and ceiling, it was apparent that this hadn't been cut into the earth but was a natural cavern that had been repurposed. The far end looked to be a jagged tunnel, but from where I stood I couldn't make out any details. I crept quietly toward the stacked crates. Some were open and heaps of straw or packing popcorn were spilled like guts onto the ground. A few were still sealed, and I began circling the stacks looking for a crowbar.

Then I suddenly lost all interest in the crates, the crowbar, the dead bodies, and every other damn thing. I could feel the blood in my veins turn to ice water. My guts clenched as I saw what sat on the far side of the crates.

It was there.

Sixty feet away. It squatted there in the center of the big cavern. Sitting out in the open, all by itself except for thick power cords that coiled like snakes toward the nearest wall.

Huge, powerful, feral. Sophisticated in a brutal and primal way.

Deadly as hell.

My heart started beating as fast as Ghost's and all the spit in my mouth turned to dust.

"God," I murmured, but I was looking at the devil.

The bomb.

Chapter One Hundred Ten

I moved toward it. I wanted to run. God, I wanted to run for my life.

I kept moving toward it, drawn to the sheer enormity of what it represented at the same time as I was totally repulsed.

Ghost was right with me, but he seemed happy to be away from the dead, which is weird. Dogs like smelly, rotting stuff. He should have been having a field day cataloging all the scents. He wasn't.

The device was larger than I thought. Four feet high, six wide, eight long. The data on these models gave a weight range between eight hundred and sixteen hundred pounds. This one looked bigger, maybe a ton. I wasn't going to slip it into a pocket and run out of here with it, and I wasn't going to sneak it out on a hand truck.

I was going to have to de-arm it.

I tapped my earbud again in the vain hope that somehow there was a signal. Nothing, and glancing over my shoulder at the heap of corpses I had a pretty good idea why. Whatever was happening, whatever the Red Order and the knights, or the knights themselves, had running—the infiltration, the communications jamming—was happening now.

The only thing that kept me from having a stroke right there was the thought that there were a couple of dozen of our unknown hostiles here at the refinery. Not the time to detonate the device.

Hopefully they were not suicide soldiers.

My inner Cop told me to shut the fuck up and pay attention to the task at hand.

I used my forearm to wipe sweat out of my eyes, then took a long steadying breath, and focused my mind on the PDA strapped to my forearm. I tapped the keys to pull up the de-arm procedures for the nuke. I scanned it to refresh my mind and then scrolled back to the first step.

"Okay," I said aloud, hoping that my voice sounded competent and calm. Maybe tomorrow I'll cure cancer. About as likely.

I have a little bit of religion. Not much, just enough to get me to church on Christmas and Easter. I wasn't much for personal prayer. Not like my friend, Rudy, who was a staunch Catholic. However, as I removed my tool kit on the cowling of the beast, I was praying as hard as I could.

My tools were all made from an ultra-high-density polymer rather than metal. Plastics are nonconductive. The steps sound easy. Remove the screws holding the cover plate in place, disconnect the wires leading from the battery or the timer to the detonator. Sounds easy, but this is where you're most likely to encounter a booby trap. Trembler devices, fake wires, micromotion detectors, heat sensors. If nothing goes boom at that phase you hit the whole red wire–blue wire thing.

I slowly unscrewed the six screws and checked to make sure that there wasn't a trip wire rigged to an anti-intrusion trigger. There was no wire visible. Sweat ran down my face and stung my eyes. Ghost smelled my fear and whined nervously. I held my breath as I removed the plate.

Nothing went boom.

I set the plate down and addressed the wires. The leads from the battery were easy to spot. And, yes, they were red and blue. Always have to appreciate the classics.

There was a second plate covering the electronic trigger device. This was the brains of the machine, a computer that operated the neutron trigger and would fire it as soon as the activation code told it to. In devices like this, the code could be radioed in or hand-entered. I glanced up at the rocky walls. No, maybe the device on the oil platform in Louisiana could be activated via radio, but no radio signals at all were getting in here. They must have come and hand-entered it. As soon as I removed the plate I should be able to determine how much time was left before detonation. With any luck it would not already be ticking. Ideally, a two-hundred-year countdown would be nice.

I gingerly removed the screws and lifted off the plate.

And stared at the digital screen display.

"What the fuck?"

The bomb was not ticking away its last few seconds.

All of the little lights were dark. The timer wires were not even attached.

I stood up and backed away from the device.

The bomb wasn't live. Not yet.

I wanted to fall down. Swooning like a Victorian maiden seemed like a proper response.

The universe so rarely cuts me a break that I usually don't recognize them, or believe in them, when they show up.

Nevertheless here it was.

"Ghost old buddy," I said. "I think we finally got lucky."

There was a sound behind me. A soft scuff.

I spun around. I knew what I would see standing in the dark behind me. A Red Knight.

But I was wrong.

There were *two* of them.

So much for luck.

Chapter One Hundred Eleven

Arklight Camp
June 16, 6:06 a.m.

Church swiveled in his chair, looking from one screen to another. On each of them the teams were in motion, but on the Aghajari screen the little glowing dot that indicated Joe Ledger had winked out.

There were two possible explanations. Either he was deep underground, or his transponder was damaged. Neither optioned seemed to be a happy one.

Church touched the communications button. "Talk to me, Auntie."

"The ball's in play. Riptide Team reports zero resistance, no apparent hostiles. They've taken the rig and are searching for the device. SEAL Team Six is in the water checking the underside and the drill head. Landshark Team is inside the Beiji refinery but no joy so far. Same for the Abqaiq in Saudi Arabia. Only resistance is at the Pakistani site. We have satellite and predator surveillance, but, as yet, bubkes. Local military were on-site for an inspection and they encountered Zulu Team. At present no shots fired."

"Keep me posted."

He turned to the screen on which the remaining identification codes were posted. V/I, M/S, and J/I. Circe's face looked at him from an adjoining screen.

Lilith had been staring at these for minutes now.

"This doesn't make senses," she said. "In the previous codes, the *I* in A/I had been Iran. But *J* doesn't fit with Iran's other refineries, nor does *V*. And there is no *M* refinery in Saudi Arabia. Why change the code in the middle of a single list?"

"It's not LaRoque's handwriting," said Circe. "Bug checked it against samples he found in the computer records at the foundation for which LaRoque sits on the board. He has a clunky style in print and a scrawling cursive. This is elegant. Toomey in handwriting says that the style and grace is indicative of a highly trained person, probably with Catholic school education. Someone who has spent much of his life writing in cursive. LaRoque's young enough to have grown up with computers and e-mail."

"LaRoque's father is out," said Lilith. "He would have been alive when the Order first tried to buy the nukes, but he's long dead now."

"It's not Hugo's," Circe said. "Grigor?"

"No. I've seen his handwriting. It's as terse and brutal as he is."

Church said, "Nicodemus."

Lilith and Circe stared at him. And nodded.

"Knowing that doesn't help us understand the code." He paused and grunted. "On the other hand, we might be overthinking this again."

"What do you mean?" asked Circe.

"What if the list is not a code but a simple uncomplicated shorthand?" He tapped a key on his console and Bug's face appeared on one of the screens. "Bug, initiate a search. Listen first. If the first letter in each pair is the name of the target—*A* for Aghajari and so on—and the second letter is the first of the location, *I* for Iran, we missed a clue right there. *I* was used to indicate both Iran and Iraq. The answer is right there and we looked through it."

"But there's no *J* or *V* refinery in Iraq, either," insisted Circe.

"Stop thinking about specifics and go general. The additional targets may not be refineries. They could be anything. And remember, these were written by two different people. The code, and even the order of the letters might not match. Allow for flexible thinking."

"If they aren't matches, how will we ever find them?" asked Rudy.

"The second letter. Bug, let's start there. Make a list of all oil producing countries beginning with the letters *I* and *S*. No, give me J as well, in case the order is skewed. Then get me a general alphabetized list of all countries. Run both through MindReader's counterterrorism assessment package and cross-reference with significant potential targets beginning with *V, J,* and *M*. Do it now."

Circe and Bug's screens went dark. Lilith put her hands on Church's shoulders and gave them a single squeeze, then she went out to deal with her teams.

Church sat back and waited, his face showing none of the tension that burned through him. His cell buzzed and he picked it up, looked at the screen display, and frowned. It read ID NOT AVAILABLE.

There were only two systems that could block MindReader's phone trace technology: the one he had provided to Lilith years ago and which he could break if he chose to, and the one that had been used as a weapon against him by the Seven Kings.

He answered the call. "Hello, Hugo."

"Sorry, Mr. Church" said an unfamiliar voice, "wrong monster."

Church straightened. "Who is this?"

"Nobody."

The accent was London, South End. That, plus the access to this kind of phone, told him a lot.

"What can I do for you, Mr. Chismer?"

"That person doesn't exist anymore."

"Should I call you Toys?"

"Toys is dead. He's burning in hell where he belongs." There was a sound. A soft sob. Then, "Can we do this without names? It won't take long. I know you can't trace the call."

"What's on your mind?"

"Hugo told me that you are a religious man. Was he telling the truth about that, too? Please tell me the truth."

"Yes."

"Hugo thinks that you used to be a priest. Was he right?"

"No."

"I need to make a confession," said Toys. "Will you listen?"

Church said, "Yes."

Chapter One Hundred Twelve

They stood between me and the tunnel that led back into the refinery. One was dressed in the orange coveralls of the refinery's general maintenance staff; the other was the major. I'd walked on the false teeth he'd dropped, and he smiled to show me his real teeth. His fangs.

And I realized that he must have been wearing contact lenses earlier and had discarded them as well. Both Upierczi glared at me with hellish red eyes.

I had a flashlight in one hand and a plastic screwdriver in the other. My pistol was in its holster. So were theirs, but that wasn't as comforting as it should have been.

Usually in situations like this Ghost would move to one side and slightly forward, preparing to defend the pack leader and launch the first wave of attacks. He didn't. Instead, shivering and whimpering, he peed all over the floor. The Upierczi may be scared of white dogs, but my superhighly trained, ultrafierce attack hellhound was a whole lot more scared of them.

The two men stared at Ghost, and their smiles grew bigger.

Swell.

"Fetch dog," laughed the major and made the same sign to ward off evil that the first goon had made back at my hotel—touching his heart and drawing a line above his eyes.

"If you kill that piece of shit dog we will make it quick for you," said the maintenance man.

He smiled when he said it.

It was bad enough that he made that suggestion. He shouldn't have smiled when he did, because until that moment I was genuinely terrified.

Now I was pissed.

"Here's an idea," I said conversationally, and I threw the screwdriver at the maintenance guy with my left hand and drew my Beretta with my right.

Two things happened at once.

The Upier in the coveralls shocked the hell out of me by catching the screwdriver.

A microsecond later I put a bullet through the bridge of his nose.

Do not fuck with my dog.

Chapter One Hundred Thirteen

Aghajari Oil Refinery

Iran

June 16, 6:12 a.m.

The maintenance man flew back. The bullet blew out the back of his head, and the force of impact snapped his neck. Hollow points. Booyah.

The major didn't stop to gape at his fallen comrade. He moved like a blur and I pivoted, firing round after round at him. Ghost barked and lunged, but he was trained not to run into a field of fire.

The Upier was stunningly fast, but he really ought to have run serpentine. I fired at the target and caught him with my fourth round. He was fast, but a nine millimeter bullet is a whole lot faster. The round hit him sideways, clipping his elbow and drilling into his hip. From the way he fell it was clear that his pelvis was shattered.

"Hit," I told Ghost, and he flashed across the concrete floor toward the screaming vampire. The major's screams instantly jumped to a higher register.

It was over very fast, and I wasn't sure if it was because of Ghost's aggression or the bullet. Jonatha Corbiel-Newton had made some very smart recommendations, and we'd used them. A drop of garlic oil into the mouth of a hollow point, sealed in place with a bead of wax. We'd used the same syringe to inject garlic into all of our shotgun shells, sealing the plastic cases with a cigarette lighter.

And we had some other surprises.

Which left a big problem.

Echo Team was still upstairs, and there were a couple of dozen Red Knights somewhere in the facility. The Knights didn't know that and I couldn't call my team. Lydia either hadn't found Echo Team yet or something was slowing up their progress up there.

My instinct was to hot-foot it out of there and find them; but that was poor thinking. Just because the bomb wasn't active at the moment didn't mean that it couldn't be activated by one of the Upierczi here in the refinery. The only way I could prevent that would be to remove the entire triggering system, and that was going to take ten careful minutes. Inactive or not, it was still a nuke and there was always the possibility of booby traps.

Ghost suddenly looked past me and barked. Loud, angry, and scared.

I spun, bringing the pistol up.

Red Knights.

And I didn't have nearly enough bullets.

Chapter One Hundred Fourteen

Arklight Camp
Outskirts of Tehran
June 16, 6:15 a.m.

Church closed his phone and thought about what Alexander Chismer—Toys—had told him. Much of it was information he already had. Some of it was Toys's guesswork whose accuracy Church doubted. Some of it, though . . .

Hugo's cancer.

Upier 531. Dr. Hasbrouck.

The disease and its possible cure explained two key parts of this puzzle. The viciousness was born out of frustration as a narcissistic megalomaniac lashed out from his deathbed. Vox wanted to light a nuclear pyre to mark his own death. Very dramatic, mused Church. Very Hugo.

Then there was the improbable amount of useful information on Rasouli's flash drive. Vox had used Rasouli to provide the DMS with virtually everything it needed to hunt for the nukes. Why would he do that?

It made no sense unless Dr. Hasbrouck's treatment had worked.

Hugo no longer wanted to burn the world because he intended to live in it.

Toys had not said any of this in plain language. The young man was more than half crazy with guilt and self-loathing—both for past actions and for betraying Vox with this call—but the essence of Vox's plan was buried within Toys's rambling confession.

One element remained obscure, however. Nicodemus. No matter how this thing was turned, the old priest—if priest he was—leered out at them.

Church called Joe Ledger, but there was no signal.

The most crucial thing was the leverage Vox had used to stall Grigor long enough in order to receive the full set of Upier 531 treatments.

The code scrambler. Without that, the nukes were dangerous, but they were sleeping dragons. He called for Lilith and briefed her and then used the team com channel to call Top Sims.

"Deacon for Sergeant Rock."

"Go for Rock."

"Sit rep."

"Cowboy is at zero point. We're converging on his location. No fuss, no muss upstairs."

"Proceed with utmost haste. High probability that the nuke is not yet armed. Grigor may be on the way there with the code scrambler. Unknown if other activation codes have been sent. Regardless, obtaining that scrambler is now priority one, superseding all mission objectives and restrictions. Confirm understanding"

"Copy that."

"Sergeant Rock, listen to me. The Red Knights are the hostiles. That is confirmed. All other combatants are secondary."

"Copy that, too. We're ready for them."

"There are no time-outs, no rematches in this game. We win this or we lose."

"Hooah. Rock out."

Church made similar calls to the other teams. It was only Toys's guess that Grigor would be coming to Aghajari. It was closest; Grigor's Kingdom of Shadows was a mile below Tehran. However, all of the teams had to be prepared to encounter Upierczi.

When he was done he called the president.

As he ended that call, Bug rang through.

"Okay, Boss," said Bug, "here goes. Oil refineries by nation are as follows. For *I* we have Iran, Iraq, Israel, and Indonesia, Ireland, and Italy. By 'J' we got Japan, Jordan, and Jamaica. And for *S* we have South Africa, Sudan, Singapore, Sri Lanka, South Korea, Serbia, Slovakia, Spain, Switzerland, and Suriname. But like you said, this mixes things from the order of the codes."

Church pursed his lips. "Give me all the countries that start with those letters."

"For *I* we have nine countries: Iceland, India, Indonesia, Iran, Iraq, Ireland, Israel, and Italy. For the '*J*s' we have six: Jamaica, Jan Mayen, Japan, Jersey, Jordan, Juan de Nova Island. And the big list is '*S*': Saint Kitts and Nevis, Saint Lucia, Saint Vincent and the Grenadines, Samoa, San Marino, São Tomé and Principe, Saudi Arabia, Senegal, Serbia and Montenegro, Seychelles, Sierra Leone, Singapore, Slovakia, Slovenia, Solomon Islands, Somalia, South Africa, South Korea, Spain, Sri Lanka, Sudan, Suriname, Swaziland, Sweden, Switzerland, and Syria."

"Did you run it through the CT package?"

"Got it, sending it to you now."

There were multiple potential targets on the list from the counterterrorism software package, but MindReader was designed to look for patterns and probabilities. It weighted its choices, and at the top of each list was the most likely target, the one that would have the greatest economic, social, cultural, or political impact.

Church scanned the list.

"My God," he said.

Lilith saw it too. And then Circe.

Rudy and Bug said, "What?"

And then they saw it.

"This isn't about the Holy Agreement," murmured Circe in a small, shocked voice. "They may have wanted the bombs for some purpose before 9/11, but this has nothing to do with that."

"No," said Church. "This is about the Upierczi. They are without doubt the ones with the bombs."

"But *why*?" demanded Rudy.

"They were monsters and slaves for centuries," Lilith said in a hollow voice. "They had become weak and almost died out. Now they are stronger than they ever were. Much, much stronger."

"But—"

"We are about to go to war with a new nuclear power. The vampire nation."

Chapter One Hundred Fifteen

There were thirty or forty of them standing at the edges of the spill of light, but I could see indistinct shapes moving in the darkness. More of them. Many more.

Their ranks parted and one of them walked toward me. He was taller and more muscular than the others. His skin was milk white, his eyes the color of bright blood. He wore black clothes and a crystal teardrop on a silver chain. In the center of the teardrop was a brilliant ruby.

I aimed my gun at him, but I heard soft, furtive footsteps on either side of me. And behind me.

The lead Upier studied me for a moment. Around him his people were whispering to each other: "White dog . . . white dog!" They all made their protective signs, touching hearts and tracing lines on their eyes.

Their leader half turned and silenced them with a growl like a wolf. The silence was immediate. He turned slowly back to me, and a slow, broad smile spread over his hideous face.

"I know who you are," he said in a voice that was every bit as cold as a Halloween wind. "You are Captain Ledger."

And I said, "Oh shit."

It is never going to be good news if a vampire knows your name.

"You are a traitor to your own people," he said, "and an enemy of mine."

"The fuck are you talking about?"

"Our friend told us," he said, smiling so that I could see his teeth. Those teeth were scaring the living hell out of me. "He said that you conspired with Rasouli and the Red Order to keep us in chains."

"I don't have a clue what you're talking about, pal. I'm here to keep this bomb from going boom. When I'm done with that, we can sit down with a latte and talk about it."

I've always marveled at my own ability to be a smart-ass when there is neither a good reason to be one or time to screw around. It's way high on my list of character flaws.

"Do you know who we are?" asked the leader. The other vampires had me completely surrounded. Ghost whimpered and shivered beside me.

"At a guess? Grigor, chief bloodsucker of the Upierczi," I said.

He didn't blink, just gave me a nod of approval.

"Then you'll know what an honor it is to die by my hand."

"That's actually not on my day planner."

His eyes cut left and right. "Bring him to me."

The Red Knights closed on me.

"Ghost—*hit!*" I yelled, but Ghost simply stood there. Trembling, drooling with terror. His bladder let loose and he peed all over the floor. Again.

Not exactly the response I was hoping for.

The Upierczi stared for a two count, and then they all burst out laughing.

"Oh shit," I breathed.

The closest Upier darted in and kicked Ghost in the side. It looked like a light kick, but it lifted Ghost's hundred pounds and flung him against the side of the bomb case. Ghost slammed into the hard metal with a terrible yelp of pain, rebounded, and fell. He lay whimpering on the floor.

The vampires laughed and laughed at Ghost, but they were looking at me. Red eyes and red mouths surrounded me.

I pivoted and shot the Upier who had kicked Ghost. I hit him in the balls because I wanted him to suffer. He screamed and fell, and the bullet punched all the way through him and hit another Upier in the thigh. Two down. Their screams were so high, so shrill that it wiped the leering smiles from every face.

I liked the effect, so I kept shooting.

I wanted Grigor, but two Upierczi threw themselves into the path of the gunfire and died for their king.

I shot the gun dry, and in the confusion I swapped out the magazines.

But I never had a chance to fire the gun. A pale figure moved toward me with such insane speed that I couldn't bring the barrel to bear. Grigor. He swatted the Beretta out of my hand and it went spinning away.

He grabbed a handful of my shirt and pulled me toward him. I used the impetus to hook a palm-heel shot across his temple. It turned his head but it didn't drop him with a sprained neck like it should have. All that I accomplished was to shake loose of his grip, though as we staggered apart the whole front of my shirt tore away, exposing the Kevlar vest beneath.

With a snarl he darted forward and punched me square in the center of the chest. The blow slammed into me like a cruise missile and literally plucked me off the ground and hurled me ten feet through the air. I hit the flat front of the bomb housing near where Ghost had struck, and a twenty-one-gun salute burst along my spine. My feet landed flat but my knees buckled and I went down hard on my kneecaps and then fell forward onto my palms.

One punch.

He was unbelievably strong. Far stronger than the one I'd fought at the hotel.

Jesus Christ. It was all I could do to suck in half a lungful of air. Kevlar stops bullets, not foot-pounds of impact.

Move or die, bellowed my inner voices. Cop and Warrior, both of them shouting at once.

As the king of the Upierczi came at me I launched myself from hands and knees and tried to drive my shoulder all the way through his midsection. I'm two hundred pounds and six feet tall buck naked, and that's a lot of PSI to absorb.

Turns out, not only was he strong as a bull, he could fight. He caught my charge and with both hands and a pivot of his hips sent me flying again. I collided with a line of Upierczi and we all went down. The impact tore a cry of pain from me; they merely grunted. They were laughing as we hit the ground and cold fingers were suddenly plucking at me.

"No!" bellowed Grigor. "Leave him be. This one is mine."

Disappointment flickered on their faces, but that was quickly supplanted by evil smiles. They shoved me to my feet and one of them even steadied me and slapped dust from my clothes. He gave me a friendly grin and a wicked wink.

"Thanks," I said, then I flicked my rapid-release folding knife from my pocket and whipped the blade across his throat. It wasn't my best cut, not even that deep, but the whole knife had been soaked in garlic oil. Mr. Friendly staggered back, clutching his throat while he gurgled a wet scream.

Everybody watched him fall, watched the blood geyser from his throat and then fade to a trickle. Then every set of red eyes shifted to stare at me.

I moved away from them and dropped into a fighting crouch, blade ready for Grigor.

"Garlic," he observed. "Clever trick."

"Come over here and let me show you how it works."

We all had a good laugh over that.

The other Upierczi began circling me again, laughing, taunting me, pretending to lunge at me. Some—friends of the dead, I guessed—told me how I would die and what I would feel. Not really necessary—Grigor was about to show me firsthand.

He lunged in and swatted at my knife. I evaded but only just. He was wary of the garlic on the blade and his hesitancy allowed me some seconds of breathing room. I pressed that advantage, leaping at him, slashing and hacking with a dozen overlapping cuts. But all I really cut was air.

Then he faked high and came in low and wickedly fast. He punched the bicep of my knife arm and the whole arm went dead. The knife clattered to the floor. Grigor rose from his crouch and hit me again in the chest. Same place. Same effect.

I flew backward into the stack of packing crates, splintering the side of one that was the size of a refrigerator.

In the movies, these crates fly apart like they're made of balsa wood. In the real world they become a network of sharp splinters and jagged edges that gouge into you, tear your skin and your clothing, and pin you like a butterfly on a display board. I was stuck fast, my shoulder caught as surely as if an alligator had its jaws clamped around it.

I couldn't free myself. Couldn't escape.

Smiling, Grigor stalked toward me as all around us the vampires howled in the darkness.

Chapter One Hundred Sixteen

Violin felt a small vibration in her earpiece and she tapped it.

"Go," she said very quietly. The sound of the refinery in full operation was like thunder. Two sentries walked along a catwalk twenty feet below her.

"Daughter," said Lilith, "listen to me. We have new intelligence. We've cracked the *Book of Shadows*. It has everything the Order has ever done. Names, places, dates. Everything. Mr. Church is going to coordinate a worldwide police action against the members named in the most recent entries. We are going to tear the whole thing down!"

"Oh my God!" cried Violin. "That's—"

"There's more. You need to find Joe Ledger right now."

"That's what I'm trying to—"

"No, listen. No matter what it takes, no matter who gets in your way—*find him.* Church is certain *Grigor is there.*"

"*What?*"

"The device is unarmed. Vox helped the Upierczi obtain and position the bombs, but he withheld the activation codes until they gave him the full spectrum of a gene therapy to cure his cancer. Upier 531. Daughter, they've made Hugo Vox one of *them.* Now Vox is fulfilling his end of the deal.

Grigor is there to activate the Aghajari bomb. He has a device for it, a code scrambler. He has to be stopped."

"I'll cut his—"

"Listen," said Lilith sharply. "The code scrambler has all of the codes on it. *All* of them, do you understand?"

"Yes."

"Daughter," said Lilith, "we figured out where the other devices are. You have to get that code scrambler. If those other devices are activated . . . God."

"Where are they?"

Lilith told her.

Violin had to clap a hand to her mouth.

Before another second passed she was moving. Leaping down to the catwalk, running nimbly along it, heading down toward the basement. Looking for Joe Ledger.

Looking for Grigor.

Racing to save the world.

Chapter One Hundred Seventeen

Aghajari Oil Refinery

Iran

June 16, 6:21 a.m.

I bellowed my pain as I tried to wrench my flesh from the teeth of that shattered crate, but I wasn't going anywhere. Grigor bent low, his body language becoming like some animalistic and predatory thing, vulpine, unnatural. His mouth was a wide, red slash in his pale face. He flashed out a hand and knotted my hair in his fist. Blood ran down my face, blinding my right eye, snaking hot lines inside my clothes. My arms were pinned by the jagged wood and I couldn't reach my back-up knife clipped inside my pocket. He could have killed me right there and then. I knew it, he knew it. My life was nothing to him, an inconvenience at worst or an amusement at best. But he paused before going for the kill.

"Your world is going to die," he snarled.

It was the kind of grandiose threat that might have sounded corny in pretty much any other circumstance. Not now. Vampires with nukes. Yeah, they get to mouth off any way they want.

The best reply I could manage was a wheezy, "Yeah . . . well fuck you."

Not original, but effective. The effect was, however, that he pulled me halfway out of the nest of splinters and then slammed me back in, deeper.

"When the bombs go off," whispered Grigor, "your own stupidity and paranoia will drive the nations together into a war that will devastate the earth. When the skies darken with ash, your kind will cower. When the fallout spreads, they will sicken and die. In the coldness of nuclear winter, the Upierczi will rise up and claim dominance."

"Not a chance," I said, but that was defiant bullshit.

His plan was a pretty good one. The war would probably start as soon as the bomb in Pakistan detonated. That government was conflicted and paranoid, and ever since SEAL Team Six popped a cap in Bin Laden on Pakistani soil, political tensions have been high and hostile. They would never believe that the bomb was triggered by vampires. I mean . . . who would believe that? Sure, I was a true believer right now, but I wasn't going to be there to testify to the existence of monsters. No, the bomb there, the bombs in Iran and Saudi Arabia, the bomb in Louisiana, these were going to be seen as acts of war, and war would be the result. By the time anyone ever figured out what the hell was going on, the whole world would have become a hell.

And the Upierczi could live in a radioactive world. They were perfectly adapted—and genetically modified—to live in the world they were making.

The fact that this was all becoming crystal clear to me right now was a pain in the ass. Would have been nice to have put this all together back at the Arklight camp, and then sipped a beer while Church called in a multinational airstrike on Grigor.

As Church said, "If wishes were horses."

"I thought you believed in God," I said, fumbling for something to use as a lever. "How does this serve Him?"

"Read the Old Testament," he said. "Our God is the God of vengeance and warfare. We are the new chosen people. We were chosen by Father Nicodemus and blessed by him in God's name. Your kind should worship us."

I had no answer to that. I'm not a theologian. So I again fell back on my old favorite. "Fuck you."

Another pull and slam. Hard enough to rattle the whole stack of crates. A whole new array of burning points of pain blossomed where my body was pressed into the splinters. He leaned in close—not close enough for me to bite his nose, though—and snarled at me to worship him, emphasizing it with another shake. I was getting chewed up pretty bad by the splinters and blood was pouring down my body. I could feel it running out of my hair and down my cheeks.

"The Red Order thought they were working to maintain the faith," said Grigor, his tone full of mockery, "but they polluted their own mission. When the bombs go off, every human who survives will be on his knees. Not the first bombs—no, that will merely start the war—but the three we have placed on the altars of faith."

"What . . . are you talking about? Where are those other bombs?"

Grigor leered at me and the other vampires laughed. This was the heart of their plan, and the delight they took in it crackled through the air like electricity.

"We will strike the very heart of the faiths whose stupidity and superstitions have made monsters of my people, and whose pointless holy wars have done nothing but drive people *away* from faith. When I have drunk your life, Captain Ledger, I will send the activation codes that will detonate high-yield nuclear devices that we have placed in tunnels beneath Jerusalem and Mecca and the Vatican." He leaned close. "Do you think that will bring the faithful to their knees?"

Chapter One Hundred Eighteen

Aghajari Oil Refinery
Iran
June 16, 6:23 a.m.

John Smith lay prone on a catwalk and tracked a dark-clad female figure with his scope. He had crosshairs on her the entire time. His finger lay along the outside curve of the trigger guard.

Without moving he said, "Company's coming."

In his earbud, Top said, "One of theirs or one of ours?"

Before he could answer, a second figure leaped out of a place of concealment and landed right in the woman's path. The second figure moved unnaturally fast and he whipped out a long, curved dagger.

One of *them*.

John Smith slipped his finger into the guard, but before he could wrap it around the trigger, the woman ducked under the swing of the knife and there was a flash of silver in each of her hands. The Red Knight seemed to disintegrate into a cloud of bloody mist. Part of him landed on the catwalk, the rest fell into the steam below.

"One of ours," said John Smith. "I hope."

Chapter One Hundred Nineteen

I thought I had heard the worst, most shocking things I could hear. I was wrong.

Jerusalem.

Mecca.

The Vatican.

God almighty.

The King of Thorns sniffed the blood on my face and then suddenly darted his head forward, his tongue slithering out like a snake's to lick fresh trickles from my cheek. It was a horrible thing, invasive, intrusive on a level I'd never personally experienced before, and deeply disgusting. He took a second, longer lick and I tried to squirm away from his hot tongue running over my jaw and cheek and all the way up to the corner of my eyebrow.

He pulled back for a moment, and his smile was truly horrifying.

I think I screamed.

His face wrinkled in disgust and he spat out the blood, but then he smiled. "Eating garlic is an old trick. You have to do it for years before your blood is poison to us."

He laughed, stretching that mouth wider still. I recoiled and thrashed and kept screaming. Then Grigor bent closer still and pressed his cold lips to my ear.

"Hugo Vox gave me a very special list, my friend. Would you like to guess what is on it?"

My heart froze in my chest.

"There are Upierczi in America. Even now, even as you die here, my brothers are heading toward Baltimore. Shall I tell you who will die?"

He whispered the names of my father, my brother, my sister-in-law, my nephew.

"If your brother's wife is still fertile, we may let her live. Our birthing cells are waiting. But she will see her husband and child torn to pieces and *consumed*."

I howled in fury and tried to tear myself free of splinters. All I accomplished was to drive the jagged points deeper into my own flesh.

Grigor was not done with me. His lips moved against the flesh of my ear. "I can spare her. She will still die, but she can die quickly . . . and whole. You can save her. I offer you a chance to assure an easy death for those you love."

"Go to hell."

He slapped me so hard that I felt a tooth crack. But the impact shifted me in the nest of splinters. I felt one shoulder suddenly slide free, greased by my own blood. The rest of me though, was still trapped.

"I'm offering you a chance to save your family. Are you too stupid or heartless to listen?"

"O-okay," I wheezed. "Tell me . . ."

"Pray to me," he said. "Fall to your knees and pray to the King of Thorns. Pray to the Upierczi. Be the first of your kind to worship us and you will earn my mercy. That's all you have to do."

Around me the Upierczi had fallen into an expectant silence.

I closed my eyes and thought of my sister-in-law. Jenny. Beautiful, sweet-natured. A schoolteacher and mother. I thought of my brother, Sean. A detective, a loving husband, and father. And Sam, his son. Cute, smart as a whip, and an expert on all things baseball. He wanted to play third base for the Orioles when he grew up.

If he grew up.

My tears mingled with the blood on my face.

"Okay," I gasped. "Okay . . ."

He moved slightly back, easing the pressure that held me within the shattered crate.

"You will be remembered as the first of your kind to—"

"*Fuck you,*" I snarled as I tore my loosened other shoulder free of the splinters and clamped my right hand around his balls.

Full-fist grab, hard as I could, backed by all the terror and desperation that howled in my mind.

Grigor's eyes flared wide and he tried to simultaneously back away and twist his body free, but I clamped down and held on with everything I had. I came out of the crate with a spray of bloody splinters, and hit him across the face with my left. Once, twice, twisting his nuts as each punch landed. His scream was so high and loud that stalactites trembled loose from the roof and fell around us.

So I spit right into his screaming mouth. There might not be enough of garlic in my bloodstream, but there had to be a lot of it in my saliva.

Even in the midst of his pain, he stared at me in blank surprise for just a moment.

Then he hit me.

A third straight punch to the center of my chest. My hands and feet went instantly numb. I lost my grip and I lost my ability to stand as the punch sent me crashing back into the crate. I hit the corner of the big one and spun off and down, landing on my face near my fallen flashlight. For a single burning moment I could not feel my heartbeat, and I was positive that the shocking force of the blow had stalled it in my chest.

I gasped like a dying fish and could not move.

The Upierczi had begun to laugh like spectators at the Roman circus, amused at my defense but delighted by Grigor's apparent victory.

Then their laughter died.

My body seemed to be catching fire. My chest was a solid knot of agony. I collapsed down as the darkness closed around me like a fist.

Behind me I heard Grigor gagging and keening as he staggered away from me, but he wasn't clutching at his groin. I could just barely see him through the gathering haze. He was clawing at his own throat. His pale face was turning red, and I could see his chest labor as he fought to suck in a breath. All he managed was a high-pitched wheeze as the allergic reaction shut down his upper airway.

It was the garlic in my spit. Maybe even what was in my bloodstream. He'd tasted my blood after all. I'd eaten a whole lot more of it than Ghost had.

At least I hurt him, I thought as I lay dying. *At least I did that much.*

Then there was a huge sound as Grigor suddenly dragged in that lung-ful of air. His chest and abdomen expanded with it and he blew it out. He took another breath. And another. His color was still bad, but my trick hadn't been enough.

He looked at me and began to laugh. It was hoarse and phlegmy, but it was a laugh of triumph.

Well, fuck me, I thought. The trick hadn't worked after all.

Then something came out of the dark and moved at me and across me and over me. A monstrous white creature that howled like a demon from the pit as it leaped into the air and struck the King of Thorns like a thunderbolt.

The vampire's laughter turned into a terrified shriek.

Ghost.

Chapter One Hundred Twenty

Aghajari Oil Refinery
Iran
June 16, 6:29 a.m.

Maybe it was that Ghost could sense me teetering on the edge of the abyss.

Maybe it was the sound of vulnerability in the knight's shrieks of pain.

Maybe Ghost just plain had enough.

Whatever the reason, my dog had clawed his way back from helpless terror. His eyes blazed with bottomless animal hate, and his teeth flashed as he bore the King of Thorns backward into the darkness.

I think that's when my heart started beating again.

The Upierczi howled in mingled shock and horror as their master went down with a white dog tearing at him. They hesitated at the edges of inaction, stepping forward but not attacking. My pistol lay on the floor and I wormed my way toward it. My chest was on fire and I knew that something inside was broken, but I stretched bloody fingers toward the gun.

Grigor tried to fend Ghost off, slapping and punching at him, but there was no art or skill in his defenses. He was absolutely terrified of Ghost. Of the fetch dog who had suddenly become the thing he and his kind truly feared.

Ghost tore at Grigor's flailing hands, slashing with his fangs, biting. I saw a couple of fingers arc through the air trailing streamers of blood. Grigor screamed for the Upierczi to help him and suddenly they were moving, rushing forward, converging on Ghost.

I clawed the pistol butt into my hand, racked the slide, rolled over, aimed.

Sudden thunder filled the chamber. The whole line of Upierczi closest to me went down but I hadn't fired a shot.

The Upierczi spun and looked up.

And more of them died as bullets tore through faces and chests.

I heard a voice, leathery and deep-chested, bellowing one word over and over again.

"Echo! Echo! Echo!"

And the slaughter began.

Chapter One Hundred Twenty-One

The Iran-Kuwait Border

June 16, 6:30 a.m.

Charles LaRoque sat hunched in one corner of the limousine as it raced toward the border checkpoint between Iran and Kuwait. Forty miles and they would be out of the accursed country.

Across from him, Father Nicodemus appeared to be dozing.

LaRoque's phone rang and he snatched it up, looked at the screen display, and punched the button.

"Where are you?" asked Vox.

"Nearly to the border. We'll be out of the country in less than an hour."

"Good. Things are going to hell here. Get out and lay low, and I'll call you when the dust settles."

"What about the bombs?"

Vox laughed. "You'll know if they go boom."

"Goddamn it, Hugo."

"Look, Kuwait's safe ground. Grigor isn't targeting that. But once you get to the airport go somewhere really safe. Outside of the prevailing weather patterns. Fallout drifts, you dig?"

LaRoque glanced at Nicodemus, who was smiling in his sleep.

"How could so many things go wrong all at once?" asked LaRoque. "I thought you said it was all under control."

"Yeah, well," said Vox. "Shit happens."

Vox was laughing as he disconnected, and LaRoque frowned. His father had trusted Vox, but his grandfather had not. Now LaRoque wondered which one truly knew the man.

"Father—?" he asked.

Nicodemus opened one eye. "What is it, my son?"

"That was Vox."

"Yes," said the priest, as if he had heard the conversation. Perhaps he had. He was sneaky like that.

"Were we wrong to trust him?"

" 'We'?" The priest smiled. "I wouldn't say that *we* were wrong to trust him."

LaRoque stared at him in puzzlement, confused by the inflection.

"I've always trusted Hugo. Ever since he was a boy."

"What? But I . . . I thought . . . you said you didn't know him before this."

"Oh," said Nicodemus. "Yes, that was a lie."

"What?"

"I do that," said the priest. "Lie, I mean."

"What are you talking about?"

The priest gestured to LaRoque's pocket. "Look at your mirror. Tell me what you see."

Deeply confused, LaRoque removed the compact from his jacket and opened it. The top mirror showed his own troubled face, mouth turned down in a frown, brows knitted. Then he angled it to show the bottom image.

It was the priest's face. It was not the first time LaRoque had seen the priest in his mirror, but there was something different about it. The face was much younger, less seamed and spotted. A healthy face that was nonetheless *un*healthy. Diseased in a different way. The face was grinning—the merry, devious grin of a trickster.

"Sir Guy was a trusting fool, too," said Nicodemus. "That's why I loved him. You, however, are a disappointment even as a pawn. I'll have to find some new toys."

LaRoque heard the words, but he could not tear himself away from the image. As he watched the trickster opened his mouth and blew out his cheeks in a huge exhalation. But it was not air that he exhaled; instead a burst of living fire erupted from between the lips of the face of the demon in the mirror.

Sixty yards above the limousine the Nightbird 319 stealth helicopter hovered without lights in the endless predawn darkness.

"Target acquired."

A voice on the radio headset said, "You are cleared to fire."

The pilot squeezed the button and launched a Hellfire missile. It struck the car in less than one second and a massive fireball blasted upward from the hard-packed sand of the Iranian desert.

"Target destroyed," reported the pilot, his voice bland, detached.

"Return to base," said Mr. Church.

The helo banked left and flew toward the Kuwaiti border. The ground-based radar looked right through it as it vanished.

Chapter One Hundred Twenty-Two

Aghajari Oil Refinery

Iran

June 16, 6:33 a.m.

I struggled to get to my feet.

A minute ago I had thought that the whole world was sliding into the mouth of hell, but now a different kind of hell had come to this place of shadows. There were screams and Upierczi running everywhere. Flares popped in the air, painting everything in bright white light.

I took a step toward Grigor and my foot kicked something. I looked down and saw the code scrambler.

I bent and picked it up.

"Cowboy—on your six!"

It was Khalid's voice, and I turned to see one of the vampires four feet away. I had no time to run. I didn't want to run. As he slammed into me I buried the pistol under his chin and blew off the top of his head. We hit the ground and I lay there, Upier blood all over me. In my face, my eyes, my mouth.

I rolled over and threw up.

Grigor was still screaming. Then I heard a sharp yelp of pain and looked up to see the Upier fling Ghost aside. Ghost hit the side of a packing crate and collapsed, spitting blood onto the floor. I saw a couple of teeth, too.

That made me mad. Maybe I needed that to shake off the damage and the pain. I came out of my daze and finally the situation gelled in my mind. The Upierczi were rushing outward from me, some were seeking cover, most were rushing at Echo Team. Bunny and Top were at the foot of the metal stairs. Bunny had a combat shotgun with a drum magazine and he was firing, firing, firing. Everything that came at him died. The heavy buckshot soaked with garlic oil poisoned every Upier that wasn't instantly killed by his blasts. The ones who took a few pellets staggered away, gagging and twitching with the onset of allergic shock.

Top was watching his back, firing a big Navy Colt automatic, the hollow points doing terrible work in the tightly packed crowd.

On the other side of the chamber, Khalid and Lydia were behind a packing crate, using it as a shooting blind to create a cross fire.

"Frag out!" Lydia yelled and lobbed grenades into the heart of the vampires.

The fragmentation grenades weren't filled with garlic, but the blasts tore the monsters to pieces.

I saw three Upierczi running along the wall toward them, well out of Lydia's line of sight. I raised my pistol but before I could fire the monsters went down, one, two, three, their heads burst apart by sniper rounds. John Smith, firing from somewhere I couldn't see.

My knife was on the floor too, and I grabbed it as well. I shoved knife and scrambler into my pocket and tapped my earbud. "Echo, Echo, this is Cowboy. I have the football and I need a doorway out of here."

"I have your back," came the reply, but it wasn't in my earbud. I whirled, and there she was.

Dressed all in black, splashed with blood, a wickedly curved blade in each hand.

"Violin," I began, but she shook her head.

"No time."

She lunged past me as several Upierczi rushed my blind side. Until that moment I didn't understand what "gifts" the dhampyri had gotten from the cauldron of their birth. Violin was not as physically powerful, but my God, she was fast.

She met the rushing vampires, and even though I am trained to observe and understand combat at any level, I could not follow what happened. Her arms moved so fast, her body spun and danced as she threaded her way through the pack, the silver blades whipped with such frenzy that the monsters seemed to disintegrate around her. It was so fast that their blood hung in the air like mist. It was hypnotic and beautiful in the most awful way that perfect violence can be beautiful; and it was horrible because there was nothing natural about what I was seeing.

Violin was a thing born from rape, torn from a tortured mother by a monster of a father, raised in a culture of rage and humiliation. If it was possible for the concept of vengeance to be embodied in one form, then that's what I was seeing.

The Upierczi did not understand the nature of their death. I could see that on their faces. They saw a woman—something that to them represented a thing to be taken and used and discarded—and they attacked her with the arrogance of habitual users. They expected her to fall. They expected her to be weak.

Then she spoke to them, a snarled challenge filled with hate. I don't know what she said, or what language it was, but I caught three words. Grigor. Lilith. And Dhampyr.

The Upierczi recoiled in terror, and then she was among them, and strong as they were they fell before the precise and unstoppable fury of this daughter of Lilith.

She killed and killed and killed.

And yet, with all of that, I knew it wasn't going to be enough. There were at least a hundred of the Upierczi in the chamber. More of them were seeded through the staff of the refinery. There were a handful of us.

We were going to lose this fight.

In my earbud I heard John Smith say, "Mother of God."

And then I heard him scream.

I raised my gun, searching the catwalks for Smith. I saw him.

I saw what was left of him fall.

Grigor, bloody, torn, perhaps dying, stood on the catwalk fifty yards away. His mouth was bright with fresh blood.

John Smith struck the hard stone floor in a broken sprawl. His throat was completely torn away.

"*No!*"

I heard that scream of denial fill the air. From Bunny's throat, from Lydia's and Khalid's. From my own.

Before I knew what I was doing I was running with my gun held in both hands, firing, firing. Bullets pinged and whanged off the steel pipes of the catwalk, but Grigor ducked away and fled out through an open doorway.

I raced toward the stairway, but Khalid was closer and he bolted up the metal steps in hot pursuit. Seven Upierczi saw what was happening and they leapt like apes onto the pipes and climbed upward. I emptied my magazine at them. One fell away. By the time I reached the foot of the stairs I had the magazines swapped out and I ran upward. I was still hurt, still bleeding. Maybe inside, too. My chest was a furnace and it felt like it was consuming me, but I didn't care.

As I reached the top deck, the last of the Upierczi turned and blocked my way.

I put three rounds through his face and kicked his body out of my way.

Behind me there was another massive explosion, and I lingered at the doorway, knowing that the blast signature didn't match our fragmentation grenades. I was right.

Smoke and fire billowed out of one of the tunnels and Upierczi bodies were flung backward. Then a wave of new figures flooded in. Thirty of them. Women.

Arklight. The Mothers of the Fallen come for justice. Of a kind.

The battle below became a bloodbath.

I turned away and ran after Khalid, the Upierczi, and Grigor.

Chapter One Hundred Twenty-Three

Aghajari Oil Refinery
Iran
June 16, 6:37 a.m.

The corridor ran straight for a hundred feet and then jagged right, and I could hear shouts and gunfire. A Upier lay dead in the hall, his face shot away. A second limped toward the fight. I put a bullet in the back of his head and leapt over him as he fell. At the corner I skidded to a stop and whipped my gun around.

Four of the Upierczi surrounded Grigor in a defensive circle. They had muscled past Khalid somehow. They were bleeding. Grigor looked bad, but not as bad as I'd hoped. Maybe Ghost hadn't done as much damage as

I thought, or maybe drinking John Smith's life had given his system a boost. Goddamn it.

Khalid had his gun on them, but he was seated on the floor in a lake of blood. He tried to fire his pistol, but the weapon toppled from his hand. He was alive, but they'd torn him to rags.

"Cap . . ." he tried to say, but blood dribbled from between his lips. His eyes were unfocused as he slumped against the wall.

I ran past him and emptied the Beretta into the crowd. The Upierczi huddled up to protect Grigor and my bullets tore pieces out of them. One went down, two, and then the slide locked back on my pistol. I don't remember firing that many shots, but I was badly hurt and my brain was full of broken glass.

I tried to swap out the mags, but Grigor shoved one of the monsters at me. The Upier staggered in surprise, but he corrected his motion and dove at me. I drove the unloaded gun into his throat and heard the cartilage snap. His momentum carried me back, but I turned to shrug him off. I was clumsy with pain and my gun slipped from my bloody fingers.

There were two Upierczi left on their feet, but both were wounded. We all were. Bleeding and panting. They looked at me, at my empty hands, and smiled, showing me the jagged weapons that would tear the life out of me.

I whipped out the rapid-release knife and showed them my fang.

They rushed me.

In my mind was the image of Violin with her two knives, moving like a ballet dancer, elegant and balanced and wickedly fast. It was nice, but that wasn't something I was capable of. Not at that moment.

When I rushed them it was awkward and dirty; it was rage with no finesse. But my blade was coated with garlic and that gave me my first real advantage. I slashed and chopped at them, cutting tendons, taking their eyes, punching holes in their throats. I used my elbows to knock their teeth out. I kicked their kneecaps off and stamped on their faces when they fell.

Not pretty, but it would do.

Grigor backed away from me. He was missing the pinky and ring finger from his left hand, and there were long gashes on his arms and chest and face. Ghost had tried his best.

He flicked a look over his shoulder. The exit door was fifteen feet behind him. If he made it into the refinery I had no chance to catch him. He had backup there, I didn't. Even hurt, he could outrun me.

He should have run.

Instead he pointed at me.

"I saw you pick up the code scrambler," he said. "Thank you for bringing it to me."

"You want it, asshole," I said, shifting my weight to run or fight, "come and take it."

He really should have run. He would have won. Vox was still out there. Vox could give him another trigger device.

But Grigor's hate was too intense. In that one way, we were alike. In that way, in that moment, hate mattered more to us than anything.

He rushed at me, once more swatting the knife from my hand with shocking speed. He punched me in the face. I tried to duck under it but the blow caught me on the forehead. The shock ruptured something in my neck and broke a bomb inside my skull. The air was filled with red fireworks that burst and did not fade.

I staggered backward, suddenly blind in one eye. Blood poured from my nose and I could feel it in my ears. Grigor came at me again, clamping his mangled hands around my throat. Even with fingers missing he was immensely powerful.

And yet . . . it was the wrong thing to do.

I dropped my chin as hard as I could, pinning his thumbs against my sternum. It wasn't enough to stop him—he was way too strong for that—but it was enough to slow him down, to buy me maybe ten seconds more life. My heart was banging around all wrong, so I figured ten seconds was probably all I had left.

I only needed five.

I whipped both arms over his and boxed his ears with full-power blows of cupped palms. The sudden inward pressure burst his eardrums, and he screamed and let go, reflexively grabbing his pounding head. I kicked him in the groin as hard as I could, channeling everything I could muster into the blow. I thought of Lilith and the Mothers and every wretched thing they had endured. I thought of the threats he made against my sister-in-law, Jenny. I thought of all the women the Upierczi had tormented. I took all of that and kicked him with the tip of my steel-toe shoe. Over and over again. Without mercy. Without stopping. The impact shattered the underside of his pelvis, pulping any tissue that was in the way. His shriek went ultrasonic and he froze, eyes goggling in their sockets.

Nice targets.

I used my thumbs on those.

He fell screaming to the floor. I stood swaying over him. He was blind, broken. But as deeply as I looked inside myself I could not find a single splinter of mercy. Inside, a black voice howled from the cold furnace of my soul. The sounds of gunfire and screams echoed down the hall.

I bent close to Grigor and whispered in his ear. "A bunch of *women* are chopping your master race to pieces. Bet that really fucking stings."

I straightened.

"This is for the Mothers of the Fallen."

And I stomped him to death.

Somewhere along the way I went crazy. Broken things inside me shifted and there were bursts of color and walls of darkness. I could hear myself laughing every time a bone shattered under my heel. While I was in that bad, bad place, the damage in my chest and the damage in my head caught up to me. I coughed and spat blood on the wall.

I reeled away from Grigor and went toward the sound of the battle, but I kept hitting the walls.

I heard a woman's voice. Familiar.

"Grace!" I yelled.

That's what I thought I said, what I tried to say. But my words came out slurred as I wandered sideways on feet that no longer understood their purpose. I made it as far as the metal stairs, but when I tried to step down I forgot how my feet worked. I fell. Rolling, tumbling, hitting the metal, spilling and sprawling as the cavern swirled around me.

I don't remember landing.

I thought I heard voices. More knights? No . . . was it the cold voice of Mr. Church speaking in the meaningless language of the knights?

My dead mother smiled at me from behind the stacked crates, her eyes weeping blood.

Rudy whispered in my ear, "I was so sorry to hear that you died, Joe."

I said, "No!"

But the darkness said, "Yes."

I fell forward into its embrace.

Chapter One Hundred Twenty-Four

Aghajari Oil Refinery

Iran

June 16, 6:43 a.m.

I heard someone calling from the other side of a wall. The wall was a million miles high and made of darkness.

I thought I heard a woman speaking. She was close, kneeling beside me, whispering in my ear, but her words made no sense.

Then silence.

A moment later . . .

"Cap'n? Jesus, Cap'n . . . are you dead?"

I knew that voice. Male, gruff. Filled with emotion. But I had no label to hang on it.

Dead?

"No," I thought, or perhaps I said it aloud.

Then there were hands on me. Another vampire? I screamed and tried to fight them off.

"Watch!" barked another voice. "Hold his arm. Hold him."

My wrists were caught. One, two. Held, though I fought against it.

"Hold him!"

"I am holding him, Farmboy!"

"Christ, he's a mess."

I tried opening my eyes, but the world was filled with lights that were too bright to look at. Then someone forced my eyelids open and let the burning sun blast me.

"Look at his eyes!"

"They're hemorrhaged. Concussion . . . might be a skull fracture."

I wondered what that was. I knew that I should know.

More hands on me, under my arms, lifting. Pain was a defining characteristic of the whole universe.

"Watch his head."

I heard a dog barking. Funny. I used to have a dog when I was a kid, but he died. How could he be barking now?

"He's coming out of it . . . watch, watch!"

"Top, hurry the fuck up. They're coming!"

A rattling sound. Loud pops. Some screams too. I wondered what movie we were watching.

"Warbride . . . get those cocksuckers!"

Pop! Pop! Pop!

I had the weirdest sensation, like I was floating along on just the toes of my boots. Gliding.

More pops and bangs.

"Go—*go!* I'll hold them here. Get him out of here."

No, I tried to say. I wanted to see the movie. I tried to pull away.

"Don't let him go!"

"Juice him, damn it. Give it to me. I'll do it, give it to me."

There was a pinpoint of cold heat on the side of my neck.

And then nothing again.

This time the nothing was wonderful. If it was death, then I liked it.

Chapter One Hundred Twenty-Five

Aghajari Oil Refinery

Iran

June 16, 7:49 a.m.

I woke up in a truck that smelled of diesel oil and fertilizer. The first thing I was aware of was pain.

Everything hurt.

Every.

Single.

Thing.

The worst was my head. It felt like the Hindenburg after the fire started. Even my eyebrows hurt.

I opened my eyes but everything was a pale and uniform white. No details at all.

My neck didn't hurt as much, but I couldn't move it. I couldn't move anything. When I was able to separate the painful things that were my ankles and wrists from the bigger painful thing that was my body, I realized that they were held fast.

I was tied down. I could feel bindings across my chest, my waist, my thighs.

Panic surged in my chest.

Who had me? The Iranians?

The Red Knights?

My mind hit a wall going eighty miles an hour.

The Red Knights. What *about* them? Why was I afraid of them?

Sure, there was the goon back at the hotel, but he was dead. Had I met another Red Knight? If so . . . where? Everything was so—detached. I fumbled for pieces of my mind but they were slippery and they rolled away.

Where had I been? If I could remember that maybe I could figure out where I was now.

I told myself not to move. My inner voices echoed this.

Don't let them see that you're awake, cautioned the Warrior.

Remember your training, whispered the Cop. *Observe first, gather intel. Process it, evaluate it. Assess the situation and determine your tactical position.*

Position? Up shit creek without a paddle.

Then I felt a presence near me. It wasn't exactly a sound; more of a sensation of awareness, as if someone was watching me and noticed that I was awake.

A voice said, "Cap'n?"

I had to concentrate to identify the voice. "Top . . . ?" I whispered.

"Yeah," he said and squeezed my shoulder very gently.

My eyesight came back slowly, slowly. It was dim and blurry, but I could see Top sitting beside me in the back of the truck.

"Where's the team? Is everyone okay?"

"We got out," was all he said. A few moments later he added, "Got a stealth helo coming for us. Be here any minute."

I licked my lips, and Top put a straw to my lips and let me drink.

"Top . . . ?"

"Yeah?"

"What's wrong with me? Why can't I move?"

There was a pause.

"Come on, First Sergeant . . . tell me."

Top said, "You're all messed up. You took a lot of—"

"Christ! Is my back broken? Is that why I can't move?"

"No," he soothed. "No. It's your head. Lydia thinks you might have a skull fracture. Definitely a concussion, and a mother of one."

"What does Khalid say, goddamn it? He's the frigging doctor."

Top's face was filled with pain. "Khalid's gone, Cap'n. You know that. You were there."

But I didn't remember.

"Gone? Christ, what happened at the refinery?"

"We got the scrambler. You did, you and Khalid. But . . ."

"But what? Stop screwing around and tell me."

"Those knights. They killed some of the staff and took their places. They were rigging the whole place. C-4 charges on wellheads, charges all over. Looks like once the nuke was active they wanted to bury it under a couple million tons of flaming debris. Wouldn't stop the nuke down there in the subbasement, but if we were an hour later we'd never have gotten to it. Not unless we knew the tunnel system, and we didn't."

"We stopped it, though, right?"

"The nuke? Yeah. Nobody's going to set it off. Not now."

I didn't like the way he said that. "What's wrong? What are you not telling me?"

Top sighed. He nodded to someone, and I slowly turned to see Bunny sitting at the back corner of the truck. There were tear tracks on his cheeks.

"Good to see you awake, Boss," he said, but there was no life in his voice.

Top said, "Open the door."

Bunny cut a worried look at me and back to Top. "Sure you want to do that?"

"Open it, Farmboy."

With a heavy sigh, Bunny pushed the door open so that I could see the bright noonday sun.

Except that it was early morning and the sun was still behind the mountains.

The big smiling face of the sun was not that at all. It was the leering demon face of a mushroom cloud. Many miles distant but massive, and it seemed frozen against the darkness, like a brand burned onto the flesh of night. Not a nuclear blast, which is a mercy, I suppose. This was the entire Aghajari oil refinery curling upward in a fireball five hundred feet high.

I said the word that I didn't want to say, asking it as a question.

"Violin?"

Top sighed.

"She and the Arklight team tried to stop the knights from setting off the charges. She . . . never made it out, Cap'n."

I could feel all of the horror and outrage and fear of the last couple of days sear that image onto my soul. I knew that I would never forget it. I would never be able to forget it.

We had won, but we had also lost.

Epilogue

I was out of it for a long time.

Church was there when I opened my eyes. He looked haggard and old.

"Christ," I said. "If you look that bad, I must be a frigging mess."

He didn't smile.

"What do you remember?" he asked.

I had to think about it, and I fell asleep a couple of times.

When I opened my eyes again it was morning and there was sunlight slanting in through the windows. Rudy was gone. Instead it was Mr. Church in the chair beside my bed.

"Where am I?" I asked.

"The trauma center at Columbia Presbyterian Hospital."

"In?"

"New York."

I thought about that. My body was swathed in bandages and, although there was pain, it was buried under a heavy layer of something. Morphine. My head felt like it was stuffed with bubble wrap.

"What do you remember?" he asked,

"Rudy asked the same question."

"When?"

I couldn't answer that, and I realized that this wasn't the same room. "I don't know."

"Do you remember the raid on the refinery?"

It took me a long time, and the memories were sluggish and reluctant. "Some of it. Maybe. Did we . . . did we win?"

Church nodded. "You had the code scrambler. All eight of the devices have been secured."

"Eight? I . . . don't remember eight."

But then I did. And that memory brought other memories. Church watched my face as each came tumbling downhill at me. Grigor. The army of Upierczi. Everything else.

"My team," I asked. "John Smith?"

"No," he said.

"Khalid."

"No."

We sat in the silence of that for a long time.

"I'm sorry, Captain," Church said eventually. "They were good men."

"They were family."

"Yes," he said. "They were."

"What about the others?"

"Everyone else took some hits, but they will all recover."

In body, I thought, but in spirit? In heart? I had my doubts. There was only so much loss a person could take.

"Ghost?"

"He's recovering. He needed some work. He had cracked ribs and lost a couple of teeth. I arranged for dental implants. Titanium."

"How——?"

"I have a friend in the industry," he said with a faint smile.

There was one more name, but I was afraid to ask; and I vaguely remembered a moment like this with Top. Or was that a dream? Church read it on my face. He shook his head.

"No," he said.

(2)

Church told me all of it.

The *Book of Shadows* was deciphered. Circe believed that it was the way the knights confessed their "sins" to God for everything they did to fulfill the Holy Agreement. Each entry was countersigned with the letter *N*. Nicodemus? Probably. Bill Toomey, the head of our handwriting analysis team, said that the same person countersigned every page, but of course that can't be right.

Can it?

Toomey was doing carbon dating of the ink on all the signatures. I wasn't sure I wanted to read his results.

Charles LaRoque was taken out by a Hellfire missile. Very appropriate. When the Iranians picked through the rubble they found three bodies. A driver, the remains of the last Scriptor of the Red Order, and the body of a man whose identity remains a mystery.

Grigor and the Upierczi from Aghajari? Like the song says, it's all dust in the wind.

There are probably more of them out there. There are always monsters in the dark.

But Arklight is out there too. Hunting them, with the full resources of the DMS at its disposal.

If I were one of those bloodsucking freaks, I'd kill myself before I let Lilith's people find me. I wonder if monsters have their own version of the boogeyman. I wonder if the thing that they dread when they go to sleep at night looks like a beautiful woman with eyes that hold not the slightest trace of mercy.

Rasouli tried to flee the country, too. Mr. Church made a phone call and even though Armanihandjob was in no way our friend, he was useful as a weapon. Rasouli will probably be in prison until the Middle East becomes a sunny center of tolerance and friendship for all.

Church, the presidents of America and Iran, and a few other key people met in Switzerland to discuss the Holy Agreement. The ayatollahs hoped to edit out Islamic involvement and lay it all on the Christian Church, but that was never going to happen.

"What will happen?" I asked Rudy, when he came back to visit me.

He smiled and shook his head. "Nothing visible. Nothing that will ever make the news."

"Why the hell not?" I demanded, but Rudy looked at me with disappointment.

"What good could possibly be served by telling the world about this? Do you think it would stop hate crimes? Do you really think that it would end the violence in the Middle East?"

I sighed and turned away from him.

"Of course it wouldn't," he said sadly. "It would throw gasoline on it."

"What happened to 'the truth will set you free'?" I growled.

He sighed. "As much as I hate to say it, Cowboy, sometimes a lie is better."

"Ignorance is bliss? Is that our stance?"

Rudy didn't answer, because there was no answer.

And the world? It didn't end. It still leans heavily on a crooked axis, and it still turns.

But as the weeks passed I saw something I hadn't expected.

Throughout the region the guns have fallen silent. Tensions are down across the Middle East. No one exactly knows why. At least, no one in the press seems to know.

Without gasoline on the fire, maybe the fire is finally going to burn itself out.

That would be nice.

We'll see.

(3)

Violin?

They never found her body, of course.

Burned, they said, along with so many others. Human and vampire. Charred to dust, blown away by the hot winds of an unforgiving desert.

I saw Lilith, very briefly, at the joint-use base. She wouldn't even look at me.

Everybody needs somebody to blame.

Maybe she's right to pin it on me. Violin wasn't just looking for the scrambler. She came looking for me. She told me that much, and it's all we ever got to have.

(4)

The name on the young man's passport was Gerald Hopkins. He did not look at all like the person he had once been; no one he had ever known would be able to pick him out of a lineup. People who had known him last year couldn't even do that. The face and fingerprints of Gerald Hopkins matched the computer records. No bells or alarms rang. The airport security officers in Germany did no more than an ordinary search of the man and his possessions before passing him through.

"Have a safe flight, Mr. Hopkins," said a cheerful man at the gate.

"Thank you," said Hopkins, but he was not smiling. He found his seat and buckled in and sat staring out the window for the entire flight. He did not fly first class.

When his plane landed in Canada there was no one to greet him. He hired a cab and, except for the name of his hotel, Hopkins said nothing at all on the drive. The hotel was a modest one, second or third tier. He checked in, locked his door, set his bags down and spent the next full day sleeping.

When he woke up, he stumbled into the bathroom and stood naked for half an hour under the hottest spray he could endure. His skin screamed and he screamed. But the spray was loud and the walls were sturdy and nobody reported it to the front desk.

Later, he ordered room service, and while he waited he looked out at the skyline of Montreal. His mind was a furnace.

When the porter knocked, he opened the door and stood looking at the floor while the young man set up a table and laid out the meal. Hopkins gave him some cash and locked the door again when he was gone.

The food was cold before Hopkins finally sat down to eat. He removed the metal cover to see how the steak had been cooked.

There was no steak. The plate was clean. But it was not empty.

Instead there was a folded piece of paper.

Hopkins rushed to the door and checked through the peephole, but the hall was empty. He parted the curtains, but he was on the ninth floor and there was no one down on the street that looked like police or military. No SWAT.

Cautiously he crept toward the table and the note.

He was sweating, heart hammering as he picked it up.

The sheet was a single piece of legal-size computer paper folded into a small square. Hopkins carefully unfolded it. Most of the sheet was given over to a printed list of charity organizations around the world, the majority of which were devoted to poverty, clean water, and other humanitarian causes in third-world countries. None of them were high profile. Nothing that would get headlines.

Below that was a printed list of forty-seven numbered accounts and the balances of each. He knew those account numbers by heart. The amounts in each were untouched.

And below that, written in a neat hand was a short note.

The road to redemption is paved with rocks.
There are no third chances.
Do it right.

Hopkins read the note over and over again. There were only two men powerful enough to have gotten this information and arranged its delivery. He had abandoned one, and he was sure the other wanted him dead.

And yet.

The note was unsigned.

But it was not Hugo Vox's handwriting.

The young man clutched the note to his chest. The first sob nearly broke the world. The tears burned like acid. He slid out of his seat onto the carpeted floor.

And, in the silence of his cheap hotel room, Toys wept all through the night.

(5)

Hugo Vox was grinning as he entered his study in Verona. Everything had played out perfectly. The Red Order was in ruins, and good riddance to the self-important pricks. The Tariqa were being hunted with quiet vengeance by their own people. Although they had been inactive since their leaders were killed during the invasion of Baghdad, many of them had old blood on their hands, and all of them were clearly willing to continue the centuries-old insanity. The surviving members of that sect would feel a wrath greater than anything Islam had leveled against the West.

Payback, Vox mused happily, was a real bitch.

He regretted that the knights were done, or as close to done as made no difference. They were interesting as all hell. They were one of the things that pulled him into this. Vox knew that he was a sucker for something with a biblical spin. Vampires. Bloodsucking hit men for the Church. You couldn't make this shit up.

Shame the real story didn't get into the press. That would have been legendary. That would be books and movies. Maybe they'd have gotten Ron White to play him. Vox loved that guy, never missed his stand-up act. Looking at him was like looking in a mirror. Well, a younger mirror.

He turned on a single light, locked the door, and crossed to his computer. He had looked for Toys on the Net, using the resources that had once belonged to the Seven Kings, but he hadn't found him. The kid was all the way off the grid.

Vox's smile flickered when he thought of Toys and the last, hard words between them.

I hate you, Hugo. I wish you were already dead.

Had Toys really meant that?

Probably.

Fuck.

He switched on the computer, entered his passwords, and accessed his banking records. His wealth was so scattered and so well protected that it was almost impossible to calculate. Somewhere a hair's breadth south of one hundred billion. Nothing to piss on.

Enough to rebuild the Seven Kings.

Or, maybe find the scattered remnants of the Upierczi.

Hell, maybe both.

If he was going to live forever, he might as well have some fun.

He was smiling as he tapped in his banking codes. The screen buzzed with an error message. Mistype, he figured, and tried again. And again.

"What the fuck?"

He switched to a different bank and tried to log in.

The same thing happened.

He tried seven more, his fingers trembling with panic. Nothing.

"Goddamn son of a bitch, what the f—?"

A voice behind him said, "You're wasting your time, Hugo."

Vox jumped and spun around in his seat. He had not seen the figure sitting quietly in the darkness of the far side of the study. Vox had not even sensed his presence. The figure was seated in a leather chair, legs crossed, body relaxed and casual, face completely hidden by shadows.

"God . . ." Vox gasped, and he felt as if a hand were suddenly clamped around his throat.

The figure reached to the lamp on the nearby table and switched it on. In the yellow glow of the low-wattage bulb he looked calm, his face without expression, the lenses of his tinted glasses reflecting Vox's shocked and terrified face.

"Deacon . . . Holy Christ, how'd you . . . How'd you . . . ?" He could not finish the sentence.

Mr. Church lifted something from his lap. A coded cell phone. A purple one. "I received this in the mail. From a mutual friend." He tossed it onto the floor between them. "My friends in the industry constantly amaze me with what they can do with reverse engineering. Even to the point of turning a simple phone into a tracking device."

"No . . ." breathed Vox. Sweat burst from his pores.

Church said nothing.

"Is Toys alive? Did you kill him?"

"What does it matter to you?"

Vox wiped an arm across his face. "You know it fucking well matters."

"Why?"

"Why what?"

"Why does he matter to you, Hugo?" Church asked quietly.

Vox glared at him. "You wouldn't understand."

"I wouldn't?"

"No, because you're a heartless prick, Deacon. Ask Circe. When's the last time you told your own daughter you loved her? When's the last time you *loved* anyone?"

"You're saying that you love Toys?"

"He's my son."

"Really." Church made a statement of it, not a question.

"Why the fuck do you think I did all this?"

"I know why you did this, Hugo. It's what you do. It's who you are."

"You're wrong. That may have been true when I was running the Kings, but this—this was different. I'm giving it all to Toys. Poor dumb kid found God again. Wants to devote his life to good works, corny as that shit sounds. So what can I do? I'm dead in a box in a few months. At least I can step out on a good note."

"Please, Hugo," said Church mildly. "It's just the two of us here, and I think it's past the time when you should be lying to me."

"I have no idea what you're talking about."

Church nodded and picked up a folder from the table. He whipped it across the floor so that it skittered to a stop with one corner under the toe of Vox's left sandal. Vox looked down at the folder but did not reach for it. Instead he kicked it away.

The label on the folder read UPIER 531.

"Christ," Vox gasped. "How the hell do you know about that?"

Church shrugged. "I know."

Vox said, "Toys?"

Church didn't answer. They sat in silence for almost a minute.

"Who took my money? You or Toys?"

"Who do you think?"

"I gave him a billion frigging dollars."

"And took it back. I checked the records. You left him with a penny."

Vox spread his hands. "He in custody?"

"Not at the moment."

"Let him go, Deke," murmured Vox. "The kid. Toys. Let him go."

Church said nothing.

"Whatever he was when he was with Gault, that's over. He wanted out when Gault joined the Kings. He tried to stop Gault. He even called your boy Ledger to warn him."

Church said nothing.

"This stuff—Kings and intrigues and all that shit—it broke him. Or . . . or maybe it healed him. I don't know. I'm not a philosopher and I'm not a priest. All I know is that he's done. He's really going to do as much good as he can with that money."

Church said nothing.

Vox licked his lips. "You know the story about the guy who wrote 'Amazing Grace.' John Newton. Started out as a slaver then one night, right off the coast of Donegal, a storm whipped up and was going to sink the ship. Newton prayed to God to save the ship and everyone aboard. They weathered the storm and by the time the ship docked, Newton had gone through a spiritual conversion. Worked the rest of his life to abolish slavery. Became a minister. That's Toys, Deke. He's hit that same moment . . . and after he left me, I think I did too. Big perspective check when your own son leaves you."

Mr. Church traced a small circle on the arm of the chair. "As usual, Hugo, you twist the truth to get what you want. John Newton didn't renounce the slave trade for four more years, and he captained slave ships until 1754. It was only when he had a stroke and feared that he was going to die that he underwent that conversion. Even then . . . he continued to invest in the slave trade."

Vox smiled. "My version's better."

"Your version is a lie."

"Toys, though."

"You took all his money and threw him to the wolves. If that's your attempt at tough love, you should reconsider your strategies."

"Hugo . . . when I look at this whole thing, all the players, all the factions, all of the secret agendas, it doesn't add up to anything. It's chaotic. But as I sat here I believe I figured it out."

"Think so, huh?"

"It's simple, when viewed from a certain distance. When you got involved in this, you were dying and you wanted to throw yourself a going away party. My guess is that the Upier 531 is working. You're going to live. You don't want anything to blow up because that would close the candy shop for you. And you used everyone—your allies, your friends, and me—to cancel each other out. I thought it was clumsy at first, but now I appreciate it. It's so utterly chaotic that no one would ever sort it out; there are too many missing pieces. However I know you, Hugo. Those pieces are irrelevant because they wouldn't make a clear picture no matter how they were assembled. Chaos is the best way to hide your tracks."

Vox smiled, but he neither confirmed nor denied Church's allegations.

"And if the nukes had gone off? What then? No, don't bother to answer. You wouldn't even wait for the dust to settle. You'd find a safe place to build your next web and start all over again. Now that you have the Upier 531, there will be no end to the chaos, will there?"

Vox said nothing, but his eyes shifted toward the door and back.

Church half-smiled. "Please, feel free to try and run."

Vox's face underwent a change. He let the mask of pretense slip away.

"Come on, Deacon . . ." he said. "Give me a pass. I'm no threat to you anymore."

Church continued to trace the circle.

"I'm begging you," said Vox. "I'll get down on my knees if that's what you want."

"Sure," said Mr. Church. "Let's see you on your knees."

The big man blinked at Church. "Really?"

"Really."

Vox licked his lips again and slid out of his chair onto his knees. The jolt knocked a single sharp cough out of him, but it was a small thing. A fading echo of what was. Upier 531 was doing its job. They both knew it.

"Please," said Vox. "I'm on my fucking knees and I'm begging you."

"Betraying me and betraying your country is one thing," Church said. "You provided the Sabbatarians and the Upierczi with lists of all of the DMS staff and their families."

Vox licked his lips. "Nobody got hurt, did they? You stopped all that shit. It was a scare tactic, a diversion."

Mr. Church studied him for a long time. An unbearable time for Vox.

"Circe's name was on that list, Hugo."

"Hey, come on, Deke . . . you know I'd never hurt a hair on her head. You *know* that."

Without comment or change of facial expression, Mr. Church reached inside his suit coat and withdrew a pistol. He shot Hugo Vox once in the heart and once in the head.

The bullets were low caliber. There were no exit wounds and Vox's body was solid enough to withstand the foot-pounds of impact. He stayed there on his knees for three full seconds before he canted backward and collapsed onto the floor.

Mr. Church laid the pistol on the table and folded his hands in his lap.

He did not move at all for over an hour.

(6)

Dr. Rudy Sanchez sat next to Dr. Circe O'Tree in the Basilica di San Giovanni in Laterano. It was midafternoon, and a tour group was following a guide up a side aisle as the man droned on about how this church had been burned, sacked, ravaged by earthquakes, and rebuilt several times over the years. Circe had her eyes closed, listening to her own thoughts, but Rudy eavesdropped on the guide. The story seemed appropriate to all that had happened.

"It's different," Circe said quietly and Rudy turned in surprise, wondering how the comment fit the speech.

"What?"

"The world," she said. "It's different."

"Ah," he said, nodding.

"Today and tomorrow and from now on. It's different." Circe wiped away a tear.

"I know."

The tour guide moved off toward reliquaries containing bones of dead saints, his flock following, cameras flashing.

"It's not fair."

"I know."

"The dark isn't the dark anymore. There are things in it." Circe bared her teeth in an almost feral snarl. "I don't want it to be real."

"No."

"But it is."

"Yes."

"Vampires," she said. "God help us."

Rudy wrapped his arm around her and held her close and looked up at the statues of the holy people who were supposed to keep them all safe.

"*Dios mio,*" he whispered.

(7)

The bishop and the gathered priests stood in the multicolored rays of light which slanted down through the tall stained glass windows. The bishop stood in the Great Entrance of the Liturgy, flanked by assisting priests, watching as the young candidate for ordination came forward, carrying the Aër—chalice veil—over his head, following the procession of other members of this holy event.

The bishop took the Aër from the candidate and covered the chalice and diskos with it. A priest brought a chair for the bishop to sit in, setting it in front and to the left of the Holy Table.

Two priests flanked the candidate and brought him through the Holy Doors, escorting him three times around the altar, allowing the young man to pause and kiss each corner of the Holy Table. At the end of each circuit the candidate bent to kiss the bishop's palitza and right hand. The priests guided him then to the southwest corner of the Holy Table. The young man knelt and rested his forehead on the table's edge. The bishop then placed his omophor and right hand over the ordinand's head and read the prayer of ordination.

The other clergy quietly recited a litany amongst themselves and the faithful in the pews chanted "Kyrie eleison."

When the prayers were completed the bishop clothed the new priest in the sacerdotal vestments. As each garment was placed, the people in the pews cried out, "*Axios.*"

He is worthy.

Throughout the ceremony the man looked slightly dazed, as if this was all such a mystery and a wonder to him. In the pews, his parents beamed at him. They had never figured this lad for the priesthood, not when he was a boy. But God has His own needs and His own ways. If the call comes, then what man of true faith can turn away?

"By what name will you be known as you serve God?" asked the bishop. It was a formality, rooted in old traditions, echoed down through time since popes had chosen not to take the name of Peter out of respect for the first of their line. These days, priests usually kept their own name. But the young man surprised the bishop.

"I will be Nicodemus," he said.

The bishop nodded, his approval outweighing his surprise. Nicodemus was a righteous name, and there had been many priests from right here in Verona who had chosen to serve God with it.

"Receive thou this pledge, and preserve it whole and unharmed until thy last breath, because thou shalt be held to an accounting therefore in the second and terrible Coming of our great Lord, God, and Savior, Jesus Christ."

The new priest turned toward the gathered people as the colored light from the stained glass windows patterned his face. His eyes no longer looked confused or doubtful. Instead, the mingled lights seemed to paint them in shades of green and brown.

He smiled and smiled and smiled.

(8)

My plane touched down at Dulles on a blistering hot afternoon in August. When I walked out of the terminal the sun felt like it was a foot above my head. Hellish hot.

Ghost walked beside me. Silent, loyal, alert. When he smiled at the tourists, sunlight glinted off of his four new titanium teeth. I think he liked showing them off.

I saw my Explorer sitting in a no-parking zone. The big Echo Team tactical vehicle, Black Betty, was parked behind it. Bunny leaned against my fender. Top sat in the passenger seat, the door open. Lydia stood near Bunny. Just the three of them. Ghost wagged his tail when he saw them.

No one said anything. I shook hands with Bunny and Lydia, nodded to Top, who nodded back.

A cop stood a dozen yards away, trying to give us the *look* for blocking a loading zone. We ignored him.

I put my bags in the back and climbed behind the wheel. Top patted me on the shoulder and got out to join the others in the TacV. In silent convoy we headed out of the airport for the ride to Baltimore. We could have gotten a DMS helo, but this was fine.

As we cleared the airport traffic I took a deep breath and let it out. There was half a hitch to it, almost a sob.

Ghost laid his head on my thigh and whined softly. I stroked his fur.

When we were on the highway my phone rang. I didn't want to answer it. I didn't want to hear from Church or Rudy or any-damn-one else. I wanted to be alone. I wanted to get drunk.

But the DMS owns my ass, so I snatched up the phone without looking to see who I was going to growl at. "What?"

"So," she said, "how many brownie points do I have now?"

Ghost raised his head and *whuffed*.

I smiled.

"Hello, Violin," I said.

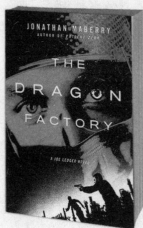